W9-BZD-310
3 2306 00338 1632

Three for a Letter

Also by Mary Reed and Eric Mayer

One for Sorrow
Two for Joy

Three for a Letter

Mary Reed & Eric Mayer

Poisoned Pen Press

First Edition 2001

10 9 8 7 6 5 4 3 2 1

Library of Congress Catalog Card Number: 2001090170

ISBN: 1-890208-82-5 Hardcover
ISBN: 1-890208-88-4 Trade Paperback

Poisoned Pen Press
6962 E. First Ave. Ste. 103
Scottsdale, AZ 85251
www.poisonedpenpress.com
info@poisonedpenpress.com

Printed in the United States of America

To Louis Henry Silverstein
1938-2001

Chairman, Editorial Review Committee
who delighted in being known as
The Poisoned Pen Press CERC

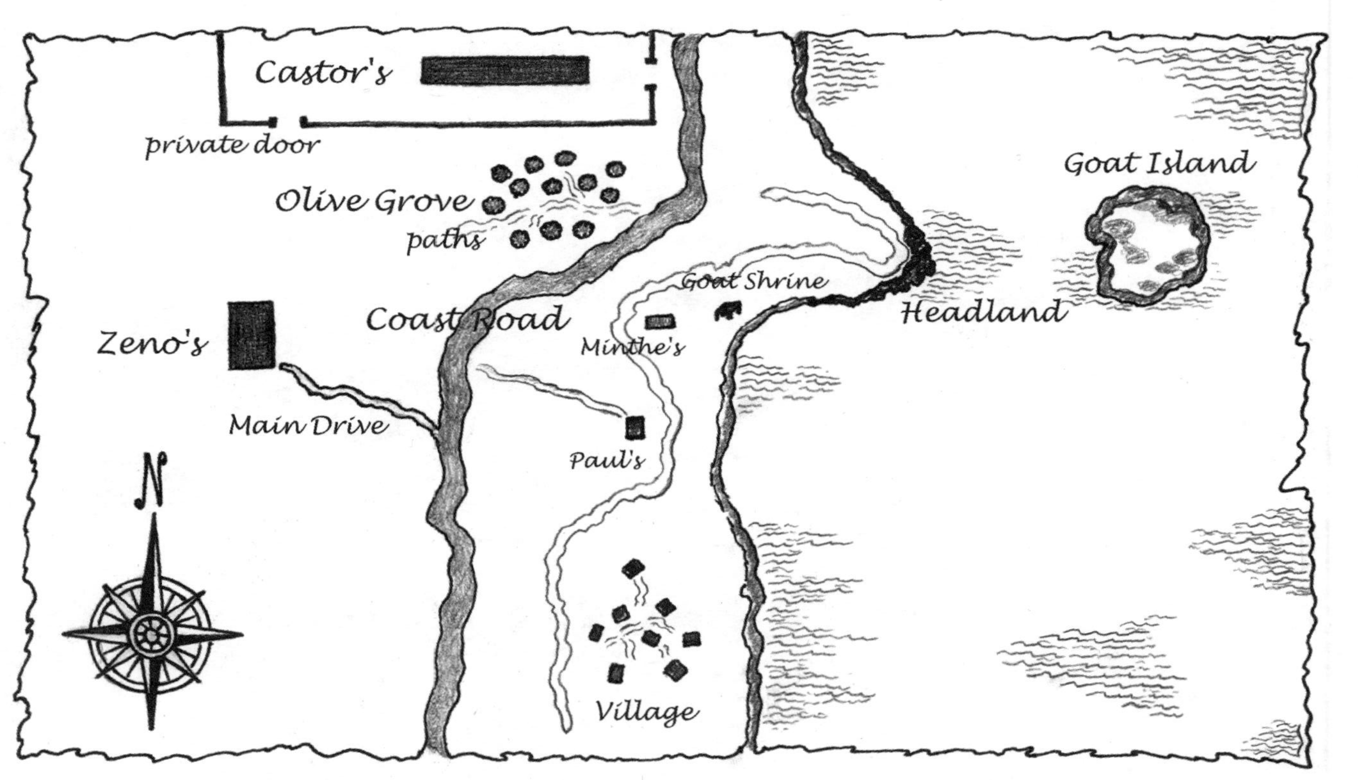

Castor's
private door
Goat Island
Olive Grove
paths
Goat Shrine
Coast Road
Headland
Zeno's
Minthe's
Main Drive
Paul's
N
Village

Chapter One

A tempest broke across the end of the dining room.

Signified by a terrible hammering on metal sheets, the raging storm tossed sailors across a makeshift deck and into blue-painted waves surging where the banquet table ended.

The impression of watery peril created by the acrobats tumbling around the motionless wooden stage was too realistic for John. While a mercenary in Bretania, the man who would eventually become Lord Chamberlain to the Emperor Justinian had seen a comrade in arms drown in a swollen stream and barely escaped with his own life. He averted his gaze only to realize his plate was graced with liver forcemeat molded into the shape of a fish.

"Uncle Zeno should have arranged to borrow one of those thunder-making machines from the theater," remarked his neighbor, a young man with dark hair and the regular features of a classical Greek statue. "It doesn't really sound as if heaven's sending a real storm. It's more like a rapping on the front door."

Recognizing his friend Anatolius' attempt to distract him, John managed a wan smile. It was, after all, just a play. Not a matter of life and death.

The mock storm intensified and the room darkened as servants covered the lamps. The wall behind the reeling acrobats had been concealed by curtains painted with a seascape to match the long room's frescoes of underwater life. The diners might have been reclining at the bottom of the Sea of Marmara. If true it would have been a great loss to the empire considering the number of senators, prominent landholders and high churchmen amongst them, not to mention Empress Theodora. As she stared raptly from her richly upholstered couch at the head of the table, her eyes gleamed like pearls in the light streaming from the illuminated stage.

Around the edge of the room shadowy figures moved quietly and John's keen hearing picked up the whisper of a sword drawn from a scabbard. Guards, he well knew, were always wary of darkness.

The smothered lamps filled the room with smoke. Its acrid odor mingled with the smells of fish, mussels, and lobsters. The food might have complemented the room's marine motif except that all had been grilled or broiled in pungent sauces.

"A shame the twins can't be here." Anatolius took a bite from a newly arrived delicacy. "After all, this fete at Uncle Zeno's estate is in their honor.

They will be sorry to miss it, the more so as I overheard my uncle telling them tall tales this afternoon. He claimed the whale they've seen occasionally from the beach was going to come ashore and dine with us. I think he had himself half-convinced by the time he'd finished. The children didn't believe a word. They were just disappointed they'd be the last to see this new contraption, the mechanical whale that my uncle commissioned." He paused for another bite. "I believe this delicious dish is mullet in quince sauce."

John nodded without interest. He would have been happier with cheese and bread. "I understand that Gadaric and Sunilda will see the play tomorrow afternoon in a form better suited to eight-year-olds."

Anatolius remarked that seemed a sensible idea.

"Yes, especially as the writer of this current spectacle seems to have placed a great deal of emphasis on the fleshly evils of Nineveh."

The acrobats had been temporarily replaced on stage by a bevy of undulating dancers.

Anatolius grinned. "If I'd been Jonah, any one of those tempestuous girls could have convinced me to be off to Nineveh at once. There'd be no need for storms at sea to persuade me." His enthusiastic utterances were cut short by a sudden bout of snuffling. "Mithra!" he muttered. "The country air is bad enough and now with the smoke in here—" He sneezed thunderously, as if heralding the prophet who finally appeared, stepping from behind the curtains as the dancers fled.

If John had ever thought about Jonah—which until this evening he scarcely had, being like Anatolius a worshipper of the soldier's god Mithra—

he would not have envisioned him as a muscular dwarf. However, there stood the mime Barnabas, a special favorite of the empress, and thus for this performance at least, the perfect Jonah.

"And just as well he's so small," Zeno had confided earlier. "Anyone else would have difficulty fitting inside the whale."

Barnabas now proceeded to demonstrate how he had gained his considerable reputation in Constantinople, staggering about the stage in a convincing portrayal of a man still groggy with sleep and horrified by a storm-tossed ship.

"Oh, ah," he wailed. "How I wish I had gone to Nineveh!"

For a heartbeat the room was silent. Then Theodora let out a cawing laugh and the other diners, who had been uncertain as to whether they should be regarding this ludicrous prophet with the solemnity befitting his position, immediately joined in.

"Look at the empress," whispered Anatolius. "When she forgets her rank she looks like any spirited girl, but Mithra help anyone who mistakes the appearance for the reality!"

Now the sailors and Barnabas were engaged in violent fisticuffs. The still-to-be-converted mariners insisted on taking the name of Jonah's Lord in vain in increasingly inventive, not to say obscene, ways only to be patiently rebuked and beaten around their heads by the small but athletic prophet.

"Uncle insisted my play contain some didactic elements," explained Anatolius.

John shot him an amused glance. "This wonderful work is your writing?"

"Do you think I should claim a reward from the empress for its entertainment value?" the other replied, unabashed.

At last Jonah was overcome and cast flailing and screaming into the painted waves. The sailors vanished and an exceptionally tall, gaunt figure sitting in the shadows at the back of the room stood and with obvious reluctance mounted the brightly lit stage.

The man's expression was grim as he began to speak. "So they picked Jonah up and threw him into the sea and the sea ceased from its raging."

His intonation was that of a prelate, John thought.

The man had to raise his voice to be heard over the titters and muffled guffaws still filling the room in the wake of Barnabas' performance. He glared out at the unruly audience and very quickly there was silence.

"Now," he continued, "whilst the servants are bringing in the final course of this excellent repast, it might be fruitful to take the time to contemplate the consequences of Jonah's refusal to do the Lord's bidding. What is the message we may all draw as we await the Final Course which our host in Heaven has surely prepared for each one of us?"

Already Zeno's servants had relit the lamps and were bustling around the long table, removing empty plates and bringing further new delicacies.

"That isn't the speech I wrote for him, John," Anatolius complained. "He was supposed to announce the dramatic finale that's planned. This is what you get with a man of religion."

"He isn't an actor? He looks and sounds so much the holy man, I thought he must be playing the part."

John rose from his couch to pace a few steps back and forth to relieve the cramps in his legs. Many of the diners were doing the same, strolling around the room, some still laughing over Barnabas' antics. Others took their opportunity to escape the smoky atmosphere and catch a breath of air in the garden.

Before long, however, all had resumed their places, the lamps were dimmed again, and the raw-boned prelate, looking even more irritable than before, continued his remarks.

"Yes," he began, "the sailors threw headstrong Jonah into the sea. Then the Lord provided a great fish to swallow up Jonah who was in the belly of that fish for three days and nights."

As he stepped down from the stage, most of the lamps illuminating it were extinguished. The eerie trill of flutes filled the air but could not hide the shrill squeal and clank of machinery.

"Now you'll see a real wonder," Anatolius whispered. "Uncle's been telling me all about it, and if it can do half of what he says..."

The curtains parted and although there was no sign of pulleys or any other device, a large, shadowy shape, taller than a man, rolled forward.

It was a great whale. The room's remaining light limned its broad, gray back and enormous flukes and gleamed off the huge glassy eyes set on either side of its head.

An admiring murmur rose from the audience as the beast's tail, moving slowly from side to side, emerged from the curtains. It was apparent that no agent propelled the leviathan from behind. Indeed, it continued forward on its own as if truly alive. There were gasps, and John tensed as the great head moved out over the edge of the stage. However, just as it appeared the whale would swim straight into the diners, it came to an abrupt halt.

There was a hissing noise. The whale spouted. To the startled exclamations of the audience, a jet of water burst up from the contraption's head and descended in a cloud of droplets that caught the dim light and glittered like stars over the sea. John, sitting near the end of the table, felt mist against his face.

The flutes keened more urgently, underscored by a new sound, a clanking and ratcheting.

Slowly and majestically, the whale's mouth opened a crack. Through a fence of huge bronze teeth brilliant light poured out across the banquet table to flash and coruscate along gold and silver bowls.

Anatolius could not contain his enthusiasm. "The beast's lit up inside like the Hagia Sophia," he declared with delight. "Uncle's really outdone himself this time."

The whale's maw opened yet further, spilling more brightness into the room. Laughs and shouts filled the air. No one doubted what the climax would be—Barnabas would leap forth, freeing himself from the creature's belly with a huge bound.

The jaws stopped moving.

Barnabas did not appear.

John squinted into the fierce light inside the whale. "He's waiting, for better dramatic effect when he finally appears," he heard Anatolius say knowledgeably.

A small shape was visible in the cramped interior of the whale amid blazing oil lamps set in the floor and the walls of the beast's head. The shape lay motionless, crumpled on the stuffed red linen tongue.

John jumped from his couch and strode to the stage. The clatter of armor and weapons accompanied him as guards moved forward quickly.

As he neared the whale he could see the face of the small, limp figure with the horribly mangled neck.

It was not Barnabas.

"It is the boy, Gadaric," John said into the quiet that had descended upon the room.

Then, before he could attempt to reach between the jaws to retrieve the child's body, the huge mouth began to close irresistibly, cutting off its lamplight. Semi-darkness descended as the mechanical leviathan, insensitive to the tragedy, rolled smoothly backwards and vanished behind the painted curtains.

❊ ❊ ❊

"Barnabas! What's happened to Barnabas?"

John turned in the direction of the agitated voice. The distraught speaker, amazingly, was the usually controlled Theodora. Next to her John recognized Anatolius' elderly uncle, Zeno, a slight man, bird-like. His hair, still dark, hung down his back. John noticed, to his horror, that the scholarly old dreamer was trying to calm the empress by gently patting her arm as if she were some young servant. John moved forward quickly, diverting her attention to himself.

"Lord Chamberlain!" Theodora said. "Perhaps you have an explanation for this strange exhibition?" The cold expression in her hooded eyes suggested it would be best if he did.

"It is the boy Gadaric who is dead, Empress," he replied with a slight bow. "Not Barnabas."

"Gadaric? Then explain to me, where is Barnabas?"

"Highness," Zeno offered her a sweet, vague smile, "perhaps he has had to return suddenly to the city?"

Theodora regarded him with incredulity. "Do you think," she began, pointing a slender finger at the elderly man, "that I am merely a foolish woman, to be patronized as if I understand nothing?" Her face reddened under its cosmetic chalk and her eyes glittered with anger. John had rarely seen her in such a rage.

Anatolius advanced to the group.

"Highness," the young man began, doubtless fearful for the safety of his uncle, under whose roof this outrage had occurred. "May I..."

The empress ignored him. "Lord Chamberlain, you will find Barnabas, and you will find him quickly. Furthermore, when Barnabas reappears, he'd be wise to have a very convincing explanation as to why he has so sorely disappointed me by departing from this festive occasion without my permission."

The room had fallen so silent that John could hear the rustle of Theodora's stiff robes as she stepped closer.

"But if you are unable to locate him," she went on with a smile that was more a snarl, "you'd best have an excellent reason as to why you failed in your search. A child has died in my presence. Not only is it a gross insult to me, it is of course—" she turned and laid her hand on Zeno's shoulder, visibly startling him, "an equally intolerable slur on my dear host's hospitality."

"Indeed, highness," John agreed. "But if I may inquire, is it possible that you can reveal anything concerning Barnabas that may—"

"You may not inquire, Lord Chamberlain." Theodora's voice was very low. "I do not concern myself with the private affairs of mimes."

John looked away from her cold glare. Zeno's guests were standing in clusters near the painted walls, silent or speaking in whispers, afraid to approach the furious empress and equally frightened to leave without her permission. The guards who had failed to prevent the tragedy stood with swords drawn but without an enemy to confront. Then he thought of one who was not present, forgotten momentarily as everyone kept their attention fixed on the enraged empress and her missing mime.

"Sunilda!" John shouted to the guard commander. "Find her immediately!"

Chapter Two

Greetings, dear Aunt Matasuntha.

I have amazing news for you! Not only has the whale kept his promise but he did it so well that even the empress has been deceived! Now she's in a foul mood although I gather that some of her dark humor is because her favorite mime is missing. Bertrada (my nursemaid, you'll recall) says the mime did something really terrible but wouldn't say what and when I get near to people they stop talking so I don't know what she means, but I shall find out and tell you when I do.

Theodora has been here three days now. We've had lots and lots of entertainments to honor Gadaric and myself but with all the bustle everyone has been cross and hardly had time to talk to us at all. Even Zeno's cook got bad-tempered and wouldn't let us stay in the kitchen. Usually he doesn't mind if we watch him at work. We like to visit because he gives us fruit or sweet dates or something nice like that and tells us wild tales about when he was young. Perhaps it was because the kitchen has been very crowded with all the boxes and baskets of food for the banquet.

I took a peek in some of the baskets as the porters brought them in and before the cook chased us out. One had a lovely pair of plump ducks in it. Their feathers were so pretty I felt sorry they would be eaten. The birds, I mean, not the feathers. There were two or three baskets full of nuts but Gadaric reminded me we're not allowed to eat them and I didn't want to get sick so I took some peaches instead. They were very nice and juicy. Most of the food for the banquet was different sorts of fishy stuff. Then the cook saw us poking about and said we had to leave. But I suppose cooking for the empress must be very hard. What if she doesn't like your sauce or says the wine is vinegary and orders your head chopped off?

Anyhow, after that we went for a walk in the garden with Bertrada. The gardeners were all rushing about trimming bushes and bringing in flowers and greenery to decorate the villa. It was so frantic it made my head ache. But even in the garden we kept getting in the way, so we went and found Poppaea and went down to the seashore. I was hoping we'd see Porphyrio but we didn't.

Zeno told us that a whale has been spied now and then for many years and that he's called Porphyrio because he's the same purple gray as the marble. I wouldn't name a whale after a piece of rock, would you? We've seen Porphyrio a few times and he's more gray than purple, it reminds me of the color of a storm cloud. Zeno says Porphyrio has been attacking ships for years and years. The sailors don't like him, it seems, which goes to show how foolish some people are. But Zeno is very kind even if he is often mistaken, although I suppose he would have to be kind since it was Theodora herself who said we all had to spend the summer with him by the sea. She's been to visit more than once and right now two of her ladies-in-waiting are helping Bertrada, if you can imagine that. They are very great ladies themselves although not royalty. I told Poppaea that some day I will make her my lady-in-waiting, just as her mother serves Theodora, but she didn't seem very happy about the idea.

The empress is not very pretty. She's quite short as well but she's got lots of beautiful clothes and jewels and attendants. Also soldiers to guard her, of course. And some men in very fine robes, all from court, are here as well. Just imagine that, all those high-born people coming to see us!

I wanted to go to the banquet, only Bertrada said it was too late for us to stay up. That wasn't the only reason, though, because I overheard her talking to Godomar—our tutor, you know, and a gloomier person than Godomar you never saw—and he told her the entertainments would not be suitable for young people. We were going to be shown how the mechanical whale works after the guests had gone back to the city but I haven't seen it yet. Everyone is going about with long faces. Bertrada cries all the time. At the banquet Theodora raised her voice to the Lord Chamberlain—at least Godomar says that's who the man is. I could tell by the way Godomar talked about him that he doesn't like him, but I don't know why. I've only seen the Lord Chamberlain briefly. He's called John. He's almost as tall as Godomar. He's thin and moves very quietly.

Anyhow, to get back to what I was saying, the banquet was very noisy and I kept waking up. Bertrada came in and went out again and then came back crying and told me Gadaric has gone away. If only she knew! You see, Porphyrio promised us we'd be taken to a safe place and when I asked him how he could do that so we wouldn't be missed, he said he knew how but that it was a secret and we would see in time. So when they took me to see Gadaric to say good-bye I knew it wasn't him, for that clever Porphyrio really has smuggled him away and left behind a figure like the ones

Hero builds all the time. It's so clever it's fooled everyone, even the empress! Godomar was shocked because I laughed when I saw it but I couldn't say why because I'd promised not to tell. But I know you will keep this secret, dear aunt.

I am sitting by the window as I write and I can see the Lord Chamberlain and another man, I think he is the palace physician, talking in the garden. I wish I could hear what they are saying.

Chapter Three

"The boy's throat was crushed. As a matter of fact, he was nearly decapitated. The neck was—well, never mind the details." Gaius took a deep breath and released it in a ragged sigh.

In the past the stout palace physician had delighted in regaling John with the most gruesome of medical details but on this occasion, in the watery morning sunlight, John could see that Gaius' normally ruddy face was as pale as the marble peristyle where the two men had paused. The airy gardens laid out before them seemed a world removed from the dim room, just a few steps down the corridor behind them, where Gadaric's body huddled beneath a coverlet in the posture of a child who has pulled his blanket over his head to escape some imagined terror of the dark.

"If the boy had been brought to my surgery," Gaius continued, "I would have guessed he'd been thrown from a horse and trampled or perhaps run over by a cart. Since he was found inside this construction—this whale you've described—I can only assume that the injury resulted from his being trapped in the mechanism. You say the mouth opened and closed?"

"Yes. Zeno's ordered the automaton back to the workshop, if you'd like to inspect it."

"No need." Gaius resumed walking, leaving John to follow. "I'm convinced that the boy's death was an accident. Now I'd like to go home. I'm accustomed to being summoned at odd hours but to spend half the night on horseback to get here, well, I'm getting too old for that. And then to find such a sight waiting for me...I'm not usually distressed by bodily misfortunes. You know that. The wagon maker can't lament every broken axle. But when a child is involved..."

They started along the flagstone path that crossed the interior garden. It was true, John thought. There was something particularly disturbing about the death of a child. He had been almost relieved when the mouth of the deadly contraption in which the boy had died had slowly closed, hiding the pitiful body from view. The death of one so young and defenseless against the whims of Fortuna seemed unfair.

"I trust you are not thinking about accepting consolation from Bacchus?" John said quietly.

Gaius assured him there was no need to worry about the possibility. "I've resolved to stop self-medicating with wine," he asserted. "Bacchus is as likely to get an audience with Justinian these days as with me."

John remarked that he was glad to hear it. The emperor, as everyone in Constantinople knew, was abstemious to a fault. "So you're certain it was an accident?"

Glossy laurel leaves, still shining with dew, brushed at their robes as they paced along. From some hidden corner nearby drifted the sharp odor of fallen pears fermenting on the ground.

"No one strangled him, if that's what you're thinking. Not unless Hercules walks among us mortals again."

"Barnabas is an acrobat, Gaius, as well as a mime. He's reputed to have exceptional strength—and he is missing," John pointed out.

The physician shook his head. "John, the child's throat was mangled. I've seen similar injuries after riots where the victims had been crushed by falling under the boots of panicked crowds."

"There weren't any riots here last night, although I noticed that Theodora's guests departed as fast as a losing faction leaving the Hippodrome."

"Do you suspect one of them was hiding something?"

"What I suspect is that they decided it was more prudent to risk being robbed on a dark roadway than to remain within striking distance of Theodora's wrath. She was as furious over Barnabas' disappearance as Gadaric's death, or so it seemed to me."

Gaius sourly pointed out that the empress was nothing if not practical. "One of the royal twins is still alive, after all. Barnabas, needless to say, is matchless. Nobody's seen him since the performance?"

"None who'll admit it," John replied ruefully. "I managed to have a few words with all the guests despite their eagerness to depart and as for Barnabas, apart from his reputation, not one of them had anything to say about him. I suppose they're all of the same mind as Theodora, taking no interest in the private affairs of mimes."

"Not since she left the acting profession herself, you mean. Let's hope he turns up soon. There's no telling what the empress will do when she's in such a foul temper. Yet what puzzles me, John, is how the child managed to get inside this mechanical whale in the first place."

"That's a mystery as well. The children's nursemaid insists she saw both of them safely to bed. She's only a girl herself and distraught. Understandably so, of course. The arrangement of their apartments is such that Gadaric would have had to come through her room in order to get out."

"Ah, but when children want to get up to mischief—well, you know how it is with children."

John smiled thinly. "About as well as I know how it is with the natives of Hyperborea."

❄ ❄ ❄

Hyperborea. As John, having bid Gaius a safe journey home, strode off to the workshops at the back of the villa he decided it wasn't surprising that the name of the dubious northern kingdom of ancient Greek legends had come to his lips. After all, he had spent the last few days surrounded by such strange marvels as doors that opened automatically, a mechanical satyr dispensing an endless stream of wine, and a serpent-slaying automaton.

The rambling garden also displayed some of its owner's previous interests. John could not begin to identify the rioting beds of exotic flowers, no doubt planted during a horticultural craze, while the small temples and statues scattered here and there bore mute witness to passing fascinations with various religious cults.

The workshops were much more mundane. Housed in a series of low brick buildings augmented by wooden sheds and lean-tos facing a courtyard, they looked as if they had been lifted straight from one of the grimier streets snaking between the Hippodrome and the sea walls of Constantinople.

Everything in this less public area—the overgrown mass of shrubbery edging the courtyard, the fountain set in its center, even the small marble statue of Eros standing in a bed of exotic flowers beside a bench under the courtyard's lone tree—retained the dreary dullness of an undusted room despite the fresh morning sunlight.

John tasted smoke in the air. It burnt the back of his throat as he entered the main building and spoke to the man manipulating the tongs thrust into an aperture in the side of the mechanical whale.

John introduced himself, adding, "I take it that you are Hero, the builder of this marvel?"

"The inventor of the creature, yes."

The man who had turned to face John had very nearly the appearance of a Nubian, the darkness of his skin enhanced by the stain of the smoke in which he must often have labored. John, having learned that Hero was Egyptian, had addressed him in his own tongue, but the man had answered in excellent Greek.

"Hero was also the name of the ancient Alexandrian inventor," John remarked. "Coincidence or fate?"

"Neither, Lord Chamberlain. I took the name myself." Hero smiled, displaying even teeth. His eyes were large and liquid, his beard spotty, and his black hair tightly curled close to his scalp. He had broad shoulders and a muscular right arm. His left arm ended abruptly at the elbow.

"Zeno informs me that you can explain the whale's workings to me."

"Indeed?" Hero bridled. "And doubtless the Patriarch of Constantinople could explain to you the nature of God if you had sufficient time."

John observed mildly that a rough description would be acceptable.

"Very well then, Lord Chamberlain. It was a rather a hurried construction, I will admit. My assistants didn't have much time." He tapped the side of the whale. "The skin, as you can see, is painted canvas stretched over wooden ribbing similar to the frame of a boat. An old fisherman from the village assisted us with that part of the work."

Hero made a circuit of his creation, opening small doors in its frame to reveal taut loops of rope, cogged gears, and labyrinths of tubing. The air in the workshop was thick with the heat radiating from the forge in a corner. Tools, as inexplicable to the layman as those in Gaius' surgery, littered wooden tables set along the walls. Beached in the middle of the timber-ceilinged workshop, the whale appeared less impressive than while swimming through Zeno's dining room. Somewhat taller at its head than John, its back sloped down toward the tail.

"The spouting action is accomplished with the aid of a sealed vessel partly filled with water," Hero explained. "When its top is removed, the liquid is forced out by the action of compressed air."

"And when the whale rolled out and then back again, with no apparent human aid each time?"

"Ah," Hero beamed. "A most striking effect, is it not? Yet easily accomplished. It's done by winding two ropes, one in each direction, around the back axle of the whale's base. Now, as you see, inside the creature are two compartments, each half filled with sand." Showing John the mechanism as he described it, he went on, "Each compartment contains a weight to which one of the ropes is tied. The weight rests on the sand. When the bottom of the first compartment is opened, the sand flows out and the weight it supports descends as it empties, pulling its rope down with it. That in turn moves the axle to which the rope is tied. Thus the whale rolls forward. Later, when the other compartment begins to empty, the process is repeated and the whale rolls backward. It's the sort of device has been used in the theater for hundreds of years," he concluded.

Nonetheless, John expressed admiration for the ingenuity of the arrangement and then questioned Hero concerning the construction of the whale's teeth. They had circled the creature and were now standing by its open maw.

"Unfortunately, Zeno insisted they be made of bronze. He liked the way the metal shone in lamplight inside the mouth. The lamps ignite automatically, by the way. Strikers attached to the gears ignite their wicks at the proper time and the gears are set in motion by certain rods governed by water clocks."

"A complicated affair indeed," John observed.

"Extremely complicated, yes, but simple enough for one as familiar as I am with such machinery. Still, even though I've given it a lot of thought, Lord Chamberlain, I just can't explain how anyone could have caused the mouth to close on the child."

John glanced up sharply. "Surely it was an accident?"

"It was no accident." Hero's voice was suddenly harsh. "Look!" He angrily shook the stump of his arm. "I lost this years ago in some fool's badly designed gears. I would never build an unsafe device. Never! In fact, the mouth was kept closed at all times. Let me show you something."

He dragged a stool over to the whale and directed John to climb up and look under the trapdoor in the top of the beast's head.

"That's where you get into the whale, Lord Chamberlain, provided you're small enough, that is. I didn't want to risk any possibility of the mouth shutting on anyone."

John opened the trapdoor and looked down into the beast's dark interior briefly. "I can see it would be a dangerous venture without such safety precautions," he agreed as he stepped back down.

"And especially dangerous for me, considering it was Theodora's favorite mime who was going to be inside. Small as Barnabas is, the empress would not have been pleased to see him diminished further."

"And as to the matter of the performance at the banquet...?"

"The beast requires considerable preparation before its few moments of life," Hero replied. "There are vessels to be filled with air and water.

The ropes must be wound correctly and tied to weights, sand has to be poured into compartments, the lamps filled with oil, that sort of thing."

"You saw to all this personally, I take it?"

"Yes, during the afternoon, right here in the workshop. A couple of servants pulled it into Zeno's dining room at the appropriate time. The wooden platform it sits on has wheels, as you saw, although I have them blocked at the moment."

"You didn't remain with the whale until the performance?"

"No." Hero's tone was curt. "There was no reason for me to stand guard. The servants had had strict instructions not to touch it. Then too, once the whale is prepared it doesn't take an expert to set it in motion."

"But if something had gone wrong?"

"Naturally I would have been sought out immediately."

John expressed some surprise that the other had not wished to see his invention's performance.

Hero laughed. "I was thoroughly sick of seeing it working, we'd tested it so often! To tell the truth, I was happy to have finished my contribution to the festivities."

"I gather that anyone could have started the whale's mechanisms?" John asked.

Hero indicated a short metal rod protruding from the side of the whale. "They can only be set in motion by removing this rod, although that wouldn't be done until Barnabas had climbed into the whale and given a specific signal. However, yes, anyone could start it—provided he were strong enough. Try it yourself."

John grasped the metal rod with both hands and pulled, feeling it move only grudgingly. "An excellent safety feature, Hero," he congratulated the man. "But let us consider all possibilities, however unlikely they seem to be. For example, a large number of servants were moving around the hall, many of them carrying heavy platters. If one had accidentally struck the whale with some force, perhaps loosening the rod...?"

"We'd thought of that as well. The whale was taken into the villa just before the banquet and positioned in the small storeroom off the end of the dining room. So it was well out of harm's way but ready to be wheeled out to the back of the stage just before it was needed."

"You seem to have considered every eventuality. One final question, then. Can the jaws be operated separately from its other mechanisms?"

"No." Hero's dark features furrowed into a scowl. "I rather suspect someone pried them apart with an iron bar. They'd close with tremendous force as soon as the bar was removed, of course. But once again it would require a very powerful man to lever them open when the safety mechanism is set." Aware of his own muscularity, he met John's questioning gaze squarely. "A man with two arms."

"But not necessarily a large man," John replied.

"You have deduced my thinking exactly, Lord Chamberlain."

"Do you have any particular reason to suspect Barnabas?"

"The most obvious one. He's run away, hasn't he?"

❋ ❋ ❋

"Wherever Barnabas may be, he's not on my estate. My servants searched all night." Zeno sounded weary as he led John through the garden. This morning the old man was plumaged like a particularly colorful bird in a fine cotton dalmatic dyed a glaring orange.

He had paused beside one of the shrines scattered around his garden. Placed beside a pine tree, it displayed a sculpture set upon a black marble boulder. John noted with some discomfit that the statue was a depiction of the goddess Cybele, flanked by lions.

"What a dreadful trial these past few months have been." Zeno sighed. "I knew no good would come of it. 'You're all by yourself on that huge estate,' Theodora informed me. 'And right by the sea,' she said. So of course this was a perfect place to send her little hostages for the summer."

"Her diplomatic guests, you mean," John replied with a thin smile.

"Oh yes, of course that's what I really meant! I am just a silly, careless-tongued old man. Certainly not a proper host for royal children."

"When I spoke to Anatolius before he returned to the city, he mentioned you got along wonderfully with the twins."

Zeno beamed. "My nephew is too kind, John. If it had been only the children who came to live with me, it would have been different. But my household has had to endure their entire entourage, including their saucy nursemaid and a lugubrious tutor, not to mention those two ladies-in-waiting Theodora foisted upon me as well. With their airs of superiority and the way they order my servants around, you'd think they were waiting to become empresses themselves!"

"Calyce and Livia?"

"You've talked to them?"

"Only briefly. The children's playmate, Poppaea, isn't Livia her mother? The woman with the round face and sharp tongue? There's a family resemblance there, in the face at least."

"Ah, John, what a horror it's been with all these women constantly under foot. And just between us, the empress has been particularly trying. In fact, she's visited me more often than her tax collectors this summer. What's worse, while she's staying here she treats my estate like her private gardens at the palace, wandering about unattended like some foolish girl. Can you imagine what it's been like, half-expecting to run straight into the empress every time you walk around a bush?"

"Very distressing, I should think," John replied.

"And Anatolius hasn't visited me at all this summer either, apart from accepting my invitation to the banquet. It's as if he is avoiding me."

"It's more likely he was avoiding the empress."

"Yes, probably. Do you suppose she is still angry over those verses he wrote about her? Still, even though half the palace guard is tramping through my garden, Barnabas is not. There isn't a stone my servants haven't turned over looking for him." He patted the large boulder beside him. "Or at least all the ones that could be turned over."

"Barnabas may still be hiding nearby," John observed.

Zeno blinked, as if surprised by the notion. "But why? If he committed this terrible crime, as it seems you suspect, wouldn't it be natural for him to flee?"

"One of the royal twins is indeed dead, Zeno, but the other is still alive and therefore could be in great danger," John pointed out.

"Yes, I see your point. Let me assure you that Sunilda is being continually watched and is quite safe from any murderous mime. You can be certain of that."

John walked on, forcing Zeno to follow. He did not care to remain in the vicinity of the representation of Cybele, whose priests so joyously castrated themselves.

They followed the winding path through banks of shrubbery and emerged into an open space graced by a small fountain before strolling down a track leading through the olive grove beyond.

"Gaius believes the boy's death was an accident, but Hero appears to think it must have been murder," John remarked.

"What do you think, John? Could it have been murder? I've been berating myself since last night for the boy's death," Zeno confessed. "To be honest, this morning I was ready to order all these automatons of mine thrown into the sea. Deadly abominations! Yet if it was a human hand that killed the boy rather than an accident brought about by my vanity, for I wanted to impress the empress, you see, well, that's a different matter entirely."

John did not point out that if Hero's whale were proved to have accidentally caused the youngster's death, both the Egyptian inventor and his employer would be likely to lose their heads, unless Theodora happened to be feeling less than merciful. In that case, they would suffer a fate far more terrible before death finally ended their agonies.

"On reflection, though," Zeno continued, "how could it have been an accident? Barnabas and Hero spent hours together. Every time I visited the workshops they were deep in discussion about the whale's mechanisms, making absolutely certain that nothing could go wrong even though it goes without saying that Hero would have prepared everything meticulously. He is not a man to leave anything to chance."

"How did you become interested in these strange mechanical devices in the first place?" John asked with interest.

"Well, it came about because my neighbor Castor has a most remarkable library. More than a hundred volumes, if you can imagine that, and not just your usual works by Homer and John Chrysostom either! Anyhow, it was in his library that I came across a copy of Hero of Alexandria's Pneumatics. It's filled with diagrams and instructions for the construction of any number of truly amazing inventions."

"Hero never mentioned this Pneumatics. He called himself the inventor of the whale."

"That's true enough. The ancient inventor did not describe a whale as such but rather useful bits and pieces that we incorporated into it, duplicating the parts as closely as possible. I can tell you, it wasn't easy when we first began. A pressurized container exploded, not once but twice. Hero had been carefully following a special instruction in his namesake's treatise. However, Castor must have been studying the work, thought he had a better idea, and amended the text! Not surprisingly, the original inventor had known better." Zeno had begun to gesticulate enthusiastically, his eyes glittering with excitement, but as they emerged from the olive grove between his gardens and the grassy headlands of the shore, his voice trailed off.

"I'm such a fool," he said sadly. "A prattling old fool! A child has died and here I am, rambling on about such things! Gadaric should be playing dodge ball out here, not lying dead under my roof. I acquitted myself quite well when we played it, you know. I'm nimble considering my age although there again I do present a larger target than either of the children."

The gentle breeze ruffling the rough grass on the headland they were crossing carried the faint smell of smoke from the workshops.

John asked if the children had displayed particular interest in Hero's inventions.

"Of course they did!" Zeno replied sorrowfully. "I must say in a way I blame myself since I allowed them to watch Hero and his assistants at work. The children were fascinated by it all. They're frighteningly intelligent children, monsters of precocity, John. I suppose it comes from being raised in isolation and tutored endlessly almost from birth."

Zeno moved suddenly, like a startled bird, his baggy orange dalmatic billowing out and his hair flying. A dull thump and the leather ball lying in the grass arced up into the sky, propelled by his boot.

John decided Zeno's estate was not a good place to ponder puzzles. Not that this particular puzzle seemed very difficult. The only missing piece was Barnabas and if he was not here, then where else could he have gone but Constantinople?

It was time to return home.

Chapter Four

John sat in the study of his house on the grounds of the Great Palace, sipping a cup of the vinegary Egyptian wine he had favored since the long-ago days when he had lived in Alexandria.

It was late afternoon, when men hastened to their homes and evening meals while those who had neither began to drift into neglected corners of the city seeking the company of their impoverished fellows and perhaps a stale scrap of bread found in the gutter or stolen while the baker's attention was elsewhere.

The rusty light of the dying sun laying a bloody hand across Constantinople spilled in through the window and across a wall mosaic depicting a placid rural scene not unlike those through which John had ridden on his return from Zeno's estate.

John had discarded his travel-soiled garments for a simple white tunic. Lost in thought as he stared at the mosaic, he could have been mistaken for a well-to-do, albeit rather ascetic, merchant pondering about the day's takings or possibly formulating plans for a family celebration.

"It seems that recent events on Zeno's estate are sadly much more harrowing than what's happening in your landscape, Zoe," John said quietly as he set his cracked clay cup aside.

The almond-shaped eyes of the mosaic girl he addressed had been given a semblance of life by the sun's rays, but she remained silent.

Zoe was a familiar figure, a confidante who knew more about John than anyone, for in times of stress he spoke to her. John knew that the habit distressed his elderly servant Peter, but he found it aided him in untangling his thoughts. Talking to Zoe allowed him to sort through untidy scraps of information. Thus, however indirectly, it helped bring him to a point where he could take the always breathtaking leap from uncertainty to clarity. It was subsequently proving what he saw to be the truth that was the difficulty, as he had remarked to Zoe more than once.

This evening, however, something in the mosaic girl's appearance troubled John. He got up and paced back and forth across the tiles through the light of the sunset. After a while he realized the source of the problem.

"It's the other girl," John told Zoe. "She looks like you."

It wasn't just the large, almond-shaped eyes that the surviving twin Sunilda had in common with Zoe, although that similarity was striking enough. He recalled the little girl he had seen only briefly. She was, if anything, small for her age, with the thin limbs of a child but blessed with long, dark hair shadowing a solemn face that seemed much older.

Perhaps that was where the real resemblance lay, he mused. Both children, the one a guest on the rambling estate by the sea and the other living on John's study wall, exhibited an air of maturity beyond their years. There was something mysterious about both of them too, as if they were not quite what they appeared to be.

"But, then," John muttered, stopping to look out of the window into the square and talking to himself as much as to the mosaic girl, "who can blame those who have been imprisoned by circumstances as much as by prison bars if they develop strange humors?"

A rising breeze carried the tang of salt from the Sea of Marmara through the half-open window. The smell reminded John of the travels of his youth, the long journeys that had taken him half way around the world. Difficult and often dangerous travel, to be sure, yet no place he had visited, not even Egypt, had struck him as more exotic than Zeno's estate.

"How long a journey from Italy it must have seemed for one as young as Sunilda," he reflected. "She's scarcely your age and already she's lost her brother, Zoe. I think you would enjoy walking with her on the beach or looking for shells or perhaps even playing dodge ball with her."

He paused, awkwardly and suddenly aware that he had not seen his own child grow from an infant to the coltish grace of the girl living in Zeno's villa, far away from any of her blood relatives. How could he be certain what such children thought or what games they would enjoy?

"It's a sad thing that the boy died so young. I fear Zeno will ultimately suffer for his carelessness, but fortunately for him he doesn't appear to realize that. No wonder Anatolius has such an unworldly streak at times. It must be in the blood."

The room was growing dark. Peter would soon bring in a lamp and announce his master's meal was prepared, just as he did each evening. The thought reminded John of the lamps that had revealed the pathetically crumpled body of the boy when the mechanical whale's mouth ponderously opened. Would the lighting of a lamp forever summon forth the same memory?

He recalled what had happened at the banquet. He had been first to realize that the figure within the great maw was not going to comically leap forward and indeed was not even Barnabas. But where could the mime have gone after performing his last scene?

And why would he have murdered Gadaric?

A tap at the study door disturbed John's ruminations. Peter entered and set his lamp on John's desk. The elderly servant averted his eyes from the glassy, hypnotic gaze of the mosaic girl as he replenished John's wine from the jug on the table by the door. He asked if his master wished his evening meal brought to the study.

John nodded and resumed pacing up and down the room as Peter escaped down the corridor to the steamy kitchen.

❊ ❊ ❊

"Some may laugh at the very idea," pronounced Peter, "but I have heard that the village by Zeno's estate is a hot bed of magick and superstition. In fact, the area's famous, or perhaps I should say notorious, for the fortune-telling goats living on a local island."

The young woman across the table from him, his assistant Hypatia, looked down at her dinner plate and tried without much success to stifle a laugh. "Oh, Peter, I'm sorry, really," she giggled, "but fortune-telling goats! Really!"

"You may find it amusing, young lady, but the fact is that no matter what guise it's presented under, it's not wise to have commerce with such unholy things." Peter's spoon rattled rather too hard against his bowl. "I know Anatolius is a good friend to our master but I can't help worrying about his uncle Zeno dabbling in all manner of strange knowledge. That's not even to mention building automatons and other such strange devices for the entertainment of his guests."

Hypatia looked thoughtful. "They sound fascinating. If they're just for entertainment, surely there's no harm in that?"

Peter's eyes unexpectedly brimmed with tears. "Zeno's infernal whale was built for entertaining his guests and it killed a little boy, leaving his sister alone. Don't forget, Hypatia, that the master has a daughter of his own. No wonder he looked so distracted just now."

The elderly servant mournfully wiped his eyes on his sleeve before mopping his bowl clean with a scrap of bread.

"At least the master's back home now, Peter, and safely away from all the things you've been fretting about." Hypatia was always kind.

"But for how long?" Peter stood and began to clear their dishes from the table. "As soon as anyone connected with the court dies, our master is immediately sent somewhere a Lord Chamberlain should never have to go. What dangerous quarter of Constantinople will he end up in this time?"

Chapter Five

John gazed down over the sea wall. The docks below swarmed with gangs of sinewy men loading and unloading the ships that rose and fell on water so befouled with floating debris that it would have been impossible from a distance to tell where land gave way to sea except for the gentle undulation of the swells.

At night flaring torches lent a lurid glow to the proceedings and prudent merchants sent deputies to count crates and bales and amphorae. Away from the harbor, the widely spaced torches kept burning overnight in front of business premises seemed only to accentuate the darkness and sense of danger, especially if the wind, or human hands, dowsed their guttering flames.

Not that the latter might necessarily mean criminal intent, John thought, as he padded down the stone steps leading to the dock. He had to shade his eyes against the sudden blow of sunlight as he emerged from the dark tunnel of the stairway. Though it was true that a man could be waylaid and dragged into the stygian depths of an alley, never to see daylight again, other sorts of commerce were transacted along those dark and narrow ways, including a variety of fleshly trades. With the number of wayfarers arriving daily in Constantinople by road or sea, there was certainly plenty of money to be made by fair means or foul.

All in all, the harbors were easy places to move around unobserved. Having already visited the larger Theodosian Harbor, John had walked east to Harbor Sophia. He had to admit that even with imperial spies everywhere and armies of informers reporting to more than one palace official, it was all but impossible to discover where anyone who had left the city in haste would have gone. Yet he must leave no stone unturned in his search for Barnabas.

The mime, he reasoned, must have realized that given his distinctive looks he could not remain hidden for long, even in the multitude of twisting byways and human warrens that crowded the houses of the wealthy and the walls of the Great Palace itself—especially once it was known that a court official was making inquiries concerning his whereabouts. The natural and correct assumption would be that anyone with the right information would be rewarded, and richly so. A prudent man would therefore have left the city, and the quickest way to do that was by ship.

The toe of John's boot stuck for a moment to the stones underfoot. An acridly sweet smell identified the sticky patch as wine from a smashed amphora, its odor mixed with the smell of the sea and the musk of the rotting vegetation being slapped hypnotically against the docks.

A burly man emerged from the arched doorway of a nearby latrine, speaking over his shoulder to someone inside. Whoever his listener was, the man had plenty to say about his antecedents and future prospects although at least he had the grace to leaven his obscene comments with a broad grin that revealed several broken teeth. An answering burst of coarse laughter and a string of Egyptian curses made John chuckle. Docks and the people who frequented them were the same everywhere, whether at Alexandria or Constantinople.

"And did you really marry the camel-driver's daughter?" John asked the man as he passed by.

The man scratched his stubbly chin. If he was surprised to have been understood by the tall, lean Greek, he gave no indication.

"No, but she thinks that I did," he replied with a grin. "You speak passable Egyptian, sir, although I can tell you're not from Egypt. Since you don't appear to be profitably employed right now, I would venture to offer you a job on my ship. However, it seems from your garments that it's more likely you own one. Or possibly more than one?"

When John shook his head, an eager expression passed over the Egyptian's face. "Then you must be a merchant, sir, perhaps seeking someone to carry your wares to Alexandria? That's my ship over there, the Osiris. A good-sized vessel as you can see. Now I admit I've just played Noah for a prominent senator who's taken a fancy to the animals of Africa, but that's a longer story even than the one about the camel-driver's daughter, and time's getting short. The summer's ending and I should be sailing south before the winds shift and my journey takes even longer than usual. So I am prepared to offer you an excellent bargain on my price for carriage of goods."

John shook his head again. "My thanks, but unfortunately it's not an offer of which I can take advantage."

The man's shoulders slumped with disappointment. "The Osiris has been well cleaned," he said persuasively. "It's as spotless as the Augean stables after Hercules finished with them. Needless to say, the senator's lion made almost as much of a mess as Hercules had to deal with, but not a trace of it remains, I assure you."

"I don't doubt that. However—"

"Sir, I've been sitting around here for three days now," the other pressed on, "asking every merchant who sets boot to dock if I may be of service and few of them have so much as even acknowledged me. This is a very unfriendly city, for all its wonders and huge buildings and beautiful women. And that reminds me of another tale I could relate." A jovial smile crossed his face. Evidently, thought John, the man's moods shifted less predictably than the winds that moved his ship across the deep waters. "But tell me, surely half of what I've heard about the empress can't be true?"

"That depends on what you've heard and which half of it you mean! But as to business. Although I can't commission you to take goods to Egypt, I can certainly offer you an opportunity to earn a few coins if you're interested?"

The man indicated great interest in the possibility.

"While you were looking for a cargo," John asked, "did it present itself in the form of a dwarf seeking a swift passage away from Constantinople?"

The Egyptian captain scowled. "Are you jesting, sir? Not that I've ever been one to object to hearing a good story myself."

John assured him that his question was quite serious.

The man continued to look dubious but replied readily enough. "A dwarf? No, I've not seen one and I would certainly remember such a thing. I could ask around the docks for you, if you'd like."

"You would perhaps be better served searching for a client, my friend, but if you should happen to hear or see anything of him, send a message immediately to Felix, the captain of excubitors at the palace. You'll be well rewarded. Here's something on account." A gold coin flashed in the sunlight as it changed hands.

The man thanked John, adding, "If this is really just a jest after all, it's at your expense, sir, and a large expense at that, if you don't mind me saying so!"

Climbing the steps away from the docks shortly thereafter John smiled to himself. He had no doubt that before nightfall every seaman and dockworker in the city would have heard about the dwarf who was worth a small fortune to somebody at the palace. In the unlikely event Barnabas had yet to take ship, his escape by that route would now be well nigh impossible.

As he reached the top of the stairway he noticed graffiti scratched into the stone of the archway leading to the street. No doubt the work of a bored mariner waiting for a companion, the simple drawing showed a beast with a fish tail and the snout of a rat, floating above several triangular waves. It reminded him immediately of Zeno's deadly mechanical whale. As John walked briskly away from the docks, he wondered what the garrulous Egyptian captain with whom he had just been in conversation would think if he knew that his minor stroke of good fortune arose from the death of a child.

❊ ❊ ❊

"Kill you? You'll wish for death before I'm done with you, you pitiful excuse for a donkey!"

The shout echoing from inside the theater distracted John from reading the inscription near its entrance:

> Donated by the goldsmith Achelous and built in the ancient style so that the cultural lives of his fellow citizens may continue to be enriched by the classics, as they are enriched by the products of his workshop, to be found near Forum Bovis

John looked away from the brass plaque and through the theater's entrance, down the corridor leading to the seating and the stage beyond. He suspected that the goldsmith would not have been pleased to hear the profane uproar spilling out into the square. It was certainly not from a classical play if, in fact, it was dialogue from a play at all.

He strode down the corridor and soon found himself in the topmost tier of the building's marble seating, the theater having been built into the side of one of Constantinople's seven hills. An awning overhead shaded the seats, while the wide stage below, backed by a tall painted façade replete with windows, doorways and several niches occupied by statues, was bright with late morning sunlight.

The overheated scene unwinding onstage would not have disgraced a rustic celebration of the grape harvest, he thought as he walked down to the stage.

He could not identify the production being rehearsed. What manner of circumstances could possibly call for three men fitted with extremely long donkey ears to be engaged in violently pummeling each other with suspiciously realistic vigor? The trio were too engrossed to notice him until he had made his way through the orchestra and up onto the stage itself.

"Fools!" bellowed the shortest actor, a swarthy man with long dark hair, extracting himself from the fray. His voice was recognizable as the one John had just heard from outside.

"What's this about?" the man shouted at him, turning and noticing their intruder. "More complaints about the noise, is it? We're just rehearsing, can't you see? There's no problem here so you can go away."

Despite his reassurance, the other two actors continued beating each other with their fists while yelling lurid curses at the top of their lungs.

"I would have thought you've rehearsed enough," John observed mildly, "for it would be hard to imagine a more realistic depiction of a brawl."

The short man grunted, "We're perfectionists!" and then turned and directed at his companions a stream of curses which John judged to be less creative than those commonly uttered by laborers at the city's wharves. The actor was a somewhat larger and more rotund version of Barnabas, short enough, no doubt, to attract ridicule but not so short as to qualify for description as a dwarf.

He turned back to John. "My name is Brontes," he said in a more normal tone of voice. "I apologize for the abysmal ineptitude of my colleagues, who cannot follow even the simplest of directions." He jabbed a long-nailed finger at John. "However, I don't think I need to speak to you about the rigors of comedy since you appear to be a man of culture. A lover of Euripides, perhaps?"

"I fear I don't have much interest in Euripides," John admitted. "In my experience real tragedy has no eloquence at all."

Brontes let out a booming laugh. "Well put! Your taste is execrable but at least you speak well!"

The two combative donkeys abruptly ceased fighting and now sat down, panting, their legs dangling over the edge of the stage. Brontes turned to harangue them again at the top of his voice.

"You are supposed to be acrobatic, not rusty-jointed," he shouted. "Remember, you're playing lascivious old crones disguised as beasts of burden. If only he was here, Barnabas would put you both to shame!"

"That's not what you said the last time the two of you traded blows," retorted one of the donkeys, embellishing his comment with a rude gesture.

Brontes gave a great despairing shrug.

"You see how it is," he remarked to John. "The theatrical profession has been moribund so long that there are no great actors left. Polus, they say, could reduce audiences to tears of sympathy for his travails. This pair just induce tears of despair. To think that I once aspired to play Agamemnon.

But then, where is the audience? With ours, the works, of Aeschylus are not popular, alas."

John refrained from pointing out that such a short, rotund actor would have made an unlikely Agamemnon, no matter the audience involved.

Brontes shook his head sadly. The gesture, being scaled for the stage, made his hair swing back and forth. "Yes, Polus would rather have been whipped the length of the Mese than undertake to play an old crone, lascivious or otherwise." He gave a snort of disgust.

"You remarked on Barnabas' absence," John said. "I was hoping to find him here as there's an urgent matter we need to discuss."

"I haven't seen him for a few days now." From the sour expression that passed over Brontes' face, John judged this to be a sore point. "He had an engagement on a country estate belonging to some old madman, from what he said. Apparently it involved something to do with a huge whale and children. It all sounded very unlikely to me, I must say. We have the most advanced stage machinery in this theater. Even so we'd be hard-pressed to present our audience with a whale. Anyway, he hasn't returned yet even though he's supposed to take the main role in this play."

John remarked that it seemed a lively enough presentation even without the presence of the famous mime.

Brontes' expression brightened. "Are you from the palace, by any chance, sir? You might mention *A Stepmother and Three Donkeys* around the court if you are. I can assure you that it's highly entertaining. The plot involves a young noblewoman who has taken a romantic fancy to her husband's slave because of his beautiful poetry, but as it turns out, the slave is only pretending to be a eunuch."

John changed the subject. "Do you have many visitors inquiring for Barnabas?"

"Why do you ask?"

"You seem unconcerned by my visit."

One of the listening donkeys called out, "There's always high-born folks coming around looking for Barnabas' services. Mostly young ladies. They just can't get enough of Barnabas." Both actors sniggered loudly.

Brontes' fists clenched and he directed a thunderous look over his shoulder, silencing the pair. "The fool exaggerates, but he's right, Barnabas is much sought after—for his talents as a mime, I mean. He has so many private engagements that he can barely honor his contract with the theater although he's managed to do so, despite his popularity. Or at least until now."

"And you say he hasn't returned?"

"No." Brontes looked thoughtful and then grinned. He let out a bellowing laugh. "Perhaps he's found a high-born lady who wants to be more than just a patron! Ha! Well, I've always liked his lodging. Perhaps he won't be needing it any more and I can get the lease!"

John asked where the mime lived.

"Just across the square. That's why I've always liked it."

The donkeys began quarreling again. One of them removed a long ear and flung it at the other, narrowly missing his target. John stepped nimbly aside as the flapping appendage flew past him. He asked Brontes to point out where Barnabas resided.

"Certainly, if it will help you to find him." Brontes jumped down from the stage. "And if you do find him," he rumbled loudly enough to be heard all over the theater, "tell him that Brontes needs his help in thrashing a pair of fools into shape! For even though he's small, he's stronger than a blacksmith. That's very useful in our profession, as you can imagine."

❊ ❊ ❊

Barnabas' lodging was a modest second floor room in a solid brick building on the opposite side of the square dominated by the theater. Brontes produced a key, explaining that Barnabas allowed him to use the room when he was absent.

"It's closer than my place and boys can be so timid once they're offstage. They often need instructing in the profession, you understand. No more than that," he added quickly. "We're all aware of the emperor's exhortations against unnatural lust. I hear he says it's the sort of thing that causes earthquakes and pestilence. We certainly don't want any of those, and in any event none of us would even think of flouting his laws to begin with."

"No, none of us would." John stooped slightly to enter the room. City apartments were not built on the grand scale of the palace.

The apartment had the appearance of the home of a person who was rarely at home. There were no coals in the brazier sitting in an alcove nor did any pots hang from the hooks on the wall behind it. The walls were whitewashed and plain. The theatre's colonnaded front could be seen from the room's small window.

"You would be able to hear the audience if you opened the window," Brontes remarked. "Especially when it's a particularly good performance. Or even sometimes when it isn't and our patrons are making their displeasure known."

The room was sparsely furnished with a chest, a table with a pair of stools, and a bed with a bright red coverlet. A tall cupboard stood against one wall. Evidently Barnabas did not feel the necessity of gathering together a large number of the world's riches, although he was certainly paid extremely well for his frequent work at the palace and elsewhere. John said as much to Brontes.

"I believe he's a frugal man, and he's putting as much as possible aside towards his retirement. He's a wonderful acrobat but we all get older. There'll come a day, not too long from now perhaps, when his body just won't do his bidding any longer."

It was true, John thought. He wondered if Brontes was also referring to himself for though he was not yet old, he was not a young man either.

John looked around again. One corner of the room was stacked with theatrical props, among them ecclesiastical garments and several large, obscenely stuffed phalluses.

"Barnabas uses those for one of his acts," Brontes confirmed John's surmise nervously. "It's very popular at the palace."

Suppressing a smile, John remarked that Barnabas was a particular favorite of Theodora's.

"Very true. What a wonderful jest! The little actress being entertained herself, rather than entertaining others. I would never have prophesied such a future for her."

"You have met Theodora?" John concealed his surprise.

"I knew her in the days when she was working in the theater, and behind the theater as well if I dare say it," Brontes replied boldly.

"Everyone dares say so but not within her hearing, Brontes." John was examining the line of erotic amulets hung along the window frame.

"Oh, I could tell you some tales about Theodora," Brontes went on confidentially. "I worked with her on more than one occasion. Yes, the empress herself and Brontes are old friends. But now she's a very great lady, all turned out in silks, gold, and jewels. Her ladies-in-waiting put more clothes on her every morning than she wore in all her years in the theatre put together! Not that I knew her except as a colleague, you understand. Of course, if you're from the palace, you'll have caught a glimpse of her."

"From time to time," John agreed. He hoped Brontes was not about to relate how he had personally witnessed Theodora remove her clothing and lie on the floor while geese pecked grain from her naked body. It sometimes seemed there was not a single person in all Constantinople who had not been present at that alleged performance, including many at the time unborn. "Did Barnabas also know her during her theatrical days?"

"I shouldn't think so, since he's somewhat younger than I am."

John opened the chest, revealing nothing more than several neatly folded tunics and other garments.

"Everything here's in its usual place as far as I can tell," Brontes volunteered.

"Have you used this room in the past week?" John dropped the lid on the chest.

Barnabas said that unfortunately he had not been so fortunate.

If Barnabas had returned here in his flight from Zeno's estate, John concluded, there was no evidence of it. The room was clean and neatly arranged, just as a meticulous person would leave it before departing for a few days.

There remained only the contents of the tall cupboard to be examined.

Expecting it to contain clothing or more theatrical props, John found instead at least part of the answer concerning what Barnabas did with the money he obviously did not spend on material comforts.

The cupboard was filled with dozens of codices and scrolls, neatly arranged in specially made racks.

John pulled out a scroll, which turned out to be Vitruvius' work on architecture. There was a codex of Plotinus' Enneads and much more besides. Any one of them would have cost more than a laborer's annual wages.

"Barnabas was always quite the reader," remarked Brontes, somewhat superfluously.

John produced a coin, twin to the one he had given the Egyptian at the docks, and handed it to Brontes with the same instructions concerning his interest in acquiring information about Barnabas' whereabouts.

As he emerged into the square, John wondered what other surprises the missing mime had in store for him.

Chapter Six

"Barnabas isn't hiding under one of the pallets here, I can assure you of that, John." Isis' smile took the sting from her waspish denial of any knowledge of the elusive dwarf.

The plump Egyptian had greeted John in the reception hall of her establishment. Its semicircular courtyard was discreetly screened from the busy square beyond by a portico housing several shops, many of which she was part owner.

"You know I would never accuse you of harboring a criminal, Isis," John protested with a smile. "However, the theater isn't too distant from here and you've often said that half the world passes through your door. Or perhaps more than half now, given that your girls stroll up and down the courtyard all day?"

"And a fair bit of the night as well, John. It does entice a few of the more timid sort of patron to venture past the little gilded Eros at our door. Once they're inside my house, few are dissatisfied with our services."

John knew that Isis took considerable pride in her new house, which had replaced one burnt down during riots a year or two before. "Yes, I can imagine it might be difficult to leave your excellent establishment before parting with a few coins." John's gaze skimmed over the closest of a number of mosaic plaques set beside the doorways along the wide corridor leading from the reception hall. The plaques depicted the particular expertise offered within each room with graphic specificity.

"Stay and talk for a little while," Isis said. "You look as if you've had a grueling morning. While I really can't help you find Barnabas I can at least offer you some wine."

John followed her down the corridor and up the stairway to her private apartments.

"Just as a matter of interest, Isis, how is it that you can be so certain you can't assist me?" John settled down on an overstuffed couch in her sitting room and took the proffered goblet of wine.

Isis, about to bite into a large honeyed date selected from a silver tray on the inlaid wood table beside her couch, drew her full lips into a pout of displeasure. "So, John, is this chat to be devoted only to business matters after all? You know how much I love reminiscing about the old days in Alexandria!"

Like John, Isis had resided for some time in that bright city although they had never actually met there, a detail she always conveniently overlooked.

"I'll visit you again very soon and devote a few hours to talking about the old days, I promise. But

I have an audience with Justinian this afternoon, so I hope you won't feel offended by my questions."

Isis finished sampling her date before answering. "Of course not, John," she finally said. "But you see I am certain that I cannot help you because I have long since barred dwarfs from my house. My rule is that if you can't see over the head of the little Eros outside, you will not be admitted."

John expressed his mystification at such a policy.

"You've lived in Egypt and so you know we consider the dwarf Bes to be a most benevolent god, for he guards against all manner of misfortunes. But what it all boils down to is a question of good business practice. Long ago I found that men of such small stature will fight my other patrons at the drop of an insult, whether one that's real or merely perceived. They seem determined to prove that their lack of height doesn't mean they are lesser men. For the same reason, they tax my girls more heavily than the emperor's collectors, and they complain."

John set down his goblet. The possibility that there was anything a Constantinople prostitute might find unnatural was one that had never occurred to him. He said so.

"You're surprised? Let me tell you, the girls in my house never entertain men working in the theater. Especially mimes. There are no men more lascivious than mimes and if anyone spurns their advances, well...and Barnabas is a famous mime. Need I say more?"

"Well, Isis, at least I've learned something from my inquiries this morning even if it isn't directly concerned with my current investigations." John got up from the couch, relieved to be freed from its overly soft embrace. "All the same, it may be that one of your employees might hear something of Barnabas from a patron, in which case I would be very interested to learn of it."

"If they should, I'll send word to you immediately. One who murders a child deserves all that he gets, but first he must be caught and I'll do whatever I can to assist you to do that." Isis waved a soft, beringed hand emphatically to underline her words.

John parted with yet another coin. He and Isis were old friends, but business was business and their friendship never interfered with that.

❊ ❊ ❊

As he left Isis' establishment, John realized it would soon be time for his audience with Justinian. He would have to attend even though his search for Barnabas or information concerning his whereabouts had so far proved fruitless. He had not really expected to find his quarry in the crowded city but he had, he hoped, contrived to provide himself with several extra pairs of eyes to keep watch for the missing mime.

His walk back to the palace took him past the theater. He briefly considered stepping in again to have another word with Brontes. However, deciding against a second visit, he instead cut down a short alley nearby. Emerging into the sunlight of another nondescript square, he had to step quickly aside to avoid treading on a three-legged cat that suddenly scuttled across his path.

The cat loped with remarkable speed to the portico of a warehouse a few paces away. Sitting there was a woman he had hoped to find. He had encountered her in the course of a previous investigation when she had provided him with valuable information about life on the streets of the city.

"Pulcheria!" he greeted her.

The woman looked up, startled. There was no mistaking her. Her hair was decorated with colored scraps of ribbon, her clothes a wild, layered collection of garish tatters. More memorable yet, while one side of her face retained a hint of its youthful beauty, the other was a shapeless mass where the flesh had melted like a guttering candle, the result of burning lamp oil flung at her by an unhappy client. She fixed John with her one good eye as her mouth made half a smile.

"Do you remember me?" John asked.

She got to her feet in a flurry of multi-hued rags. "Who could forget such a tall, handsome fellow? And a man of mystery, no less! I see that you're much better dressed than when we first met, excellency. Perhaps your fortune has changed for the better? Though I think it's much more likely that it is now exactly as it was then."

"I apologize if you feel that I misled you when we first met, my friend."

"Friend? When was the last time you visited me? Come now, you're here on business, plain and simple, and nothing more. Am I not right?"

It was true, John admitted. "Then tell me, you're familiar with the theater in the next square?"

"Of course. When there's a performance there's not a street anywhere near it that can boast a single one of us working folks. We all go over there where we can easily find clients."

"Do you have an acquaintance with any of the actors who work there?"

Pulcheria nodded, the bright ribbons in her black, matted hair fluttering.

John quickly described the man he was seeking.

"Barnabas, you mean?" Half of the woman's face creased into a grin. "Sometimes on a summer day I hear what sounds like thunder, as if a great storm is approaching over the sea, yet there's not a cloud in the sky. Then I realize that Barnabas must be performing and the thunder I think I hear is the laughter of his audience. I remember when I first came to live in this square, excellency. I was rendering service in that very alley and my client suddenly became incapable from laughter. I was mortified, fearing he would not pay me, but he told me not to mind, he was just recalling Barnabas. He'd seen his act with the phalluses not long before. And in fact he did pay me, despite lack of satisfaction."

Her one good eye looked intently at John as she continued. "Of course, excellency, if I should hear anything that would assist you..."

John pressed two coins, rather than the single coin he had planned to give her, into her grubby hand, and said he would visit again soon. As he went back along the alley he found himself thinking that a man as famous and recognizable as Barnabas surely could not hide for very much longer.

❄ ❄ ❄

"Look out!" the emperor cried.

A small round object flew in a rising arc past John's face to explode in a shower of twigs through the canopy of one of the tall cedars edging the sea wall. It vanished into the heat haze shimmering over the Sea of Marmara.

John's glance at the grassy playing field to his left revealed a horse being reined to a halt a short distance away. A polo stick was grasped in its rider's hand.

"My apologies, Lord Chamberlain. I've only just learned this particular athletic activity and I'm not fully expert at controlling the direction of the ball."

John recognized the rider. It was the boy Hektor, now grown perilously large for his duties as an ornamental court page. There were several mounted players on the field, on the far side of which two other pages and three girls stood giggling together in conspiratorial fashion. Hektor wheeled away to rejoin the game, giving John no opportunity to reply.

Justinian strolled up to John, clapped him on his shoulder and laughed.

"It's a stroke of good fortune, so to speak, that that ball didn't hit your head, Lord Chamberlain." The emperor's tone was almost jovial. "Yes, I've put some of the older pages to work entertaining the young ladies. Less paint on their faces and more perspiration, that's what I've advised for those youths."

John looked thoughtfully after the players. In the oppressive stillness the shouts of the players announced a new ball was in play. Beyond the far edge of the field, dusty landscaped grounds rose in terraces toward the stolid rectangular mass of the Daphne Palace. Several buildings, his house among them, could be seen scattered here and there amid groves of trees and flower gardens on the slopes above. Here by the sea wall the sultry air smelled of brine, trodden grass and the nearby stables, beyond which the cages of the imperial menagerie lay in quiet shadow. Only one of its cages was occupied and its resident, a large bear, was fast asleep, half buried in a bed of straw. John wished he could likewise lie down and rest but unfortunately for now that was not going to be possible.

"Is it wise to encourage that young man's development, excellency?"

"He is a favorite of the Master of the Offices," Justinian replied, "and I always like to keep an eye on court officials' proteges. But it's too hot to be standing about in the sun. Sit." He indicated a marble bench set in the shade of the cedars, waving his ever-present guards away. They stationed themselves watchfully at a distance of several paces.

Wiping his ruddy face with a piece of purple silk, Justinian suddenly chuckled. "I suppose you're wondering why I am not hearing petitions, Lord Chamberlain? It's because I decided to abandon the task when the reception hall became so hot that its bust of Constantine began sweating."

John offered a thin smile with the comment that the petitioners waiting to be heard were doubtless disappointed not to have been granted an audience with their emperor.

Justinian sat down next to John. He was in an unusually expansive mood, it seemed, for usually he explained his actions or reasoning to no one. Nor was it necessary, for as emperor he held absolute power over the life and death of everyone within the empire.

"There were nothing but minor matters to be heard," he said. "Tax abatements, license disputes, that sort of thing. So just for today I empowered a silentiary to render a positive verdict in every case.

Tomorrow I will be extolled in every corner of the city as a paragon of magnanimity. If only the sun god would have such mercy on me, as pagans would doubtless say, would they not, Lord Chamberlain?" He gave John a sly smile.

John nodded silently. He had no doubt the emperor was aware that his trusted Lord Chamberlain practiced Mithraism, a proscribed religion. However, it was a fact that could never be articulated—at least not until Justinian opened the topic.

Justinian's smile passed quickly into a graver expression as he continued. "Concerning the boy, Gadaric. His death greatly distresses me, John. It's been some years since I promised to defend his grandmother Amalasuntha, yet she was found strangled in her bath. And now, with General Belisarius at the gates of Ravenna, with Italy almost reclaimed from the Ostrogoths and Amalasuntha all but avenged, it seems that I have failed again."

"Gadaric's sister is still alive," John pointed out. "Although she has a lesser claim to the Italian throne, her marriage to an ally would certainly go far towards mending the empire as well as ensuring you have honored your promise."

For all Justinian's public declarations of avenging Amalasuntha, John and most of Constantinople were aware that her murder had been little more than a convenient excuse to allow Justinian to pursue his dream of returning the empire to its former glory. The loss of Italy, to the emperor's way of thinking, had been only a temporary defeat in a protracted war. There were, after all, old men who could still remember a Roman emperor in the west.

It was true, he thought, that while the Ostrogoths had grudgingly accepted King Theodoric's daughter Amalasuntha as regent for her son Athalaric, after Athalaric's death they had refused to allow her to reign as queen. Now there were signs that the new regime would be less sympathetic to Roman culture—and Roman landowners and business interests—than Theodoric and his daughter had been. Then too, the Ostrogoths were of the Arian faith and thus heretics in the eyes of the church. So if Justinian wished to be ruler of an empire made whole again, he would certainly have more than sufficient support in his quest from more than one quarter.

Then too, since Belisarius, his most trusted general, had long since wrested Africa back from the Vandals was now on the verge of reconquering Italy, Justinian had considerable interest in protecting Amalasuntha's grandchildren and advancing their claims to Theodoric's throne.

The polo players approached again as the girls squealed and the boys shouted. John noted that Hektor was now wielding his stick with some skill, not to mention an accuracy apparently miraculously acquired just after the recent near accident.

Once the riders had passed by, Justinian resumed speaking. "I have been contemplating a diplomatic solution. They say the Goths' general Witigis is a most estimable leader. I am considering marrying the girl Sunilda to him and then dividing Italy between us. Your objection will doubtless be that he is already married to Amala-suntha's daughter Matasuntha. But she was an most unwilling bride, was she not?"

"Perhaps she would be a more willing wife if you were to elevate Witigis in the manner you suggest, but I confess, excellency, that I do not see why it would be politic to employ the granddaughter instead."

"Matasuntha cannot be relied upon," Justinian replied, his voice surprisingly sharp. "It is not generally known, Lord Chamberlain, but when one of Belisarius' commanders was approaching Ravenna, that vile woman offered herself to him if he would deliver her from Witigis! Such treachery of a wife toward her husband is unthinkable."

"I see." John fell silent. Justinian sounded genuinely distressed by the woman's not-uncommon faithlessness. He reminded himself that the emperor was still only a man, an ordinary man once known as Petrus Sabbatius but now possessed of limitless power. His view of the world was, like everyone's, colored by his own experiences and his marriage to Theodora was, so far as anyone could tell, an ideal match. Justinian remained besotted with her, and, so it seemed, she with him, despite their often clashing views of religious and political matters. Those at court often whispered that the emperor gave her too much freedom, that she was allowed to say or do anything she pleased, even to engage in machinations entirely contrary to official policy. John knew this was not entirely the case. The empress hated him and if Justinian were so malleable, Theodora would have been granted John's death long ago.

"Well, John?" Justinian prompted him.

"I would strongly advise against this particular diplomatic solution," John replied. "It seems to me that Witigis might prove too strong to be a reliable ally in the future."

"Possibly. However, time to find a solution is short. The Persians are threatening to break our truce in the east and I may well have need of Belisarius and his troops there."

"Still, excellency, it seems to me that there is nothing to be gained by dealing with Witigis. Ravenna cannot withstand Belisarius' siege. It must fall, and that very soon."

Whatever Justinian's ruddy features might have revealed of his reaction was concealed as he wiped his face again with the purple silk cloth. John knew, however, that he would consider the advice. Justinian was a reasonable man, so far as an all-powerful emperor could be reasonable. He valued his advisors for their personal qualities rather than their backgrounds and John respected him for that. He also admired the fact that despite the pomp required by court ceremony, the emperor remained, in many of his private ways, an abstemious man.

Justinian stood abruptly and John followed him along the path around the playing field, their armed escort a few paces behind. They were accompanied by the muffled thud of hooves, the exclamations of the players rising and receding as the game approached them and then veered away. Even the waves breaking at the base of the sea wall seemed to be more sluggish and quieter than usual in the hot air.

At length, Justinian spoke. "The empress left several of her most trusted guards to watch over Sunilda. However, you will immediately accompany Captain Felix and an attachment of excubitors to Zeno's estate where you and the captain will take personal responsibility for the girl's safety until her brother's murderer has been caught. In addition, as instructed by the empress, you will continue your investigations into the matter of the mime."

John felt fortunate that he had had enough time to put a number of eyes and ears around Constantinople on watch. He had hoped for a different assignment. The task of acting as a glorified bodyguard for an eight-year-old girl while simultaneously attempting to find the missing Barnabas was not one he relished. "As you direct, Caesar," he replied formally.

"Sunilda is extremely important to the empire, in fact just as important as defeating the armies of the Goths. To think how many glorious victories on the battlefield have been undone by events transpiring quietly within the walls of estates and palaces," Justinian mused. "And, besides, Theodora is most distressed by this affair. Barnabas was her favorite performer, you know."

The emperor directed his gaze into the distance, toward the far reaches of the polo field and the buildings of the Great Palace beyond, their stolid forms softened by the heat haze. "I would not set you a task that was unimportant, John," he finally went on. "From the very first, from that service that commended you to my attention, I have trusted you only with the most sensitive and vital assignments."

"I was a slave at the time, Caesar," John reminded him. "You needed someone expendable, did you not?"

Justinian laughed softly. "You are always compelled to tell the truth, aren't you? Yet you are still alive. And there are those who do not believe there is a God!"

The polo players clattered by again. John noted one of the girls standing on the edge of the field was stealing meaningful looks at Hektor. The boy's face had thinned in the past year or so and was handsome enough, despite several patches applied by the palace tonsor to hide small skin blemishes.

A strong swing of the stick and the players were off again.

"Have you considered taking up playing polo?" Justinian asked.

The original topic of discussion had been closed, John knew immediately. "I prefer the exercise ball, excellency," he replied.

Justinian's florid face blossomed into a cheerful smile. "I avoid arduous exercise, Lord Chamberlain. I find it incites a pain in my side that causes me to bend so much that I resemble one of the empress' pet dwarfs. It seems to me it would not be wise for the emperor to be observed in such a guise."

John smiled wordless agreement.

Justinian clapped John on the shoulder again. It was a familiarity the Lord Chamberlain always found distasteful. "You see, that is why you are best dispatched to Zeno's estate," he went on. "No one else at court possesses as much discretion, John, even if many would say that you are often too frank. You remind me of an acrobat, balancing between truth and discretion." He started to laugh.

John looked at him quizzically.

"I wasn't thinking about you as a circus performer. Something rather humorous just occurred to me," Justinian explained. "It concerns my instructions to the silentiary today. Perhaps I shall desert my post on the next petition day as well but if I do I shall order that all the petitions presented are to be denied."

As Justinian laughed at his own jest, John forced himself to smile. He couldn't help thinking that it was a poor time to be absenting himself from the palace and his frequent meetings with the unpredictable emperor, since it left Justinian open to the uncontested arguments of the empress.

He hoped the emperor would not have another sudden whim and grant one of Theodora's venomous petitions against the Lord Chamberlain she so hated.

Chapter Seven

John and his companions rode away from Constantinople at sunrise. Remnants of the ragged mist veiling the Sea of Marmara swirled like white silk around seaweed-strewn rocks and tidal pools along the shoreline. Drifts of broken shells and bleached bits of driftwood undulated at the high water mark. Patches of rough grass and stunted, gnarled trees testified to the winds that regularly scoured the coast.

John took little notice of the scenery, devoting his thoughts to the furious empress back in Constantinople, doubtless conveying her anger to Justinian over the recent tragic events at Zeno's estate.

"So, John," Felix was saying, raising his voice slightly to be heard over the clattering hooves of their excubitor escort's horses, "which of your missions has priority?"

"I believe that finding Barnabas is the key to Sunilda's safety, so in fact Justinian hasn't ordered us to march in two different directions as you've been complaining ever since we left Constantinople, Felix," John replied.

"Well, perhaps that's so. Mind you, if the empress asked him to, he definitely would. She's got far too much power if you ask me. Take this matter of her support for the Monophysites, for example. The faithful say they're heretics. Yet the emperor ordered General Belisarus to Italy to bring Ostrogothic Arians to heel. But you won't find Justinian sending the general into Theodora's apartments to quell heresy there! Why does he let her get away with it?"

"He's in love with her." Breaking off the conversation, John glanced back at Peter. Constantinople was a relatively short ride from Zeno's estate but he was nevertheless concerned at how Peter was faring.

He had begun to regret his decision to take Peter with him. His intention had been to provide the elderly servant with a visit to the country and a rest from his usual household labors. Instead, Peter had grown visibly more fretful the further they traveled from the city. Perhaps he would be more cheerful after he had rested from the journey.

They were now riding past the high walls of the estate next to Zeno's. Looking down the coast road, John could see the edge of an extensive olive grove and beyond that the beginning of the road leading up to Zeno's villa. On the seaward side the land sloped down to the beach, gently in some places, more abruptly in others. Farther in the distance a few smudges of smoke rose lazily into the sky, evidence of a village hidden by the hilly terrain.

Peter was staring glumly out to sea across a headland that dropped abruptly toward the water. A craggy island was visible through the departing mist. No doubt it was the goat island about which the servant had muttered darkly when he learned of their trip, John thought. His servant's reaction had not surprised him, however, since Peter, good Christian though he might be, was also highly—and frequently—superstitious.

"I must say that I didn't expect to be enjoying Zeno's hospitality again quite so soon, Felix!" John observed.

"At least it's a chance to get away from court for a while," the other replied, "although from what you've told me, it's obvious the mime accidentally killed the child and then departed as hastily as his miserable short legs could carry him. After all, we all know that the children were only political playing pieces for the imperial couple and worth much more to them than a mere mime—even if Barnabas is Theodora's favorite—so can you blame him for fleeing? I would have done the same if I were in his boots."

"If I may say so, master," Peter put in, "the little boy should have been abed, not wandering about the estate at that time of night."

"The nursemaid certainly seems to have been somewhat negligent with her charges," John agreed thoughtfully. "I intend to question her more closely about that when we arrive."

"Yes, and—" Felix began to reply before Peter interrupted him.

"Master! Look!" he quavered. "Out there beyond the island!"

The party reined their horses and stared as the last shreds of mist steamed into nothingness above the swells of the sea. The water roiled as a huge shape broke the surface. Squinting against the sun, John glimpsed an enormous head and a broad, glistening back. Outlined against the bright sea, the whale moved majestically out of sight around the curve of the island, as silently as an apparition.

Peter could scarcely contain his excitement. "It is a great fish such as the one that swallowed Jonah. That I should see it!"

John glanced over at Felix, who seemed no less transfixed at the sight. It was nothing but a simple sea beast, John reminded himself, yet he had to admit that there was something awe inspiring about the creature, even when viewed from a distance.

"That must be the famous Porphyrio," he told Peter. "It will certainly be something to tell Hypatia when we get home."

His servant looked horrified. "Oh, but I would not dream of mentioning it to her, master. She would be terribly frightened. Indeed, I wish now that I hadn't seen it. Such a creature, although it was man-made, killed an innocent child. Now seeing this other whale as you journey to seek out the culprit—" the old man hastily sketched the sign of his religion—"how could it be anything but an ill omen?"

❄ ❄ ❄

"The villagers believe that seeing Porphyrio brings good fortune," Zeno remarked as he watched Hero hammer out a sheet of metal red hot from the forge.

"So I have heard." Hero quickly discarded his hammer and, dexterously retrieving the tongs held ready under the stump of his arm, grabbed the metal plate and dowsed its glow in a bucket of water. Steam hissed and spat, emphasizing his words. "However, I fear that they may now decide otherwise, given the recent events."

"Yes, yes, a terrible business, to be sure." Zeno shook his head sadly, his momentary good spirits destroyed by this reminder of Gadaric's death. "But Anatolius has often praised John's reasoning abilities and I for one am confident he'll soon find the murderer. Then the cloud of suspicion will be raised from us all." His eyebrows twitched into a scowl as he continued. "It is so tragic to see a child die and in such a manner, but I think it's best to keep ourselves busy while waiting for the person responsible to be found and punished." He sighed and changed the subject. "Are you certain that the automaton will be constructed in time for the festival, Hero? There's only a little more than a week left now."

Hero laid the metal sheet aside. "It will be ready. Indeed it had better be ready, since Theodora has ordered that the festival is to be held despite the boy's death. I do admit we are a little behind schedule." He wiped sweat from his dark forehead. His clothes were wringing wet from the heat of the workshop, while the tight curls on his scalp and the hair of his sparse beard glistened with perspiration.

Zeno plunged ahead enthusiastically. "Straw men are all very well, but mechanical figures, especially those whose movements are not prompted by obvious devices, will be even more interesting and add much to the festival. I'm certain that the villagers will be delighted with them."

"I hope so, especially as I've thought of a method to overcome the difficulty of hiding the mechanism operating the archer automaton. He could be carried on a litter, and its base will serve to conceal the necessary machinery."

"You've solved it!" Zeno's lined face lit up with excitement. "And now instead of a straggling rabble of villagers dragging their straw effigy up there with very little ceremony except that old song of theirs, I shall organize a proper procession. We'll have musicians as well, and speeches. The empress will be as enthralled as the villagers."

He paused and then said with pain in his voice, "Oh, dear, do you think that that might seem callous under the circumstances? I shall have to consult the Lord Chamberlain about it." He blinked as another thought occurred. "But what exactly do you propose your archer will do?"

Hero smiled. "I've devoted some thought to that and decided that when the litter arrives at the cliff top, the figure will draw its bow and fire an arrow out over the water."

"Didn't Hero of Alexandria design something like that for a different sort of figure?" Zeno interrupted. "I believe I recall the diagram. You can adapt the mechanism, so that part at least is already done."

Hero's smile diminished. "It's constructing the figure that will be difficult. However, my thought is that as the arrow leaves the bow, it will be the signal for the villagers to throw their straw man off the headland into the sea, thus providing the required symbolic sacrifice for a fruitful harvest, or whatever these ancient festivities were designed to accomplish."

Zeno agreed that it sounded appropriate and dignified. "I really must invite some palace dignitaries to attend as well. Senator Balbinus for one," he added. "After all, Castor is his nephew and Balbinus will be very impressed when he sees how well you've brought the figures from Castor's volume to life. Then perhaps he'll stop lecturing the poor man about wasting so many nomismata on codices and scrolls. Balbinus treats him like some wayward son at times." He sighed. "But now the senator will spread your fame, my friend!"

Hero had no opportunity to respond since the nursemaid Bertrada ran into the workshop, pulling Poppaea by her hand.

"The whale came back! It's chasing us!" shrieked Poppaea. Her light curly hair, usually pinned up, was disheveled and her round face was pink with excitement. Zeno thought the little girl appeared as much exhilarated as terrified.

"It's true," Bertrada gasped breathlessly. The plaits in her blonde hair were coming loose, as if to match her young charge's unruly hairstyle. "We saw it! It was swimming right to shore, looking straight at us!"

"It won't harm you, my dears," Zeno reassured them kindly. "It's a creature of the sea and therefore cannot venture on land."

"Indeed," Hero added, "the beast can't do much more than put a pretty flush on your face, Bertrada. But what were you doing, walking on the beach at this hour?"

"It gets so hot later in the day that we thought we'd go to the shore early for a picnic and then look for shells. But it's true, Hero. The creature was swimming right toward us!" Bertrada pushed back a loose strand of hair, directing a coquettish smile at the brawny man.

Poppaea began to hop up and down and scream even louder before slyly loosening her hair further so that its curls fell down over her plump cheeks. From the corner of his eye, Zeno caught her glancing furtively at him, as if to judge what effect her display of mock hysterics was having.

"Now then, don't be so loud, Poppaea," he chided her gently. "You'll hurt my old ears. It's just as well Sunilda isn't here or I would be deaf between the two of you screaming!"

Bertrada looked horrified. "Sunilda! Where is she?"

Poppaea suddenly looked genuinely frightened and burst into tears.

"She was running along right behind us," Bertrada stammered. "Or at least I thought she was."

"Don't worry," Hero reassured her quickly, "I'll go right away and find her."

"No." Zeno placed his hand on the younger man's shoulder. "I'll go. You have work to do."

Hero's jaw tightened with anger. "Do you think I'm incapable—"

Zeno pulled his hand away from the Egyptian's shoulder as if from the glowing forge. "Sunilda is in no danger," he said as he turned and hurried out of the workshop.

❄ ❄ ❄

Zeno trotted briskly along the track through the olive grove until his weary legs reminded him he was much older than he had temporarily imagined himself. He emerged, panting, on the headland not far from the spot where Hero's newest automaton would shortly be staging its first and final performance. From the high ground he scanned the sea, empty now save for an occasional bobbing seabird and the sharply upthrust crags of the island. The beach, running away in a curve toward the village, appeared likewise devoid of life.

Reaching a point where the land sloped more gradually, he made his way down to the beach. He walked along the shore, calling Sunilda's name repeatedly. His heart pounded from exertion and he began to feel panic swelling with each heartbeat.

He finally stopped at the shrine sitting opposite the island. The shrine was a simple, open-sided, four-pillared structure with a small pedestal sheltered under its flat roof. Soggy ashes lay in a deep bowl set into the top of the pedestal, the remains of a question addressed to the goats that someone had written on a scrap of parchment and burnt before sunrise in keeping with tradition. It was all superstitious nonsense, of course, but entertaining enough.

Zeno blinked. The strengthening sunlight glinting off the incoming waves hurt his eyes. Had Porphyrio really come for the child? Could the sea have swallowed her up? He was struck by an inexplicable sense of doom. He would never see her again. Another young life was gone, snatched away from under his roof.

Then he heard laughter carried on the freshening breeze and he reminded himself that he had known all along where he would find her if he had just paused long enough to think about it.

Minthe's house sat at the base of a hill that thrust out toward the water. Surrounded by herb beds, her home was a strange dwelling, originally a small half-ruined temple to some forgotten god and now repaired in a makeshift manner.

Minthe and Sunilda were looking out to sea, sitting on a fallen marble column that served as a bench.

"We just talked to Porphyrio," the girl called to Zeno as he approached.

"And what did he tell you?" Zeno spoke calmly but shot a glare toward Minthe.

"That's a secret," replied the girl, wrinkling her nose as if annoyed he'd asked. Though Zeno had heard her laughing not long before, her solemn little face revealed no sign of humor.

"We've been having a pleasant little chat, sir," put in Minthe. "I was just about to bring her back."

She stood, a short woman but straight and angular, with long silver hair that stirred in the sea breeze. Zeno couldn't help thinking that her bony face with its high cheekbones must have given her a most striking appearance when she was young. If she lived long enough she would again be beautiful.

"Would you like me to make a protective charm for her?" the woman inquired.

"Certainly not," Zeno snapped. "We mustn't undo all of Godomar's tutoring, Minthe. And as for you, young lady," he said, trying without much success to look and sound severe, "I fear I must forbid you to wander about unaccompanied until we can be certain it's safe to do so."

The child hopped down from her perch. "I know what you're thinking, Zeno. It's about Gadaric, but you don't need to worry. Why, what do you suppose Minthe and I were laughing about just now? But don't ask. That's a secret too!"

❊ ❊ ❊

Peter followed John to the front door of Zeno's villa. Having posted excubitors along the paved drive leading up from the coast road, Felix accompanied them, but even though they were protected, Peter glanced around the lush surroundings with increasing trepidation. As they passed through the gardens, he had noticed several statues of horrifying blasphemy set here and there among the riot of flower beds as well as numerous shrubs pruned into the likenesses of fantastic creatures. A bronze mechanical owl that unexpectedly hooted at the visitors from its perch on a marble tree stump near the wide terrace in front of Zeno's house had given him a terrible fright.

Worse, the villa's polished wood door had swung open as the men stepped up to it, but no servant waited in the exceedingly narrow and unusually short vestibule. The door had opened of its own accord.

Peter trod stoutly forward anyway, determined to accompany his master to the end, even into Hell itself.

He was therefore not completely surprised when the outer door thudded shut behind them without apparent aid, but he was certainly shocked when the lamp set in a wall alcove sputtered and suddenly died, leaving the vestibule in darkness.

Felix cursed in a disgustingly obscene manner and John uttered a short, sharp phrase in a foreign language that, going by the tone his master used, Peter was happy he was not able to translate.

There was a grating squeal and the marble beneath Peter's feet vibrated in the manner that the pavement of a forum moved when a heavy cart passed by. The inner door of the vestibule opened a crack, spilling some light into the space in which they were trapped.

It stopped moving.

Felix stepped to the door and tried to force it open, his shadow swimming around the now dimly lit vestibule as he struggled. Instead of obliging, the door clanked shut again.

"Stand away," he finally growled. His sword came out of its scabbard. "This could well be a trap."

He pounded on the inner door and shouted a command that it be opened in the emperor's name, his voice booming around the enclosed area.

Again the floor vibrated slightly and again the door creaked open just enough to allow a little light to enter.

Footsteps approached and then a woman's voice spoke reassuringly.

"Don't worry, you in there. It keeps jamming even though Hero's tinkering endlessly with the mechanism. I'll have you out very quickly."

A thinly shaped object was thrust through the narrow illuminated opening. Felix raised his sword but the object proved to be an iron bar with which the woman on the other side proceeded to lever open the recalcitrant door.

Their rescuer had dark hair dressed in an elaborately rolled fashion. Her silk garments were obviously not those of a servant.

"We keep this useful item to hand," she explained with a hint of a smile, setting the bar back against the wall as the erstwhile captives emerged into Zeno's bright atrium.

"Thank you, Calyce," John said with a slight bow.

The woman looked surprised. "Lord Chamberlain! We spoke only briefly on the night of the tragedy. You have an excellent memory for names and faces."

He smiled. "A very useful skill, considering many of my court duties."

Calyce bent to place a wooden wedge under the inner door. "We generally keep it open this way," she explained, "but it must have been knocked aside by accident."

Felix was looking around suspiciously, sword still half raised. "There seem to be rather a lot of accidents on this estate," he remarked dourly, finally sheathing the weapon.

"What about the outside door? Have there been problems with it?" John asked the woman.

She shook her head. "No, it's only the inner one that's given occasional difficulty—at least up until now."

"Calyce! What are you doing?" Another woman swept into the atrium in an impatient flurry of rustling robes. She was shorter than Calyce and as plump as a dove. She sounded angry.

"I am admitting guests, Livia."

"That is a servant's duty! The empress would be appalled to learn that one of her ladies-in-waiting had decided to act as a doorkeeper."

"Livia, my felicitations," John intervened. "We spoke on the night of the banquet, didn't we? I'm afraid Zeno's servants are not so attentive today as they were then. Indeed, they all appear to be otherwise occupied at present. However, I can find my way now that Calcye has so graciously released us from our temporary imprisonment."

"Thank you, Lord Chamberlain," replied Livia. "Needless to say, I shall have a very stern word with the servants about their negligence."

Having been spared the need to resolve the dilemma of whether an empress' lady-in-waiting should wait upon the emperor's Lord Chamberlain, the two women then departed into the depths of the villa, muttering irritably at one another.

Felix looked even more annoyed than the women. "I doubt that was an accident, John," he said bluntly as soon as Livia and Calcye were out of earshot. "Surely even Zeno must be tired of all these malfunctioning mechanisms by now? It seems extremely suspicious to me."

John agreed it was certainly very odd.

Much relieved, Peter finally spoke. "If I may say so, master, visitors should always be escorted immediately to the presence of the master of the house and not abandoned to stand around in the atrium. After all, you never know what some of them might get up to if they're left alone to wander about the halls." He gave a sniff of censure but did not offer his entire opinion, which was that apart from Zeno's estate being a stew of blasphemy and black arts, its master apparently oversaw it very carelessly, not to say with dangerous negligence.

Following his own master and Felix down the corridor, Peter prayed silently that they were not walking straight into disaster. But then, with the arrival of the Lord Chamberlain and a captain of the excubitors, not to mention a contingent of trained military men joining forces with the guards already present, what could possibly compromise the safety of the estate?

Chapter Eight

"You want your men to patrol my estate?" Zeno flapped his hands in horror. "It's impossible, Felix! Some of my servants live in the village. How could an excubitor possibly tell one of my gardeners from a prowler lurking in the shrubbery with evil intent?"

"The village is part of your estate, Zeno," put in Livia. "I'd expect it would be patrolled as well."

The lady-in-waiting made a valid point, John thought. He said as much.

Felix had spent hours surveying Zeno's estate. The main house was a rambling edifice with multiple wings and interior gardens connected by colonnades. A maze of ornamental gardens interspersed with groves and meadows in which stood workshops, baths, and shrines surrounded the large dwelling. Beyond, the estate proper gradually merged into fields and the outskirts of the village with no clear demarcation between them, let alone a wall.

Now Felix had convened a meeting to discuss this security nightmare. The gathering was in an unadorned office looking out into an interior courtyard. Even with the writing desk pushed against its back wall, with several members of Zeno's household as well as the visitors from Constantinople present, the small room was crowded. It did however have the advantage of being devoid of any of Hero's mechanical monstrosities.

"Yes, that's right, the village is part of my estate," Zeno said vaguely. "I've never paid much heed to the matter. My servants have always come and gone as they wish and I'm certain they won't want armed men patrolling on their doorsteps."

Livia glared. "But surely if their master says they'll have patrols, they'll have patrols—and be glad of them, too."

"Oh, Livia, what I am going to do with you? We've only been guests since summer began and already you want to run the entire estate!" Calyce spoke laughingly but her smile looked forced.

John's gaze passed wearily over the two women. They formed a marked contrast. Calyce was slim and dark with an overly prominent jaw, while Livia was shorter, fairer, rounder in figure and face. He had no doubt that the empress had chosen them deliberately. It was the sort of pairing she'd find highly comical and if they also happened to dislike each other, well, the imperial mistress of the disgruntled ladies-in-waiting would doubtless find that even more amusing.

Bertrada, the nursemaid who had hitherto remained standing near the door, now took a couple of steps forward and spoke. She was, John noted, an angular young woman, balanced precariously between the girl she was no longer and the woman she had not yet become. She had the blonde hair and blue eyes of the northerner.

"I'm in favor of extended patrols, sir," she timidly addressed Felix. "As Sunilda's nursemaid, her safety is always my first responsibility."

"And an excellent job you've done so far," remarked Livia sarcastically.

Bertrada looked as if she was about to cry. "Gadaric wasn't...it was an accident..." The girl's lips began to quiver. Her eyes filled with tears and she whirled and ran from the room, closely followed by Calyce, who shot Livia a look of hatred as she left.

John exchanged glances with Felix. Behind his shaggy beard the excubitor captain appeared pale, strongly suggesting that he would rather face twenty armed foes than one hysterical woman.

"I think it would be wise to have wider-ranging patrols," John advised, turning to Zeno. "You were just relating to us what a terrible fright you'd had when Bertrada and Poppaea came back from the beach without Sunilda. This time you were fortunate to find the girl safe with her friend, but next time you may not be so lucky."

"I suppose you're right, John." Zeno's uncertainty grew. "Only you don't suppose that all these new arrangements and guards and patrols going about will impede our preparations for the festival, do you?" He stared out at the sunny courtyard as wistfully as a child toiling over its lessons while longing to go out and play. "Hero seems confident that everything will be completed in good time, but the day is fast approaching."

"I'm happy to hear that your plans are going forward, Zeno," observed Livia. "Theodora doesn't want her personal tragedy to ruin the villagers' little bit of rustic joy, you know. That's why she intends to attend the festivities herself, although of course it will be with a heavy heart."

John suppressed a sigh. His visit to Zeno's villa was going to seem exceedingly long, however short a time it might turn out to be as measured by a water clock.

❄ ❄ ❄

"I don't suppose you'll require this, Lord Chamberlain."

Entering the guest room Zeno had allotted him, John was surprised to see the tall man whose words had prefaced the appearance of the whale at the banquet reaching up to remove a wooden cross hung high on the wall.

"I am Godomar, the twins' tutor, and a plainspoken man, as you can tell from what I just said." Godomar bent to add the cross to a crate almost filled with codices and writing materials. "I make no apologies for that. After all, my host Zeno is a plainspoken man himself in his own way."

"Do you mean he has a loose tongue?" John replied with a smile.

Godomar did not return it. John wondered if the man were capable of such an expression or whether his starved features had been paralyzed by disuse, like the legs of stylites perched too many years atop their columns. He was one of the few household members John had not yet interviewed.

John moved to the small table by the window and picked up a wax tablet, reading aloud the Latin scratched thereon. "Thy hair is like the wool of goats."

"One of Bertrada's exercises," growled the other impatiently. "She's also my pupil. I've had to instruct her to confine herself to appropriate works to study repeatedly. However, I fear that, like goats, she tends to stray and I regret to say that I have had to correct her about that tendency on more than one occasion."

As he handed the tablet to Godomar John caught a faint hint of the perfume wedded to the wax. "My taking this room won't inconvenience your lessons, Godomar?"

"No. I'll just tutor elsewhere. Zeno has a very large residence and the only reason I used this particular room is because it's next to mine."

The room was hot. Looking out of its small window, John noted shrubbery and ornamental trees as still as the bucolic scene surrounding the mosaic girl on his study wall.

"Lord Chamberlain, I must speak frankly with you," Godomar said abruptly. "It is about your religious inclinations."

John wondered who could have mentioned his religious beliefs to Godomar. Zeno's careless prattling, perhaps.

"You and the excubitor captain have been ordered to protect Sunilda from physical harm," Godomar went on. His deep-set eyes gave the impression of having seen much pain, John thought. The eyes of a martyr—or of a torturer. "My duty is to guard her spiritual welfare, for how can it benefit us to prolong our ephemeral sojourn in this earthly realm if we lose our immortal souls in the process?"

"Sunilda is only a child, and thus I would think hardly in danger of losing her soul," John observed.

"Evidently you do not realize that although yet an innocent child, the blood of heretics runs in her veins."

"But surely the Ostrogoths are Christians?" John pointed out.

"Their blasphemous beliefs have been proscribed for two centuries," retorted Godomar. "I have traveled to Ravenna, Lord Chamberlain. In a church in that city there is a depiction of our Lord being baptized, and whereas the workmanship is undeniably exquisite, yet consider how the Arians view Him." Outrage and agitation became increasingly obvious in his expression and voice as he continued. "As a created being—admittedly the highest of all such creations—rather than one who shares the substance of God, that's how they see Him. And this disgraceful work was commissioned by King Theodoric, my remaining charge's great-grandfather."

"The young Theodoric did not have the benefit of your excellent guidance," John replied tactfully.

Godomar swept a codex off the table and into his crate. "Someone should have guided him, Lord Chamberlain. He grew to manhood in Constantinople, after all."

"Yes, he was an imperial guest just like the twins. Therefore I think you'll agree that we have an even more compelling common interest in seeing that his great-granddaughter comes to no harm."

"Indeed we do. This has been a most rigorous summer, Lord Chamberlain. My patience has been sorely tried between infernal machines on one side and fortune-telling goats and magick on the other. Now there has been the unspeakable tragedy of Gadaric's death. But at least he died uncorrupted. I am convinced that this estate is situated in the atrium of Hell."

He hefted the heavy crate with a slight grunt and proceeded to bear his burden out of the room.

❄ ❄ ❄

"You must have suffered from far worse neighbors than Godomar in all those military camps you lived in during your years as a mercenary, John."

Felix' remark sounded humorous but he looked as morose as Godomar. The Lord Chamberlain had found the stalwart captain looking around the back of the villa, not far from the workshops where one of his excubitors was stationed. The occasional clang of metal striking metal broke the stillness of the hot air.

"You look unwell, Felix," John replied. "Perhaps you should get out of the sun? There's a seat under that tree."

Felix followed him silently across the courtyard and sat down on the lion-footed marble bench. He appeared distracted. After tugging unhappily at his beard once or twice, he finally burst into speech. "I've seen something that has greatly disturbed me, John."

John remarked that he was not surprised since there was much to be disturbed about on the estate, especially from a security viewpoint.

"True enough, but it isn't anything to do with that. I'm ashamed to admit it. I—" Felix broke off and shook his shaggy head silently.

John waited, hoping Felix would continue. Beside their bench unfamiliar flowers on slender stems swayed, not in the breeze, for there was none, but bent by the arrival and departure of bees. John could hear the insects' buzzing in the short, quiet intervals punctuating the sound of Hero's metalworking.

"Well, here we are, two followers of Lord Mithra who have also been comrades a long time," John finally said. "What could there possibly be that you would be ashamed to confide to an old friend like me?"

Felix attempted a smile. "It's the sight of the girl," he finally muttered, looking away from John at the nearby statue of Eros as he spoke. "The young blonde. Didn't you notice her?"

"The nursemaid? Bertrada?"

"Yes, Bertrada." Felix looked as if about to strangle on the name. "It is she, John! She's Berta. The very likeness of my love, even to the name! She has come back to me."

John thought of Isis' young employee Berta, a blonde like Bertrada and the girl Felix had wished to marry. "Berta has gone from you, my friend," he said gently, "and I must say that I do not see any likeness between the two women."

He tried to persuade Felix of the folly of his strange delusion but his words sounded unconvincing to his own ears. Even as he spoke them, he could not help thinking how much Sunilda resembled the mosaic girl, Zoe.

He did not have time to reflect further on these enigmas because Calyce suddenly appeared, running toward them in a panic. A thin strip of her silk tunic, doubtless torn by some thorn in her hasty passage through the garden, was flying out behind her.

"Lord Chamberlain! Captain Felix!" she gasped out. "It is Poppaea! Someone has tried to murder her!"

Chapter Nine

Greetings, dear Aunt Matasuntha.

Things here are very exciting! Poppaea was found dead in the garden, or so everyone thought because she was so still, but then they saw she was just ill and put her to bed. Livia screamed until she was hoarse and Zeno stood about looking as if he wanted to weep. Bertrada said not a word, although it would have been difficult to hear her if she had, because Godomar said a great deal and sounded worst of all. As for the Lord Chamberlain, he looked very stern and Captain Felix swore in the most awful way, or at least until he saw me listening.

Did I tell you about Captain Felix? He is a big soldier with a beard. He reminds me of the bear that Theodora showed me, the one she keeps in a cage at the palace. The estate is swarming with the soldiers Captain Felix commands. Justinian does have ever so many soldiers, doesn't he? I would have thought with all the ones he's sent to Italy he wouldn't have any left, but they're everywhere. Ever since Gadaric went away I can hardly go anywhere without someone watching me. It's very tiresome.

Poppaea is still sleeping so I have nobody to talk to right now. Zeno doesn't want to play dodge ball any more, Hero is busy in the workshop and that funny little man Barnabas has run away. Livia sits sobbing by Poppaea's bed or gets into awful arguments with Bertrada and Calyce. I did try to listen to find out what they were arguing about (and why not, when they never tell me anything?) but Bertrada caught me and scolded me for ages.

After that she took me to the atrium and we sat there for hours and hours doing nothing at all. Captain Felix went by more than once and stared at Bertrada very boldly every time. She just pretended not to notice but she did really. When I asked her about him she scolded me again.

Well, since nobody tells me anything I'm not going to tell them that Porphyrio promised he is going to take me to Gadaric very soon. It was on the morning we went to the beach for our picnic. There was a great flock of seabirds sitting along the shore, just like a white carpet. Poppaea and

I ran along the edge of the water scaring the silly things and they went flapping off in a big, noisy cloud.

By the time we had done that, Bertrada had unpacked our picnic basket and we started to eat all the nice things she had got for us. Then we saw Porphyrio, swimming out by the island where the goats live. He sprayed water up into the air, just like Hero's whale does, or so Hero says. I still haven't seen it working, you know. Anyhow, the water Porphyrio spouted sparkled like the jewels on Theodora's robe, it really was very pretty. Then he swam right towards us.

Out in the sea he looks like a toy but when he got closer to the beach we could see how huge he is and Bertrada and Poppaea got scared and ran away. I pretended to follow them but hid behind a bush until I couldn't see them any more because I knew Porphyrio wanted to speak to me privately.

How Porphyrio and I speak is magick and with his magick he explained how I shall soon meet my brother again. Don't say anything about it yet as I want to surprise everyone, especially Bertrada. I expect she'll cry a lot when Theodora finds out and she can't explain where I went, but it will serve her right for being so nasty to me. After all, she's just a servant.

Now I am going for a walk in the garden.

Chapter Ten

"Why do you stare at me, Lord Chamberlain?"

Sunilda's remark took John by surprise. He was speechless for an instant for he was a man seldom taken by surprise, and especially not by eight-year-old girls.

"I'm sorry, I didn't realize I was staring. It must be because you remind me of someone, Sunilda," he said.

"Almost everyone looks like someone else you know. I've noticed that myself. Who do you think I look like?"

They were strolling around Zeno's gardens, Sunilda leading her companion confidently through the maze of paths. John had intended to take a walk and ponder the situation, made even more complicated by the apparent attempt on

Poppaea's life that afternoon, but Sunilda had come running after him, disrupting his thoughts.

"You look like another little girl I know." He didn't care to answer her question more fully.

Sunilda looked round at him with disturbingly wise eyes. "She must be a servant or some other ordinary person, Lord Chamberlain. If she was a great lady, you'd say more about her."

"She isn't ordinary but she's not a great lady either."

"What makes you think I look like her?"

One difficulty in talking with children, John thought, was that they genuinely expected answers whereas most of the adults he dealt with every day at court only pretended to expect them. "Your eyes are like hers. Very dark and large. Very pretty," he said.

Sunilda smiled at his reply.

The sun had begun to set. A cool breeze carried the sharp smell of the sea to them, mingling with the light, delicate scent of flowers. The faint rustling of leaves and the chirping of birds returning to their nests had replaced the earlier humming of industrious bees.

"Don't worry about Poppaea," John went on. "The palace physician has been summoned. He'll know what to do. She will soon be well enough to play with you again."

"You shouldn't be sad about my brother, Lord Chamberlain," Sunilda replied as if she had read the way his thoughts were turning. "Everyone is upset about him but it really isn't necessary."

John wondered if Godomar had been talking to the girl about the after-life, but said nothing. In this particular case such beliefs would surely be very helpful. Sunilda would, he supposed, feel grief over her brother's death soon enough.

He had questioned her at length about the picnic but learnt nothing he had not discovered already from a similar interrogation of Bertrada and the cook who had supplied the treats, not to mention the servant who had packed them into the wicker picnic basket. As in any wealthy household, only the most trusted servants were allowed to prepare food. Unfortunately there were any number of ways a determined and clever poisoner could circumvent every precaution taken.

Yet although Poppaea had fallen ill some time after the ill-fated outing, the honey cakes and sweetmeats left on the beach by their hasty departure had no strange appearance or odor. Neither Bertrada nor Sunilda had displayed any symptoms. Moreover, the abandoned treats had been fed to a local farmer's swine without any visible effects to date.

They had passed through the olive grove and reached the headland. Twilight was fast advancing. John suggested it was therefore time to return to the villa.

"I'll race you back," Sunilda proposed. "Zeno says you're a good runner."

John laughed. "I used to be, but that was years ago."

"You aren't so very old, Lord Chamberlain, and certainly not as old as some people seem to think you are," Sunilda observed.

"What do you mean by that?" John asked in a suitably serious tone, suppressing a smile.

"Everyone treats you as if you were an old man. You can tell by the way they talk to you. They always call you sir or excellency and they're always careful about what they say."

"That is just respect for the office I hold, Sunilda."

"I don't think Godomar respects you at all," the girl contradicted. "I heard him telling Livia you were not to be trusted because you were a eunuch. I was not certain what he meant, so I asked Bertrada. She told me that it means you can't father children but when I asked why, she just said you were badly hurt."

"That's true," John admitted, "but in fact I do have a daughter."

"But how did you get so badly hurt?"

It was not a question a Lord Chamberlain should have to answer for a little girl, John reflected, but her solemn gaze demanded some response. Still, he could not very well explain to her that he had desired to buy silks for his lover and that, in pursuit of his quest, he had strayed into Persia and been caught, only to be sold back over the border some time later to traders who had come to buy slaves for the palace. Gelded slaves. In the dark hours when he could not sleep he had endlessly debated why Fortuna had decreed that he was not immediately executed upon capture, as was the usual practice. The only answer at which he arrived was that Fortuna had been playing with him. Or perhaps, he suddenly thought, it had been because the Lord of Light, Mithra, had been watching over him.

"A long time ago, I went looking for something I urgently desired," he finally began, "and I strayed somewhere I shouldn't have. Across the Persian border, in fact."

"The Persians are enemies of the emperor and godless heathen," put in Sunilda.

"Indeed. Well, they caught me and I was wounded most grievously. So you see, Sunilda, when you are repeatedly warned you must not run off or stray away from Bertrada, you must pay attention. Doing so might put you into great danger, just as it did me."

"There aren't any Persians anywhere near here," the girl pointed out. "Why did they hurt you, Lord Chamberlain?"

"Because it would gain them a few coins."

"People do many bad things for money. That's what Godomar says."

"He is certainly right in that at least."

Apparently satisfied with his answers, Sunilda grabbed John's hand. "At least do hurry up a bit even if you don't want to race!"

She tugged him back along the shadowy path. She at least was not awed by the high court post he held, it seemed. John felt a hint of wetness at the corners of his eyes. He was thinking of another real girl now, not the mosaic Zoe. Far away across the sea his daughter lived with her mother. He might perhaps see them again one day, but by then Europa would be a grown woman. If they ever met once more, he hoped they could spend more time together than they had during their one brief encounter. But he had never known her as a child and the child she had been was already gone, as dead as the boy, Gadaric.

But then, so was the man he had once been, the man who had fathered a daughter.

❊ ❊ ❊

Arriving at his uncle's estate to see how his elderly relative was coping with the aftermath of Gadaric's death, Anatolius was greeted by the strange sight of a grim-faced Lord Chamberlain being dragged towards him by a small girl.

"What's the matter, John?" he asked with a chuckle. "You look absolutely morose. Is your captor here hauling you off to the dungeons?"

Short as she was by comparison, Sunilda nevertheless contrived to appear as if she was looking down her nose at Anatolius.

"Sunilda and I were just having a little talk." John extracted his hand from the girl's grasp and handed her over to the servant who arrived in response to Anatolius' rap on the villa door.

Before going inside, Sunilda turned and gave Anatolius an appraising look. "You are the one Calyce is going to marry, aren't you?" she remarked suddenly. "I must say that you look very young and not very rich."

When she had vanished inside John gave Anatolius a questioning look.

"The child is certainly not going to rival those famous goats as an oracle," Anatolius told him with a grin. "I spent the whole day of the banquet trying to avoid that woman, as you may recall. She's not unattractive in a patrician sort of way, I suppose, but I've decided it's wise to keep away from those sorts of entanglements."

"It would appear that the lady in question has other plans," John remarked dryly.

"Romantic fantasies, you mean. It really is embarrassing, John. A pity, too. I understand Calyce's family had considerable holdings in Italy but they've all been lost to the Ostrogoths.

Apparently Theodora magnanimously granted Calyce the privilege of remaining at court in order to serve as one of her ladies-in-waiting. Theodora's gifts always come with a heavy price." Anatolius gave a rueful laugh.

The last of the light stole from the sky. One of the torches flanking the doorway flared briefly. Startled, John looked quickly around. His reaction made him realize just how exhausted he had become.

"Being lady-in-waiting to Theodora might be even more perilous than you think," he said.

"Especially when the two of them dislike each other intensely," observed Anatolius. "You may think Livia looks like a dove but she's got a vulture's temperament, according to Calyce. It seems that Livia has made it plain to her on more than one occasion that she's convinced that Calyce is one of Theodora's favorites. You know how women go on about these things, seeing even the slightest comment as a deliberate slight and half the time it's all unfounded." He heaved a sigh at the strange ways of the other sex. "However, so far as I can tell the acrimony seems to have arisen mostly because Livia is the one who's always being ordered to get Theodora sweetmeats at ungodly hours or clean out her carriage or run errands here and there. Livia objects to being forced to be continually fetching and carrying—like a common servant is how she puts it."

"And how does Calyce view it?" John asked with a slight smile.

"Oh, she agrees it's true. She says it's because Livia has no real skills or talents. She can't cook tasty tidbits or arrange Theodora's hair or embroider as beautifully as Calyce does. Personally I think

Theodora keeps Livia running about so much because the poor plump woman's just not suited for physical activity. She gets out of breath and red in the face and so on. With her nasty sense of humor, it would be just the sort of thing Theodora would delight in."

"Judging from all this information, I gather you were not entirely successful in evading the romantically inclined Calyce?"

"Sadly, no." Anatolius' expression clouded. "You mentioned peril, John. What did you mean by that?"

"Apparently Theodora also kindly decreed that Livia's daughter serve as a playmate for the twins and today someone tried to poison her," John said, quickly describing the attempt on Poppaea's life.

"She was definitely poisoned? It couldn't have been over-ripe fish or green fruit, that sort of thing?"

John shook his head. "It's unmistakable. She's sleeping now but it isn't a natural slumber."

"And here I was, putting aside my labors to see how my uncle was coping only to find out it appears he has yet more worries on his hands." Anatolius looked at John with concern. "Will Poppaea recover?"

"That remains in Mithra's hands. Gaius has been sent for and will no doubt have some notion of what needs to be done."

"Perhaps you could also consult Hypatia," Anatolius suggested. "She has considerable knowledge of herbs." He suppressed a sneeze. "I'm starting to think I should seek some remedy from her for this dreadful affliction. It always seems to come upon me as soon as I venture beyond the city walls." He paused as a new thought struck him. "John, is it possible that Barnabas could be behind this new attack?"

John replied that he had initially dismissed the possibility since he had been convinced Barnabas had fled. "However," he went on wearily, "now I'm not so certain he's gone. Yet we cannot find him even though we've looked everywhere on Zeno's estate."

"Have Felix's men searched Castor's estate next door?"

"Castor? He attended Zeno's banquet, didn't he?"

"Yes, he was seated on the other side of Theodora. I'm surprised you noticed him, John. She has a way of overshadowing everyone in her vicinity and Castor is not the sort who calls attention to himself. In fact, I suspect he would have preferred to be communing with a volume from his library rather than chatting with the empress."

John observed that there were many who would prefer not to get into conversation with Theodora. "I intend to pay Castor a visit as soon as possible," he added.

"I don't think he's in residence right now. There were only one or two lights visible in his villa when I passed by his gate a little while ago."

"Isn't that unusual?"

"Not for Castor. He always dismisses most of his servants and leaves the place practically deserted while he's off on one of his business expeditions. He's almost as careless in his own way as Uncle Zeno although at least he's had the sense to surround his estate with a good high wall."

John's fatigue was suddenly suffused with anger. "Zeno didn't mention Castor was away! If the place is as deserted as it sounds, Barnabas could easily be hidden somewhere over there without the estate manager's knowledge."

"Zeno and Castor have been friends as well as neighbors for a couple of decades, John. I saw a lot of him during my visits here when I was a boy because he was always dropping in to hear about Zeno's latest enthusiasms. But even so, I do think that with everything that's been happening, Zeno wouldn't have realized he'd gone off on one of his trips."

John agreed tiredly that Anatolius was probably correct. The young man turned to go into the villa but John hesitated at its entrance, staring into the darkness in the direction of the neighboring estate.

"There's no point searching in the dark, John, and especially not after all the time that's passed," Anatolius pointed out. "We can pay the place a visit tomorrow morning."

John agreed reluctantly, realizing that raising a fresh commotion would only serve to warn the mime—if indeed he was hiding on Castor's estate—while giving him the opportunity to escape under cover of darkness.

He wearily followed Anatolius into the treacherous vestibule in which he had been trapped that morning. As he stepped through its small space he thought he heard the grinding of gears and paused as Anatolius entered the atrium.

Anatolius looked back over his shoulder in puzzlement. "What is it? Is something wrong?"

"No," the other replied. The odd sound must have existed only in his imagination. "Nothing's wrong, Anatolius. We'll visit Castor's estate tomorrow. If it holds any secrets, they will doubtless wait until then."

Chapter Eleven

"A banquet for the mind."

According to Anatolius, that was how Zeno had described his neighbor's library. Briarus, the manager of Castor's estate, threw open the room's plain wooden doors with a flourish as if he were indeed ushering John and Anatolius in to sample a feast of rare delights.

The room itself was attractive enough although not impressive, at least to those accustomed to the palace. The library's furnishings were simple. Chairs surrounded a long polished table in the center of the room and a single richly upholstered couch sat beside the wall where tall, latticed windows looked out over a garden smaller but more orderly than Zeno's overgrown grounds. Bright morning sunlight streamed in across an equally tidy array of flowers and foliage depicted on the tiled floor and along the lower portion of painted walls which were otherwise a subdued blue and punctuated by niches at waist height.

It was what filled the wall niches and lay scattered on the table that might have brought a word of admiration to the lips of Justinian himself.

Codices and scrolls, the largest private collection John had ever seen.

The library might have belonged to Briarus, to judge from his expression of pride as he led his visitors inside. He was a thin, dark haired man with a brisk air and, until now, what John suspected was a perpetual scowl.

"As you can see," Briarus told them, "the Greek texts are kept on one side of the room and the Latin on the other." Although his sharp features softened somewhat as he proudly described the contents of his master's library, his disapproval of their unannounced visit remained obvious in his tone.

Anatolius, careless of the estate manager's feelings, plucked a scroll from the table and pulled it open just far enough to glimpse its contents. "This is certainly very old, John, and extremely valuable. You see the lettering is all capitalized, like a chiseled inscription? It's just as well we no longer write in this fashion. If we did, it would take me all day to transcribe even the most minor of the emperor's proclamations."

Briarus, standing anxiously at Anatolius' elbow, relaxed at the care with which the young man handled the ancient scroll. John decided he was dealing with one of those servants who was proud to serve and looked upon his master's possessions as a mark of his own standing. Unfortunately, in his experience such men were not very forthcoming.

"Zeno mentioned that Castor is a man after his own heart," John said, "and that he takes frequent excursions into Constantinople for the purpose of collecting antiquities or commissioning manuscripts. Your master must be a very learned man."

Briarus's tight lips curved into a slight smile. "Indeed, sir, that exactly describes him. He has no time for the tedious affairs of court or the vanities of idleness. No, the master is a lover of history and learning and rarely returns from one of his forays into the city without another treasure. As you see," he gestured expansively around the room, "although this is where he spends most of his time, our library is not full of gaudy statues and carved panels and other such frivolous items."

John strolled around the room, inspecting Castor's collection. He noted not only ancients such as Homer and Aristotle but also several authors less familiar to him. He opened the leather cover of a codex lying on the table and discovered it to be Athenaeus' Deipnosophistae.

"That is a brilliant account of conversations at banquets, though I believe many would find it too complex for their taste," Briarus observed without so much as a hint of a smile.

"You are a scholar yourself, then?" John gave him an inquiring glance.

"I am a man of modest intellect, sir, but through my master's generosity I have had some opportunity to educate myself."

John returned his attention to the long table that was room's centerpiece. In addition to scrolls and codices from the library there was a neat stack of loose parchment. Castor's own notes, apparently, although as John soon realized not anything so mundane as to be of value in his investigations. Rather, the writings consisted of reflections on the cosmos, poetic form, horticulture.

"No mention of mimes, let alone dwarves." John set down the parchment he had been scanning. "Not that I would have expected any."

"The subject is probably too low for one of Castor's tastes," remarked Anatolius.

One or two codices lay open and John noticed that Castor had made notes in these also. Looking more closely, he saw one page displayed a boldly penned "No! The very idea is to admit defeat! Let us, instead, laugh in the face of eternity!"

It was written on a copy of Marcus Aurelius' Meditations. Looking over John's shoulder, Anatolius noted it was safer to disagree with dead emperors than living ones.

While John silently continued his inspection of Castor's intellectual labors, Anatolius moved to a window to gaze out into the garden. "The grounds are certainly well groomed, Briarus," he said. "There is hardly a leaf out of place."

"Thank you, sir. The master does like everything kept in good order, although it is not everyone's way."

John wondered if the man was thinking of Zeno's untidy estate next door.

"I do however notice several unkempt bushes over by the wall." Anatolius was smiling as he spoke but Briarus seemed not to notice as he hurried to the window and followed Anatolius' amused glance.

"Those are caper plants," the estate manager informed him. "This past year or so the master has become very interested in growing them. I understand that they are excellent against afflictions of the joints. Alas, the master does sometimes suffer that way."

John expressed regret, adding that he occasionally experienced similar painful twinges.

"We have an excellent gardener. He's a retired fisherman from the village who taught himself about pruning and bedding plants and all the rest," Briarus continued in a burst of confidences. "Unfortunately Paul, that's the gardener, has lately been greatly afflicted by a similar malady to the master's and so that particular bed has become very overgrown. It seems that the plant is extremely difficult to establish and the master won't allow anyone else to so much as touch the bushes. However, I understand that Paul is in somewhat better health and should be back at work soon—if he can be persuaded to return."

Briarus's loquacity on the subject of the untidy bushes reminded John that a prideful servant was as quick to respond to any perceived criticism as a mediocre poet. He asked about why the gardener might be reluctant to return to work on the estate.

The scowl Briarus had worn prior to entering the library returned. "I must admit that perhaps I was hasty of tongue and said things that were regrettable, sir, but the fact is that last time Paul was working here, we exchanged some rather hot words. I thought of bringing the matter to the attention of the master but did not. Perhaps I was lax in my duty."

John, wondering what else had happened on the estate of which Castor had been kept blissfully unaware, encouraged the man to continue with his tale.

Looking dubious, Briarus complied. "It may have been that the pain in his joints caused Paul to speak out of character. It all began when we got into conversation while he was weeding." An enraged note entered the man's voice. "Nothing would do but that he felt he must express dismay over what he called all the local evil goings-on."

"Indeed?" Anatolius said with great interest. "Did he point to anything in particular?"

"Forgive me, sir, but your uncle Zeno's automatons were most critically mentioned in his diatribe. Then there was the matter of the fortune-telling goats, which he declared sheer superstitious folly. Now, I would have been inclined to agree with him on the matter of the goats, but then he went on in the same breath to condemn what he called the master's blasphemous collection of old pagan philosophers, if you please." The man's face had reddened with outrage as his story unfolded and was now almost as dark as a radish.

"Evidently the fame of your master's library is wider than you realize, although its contents are perhaps not entirely understood," John replied tactfully. "And as you say, it was doubtless his pain that caused Paul to speak in such a manner."

Having said which, he indicated he had seen enough of the library and Briarus resumed guiding them on their tour of the house. He had little else to say. His admission regarding his argument with the gardener appeared to have rendered him even more surly than before. Perhaps he regretted speaking so freely about his master's affairs.

As they moved through one spacious room after another John, a man of simple tastes, admired their furnishings. They were stark but of the finest workmanship. There was evidence, too, of Castor's penchant for collecting which Zeno had also mentioned, in the array of statuary gracing many of the rooms as well as the peristyle and the villa's inner garden.

There was no room John did not look through, no alcove or corner he did not inspect, but it was soon evident that Castor's home was compact and well-ordered compared to Zeno's rambling and chaotic villa. It was equally obvious that it could not offer even a temporary hiding place.

"Does the estate have an underground cistern, perhaps, or any disused structures?"

Briarus sniffed his disdain. "We have no need of a cistern as city-dwellers do, sir. As to the rest, my master would never countenance a ruin on his property although doubtless many consider such things picturesque."

John had initially thought that Castor's estate, protected behind high walls and with a front gate kept securely locked, would afford a good hiding place for Barnabas. After their walk around it, however, it seemed much less likely.

The estate was certainly well guarded, as much by Briarus's eagle eye as by bars and bolts, John thought as they returned to the gate through which Briarus had admitted them an hour or so before, carefully relocking it afterwards.

"Leave it with the others outside by the gate!" Briarus suddenly shouted. A farmer who had just arrived at the estate followed the estate manager's bellowed instructions and set down a small basket of lettuce in the place indicated. It joined one or two others that had apparently been left by similar callers during Briarus' absence.

"The master has fresh lettuce delivered regularly. He says it is good for the digestion," Briarus explained.

"The farmers walk straight onto uncle's estate," Anatolius remarked casually.

"When the master is away it is appropriate that everything be kept securely locked, sir." Briarus's tone was curt.

John agreed, adding that since the estates were situated in a less inhabited area there was no telling who might decide to visit by stealth.

"Indeed, that's true." Briarus looked pleased that this holder of high office would share his opinion on such an important matter. "For you never know," he went on, "what vagabond may decide to take the coast road. Sometimes even welcome visitors are not correctly announced. The house servants are constantly being startled when they go into the library in the morning." He glanced uneasily toward Anatolius. "I regret to say that they often find our neighbor Zeno sitting there calmly reading the master's priceless scrolls and the master nowhere to be seen!" His expression clearly conveyed his opinion of such abuse of hospitality.

Anatolius laughed at the revelation. "It doesn't surprise me at all, Briarus. When Zeno's thoughts fasten onto some fancy, it engages his attention to such an extent that he doesn't know whether it's day or night. Besides," he added, "he does love knowledge and has often praised your master's wonderful collection of works."

"His library is without compare," Briarus agreed. "In the usual course naturally I would see all the visitors entering the estate, but usually your uncle uses the private door at the back of the garden."

"Barnabas couldn't have got in that way. It's always locked," Anatolius observed.

Briarus glowered at the young man. "Unless your uncle told this fugitive you're seeking that he has a key to it, in which case the man could simply have stolen it!"

"Zeno still has the key, as a matter of fact," said John, "for he offered it to me this morning, thinking that we might prefer to simply let ourselves into your grounds. However, I felt it better that we enter formally by the front gate rather than skulking in through the back. After all, we must always be careful to observe the proprieties."

If the remark mollified Briarus, his frown didn't reveal it. "I will not say I doubt our neighbor's judgment, sir. All the same, we were shocked to find a pile of scrolls knocked all over the floor a few days ago. The servants are not permitted to touch them, of course, although the room is cleaned daily. The master is very particular about that. And to make it worse, there were leaves and mud and such trodden in from the garden all over the tiles. He was furious. I have never seen him so angry."

"An intruder, perhaps one who was disturbed, do you suppose?" John asked with interest.

"One of the house servants had told me that very morning she thought she'd heard voices in the library very late the night before, but I pointed out to her that possibly the master was entertaining a visitor."

"And when you were called in and shown the scene next morning you felt it would not be discreet to mention her remarks?"

"Indeed, sir, that is so," Briarus confirmed.

John suddenly asked the estate manager to show them the private door between the two estates.

Briarus unlocked the stout, nail-studded door set in a brick wall just beyond the overgrown bushes Anatolius had spotted from the library window. Capers dangled untidily, obscuring the door, which opened onto a path on Zeno's estate, half-concealed in a particularly overgrown laurel thicket.

Relocking the door, Briarus emerged from behind the caper bed fussily brushing off his clothes and grumbling under his breath about ruining his garments just to further prove the utter unlikelihood of a famous dwarf going unnoticed by his well-supervised staff of servants. John thanked him for his assistance and dismissed him to his other duties.

Anatolius, wiping watering eyes with his tunic sleeve, pointed out that lingering overlong in Castor's garden was bringing on an attack of his malady. "And what's worse," he went on mournfully, "either my vision is even worse than I imagine or else Zeno has managed to persuade Castor to harbor one of Hero's more peculiar inventions."

He pointed at the nearby fountain. A bronze ibis stood on the edge of its basin. Smaller silver birds and fruit swinging from chains occupied the branches of an intricately carved marble tree growing from a facsimile of a cliff face set in the middle of the basin. "This must be the contraption for which he showed me the diagram just a few weeks ago. When the fountain is working, the small birds sing and the fruits act as chimes. I understand that the effect is very melodic although after some hours it must become rather annoying."

"Then it's an excellent arrangement for it to be set out of earshot of the villa. And what about the ibis? What does that do?"

Anatolius shook his head. "I'm not certain. Perhaps Hero and Zeno haven't decided yet. I gather this is only a working model." A worried look crossed his face. "I hope that I'm not eventually going to be presented with a fully functional version for my own garden!"

As they returned to the front gate, John observed that he would have liked to have examined the papers in the missing estate owner's office more closely. Solicitous of his master's privacy, however, Briarus had seemed particularly anxious for his visitors not to linger there.

"On the other hand, Castor is Senator Balbinus' nephew so it would be wise to proceed with caution. All the same, it seems very odd that Briarus doesn't know where Castor has gone, or at least claims not to know."

Anatolius snuffled miserably. "Since you appear to suspect everyone and his brother, I believe I can lend you a hand, John, especially as I intend to escape back to the city as soon as possible."

"No," John cut in firmly, "I do not wish you to question Balbinus about his nephew's whereabouts."

"But it would be so helpful to your investigations and I would be happy to visit Balbinus as soon as I arrive back in Constantinople."

"Anatolius, I appreciate your kind offer but I fear that your leap into action is connected much more with the prospect of visiting Balbinus' wife than of interviewing her husband."

"Lucretia? That was years ago. She'll most likely be elsewhere when I call anyway." The expression in his eyes betrayed his hope that this would not prove to be the case.

John's lips tightened. There were enough pitfalls strewn about court for a young man without inviting disaster by becoming involved, again, with a woman who was now a senator's wife. Even so, he chided himself, it required the consent of both parties to have an affair and Lucretia had always conducted herself in an honorable way despite her less than happy arranged marriage. Then too, it might be the only way to find out quickly why the owner of the estate next to the one on which a young boy had been horribly murdered had suddenly departed for a destination unknown without even leaving instructions for his estate manager. That is, if what Briarus had said was true.

"Very well, then," he finally said, "if you insist. But promise me you will do nothing that might be misconstrued, not a single word or an inappropriate look, however romantic it might strike you at the time. The situation is difficult enough. Inappropriate relationships only bring trouble. We don't need any more of them."

Chapter Twelve

Bertrada discovered Hero sitting on a bench outside the workshop, gazing glumly at a diagram spread across his knees. A frown nagged a deep bridge between his eyebrows. She sat silently down beside him, trying to compose herself.

"There's something I have to tell you, Hero," she finally managed to say. "About us. Something important."

Distracted from his musing, Hero looked up and smiled. "Bertrada, my dove. What did you say? Have you escaped from your nursemaid duties for a while?" He leaned toward her for a kiss.

Annoyed, she glared at him and then spoke, attempting to imitate the withering tones she had often heard Calyce and Livia use to each other. "I certainly haven't left Sunilda alone, if that's what you mean. Do you think me nothing but a foolish girl?" She realized she couldn't recall exactly how she had planned to convey her decision to him in the kindest possible manner.

Hero gave a deep chuckle of merriment that creased his dark face, banishing the frown that had greeted her. "Ah, Bertrada, you may be a girl but never foolish. However, I'm glad that you came to visit even if it's just for a short time. Would you like to inspect my latest inspiration?"

The girl blushed. Now her carefully composed speech vanished entirely from her memory. "Unfortunately, I—"

Another chuckle. "No, I didn't mean that sort of inspiration although certainly you inspire me in more ways than one. However, since we agreed we must be discreet, I shall forgo the opportunity of being inspired in daylight at least!"

Bertrada's smile was as frosty as her blue eyes. "Some of your mechanical marvels have certainly been inspired, although in need of one or two adjustments to make them perform the task intended. Or perhaps even three or four, in some cases."

"Yes, the lyre-playing automaton was not supposed to serenade us all in the middle of the night," Hero replied gloomily, "although I did ascertain the nature of the problem. And just as well, as Zeno is most insistent that it is to be one of the figures accompanying the procession for the village celebration. He's spending almost as much time in the workshop as I do, you know. Personally, I would have thought he has enough to worry about right now having to arrange the boy's funeral rites."

Bertrada's eyes filled with tears at the mention of Gadaric. "I hope there will be a little ceremony at least."

"Well, I don't think Gadaric would care much for something so simple as that, considering how much time the boy spent prowling around my workshop gaping at my inventions. I suspect he would have much rather had fire-breathing monsters or some such to see him off on his final journey. Is this why you are in such a bad humor?" He patted her hand. "I keep telling you, you shouldn't blame yourself, Bertrada. You couldn't have known Gadaric was intent on creeping out as soon as he could."

Bertrada silently wiped her eyes.

"Try to keep busy," Hero advised kindly. "Look at Zeno. Now I think on it further, it's just as well he has so much to occupy his mind. Or perhaps he's just blessed with ignorance and doesn't realize how quickly Theodora could easily decide that it's his fault the boy is dead. She's insistent that the wretched festival go forward. Perhaps that's what's saved him so far, since she wouldn't want to risk his loss spoiling her entertainment. The empress was fascinated when she toured my workshop, you know. She told me she was eager to see all my half-wonders completed and in operation."

"I'm certain it will be a fine spectacle indeed, Hero, but I hear not all the villagers are happy about it. There's been much grumbling about not tampering with ancient tradition, especially when ungodly machines are going to be involved."

"Ungodly machines!" Hero was outraged. "Who said that? It was Godomar, wasn't it? Why, they're the finest automatons that can be constructed! They'll make an astounding display for Theodora. Zeno plans not only to include two or three of my lyre-players in the procession but also the flautist I'm working on at the moment. They'll be pulled along on a cart so their music can accompany the singers. I'm also making a magnificent archer to be carried on a litter. We were discussing that just recently. And when the procession arrives at the headland, there will be speeches and so on. It's going to be really spectacular, especially since it's all done by torchlight. The straw man is thrown off the cliff just as the sun rises, you see."

"We've heard something about it from Minthe," Bertrada replied. "I gather it's been going on for centuries. A celebration of the end of summer, she said, the straw man being its representation and having to be sacrificed to the autumn gods for a good harvest, or something like that. But really it's just one of those interesting old customs that Zeno loves so much. Nobody believes in such sacrifices these days and even if they did, they could hardly say so, could they? And yet," she concluded thoughtfully, "do you suppose that in the old days, real people were thrown off the cliff into the sea?"

Hero shrugged powerful shoulders. "Possibly, one might say almost certainly. However, Zeno's improvements, as he calls them, will certainly enliven the festival without posing any danger to anyone."

He continued enthusiastically, explaining the mechanical archer's role to the girl, and then paused, ruefully contemplating the destruction of the result of so much of his thought and labor.

"If it were not for the honor of enhancing the occasion," he went on, "I would much rather not lose the archer. But there it is. I gather it's going to be dressed in some of Zeno's finest clothing, with not a wisp of straw about its person. Needless to say, Zeno's been fussing about like a mother hen, chiding me for my slowness in completing the musicians. And they do need to be tested before the day. There's only a week left."

Bertrada rearranged the folds of her linen robes daintily, imitating the oft-observed actions of Theodora's ladies-in-waiting. "Life continually seems to swing back and forth between haste and wait and rarely continues for any space on an even keel, as seamen would say," she remarked. Her philosophical comment began a chain of thought that leapt rapidly from sailors to soldiers and then she suddenly remembered her reason for seeking Hero out.

"Did Zeno mention anything about guards for the procession?" she asked with over-elaborate casualness. "After all, we can't afford to take chances with Sunilda's safety."

Hero nodded. "He was complaining about the estate swarming with excubitors. Not so much because of their presence but because they aren't always very careful where they tramp during their patrols and the gardeners are constantly complaining about damage to the flower beds. Then he said that their captain has been very insistent about the need for extra caution, what with the estate being more or less unprotected and open to the world, not to mention the business of the procession. Apparently he thinks it is the height of folly in the circumstances."

"Captain Felix carries out his duties faithfully, doesn't he?"

"Yes, and he also stares a lot at a certain young lady," Hero snapped. "Quite the barbarian, if you ask me."

"Some might call Sunilda and me barbarians," Bertrada flared, color tinting her cheekbones. "He is polite enough and after all he and his men were ordered here to protect Sunilda. No doubt he would much rather be at court."

"And so would you, wouldn't you?" Hero retorted hotly. "Your strange humor has something to do with this ignorant soldier, doesn't it? A man who's grizzled enough to be your father, at that."

Bertrada said nothing but stood and began to walk away.

"Wait, Bertrada," Hero called after her. "I'm sorry, I shouldn't have spoken so hastily."

She half turned. There was something in what he'd said about Felix, she admitted to herself. The soldier was certainly a lot older than she.

"Come inside and let me show you the improvements I've made to the hand. You know I'm making it only for you. A woman naturally wants a man who is whole."

Affecting an expression of irritation, she nevertheless followed him into the workshop. "If you're making the hand on my behalf why are you so eager to boast about it to everybody, Hero? Do you think I don't know that everyone in the villa has seen it?" Her complaint sounded weak, even to her own ears.

"Ah, but nobody has seen the latest adjustments I've made to the leather straps and wires," Hero explained. "Soon I will be able to hold you with two hands and not just one."

The girl reddened again.

Hero looked around a cluttered work table, scowled, and walked over to an equally overburdened shelf by the window.

"I must have put it away." He reached for a large box set on the low shelf. "Now, it's only in the very early stages and there are still some problems to be resolved, but wait until you see—" He hefted the box onto the workbench and then removed the lid as he spoke. As he looked down into the container his flow of words was suddenly cut off as cleanly as his arm had been severed.

"It's gone! Setesh take the bastard who's stolen it!" His shocked expression presented a ghastly sight as he turned toward the girl, his remaining huge fist clenched in a knot of fury.

❄ ❄ ❄

Godomar tugged at the stubborn door of the low wooden cupboard beside Bertrada's bed. He gave a harder yank and the door came partially open with a loud creak. For an instant he held his breath and listened intently. Through the open window he heard Sunilda's faint laughter. So Bertrada was playing with the child in the garden, he thought. It was remarkable how little heed the young paid to mortality. It seemed strange that with her brother dead and her young playmate lying desperately ill the child could even laugh at all.

He eased the cupboard door open. The lone shelf held only a terra cotta lamp and a small box that investigation showed contained Bertrada's few pieces of jewelry.

Crouched beside the bed, he peered around the room. Its whitewashed plaster walls were bare. Aside from the bed, beneath which he had discovered only dust and a baked-clay playing piece from some board game or other, its furniture consisted of a wooden stool, a storage chest holding several robes, and the small cupboard just inspected.

The same perfume that so often accompanied the young nursemaid faintly permeated the air although Godomar had not found any perfume bottles or unguent jars. He sniffed again. Calyce. It was the scent in which the lady-in-waiting habitually soaked herself. Yes, he thought sourly, she was exceptionally concerned with worldly vanities, was Calyce, and thus doubtless a bad influence upon Bertrada.

A pile of discarded clothing lay in the narrow space between bed and window. He bent over the untidy heap. Overseeing the proper upbringing of children was an onerous affair indeed. However, it was the task he had been assigned by Theodora personally and he dared not shrink from even its most distasteful aspects, such as searching a woman's bedroom.

The odor of perfume assailed him more strongly. Gingerly he plucked up a thin linen tunica. His lips tightened as he discovered what the artfully disarranged clothes concealed.

It was a stack of codices topped by a collection of John Chrysostom's homilies. The volumes below were much less commendable. Moving aside a history of the Goths he pushed open the leather cover of the codex lying beneath it.

He noticed first the curse inscribed within:

> "May long-clawed demons rend out the eyes of whoever steals this from the library of Aulus Livius Castor"

Then he read its title. It was Ovid's Art of Love.

His long fingers twitched as he hesitated, debating whether or not to continue. He lifted the volume and noted it fell open at a certain place, no doubt because it had been consulted often. Here was something he did not wish to know, as a decent man. Yet, however unpalatable it was, would he not be remiss if he failed to learn the precise nature of the vile error into which his charge had obviously fallen?

The verse was nearly illegible, words and whole phrases had been crossed out, others substituted between lines and in the margins. It looked as if someone had been correcting Ovid's meter. He had no time to reflect on this before a voice interrupted him.

"Why don't you read a few verses to me?"

Mortified at being discovered, Godomar twisted around to see Bertrada standing in the doorway.

"You've left Sunilda unattended!" He spoke brusquely.

"She's with the Lord Chamberlain, Godomar. Surely you have no objection to that?"

"How dare you speak to me in that tone! Furthermore, I insist on knowing where you obtained this pagan filth."

"Ovid? He's the finest of poets, pagan or not. Besides, what are you doing creeping about in other people's bedrooms?"

"The Lord will forgive your disrespect because you are as yet an uneducated child," the prelate replied wearily. "But as for the woman whom I suspect obtained this obscenity for you, I cannot venture to say."

"I think that poetry is beautiful. With all the awful things that have happened here lately, is it so wrong to be reminded that there are beautiful things in the world too?"

"I shall instruct a servant to return these to our neighbor immediately," Godomar said. "In the meantime, I remind you that I am not only Sunilda's tutor but also her guide in spiritual matters. Any reading material that enters these apartments must first be approved by me. There are enough wholesome writings to keep you occupied during your remarkable apparent idleness without the possibility of the child finding such disgusting works as this."

Bertrada made a face. "More than enough. The church fathers wrote so much it's a wonder they ever had time to pray. What a lot of boring old men. Is the world a better place for all their writing? Not one of them could use a sword to any great effect, I'll wager. Or anything else, for that matter."

"What sort of talk is that?" Godomar was horrified. "And pin up your hair, Bertrada. Why is it hanging down like that? It isn't seemly."

The girl patted her long, blonde hair, which was rioting past her shoulders rather than plaited in her usual style. "Some people might prefer my hair this way," she said with a sly smile.

Godomar began to speak, then decided against it.

"I know what you're thinking," Bertrada told him. "She looks just like the Whore of Babylon! Isn't that right?"

"You are obviously distraught by the tragedy that befell your charge, Bertrada. That's entirely understandable. Nevertheless, I shall have to speak with Livia about your behavior."

With that Godomar picked up the offending works and stalked out, hoping that Theodora would forgive him if Sunilda should innocently repeat any of her nursemaid's blasphemous nonsense in her hearing.

He was halfway down the corridor when he met Peter. The servant seemed to have so little to do that one might have suspected the Lord Chamberlain had brought him to the estate just to give him a holiday, Godomar thought sourly.

"I was assisting in the kitchen but Master Zeno's cook is a very insolent man, and careless to boot," Peter explained when Godomar questioned him concerning his duties. "He refused to follow any of my suggestions and in fact just said, very rudely indeed, that I must have something more pressing to attend to elsewhere. Everyone seems eager to put me to work except my master. I am becoming weary from not having enough to do. Besides which, I find my thoughts are constantly turning to the things I see all around me. It makes me very uneasy, sir. I imagine it must give a pious man like yourself a great deal to ponder on also?"

"What is it that particularly troubles you?" Godomar inquired.

Peter frowned. "For one thing, there are far too many comings and goings and people creeping around during the night. It's said that the flesh is weak, I know, but on this estate it seems absolutely helpless."

"But you serve in the palace, Peter. Surely you have seen such behavior before?"

"My master has his own house, thanks be to heaven," Peter replied fervently, "and a well-ordered house it is too. Indeed, while I've served in many places in my time, I've never seen such brazen impropriety since I was—well, even then—" He paused and frowned. "It must be something to do with all these mechanical abominations, sir. I know it's not a servant's place to question his betters but is not creating a thing that mimics life almost blasphemy? Perhaps that was why the poor little boy died and Poppaea is now so ill."

"That is possible," Godomar acknowledged. "However, you appear to be devout, Peter, so I doubt you'll come to any harm in this place."

"But were not Gadaric and Poppaea also devout?"

"Indeed," the other confirmed, "yet even those of us who are firmly bound to goodness must be always on our guard."

"If you would be good enough to offer a prayer for me and for my master I would be most grateful," Peter said hesitantly.

"I will do so gladly."

Thus reassured, the elderly servant continued on his slow way down the corridor.

Watching him go, Godomar wondered how loyal such a devout man could be to a pagan master who was certainly beyond salvation. Indeed, he suspected that the twins' Christian but sadly Arian forebears, including even the great ruler Theodoric himself, were presently crying out in agony in their eternal punishment.

The thought reminded him of the preparations he had yet to make for Gadaric's funeral. Thanks to his ceaseless labors, he thought with some satisfaction, the innocent boy had been a good, orthodox Christian. His rites would certainly reflect that. Given the godless enticements of the world—especially those of the court, not to mention Zeno's estate—it was almost as well that Gadaric had died so young. The road to salvation was a difficult one but his had been shorter than most. Now his sister must continue on that road alone.

Yes, thought Godomar, the road to salvation would be an excellent topic for the address he would give at the boy's funeral. He wondered if the unrepentantly pagan Lord Chamberlain would deign to attend.

Chapter Thirteen

John walked away from Gadaric's grave. Although it was past mid-morning the grass of the small clearing in an inconspicuous corner of Zeno's garden was still soaked with heavy dew. John could feel its moisture seeping uncomfortably through the soft leather of his boots. He chided himself for even noticing such a petty annoyance under the circumstances. After all, life was full of trivial irritations, all endless distractions from its tragedies and joys.

Those who had attended the brief ceremony began to drift away back to the villa. A few remained in the clearing and talked in hushed tones. Godomar's voice rose above the others. Birds sang cheerfully, unheeding, in the surrounding trees.

The boy's funeral had been slightly delayed while messages went back and forth between the estate and Constantinople. There had been some concern over where Gadaric should be laid to rest since the twins had no family, or at least not outside Italy, and no permanent residence, having been shifted from one host to another during most of their brief lives. Finally it was decided that burial on the estate where Gadaric had spent his last summer seemed as appropriate as any other place.

"I'll have a fitting memorial built," Zeno had said. "With an ever-burning flame. Or perhaps it could include a replica of one of those toy animals Hero made for the children. Gadaric had such fun with them, you know. Hero could make it so that it would move in the wind. I think the boy would have liked that, don't you?"

John did not remind the kindly old man that Gadaric would not be able to enjoy such a creation. He had noticed that during Godomar's graveside remarks Zeno had shifted from foot to foot, looking like a lost child.

The boy's sister Sunilda, on the other hand, had appeared utterly composed, standing between her nursemaid and Calyce. The women repeatedly wiped away tears and directed concerned looks at their charge, but the child had remained dry-eyed. She appeared bored. Once John thought he saw a hastily suppressed smile begin to form on her lips.

John had now spoken to the kitchen staff and the gardeners, not to mention estate laborers and house servants and slaves, concerning the night of the banquet. Predictably, they had neither seen nor heard anything of assistance, their attention having been occupied with their master's wealthy, high-born guests. Although this famous senator or that renowned lady had been mentioned in passing, the merest glimpse of the empress had been enough to drive any possibly useful information from their collective minds.

John was contemplating the task ahead when Calyce caught up with him.

"Lord Chamberlain, I didn't see your young friend Anatolius at the ceremony." Her mouth was set in a grim line which accentuated her prominent jaw.

"It was necessary for him to ride for Constantinople, Calyce. He asked me to express his condolences to the boy's family at an appropriate time after the funeral. I should be grateful if you would accept them on his behalf."

"But of course. How considerate of Anatolius. Poor Gadaric, he doesn't have much of a family. Or didn't have, I should say." She dabbed at her eyes. "Bertrada is only a nursemaid but I've tried to help her as much as I could, or at least when I am not waiting on the empress when she's in residence here. Bertrada's little more than a child herself, you know, and has to deal with that overbearing man Godomar, although I suppose I shouldn't have such harsh words for a man of religion."

"Do I understand Bertrada is an Ostrogoth herself and came from Italy with the twins?"

"Oh, yes. She was in Amalasuntha's household but there is no family connection as such. Italy became very dangerous for anyone connected with Amalasuntha and Bertrada was fortunate she was sent to Constantinople with the twins when they were taken under the emperor's protection. She makes a fine nursemaid for them, being their countrywoman. However, she was young when she left Italy and had really had no opportunity to gain an appreciation for the finer, more elegant ways of court. So I've tried to take her under my wing and instruct her a little."

"You and Livia are also originally from Italy?"

"Yes, we are. Indeed, that was the reason Theodora chose us from among all her ladies-in-waiting to stay here with the children this summer."

Godomar strode past them at a great pace. He said nothing but his gaze lingered on John and Calyce as they walked along together and his mouth tightened.

"Is the prelate also Italian?" John asked as Godomar swept silently by.

"I believe so. Why, Lord Chamberlain, just think! We appear to have almost rebuilt Rome on the shores of the Marmara!"

"Please don't give Zeno any more wild ideas, Calyce. Tell me, had you met Godomar before you arrived at this estate?"

"No, I hadn't. I suppose Justinian chose him to tutor the children because of his obvious piety—not to mention his orthodoxy."

"I haven't seen Livia this morning," John noted.

"She's sitting with Poppaea. The girl still hasn't woken up. Do you think it's that awful dwarf creeping about, up to no good? We're all in danger so long as he is loose."

"The search for Barnabas continues and Captain Felix's excubitors are guarding the estate," John reassured her. "There is nothing to fear. As to Poppaea, Gaius was of the opinion that she would soon awaken of her own accord."

Calyce looked dubious. "Gaius? You mean the palace physician? I was there when he examined the girl. He was full of talk about an excess of yellow bile. Apply cold compresses, he told us, and meantime if her condition worsens, we are to summon him again. Yet how long has she slept now? And we are merely to apply cold compresses! I think it is past time we sought a physician's help again. Preferably a different one."

"Poppaea still sleeps, but her condition has not worsened. Gaius did not think it would. He does have some experience in treating the effects of poison, Calyce. In fact, he told me that in this particular case, Poppaea's youth will serve her recovery better than any treatment he—or any physician—could administer."

Calyce gave a sniff of disdain. They walked in silence for a while. "And when will Anatolius be returning?" Calyce finally asked.

"Soon, I'd think. Tell me, Calyce, is Bertrada trustworthy?"

"Trustworthy? Certainly. A bit flighty, perhaps, but she is young. She has handled the twins very well. They were a difficult pair of children, Sunilda in particular. She seems to live in a world of her own invention."

"I've noticed that. Could it be due to Bertrada's influence in some way?"

"Oh no, excellency. My only concern for Bertrada, although really it's none of my business, well...I shouldn't say."

"What is it that worries you?" John prompted her.

"Well, it's this inexplicable fancy she's taken to the excubitor captain, Felix."

❊ ❊ ❊

As Felix approached a bend in the flagstone path he detected the sound of running. He drew his sword as he looked keenly around.

Despite the light remaining in the sky, dusk had already settled under the surrounding shrubbery and insects had begun their discordant night songs.

A small form crashed through the bushes. Felix leapt back, raising his sword. Then he himself looked down at Sunilda, who returned his surprised stare with a wide grin.

The girl uttered a piercing shriek and then bolted away down the path behind Felix just as John strolled around the bend after her. He seemed remarkably untroubled by his charge's flight. Turning to look after the child Felix saw the reason for the Lord Chamberlain's unconcern. Bertrada was approaching.

Sunilda raced to her nursemaid's side and clung to her tunic, hopping up and down and looking over her shoulder in mock terror.

"It's a bear," she cried. "Help! Help! A big bear's going to get me." She began screaming again but the screams dissolved into laughter.

Bertrada leaned over. Her blonde hair swung down fetchingly as she put her slim arms around the girl. "Oh, my! You're right!" she smiled. "But he's such a handsome beast, don't you think? He won't harm us. See, he's putting away his sword. Why, we might even be able to lure him home and keep him for a pet."

Sunilda giggled. Felix felt his mouth go dry. He stood speechless, tugging at his beard.

"It's a pity you don't have any honey, Bertrada," John smiled. "You could have lured that bear away with it! Still, Sunilda and I have had a fine walk."

"Yes, we talked the whole way," the girl said, suddenly solemn.

The nursemaid wondered what topic could have occupied them for so long.

"Philosophy," Sunilda told her.

The two men looked after Bertrada and her small companion as they vanished along the shadowy path toward the villa. Felix wished now he had not confessed to John how much Bertrada reminded him of Berta. The Lord Chamberlain did not say much, however, but merely stared thoughtfully into the thickening shadows and then, after a word of encouragement, left Felix to complete his patrol and departed down the path himself.

Felix continued through the darkening garden. As he marched along, he turned his bushy-haired head this way and that in a semblance of alertness, but in fact King Khosrow could have led half of the Persian army past under his nose and would still have remained undetected. No matter how much he tried, Felix could not put Bertrada out of his mind. He muttered a curse or two and then began tunelessly humming a marching song.

The figure appeared before him as silently as an apparition, a glowing vision set against a dark background of shrubs. And as impossible as it seemed, she was completely naked. Her form was more perfect than Felix could ever have imagined.

It was also sculpted in marble, he realized, even as he felt his heart jump like a rabbit in a snare.

All the same, as he passed by the statue he couldn't help but touch her reassuringly cool hip. The ancient Greek artist had certainly done a remarkable job, he told himself, although the effect had been aided more than somewhat by his, Felix's, unrestrained imaginings.

And his imaginings now turned to other matters.

Felix felt uneasy. Who or what threatened the little girl? As commander of the men guarding the palace, he was accustomed to shadowy enemies that could not be confronted directly and honorably on a field of battle, but in this instance the enemy seemed even more nebulous, not to say ludicrous. He and his men had been dispatched to secure an estate against a venomous dwarf who seemed invisible, able to come and go at will. How would his next attack materialize? By poisoning the entire household? Or letting loose another mechanical device to wreak mayhem?

Felix turned and began to march back along the path. He had gone only a few paces when he spotted the second figure moving across the garden. For an instant he wondered if it was his overactive imagination at work but at the crack of a dry twig as the figure stepped forward, Felix knew this was not a vision.

Barnabas!

He sprinted toward the intruder.

Then he realized that the figure was not as short as the mime but rather more the height of the nursemaid who had been tormenting his thoughts until recollection of the accursed dwarf had driven her out of them.

The figure had long, light-colored hair.

It was Bertrada.

Running swiftly up, he lightly grabbed her arm to turn her around. "Bertrada, you shouldn't be out here alone! You know it's dangerous!"

The face that turned up toward his was wrinkled. The light hair was not blonde, but rather silver.

"My name is Minthe," the woman informed him with quiet dignity.

❊ ❊ ❊

Calyce was waiting at the back of the villa as Minthe had said. The herbalist had scorched Felix's ears on the way there. Didn't he know she would be treating Poppaea?

Felix had quickly regained his senses. "But if you're going to be healing the girl, why do you have to come skulking in like this, not to mention in the dark?" he asked shrewdly.

"Poppaea's mother has expressed some misgivings about the origin of Minthe's skills," Calyce explained. "So we thought this would be the best way."

Minthe was blunter. "The truth, Captain Felix, is that if she knew I was here, Livia would not allow me to set foot in the poor child's room. Yet it is my potions that will bring her daughter back to full health. I've come to see how she's doing. She will be awake soon, and there are certain mixtures to be prepared for her."

"Livia is distraught and hardly knows what she is saying right now. She'll be grateful to you in the end, you'll see," Calyce assured the woman.

Felix's orders from Justinian had not included instructions concerning dealings with Theodora's ladies-in-waiting. After their brief discussion and reassured that Minthe was expected, Felix allowed them to go inside, glad to see them go. Glad to be entirely free of women, young, old and in-between for a while, he thought wearily.

The torches set in brackets by the villa door sputtered and flared. Something brushed his cheek, as lightly as a memory. It was a moth, now circling one of the torches, its fluttering shadow on the wall looking larger than a bird's.

A vision of Bertrada returned, painfully, to flutter in his mind's eye. No, what was he thinking, he scolded himself. The well-loved face smiling in his memory was Berta's.

Surely there could be no other man in the whole of the empire so sorely distressed.

Chapter Fourteen

Anatolius felt his throat tighten as Senator Balbinus' wife stepped into the reception room with a whisper of fine silk. The embroidered hem of her white dalmatic, its broad blue edging matching a narrower strip of decorative border at the neckline, floated behind her like memories and old regrets.

"Lucretia! I didn't expect to see you!" Anatolius blurted out. She regarded him silently.

"Well, that's not exactly true," he admitted, forcing a smile. "I was hoping for at least a glimpse of you. It has been some time since we last met." He ended in a forlorn tone, "Actually I'm here to see your husband."

Did his former lover's pale patrician face betray some fleeting emotion or was it only his imagination? Anatolius had put this visit off and gone to his office instead. No matter what assignment John might give him, his duties to the emperor came first, he had told himself, but the fact was that as he neared the city his eagerness for this reunion had begun to turn to fear.

"Yes, it's been a very long time," Lucretia said. The neutrality in her tone pierced him as sharply as a blade. It was more terrible than the coldness he had dreaded he might hear. "Please sit, Anatolius." Lucretia sank down into the cushions of a couch. "I have ordered wine be brought for you." Her voice still held the same husky quality he recalled too well.

The young man sat awkwardly next to her, his stiff posture betraying his unease. "Thank you. The senator will be here soon?"

She shook her head. She still wore her dark hair in ringlets, Anatolius noted. "He is attending a business meeting."

"Then I had best not linger, Lucretia."

"Stay a little while longer, Anatolius. Tell me all about your latest escapades. I hear that you have visited Severa Flavia quite often lately?"

Anatolius reddened. "She is a very gracious lady."

Lucretia smiled. "It seems you have learned discretion. She often dines here as my guest and has mentioned your affectionate nature increasingly of late. Alas, she is not as careful with her confidences as you seem to have become with yours." Her voice was warmer, with that hint of breathiness that he so fondly recalled. She patted his knee playfully.

Anatolius was thankful for the distraction of the arrival of the servant bringing wine. He got up from the couch, cup in hand, to inspect the reception room's frescoes.

They had obviously been inspired by tales taken from mythology. Here, a handsome Narcissus leaned down to admire his reflection in a tranquil pond. There, Paris presented the golden Apple of Discord to voluptuous Aphrodite while Athena and Hera looked on vengefully. In the background the misty towers of Troy slumbered peacefully, unaware of their terrible fate.

Relieved to move away from Lucretia and be less tormented by the musky sweetness of her familiar perfume, he took a hasty sip of wine and stared at a scene showing the abduction of Proserpina. "What wonderful artistry," he said with the poet's appreciation for beauty. "I have rarely seen finer."

"Neither have I, Anatolius. My wife chose the scenes to be depicted and I am well pleased with the artisan's work."

Senator Balbinus strode into the room. His regal features were familiar to everyone at court but Anatolius noticed only how much older the senator was than Lucretia.

"I am happy to see you extending hospitality to a guest, Lucretia, although I would have preferred that you asked him to return when I was at home. Servants will gossip."

"Anatolius has come to see you on a matter of business," she replied serenely.

Anatolius set down his cup on the table by the door. "Senator, I regret the intrusion but I am here on an errand of some urgency."

"I shall leave you gentlemen to your discussion," said Lucretia. Eyes averted, she brushed past Anatolius and disappeared down the hallway, leaving only a faint memory of her perfume.

Balbinus had helped himself to wine and was pacing back and forth. His deliberate tread and stiffly set shoulders expressed his disapproval of Anatolius' irregular visit to his wife, but he said nothing more, contenting himself with inviting the young man to state his business. "However, I would appreciate it if you could declare it quickly for I have another meeting soon and must not be late."

Anatolius hastily gathered his wits. "I have the honor to convey a personal request from the Lord Chamberlain." His formality covered his severe discomfort at being discovered chatting with Lucretia even though, as he reminded himself, their affair had ended before she married Balbinus.

Ah, but was it truly over came a whisper from the depths of the past. Pushing such treacherous notions aside, he quickly outlined John's request for information that would be of assistance in locating Balbinus' nephew.

The senator was not helpful. "Castor often travels, Anatolius, and when he does he does not provide me with his itinerary. Indeed sometimes he does not visit my wife and me for a month or more. He is not a gregarious person. We are more liable to receive a note from him than a personal visit."

"He does seem the sort of scholar who is most comfortable with word delivered by the pen," Anatolius acknowledged. "You haven't seen him during these past few days?"

"If I had I would have said so, would I not? And before you ask, no, Castor and I have not fallen out. Our relationship is amicable enough, even though I feel I must lecture him now and then on his—well, on his lack of worldliness, his intellectual extravagance. There is nothing my nephew doesn't know about, or at least have an opinion on, except getting along in the world in which he finds himself. So I have tried to be something of a father to him."

Balbinus fell silent. Anatolius was taken aback by the senator's sudden vehemence, but before he could give it much thought, the man began speaking again with his usual bluster. "I'm sure you have heard of my brother Bassus, Castor's father, or at least know his reputation," he said. "Everyone at the court considers him a dreadful embarrassment to my family. My brother died much too young, of course, and I barely knew him. He barely knew himself. Had he lived longer he might have become wiser. Needless to say, over the years I have done my best to see that Castor avoided his father's fate. But then, we all have our weaknesses, don't we?"

Was Balbinus making a remark directed at him, Anatolius wondered uncomfortably. But perhaps the senator's comment came because his gaze had settled for an instant on the frescoes. It was obvious Balbinus had no inclination to talk about his nephew further, presumably because doing so would remind him of his wayward and dissolute brother, surely a painful topic. However, Anatolius was thankful to make his escape although he felt vaguely guilty without, he told himself, any reason he should.

Leaving Balbinus' house, he looked over his shoulder into the cool atrium. Did he catch a glimpse of pale silk there as the heavy street door swung shut behind him?

As he strode away down the street the thought came to him that the frescoes in Senator Balbinus' exquisitely decorated reception room had a common theme, and it was that of love and loss.

❄ ❄ ❄

The door of John's house opened a crack to reveal Hypatia's tawny face peeking out.

"Master Anatolius!" Surprise and, oddly, what sounded like relief were obvious in her tone. She opened the door wider and stood back to allow Anatolius to step into the tiled entrance hall. He was one of a very few people admitted without question to John's home at any hour of day or night.

"I decided I'd make a brief visit since I happened to be passing this way," Anatolius lied valiantly. In fact, his steps had brought him to John's house without conscious direction, just as he had first wandered back to his office on the palace grounds. Two blotched parchments later, he had abandoned his task of copying Justinian's letter to the Patriarch of Antioch and gone out to walk around for a while. Unlike John, who often walked to think, Anatolius usually walked to forget.

The air in the atrium of John's house was sweet, pleasantly imbued not with perfume but rather honey and a hint of spices.

Following the lithe Egyptian woman upstairs to the kitchen, Anatolius noticed anew that her hair was the same raven's wing color as Lucretia's. She offered him a cup of wine, seeming ill at ease.

"Just continue with whatever you were doing, Hypatia," Anatolius said. Various chopped herbs were set out on the kitchen table. "What are you making? A new kind of sweetmeat, perhaps?"

"Not exactly, sir. I'm experimenting with one of Peter's recipes while the master is away."

"And also while Peter is absent." Anatolius grinned, well aware of the elderly servant's aversion to sharing his kitchen.

"As you say. However, I think Peter will enjoy this new dish. He has something of a fondness for sweet things, unlike the master, although he does occasionally indulge in honeyed dates."

"They're probably the Lord Chamberlain's only indulgence," Anatolius remarked.

Hypatia raised her eyebrows but, as befitted a servant, made no comment on his observation, merely continuing to stir the mixture bubbling gently in a pot set on the kitchen brazier.

Glancing idly around the room, Anatolius noticed a small clay figure sitting on a shelf.

"What's this, Hypatia?" Picking up the statuette he saw, with some alarm, that it was a crudely fashioned scorpion. The creature was significant to Mithrans and was to be seen in bas reliefs and mosaics of Mithra's battle with the sacred bull. He could not imagine John being so careless as to leave such an emblem of his pagan beliefs lying about in plain sight. Obviously it was not his.

"Peter won't like you cluttering up his kitchen with this, Hypatia," Anatolius said in a jocular tone.

The woman gasped and dropped her ladle. It landed between them, spattering hot liquid on both Anatolius' boot and her bare foot. She did not seem to notice. "Sir..." she said faintly, "I..."

Anatolius, seeing her so distressed, carefully replaced the scorpion on the shelf. He seemed to be blundering into all sorts of difficulties with women today, he thought ruefully. "What is it for, Hypatia?"

The woman suddenly burst into tears. "It's a charm against demons, such as we swear by in my country. It has to be displayed in order to drive them away."

Anatolius stared at her. "Demons?" he repeated.

"Demons," Hypatia nodded, sniffing and swiping tears from her cheeks with her knuckles.

Anatolius considered putting a comforting arm around her but decided the action might be misconstrued. He had displayed some fondness for her before she had entered John's employ. No wonder he was always having difficulties with women, he thought. Sometimes he thought he had never encountered one who hadn't turned his head for a day. He stood looking awkwardly at the girl, not knowing quite what to do or say.

"I myself don't believe in demons," he finally said. "It must just have been your imagination. You're all alone in this big house—"

Her tears began to flow again. "No, pardon me but it's not that, sir. Something very upsetting happened early this morning. I was woken up by a strange noise. It sounded like the scratching of a beast's long claws. I'm not certainly exactly how to describe it. I was half asleep, you see. It was just a dream, I told myself. The house creaks terribly in the wind at night. You'd think that vile tax collector who first owned it had decided to return and was walking about, looking for the head Justinian relieved him of. Then that horrible, strange noise started again."

Anatolius, intrigued, asked her to continue.

"Well, sir, I got my lamp lit and crept down to the entrance hall but by then the noise had stopped. It must surely have been a rat, I thought, a rat that sounded much louder than usual because I heard it when I was half asleep."

"That would certainly be what it was, I'm certain of it," Anatolius said.

"But it wasn't a rat!" the woman blurted out in a panic-stricken voice. "Because as I turned to go back upstairs, that terrible sound started again and I could tell that the creature was right on the other side of the front door!"

Anatolius tried to reassure her. "Surely if it were really a demon it would have burst straight in, not politely scratched on the door waiting to be admitted, Hypatia. Don't you think if it wasn't a rat it must have been one of these feral cats that prowl the palace grounds?"

Hypatia shook her head. "I wish it had been. But it wasn't. You see, whatever it was, I felt I had to see it, so I went into the master's study." She suddenly blushed. Her next words explained why. "Lamplight brings out, well, to be blunt, obscene details in the wall mosaic in there that I would not even dare to speak about. I'd never seen something like that before."

Anatolius immediately pointed out that it had been the tax collector who formerly owned the house who had commissioned the mosaic in question and not John.

"Oh, yes, I know that, sir," Hypatia nodded. "I blew out the lamp but that scary little girl still seemed to be staring at me out of those big eyes of hers...But anyhow I crept to the window and peeked out. And then I saw the thing...the demon...scuttling off across the square. It wasn't human. So I made a charm to protect the master and his house and everyone who lives in it," she ended simply.

Anatolius put his arm around her shoulders. She pressed her face into his chest and sobbed.

Meant to comfort her, his gesture made him distinctly uncomfortable. He reminded himself that there was absolutely no possibility that John would suddenly burst into the kitchen and find him standing there with his arms around his servant.

The Lord Chamberlain was on Zeno's estate. Anatolius wondered whether John's investigations had been more fruitful than his own. At least John was not having to deal with hysterical women who believed in demons and magick, he thought with a sigh.

Chapter Fifteen

"She's wedded to evil! I won't allow the woman in here. Potions and magick indeed! There's too much magick in this cursed place already!" Livia burst out of her daughter's room, sweeping imperiously by John without so much as a second glance. The round moon of her face was shadowed by clouds as sullen as those gathering over the sea.

John stepped through the doorway into the glare of Theodora's other lady-in-waiting. "Let Poppaea die then," Calyce was shouting after Livia. "Your stupidity—" She broke off in embarrassment at the sight of the Lord Chamberlain.

"They're arguing about Minthe," Sunilda put in helpfully from her seat beside Poppaea's bed. "They always do, you know. Minthe will make Poppaea better. She isn't married to anybody, either," she added as an afterthought.

John bent over the sick girl. He could detect no improvement in her state. She lay as still as Gadaric had been when pulled from the mouth of the whale. Her eyes were closed, the lids bluish, almost translucent. There was a terrible pallor to her cheeks, cheeks that were no longer rounded but sunken. Her breathing was barely discernible.

"Has she been awake yet?" John asked Calyce.

The woman shook her head. "Not fully but she stirs occasionally. I've managed to get some of Minthe's potion past her lips, and her sleep seems much more natural now, whatever her mother says!"

John realized that Livia had somehow learned of Minthe's stealthy nocturnal visit, which Felix had reported to him. He didn't propose to discuss the matter further right then, however, since he had as little desire as Felix to place himself between Theodora's warring ladies-in-waiting.

"We should let Poppaea rest," he told Sunilda. "Calyce will stay with her. Would you like to take a walk along the beach before the rain arrives?"

The girl hopped out of the chair and accompanied him outside, talking all the way. She was wearing a plain linen tunic that contrasted strangely with the golden comb in her dark hair.

"Bertrada says it's my crown," she explained, when John complimented her on her hair ornament. "That's because I will be queen of Italy someday. But Livia contradicted her. She's just jealous because Poppaea will never be queen even though they're from a very old Roman family. Poppaea can be my lady-in-waiting, though. Her mother I think I will throw in the dungeons unless that would make Poppaea too sad."

They followed the path leading through the olive grove while the girl chattered. Brilliant sunlight accentuated the dark clouds massing along the horizon as they emerged and began walking towards the shore.

"My father and my great-grandfather were kings, of course," the girl said airily, as if everyone had royal blood. "My grandmother ruled too. Then again, I might decide to marry a general. Bertrada says she wants to marry a general. She likes that big bear Felix, you know."

"Felix is neither a bear nor a general but an excubitor captain," John pointed out.

"Ah, but a man can better his position in the world if he sets his mind to it, isn't that true, Lord Chamberlain?"

John admitted that it was so, thinking that he doubted the phrase was one that the child would normally have used.

They had arrived at the beach and were strolling along it, the murmur of waves sounding hypnotically in their ears. "It will be a long time before you must concern yourself with matters of queenship, Sunilda," he concluded.

"My father became king when he was only a boy," she said pertly. "Bertrada has told me many stories about him."

"I see," John replied, positive that the nursemaid had not told Sunilda that her father had almost certainly been murdered because he was unprepared to rule at a tender age. "And your great-grandfather Theodoric grew up in Constantinople. Just think, he might have gathered shells on this very beach."

"Yes, he might have. I've heard many stories about my grandmother too."

"From Bertrada?"

"Some of them."

A patrolling excubitor stopped to greet them. John exchanged a few words with him before he continued on his way.

"Is he searching for Barnabas as well?" Sunilda asked. "Bertrada says everyone is looking for him."

Without waiting for a reply she ran down to the string of debris at the high water line that delineated the disputed border between the kingdoms of land and sea.

It occurred to John as he followed a few paces behind that he could barely remember being eight. Of his own daughter at the same age—the child conceived before his terrible fate—he knew nothing. His only meeting with her had lasted just long enough to open an aching wound of a sort he would never have thought he could suffer, one that still caused him pain.

Would Europa have been so wise beyond her years at that age? Or at least grown so skilled at repeating the words and sentiments of her elders as to give an appearance of wisdom?

"Oh! It's horrible! Quickly, Lord Chamberlain! I've found a monster!"

The girl's shrill cry brought John to investigate the thing she was prodding with a piece of driftwood. The dark lump was partly concealed by seaweed; from it the ends of several appendages protruded like fingertips. Another prod revealed them to be not fingers but rather half-decayed tentacles.

"It's just a sea creature, Sunilda, something your friend Porphyrio would have for his evening meal."

"Porphyrio isn't here today or he would have come to shore to meet me," the girl said confidently, throwing the piece of driftwood into the sea.

John looked out over the choppy water. There was nothing to see but rapidly advancing thunderclouds and the jagged peaks of the island.

"We'll have to cut our walk short," John told her. "The storm will be here soon."

"But I wanted to visit the goats' shrine," the girl complained petulantly.

"There isn't going to be time." John gently took the child's hand. She pulled it away.

"I must visit the goats' shrine," she said in a louder voice.

Powerful as he was, the Lord Chamberlain was not accustomed to giving orders to children, an action even the poorest peasants took for granted. Apart from his absent daughter, the only child he knew was Zoe and she was always perfectly quiet and attentive on his study wall. Well, there were also the court pages, he reminded himself, but those painted and powdered creatures could hardly be classified as children, young though they were.

"We'll walk down to the shrine for a very quick visit, Sunilda, but you must answer a question on the way."

"Is it about my brother?"

John indicated gently that it was.

"Let's not talk about that," she replied firmly.

"I am sorry but we must," John replied softly. "I want you to tell me what you remember about the night your brother had his accident."

"Bertrada put us to bed early. I went to sleep. I don't know when Gadaric went out. I've told you all this already." With that she was off, running, the sticks of her bare legs flashing beneath her tunic.

John strode rapidly after her. A cold, isolated drop of rain landed on his face. The downpour would soon arrive. They would have to hurry.

When he reached the shrine Sunilda was standing on tiptoe, peering into the bowl set into the pedestal. John ducked in to see what she was staring at with such interest.

"Someone left a question for the goats." A few burnt scraps of parchment lay at the bottom of the deep bowl. The girl poked at them. "I wonder what it said?"

"Only the person who left it and the goats who answered know exactly what it was," John told her.

"I'll ask Minthe about it next time I see her," the girl said thoughtfully.

John refrained from commenting on the perils of superstitious belief. Godomar was surely better qualified than he to offer that sort of guidance. He felt relieved that the girl's gloomy tutor had not observed her interest in the shrine.

Sunilda grabbed John's hand. "Let's go and visit Minthe right now!"

The light was fading quickly, as if torches were being extinguished one after the other along a long hallway. The wind was rising ahead of the fast approaching storm, blowing sea spray into the shrine.

"We don't have time now, Sunilda." John led the girl back up the gentle slope to the road. As they went toward the villa, there was a clap of thunder.

They increased their pace, passing Minthe's strange house, and proceeded quickly on up the road as repeated drum-rolls of thunder grew closer.

Then a dazzling bolt of lightning struck the greenish-gray sea. John's ears rang. Another deafening peal drowned out Sunilda's shout.

"...over there." She gestured excitedly. They had reached a spot where the high ground extended a blunt finger out toward the beach, ending in a steep hill rather than the cliffs that lay further up the road. A stone hut was barely visible at the seaward end of a path leading across the promontory. Lightning forked over the sea again, followed almost immediately by the concussion of thunder.

"Very well," John agreed.

Sunilda jerked her hand free of his grasp and ran ahead. John followed her down the path, through the weedy garden behind the hut and past an overturned rowboat sitting beside it. They arrived at the hut's rough plank door just as the heavens opened and sea and sky were lost in a waterfall of water.

John stepped warily forward, hand on the blade at his belt.

"Don't worry, Lord Chamberlain. I know Paul very well," the girl assured him. "He'll be glad to see us."

The room they entered was empty, pungent with the mingled odors of garlic, onions and cheese.

Rain thrummed loudly on the roof. The shutter covering the small building's single window banged back and forth as the wind dashed its fury against it. John looked out into shifting, translucent sheets of water. It was the view one might have from the mouth of a whale, he thought uneasily.

Orange light flared into the corners as the door to the other room creaked open and an old man, short and squat, emerged from it, carrying a clay lamp.

"The storm has brought me some callers, I see," he said jovially. "The queen of Italy, for one. And who is the other? Her faithful servant?"

"Paul!" the girl giggled. "He's the Lord Chamberlain."

Paul shifted his lamp to illuminate the taller of his two visitors more directly. "Yes, I see," he agreed amiably. "You must excuse me, for I don't entertain Lord Chamberlains very often. Who will you bring next time you call? The emperor?"

"I don't know Justinian very well," Sunilda replied severely, "but Theodora will be visiting soon to attend the village festival. I'll ask her to come and pay her respects to you then, if you'd like."

Paul looked alarmed. "A very kind offer, my dear, but I'm certain that the empress and I will have many opportunities to chat during the celebrations." John noted the humor in his words but Sunilda did not.

"Oh, good! Then you'll be coming to see it after all!" she said with a grin.

"I regret the intrusion, Paul. The storm arrived very suddenly," John explained to their host.

"You certainly wouldn't want to be walking about in that tempest." Paul's observation was emphasized by a gust of wind groaning through the half open door, bringing a spray of rain with it. "We don't want it in here with us either. If you'd just close the—I beg your pardon, excellency—"

John pulled the door shut, muffling the sound of the storm. Briarus had mentioned a Paul who gardened, John recalled. "You are Paul, the gardener?"

"These days I grub in the dirt a bit, yes, excellency. I don't care for it personally. I'll always want to return to being a fisherman, although I can hardly remember when I last ventured out onto the sea. It just got harder and harder, what with the pain in my joints making it so difficult to even get my little boat down to the beach. In the end I just had to give it up."

John did not ask Paul about his argument with the prickly estate manager. It was possible too, he thought, that it was Paul who had assisted Hero with the framework of the whale, but he thought it better not to mention the matter in front of the girl. He could question Paul on another occasion if need be.

The former fisherman's skin was weathered as dark as a worn leather boot. His thinning hair and the disorderly collection of bristles springing from his cheeks and chin were like the yellowish white of spume on the beach, his eyes, appropriately, a watery blue.

Paul grimaced as he set the lamp on his table. "Old age is like a storm, one that's tossed me up on this miserable patch of dirt when I would much rather be at sea."

He sighed heavily before continuing. "Please sit down. I am happy to offer what I have to such distinguished visitors."

Sunilda promptly plunked herself on the bench beside the table. John sat down beside her as their host bustled about, producing rough pottery plates and cups along with a small loaf of bread and jugs of wine and water. He apologized for the wine as he cut a chunk from the cheese hanging by a rope over the brazier. "It's poor stuff, I fear, excellency."

"Yet very much to my taste," John replied truthfully, setting his cup back down, "although it may not suit everyone."

Paul expressed amazement at this unexpected pronouncement. "Then would you perhaps care for some of my garlic paste?" he ventured.

"Yes, he would, Paul. And perhaps we could have some of those fine olives you usually have?" put in Sunilda.

"Yes. I'd forgotten about those." Looking flustered, he produced a pottery bowl of plump olives. John wondered if they had come from Zeno's grove. They were certainly excellent.

"This is a fine banquet indeed," pronounced Sunilda through a mouthful of bread.

"You two are friends, I take it?" John directed the question to the old fisherman, who had lowered himself painfully onto a stool at the other side of the table.

"Minthe has brought the young lady to visit more than once." Paul poured himself a cup of wine.

"You know Minthe well?"

Paul did not answer immediately. In the ensuing silence John became aware that the sound of the rain was diminishing. Thunder rumbled still, but its muted grumbling came from further away.

"Everybody in the village knows Minthe," Paul finally replied. "She offers all sorts of services of a herbal nature and has for many years. Ever since she arrived, in fact. The village girls consult her a lot. I think you know what I mean."

"Minthe is a very wise woman." Sunilda popped a fat olive into her mouth and chewed enthusiastically.

"Some do say so," Paul nodded, "but I've got to know her because she often buys produce from me."

"You grow herbs?" John asked with interest.

Paul shook his head. "No, I don't. Minthe grows whatever she needs for those potions of hers. It's vegetables she buys from me. A few radishes, some beetroots, a cabbage now and then, that sort of thing. She doesn't bother to plant such sensible things as vegetables."

"Minthe prefers to devote all her garden to herbs and flowers." An olive pit rattled onto the girl's plate. "Someone left a question for the goats, Paul," she went on. "Is it true that the omens have been very bad these past few days?"

John gave Paul a questioning look.

"I put no faith in those goats, excellency," the man said, avoiding a direct answer, "although I've heard quite a few villagers say on more than one occasion that the animals are always right."

"The rain has stopped," Sunilda said, bounding off the bench and outside in a instant. "Look," she said as they followed her, "you can see the goats from here."

Ghostly pillars of mist were swirling slowly up from the dark water. John could barely see the rocky island and said so. "The young have much better eyesight," he remarked to Paul. "But what are these terrible omens that the villagers have apparently been talking so much about lately?"

"Among the ignorant it's said that the patterns the beasts are forming as they graze on the slopes have not been glimpsed within living memory," Paul replied slowly. "Some terrible disaster is to be expected, or so it's being said. However, it's my opinion that we have already had a catastrophe, for what is worse than the death of a child?"

"Don't be sad about Gadaric, Paul." As Sunilda spoke, John felt her small hand grasp his arm. "Now the Lord Chamberlain and I must be off to another engagement. Thank you for your kind hospitality. I shall expect to see you at the celebrations."

Paul, concealing a smile, gave a stiff little bow of farewell.

Watery sunlight broke through the clouds as John and the girl reached the road.

The Lord Chamberlain's young charge whirled to face the sea again. Her golden hair comb came free and John plucked it from the grass. As he did so he heard laughter drifting on the wind.

He looked along the beach in the direction in which Sunilda was now staring intently.

Two figures moved near the water. They had obviously been unable to find shelter from the storm as their sodden robes hung about them. One was pacing stolidly along while the other darted ahead and back and then ahead again. The big bearded figure was unmistakably Felix and his companion, doubtless, was Bertrada.

It was a sight John wished he had not observed. A soldier could not allow himself such indulgences while on duty and under special orders from Justinian. Much as he disliked the notion, he knew he would have to speak to Felix about the matter.

Chapter Sixteen

"I fear I was ambushed by Bertrada," confessed Felix.

On his way to Zeno's bath house shortly after sunrise John had encountered his visibly agitated friend in the open air gymnasium.

"You were strong enough to fend off the young woman's attack, I presume?"

"As you well know, a weaker force sometimes prevails against a stronger when it is allied with surprise. On the other hand, perhaps it was more an enchantment than an ambush," Felix replied.

The big captain picked up a leather exercise ball lying in one of the puddles left on the concrete by the previous day's downpour. He eyed the oblong ball suspiciously. "This looks normal enough but you never know, it might suddenly burst open and birds fly out. You can't take anything for granted on this estate."

He heaved the heavy ball at the Lord Chamberlain, who caught it and threw it back with a grunt of effort.

"That at least doesn't work automatically," John noted.

"Probably because Zeno hasn't thought of it yet."

The two men tossed the ball back and forth in silence for a while. When in Constantinople, John habitually spent an hour or so daily in the gymnasium at the Baths of Zeuxippos, determined to avoid any hint of the softness that the ignorant typically associated with those whom they carelessly lumped together under the name of eunuch.

The early morning sun had not risen far, but although the enclosure was still in cool shadow, the back of his tunic was soon damp from effort. The sharp cawing of crows roosting nearby formed a raucous counterpoint to the regular thump of the leather ball.

"I should not have to warn you about the dangers of becoming entangled with anyone even remotely close to Theodora," John eventually remarked.

Felix pointed out that Bertrada was merely a nursemaid.

"But she is nursemaid to a child who is a future queen, and a child, moreover, who is an imperial hostage."

"Perhaps you're right, John," Felix admitted. "Even so, Bertrada is so like my Berta..."

"But only like her," John reminded his friend. "And how is Bertrada so like her? Close to her age? Similar hair color? You might as well say that Sunilda is like my daughter at the same age."

Felix stepped swiftly forward to catch John's short throw. "I've seen the wistful way you sometimes look at your young charge, John. I knew you were thinking of Europa. As to Bertrada, she looks exactly like Berta. The face, the hair, they could be twins."

"To your eyes, perhaps."

"She has the same enthusiastic temperament," Felix responded with a grin.

"But didn't we all when we were her age?"

Felix looked exasperated. "She is my countrywoman as well!" he declared. "We're of the same blood!"

John began to reply but the velocity with which the heavy leather ball hit his chest convinced him that there was no point in saying anything further about Bertrada. He decided to change the subject. "Have you had any other thoughts about where Barnabas might have gone, Felix?"

"He's probably in Egypt by now, John. Or Crete. Who knows where he's fled? Now, what about this? Everyone is convinced that Poppaea was poisoned, but if the murderer's also a poisoner, then why didn't he poison Gadaric? No, I'm not entirely convinced that Poppaea's illness was an attempted murder."

"I'll bear that in mind, Felix."

The flush of exertion visible above Felix' thick beard suddenly deepened. He failed to intercept the ball on its next return, and it splashed into a puddle.

"You think that I've revealed weakness, don't you, John? You have my oath that I haven't been that weak. Not yet, at least. How often do we get a second chance? Even if she is not Berta, she is as near to her as I will ever meet again."

John remained silent.

"I'm extremely tired of being a glorified guard!" Felix snarled.

The statement took the Lord Chamberlain by surprise and he said so.

"I don't mean just this particular assignment. I'm a fighting man, or at least I used to be one. When I was given the opportunity to join the excubitors, to have the honor of serving directly under Justinian, stationed inside the palace at the very heart of the empire—how could I have refused? Besides, I was tired of campaigning."

"You certainly made the best of your opportunity, Felix. Few have risen so quickly to be captain. There's no doubt it was as a result of your heroism during the riots. You are a powerful man now, my friend, and many must envy your success."

"Powerful? Where is my power? Unless I were to rally my excubitors to place me on Justinian's throne—as more than a few military men have done in their time—I'm nothing more than a bodyguard, and one with Theodora's venomous gaze on him at all times at that."

John had never heard Felix voice such sentiments before, even when the gruff captain was intoxicated. "If you truly desired more power, you'd be seated on the throne already or, what's much more likely, your bones would be crumbling away in the earth. What is it that you really desire?"

Felix said nothing at first but walked over to retrieve the wet exercise ball.

"To be with Belisarius in Italy," he finally admitted slowly. "Or even to be Belisarius, camped with my troops outside the gates of Ravenna. If I'd remained with the army, I might be there in his place. Instead I let myself be enticed to Constantinople, to breathe the perfumes of the court. They're like an enchantment, putting a man to sleep."

John said that he suspected that it was not so much the perfumes of the court but rather the one worn by Bertrada that had affected Felix.

The big man glared at him. "We sometimes lose sight of the road Fortuna has laid before us, John, and sometimes our friends do the same." He put all his weight behind his throw. John stopped the ball but its force drove him back a step. As he recovered his equilibrium, Felix whirled and stalked away across the wet concrete.

John thought of calling after him, but the captain had no sooner vanished around the corner of the bath house than Anatolius appeared, accompanied by Zeno.

"What's the matter with Felix?" Anatolius asked immediately. "I greeted him in a perfectly civil manner and he practically knocked me down."

"He's suffering from an enchantment, or so he says," John informed him. "And what are you doing here at the first hour of the morning, Anatolius? You bring important news perhaps?"

Anatolius shook his head. "I fear not. I couldn't sleep at all, thinking about Lucretia, so I thought I might as well ride out here immediately." Looking shamefaced, he recounted what had transpired during his visit to Balbinus' home.

"You shouldn't be risking life and limb on the road in the middle of the night just to bring a report, although I appreciate your efforts on my behalf." John did not care for the sound of Lucretia's name on Anatolius' lips, nor the way he said it, but made no comment. One argument with a friend about a woman was enough before breakfast. He would broach the topic tactfully later, when he could speak to Anatolius in private.

"Speaking of enchantments," Zeno put in suddenly, "I got up with the sun also and I have wonderful news, John. You need no longer concern yourself about Barnabas."

"I do wish you had mentioned that on the way over here, uncle," Anatolius chided him. "Why, I was positively gripped with fear every time we passed by a bush tall enough to hide a dwarf."

"That's rather a startling statement, Zeno," John observed in a mild tone.

Zeno beamed. "But quite true, John. I just consulted Minthe. I left a question for the goats, you see. You've all been working so terribly hard, searching everywhere for Barnabas and patrolling the estate and so on, and everyone in an uproar and terribly worried that he might be creeping about waiting to strike again. I know you blame him for poisoning Poppaea, but all the children doted on him. He was wonderful with them, too. So I decided to ask the goats if we would ever find out his whereabouts."

Anatolius suppressed a grin. "Don't tell me they've told you where to find him?"

"No, but they've done almost as well. The searching and patrolling can be called off now. Barnabas definitely isn't here."

John looked skeptical.

"You doubt the goats, don't you?" Zeno was genuinely hurt. "Well, Minthe was waiting for the sun to rise when I got to the shrine, so that she could interpret the placing of the animals. Luckily for us it's a clear morning so as the sky lightened I could just make out the goats. To me they were just specks scattered all over the hillsides, what with my eyesight not being what it once was and the distance and all, but even I could see they had wandered into a most peculiar arrangement."

"This fortune-telling by goat arrangement sounds rather like reading the twisted entrails of a chicken," Anatolius said with interest.

"Indeed it is, and Minthe has the skill to read the meaning of the patterns," Zeno replied enthusiastically. "Now, it seems when the white goats graze high—"

John broke in, sensing a rambling lecture in the offing. "And what exactly did the goats have to say?"

"Their message was that Barnabas has crossed the waters. In other words, he's definitely gone away," Zeno replied.

"They're probably right," John agreed. "Felix and I have come to the same conclusion. The mime most likely took ship within hours of the boy's murder."

"So now will Felix call off his patrols, and we'll be able to concentrate on arrangements for the festival?" Zeno asked hopefully.

"You've overlooked one thing," John replied. "Even if the goats are correct about Barnabas, the patrols must continue until we catch the person who attempted Poppaea's murder." John sighed. "And as far as Gadaric's death is concerned, we still don't know who was responsible."

Zeno looked downcast, but only for an instant. "That can be my next question for the goats!"

❊ ❊ ❊

Hero had decided he could put off his task no longer.

He crept softly down the long corridor. The sun had been up long enough so that the occupants of Zeno's villa would have risen from their beds, or so he supposed, but not so long since that they would have finished eating their morning meal. What a luxury it must be, to be served breakfast in such a grand dining room. Not that he would care to be stuffing himself with bread and dates at such an early hour, let alone wine, and especially surrounded by painted schools of fish and octopi and other such creatures as a drowning man might see as he sank to the depths to die. The very thought made him lose his appetite.

No, he corrected himself, he had lost it because of the task he had to do. He had kept putting it off, trying to banish it from his mind, but now the unfortunate necessity could no longer be delayed.

He was absolutely certain that his mechanical hand had not been misplaced, as Bertrada had repeatedly assured him. He had searched every shelf and cupboard and cranny in the workshops where it could possibly have been mislaid, not that he had ever have done such a thing before. What, was he becoming a forgetful, doddering old man like Zeno?

No, someone had definitely stolen it. But who? And why? He could only speculate and none of the conclusions he drew were pleasant. Thus his current quest.

He padded into the wing where the Ostrogoths had their apartments. Passing by Bertrada's room, he turned around a corner and continued down a shorter corridor whose walls were washed in bright morning light. His foray had been as meticulously planned as one of his mechanical contrivances. If he were to be stopped by a house servant, he intended to say he was in the villa to repair one of Zeno's automatic wine dispensers, the one in the form of a satyr, and was seeking the master to discuss the matter. The excuse would be accepted. After all, he was known and trusted—not to mention that the mechanical devices were constantly malfunctioning one way or another.

As he went along the corridor, he met no one. The fact was, he thought, that Zeno did not have a sufficient number of servants for the size of the estate, nor did he keep a tight enough rein on those he employed. The ones who weren't serving breakfast to the household were doubtless currently lolling around the kitchen, shirking their responsibilities. He'd seen it often enough.

Poppaea would not be at breakfast, of course. Someone would be sitting with her. That might present a problem, but he had never shrunk from dealing with problems.

He slowed his steps as he approached Poppaea's room, then stopped and listened intently before moving forward and peering through its open door.

The girl was alone. Hero smiled to himself. For once he was benefiting from his employer's remarkably negligent regime.

He moved swiftly to the sleeping girl's bedside. The solemn little face was almost as white as the linen sheet pulled up under her chin. Hero glanced around. It wouldn't take long, he thought.

He heard the rustle of stiff fabric.

"What are you doing?"

Livia, Poppaea's mother, was suddenly standing in the doorway.

Hero straightened up. Panic filled his chest.

Godomar loomed behind the woman's shoulder. "By what right do you dare to enter this room?" he thundered, then fell silent. Livia also stared speechlessly.

Hero realized that he had lifted his left arm and was gesturing wildly toward them with the stump. "My hand," he stammered. "Who has stolen my hand?"

Chapter Seventeen

Anatolius lingered in the bath. His head felt as full of wool as an overstuffed exercise ball and the steaming caldarium seemed to relieve its distress somewhat.

The water temperature was kept exceedingly high, probably in deference to his uncle's old bones, he thought as he lolled in the water gazing up at the steam coiling around the marble vines decorating the dome of the ceiling. His drowsy mind saw ever-changing shapes in the shifting mist, yet each was a reminder of Lucretia. The pale hand that had brushed his hair away from his eyes, a white shoulder, the curve of a breast caught by a stealthy beam of moonlight. All of them part of a past as irretrievable as the days of Augustus.

She had been warm flesh and whispers and sweet skin and now she was another man's wife, greeting her former lover politely in a house where he was not welcome. It had been only a few years since they were intimate and he thought he had long since come to terms with his feelings for Lucretia. But his visit to Balbinus' house had stirred his blood—and his memories.

By the time he arrived for the morning meal, Zeno's dining room was empty but the serving girl clearing the table was happy to scamper away to the kitchen to seek viands on his behalf. He slumped down to await their arrival. To his consternation, the tall woman who had attempted to flirt with him at his uncle's ill-fated banquet swept in shortly thereafter, bearing his breakfast on a silver platter.

"I met a servant in the corridor, Anatolius, and thought I'd bring this in and keep you company for a while." Calyce sat down next to him, so close that her light yellow sleeve brushed his arm. "Zeno has been telling everyone his nephew is unwell, but I must say that you look positively glowing."

"I've just come from the bath. I'm probably better cooked than that egg." Anatolius stared at his plate gloomily. "It looks as if one of those painted jellyfish decided to leap down off the wall and onto my plate."

Calyce gave a throaty laugh. "Oh, Anatolius! The reports of your wit are vastly understated." Her narrow fingers patted the back of his hand, then daintily retreated.

Anatolius was suddenly reminded of Lucretia. Perhaps it was the way Calcye's impeccably reddened lips had shaped his name, pronouncing it with a slight breathiness he had not noticed before. Perhaps it was her husky laugh. No, he corrected himself, she was not Lucretia. She did not even resemble her physically. On the other hand, she was smiling at him.

"I've caught an occasional glimpse of you at the palace, Anatolius," Calyce was saying, "and whenever I did I always wondered why that good-looking young man with the dark curls looked so sad. But I'm repeating myself, for I surely mentioned that during our delightful discussion on the night of the banquet. Alas, that an evening that began so auspiciously for the two of us should have ended in such a terrible event." She dabbed at her eyes and when she again fixed her gaze on him he noticed how large her pupils were, no doubt dilated with belladonna as was the fashion among women of the court.

Anatolius took a bite of the undercooked egg. He now recalled he had done his utmost to avoid Calyce on the occasion in question, moving from atrium to garden to courtyard. She seemed to appear everywhere he went.

"Do you know the empress very well, Anatolius?" she offered with another sweet smile that made him wonder why he had tried to escape her.

"I have the honor occasionally to speak with her," he replied politely.

"How wonderful! But then I imagine you are familiar with everyone of importance in Constantinople, being a senator's son as well as working at the palace. My family is also highly placed, you know. We own land in Italy as well as interests in shipping. I expect our property and businesses will be returned once Roman rule is restored. Then I shall go home although I must say that Italy will seem barely civilized compared to Constantinople."

She chattered on amiably but Anatolius hardly listened. He was too busy asking himself, now, not why he had tried to avoid her, but rather how he could have overlooked her.

Perhaps his painful visit with Lucretia had been a gift from Fortuna. Having heard his lost love's voice once again, he recognized a similarity in Calyce's speech, one he had managed to miss on the night of the banquet. Thus encouraged, he looked at her anew, noting the aristocratic elegance he had dismissed as an overly prominent jaw. How strange that he could have been so blind.

She clasped her pale hands together. "It seems to me that we have a lot in common, Anatolius. I wait upon the empress and you labor on behalf of the emperor. Not that you are a mere attendant like myself, of course. What was it dear Zeno said, that you are Justinian's legal advisor? How very exciting!"

"My uncle exaggerated a little, I fear. I am Justinian's private secretary."

"Oh. Better yet! A man of letters. And poetry also perhaps? I do so love the ancient poets."

The wool stuffing seemed to be creeping into Anatolius' head once more. When he spoke his words sounded to him as if they emanated from far away. "It's true that my father favored a legal career for me, but I believe there is more truth to be found in any one verse of Ovid than in all the orations of Cicero."

Calyce's long—some would say patrician—face grew serious. "Ovid? You admire Ovid? Why, this is most remarkable. Are you certain you are not my long lost brother?"

As had too often happened, Anatolius was suddenly acutely aware that his breakfast companion was female, aware of the warm breath carrying her words and the smooth flesh beneath her fine silk garments.

"Your brother?" he replied with mock alarm. "I do most sincerely hope not."

Calyce, surprisingly, blushed rosily.

❄ ❄ ❄

"And then," Anatolius told John, "she said there was something on my face and ran her finger along the edge of my mouth even though I'm certain there was nothing there. Actually, I think it was just an excuse."

"You do have something on your face," John told him impatiently. "It's on the side of your nose. What did you have for breakfast?"

Anatolius, who had searched the garden for John in order to regale him with an account of his newfound joy, was disappointed at his friend's reaction. The day had hardly begun but already the sun felt hot. Even so, the seasons were turning inexorably. There would be few more mornings such as this before autumn arrived, he thought as he rubbed his nose petulantly. "Still, I do think Calyce is quite fond of me," he grinned as they strolled along the shady path.

"I thought that was obvious, given that on the night of the banquet you were practically hiding behind me to escape the attentions of the—what was your term? Sharp-beaked harpy?"

"You're in a foul mood, John. However, I shall forgive you." Anatolius glanced at the statue of Venus, a shapely reminder of one of Zeno's past passions, standing in front of a tangle of rose bushes at the fork in the path at which they had just arrived.

John gave a grim smile but did not respond as they strolled down the narrow way on their right. A few turns back and forth and they found themselves looking at the stout door leading to Castor's estate.

Anatolius tested the door, finding it locked. "Briarus certainly keeps his master's estate well secured," he remarked.

John regarded the high wall between Zeno's overgrown grounds and those of his more security-conscious neighbor.

"I intend to visit Briarus again and ask if there is any news of Castor," he finally said.

❄ ❄ ❄

The overbearing estate manager was even less happy to see John and Anatolius than on their earlier visit. The sound of their approach brought him out of his stone lodge before they had reached the entrance of the estate. He was brandishing a broom. In response to John's question as he unlocked the gate to admit them, he explained he been sweeping out his home.

"I'm glad to hear it," Anatolius told him. "When I first saw you, I was afraid you intended to drive us off with that domestic weapon."

Rather than looking abashed Briarus glowered. It was a pity the man was a servant, Anatolius decided. He would have made an extremely effective dictator.

"We have had problems with unruly village children, sir," Briarus said. "It's because of the dog." He pointed at the mosaic adorning the archway over the gate. Below the ferocious black beast was the expected legend warning passersby to beware of the dog.

"Every time children from the village go by they insist on coming up to the gate," Briarus explained. "They know that we have no dog but they pretend to suddenly notice our guardian here and go staggering sideways from the shock or fall down and roll in the dust. Then they get up and scream and run away."

"Sometimes life can take you by surprise like that," Anatolius observed.

"They think it's a great joke, sir," Briarus said morosely. "It almost appears to have become something of a tradition. Of course, it's extremely disruptive of my duties for if I hear a commotion I am duty bound to investigate it."

"This area is certainly rich in tradition," put in John, "but we're here for another reason. Have you had word from your master?"

Briarus shook his head silently. Without further word, John strode through the opened gate and stepped briskly toward the stone lodge. The agitated estate manager rushed after him. Anatolius followed, puzzled by his friend's uncharacteristic abruptness.

"You will excuse me, Briarus," John said quietly as he entered the lodge. "I am afraid that this is necessary."

In contrast to its rough-hewn exterior, the building's interior was smoothly plastered. John seemed little interested in the brazier set against one wall, the neatly made bed or any of its other sparse furnishings. His gaze had immediately fastened on the one unexpected aspect of the small dwelling—the boxes and baskets stacked carefully in two piles just inside the door.

"These were all delivered for the master during his absence," Briarus informed his visitors. "I am storing them here where I can keep a close eye upon them. The house servants are sometimes rather careless and to tell the truth, with one or two, I'm not sure they're entirely honest."

John hefted a basket from the top of the closest pile. A quick glance showed it contained only dark green apples. "If you'd care to assist me, Anatolius?"

Anatolius made the discovery before he had finished asking John what it was that he sought. It was in a wooden basket with a tight-fitting lid sitting atop the other stack.

He lowered the basket to the floor, cut the thick cord tying it shut and, assuring the outraged Briarus that Castor would not hold him personally responsible for allowing such freedom to be taken with his possessions, he pulled off the lid.

Lying inside the box was one of strangest contraptions he had ever seen, a bizarre construction of metal, wires and leather straps. At first he thought it merely a particularly elaborate set of pincers but then he realized it was a fair simulacrum of a human hand.

The fingers were curved as if ready to grasp hold of something but by the dried blood covering them, they might as well be pointing to a murderer.

Chapter Eighteen

Hero stood defiantly beside the forge, a hammer in his one soot-streaked hand. He looked away from John, Zeno and Anatolius, toward Felix and the two excubitors accompanying him.

The anger in the brawny inventor's eyes was as hot as the forge. He looked swiftly around the workshop, as if weighing what chance he and his hammer might have against six opponents, but when he finally moved it was to raise the stump of his arm to wipe sweat from his glistening forehead.

"What did you mean when you said you weren't going to hurt the girl?" John asked him again.

"It was a misunderstanding, Lord Chamberlain. I admit I was going to look around Poppaea's room. I was searching for my mechanical hand. The children have hidden things before and so I thought perhaps they were playing another little joke on me. Then Godomar accused me of intending to harm the child. So naturally when you arrived with guards..."

"You gave me a terrible fright as well." Zeno's tone was as sharp as John had ever heard it. "How are we supposed to get anything done with excubitors constantly getting underfoot? And what's this about your hand being missing, Hero?"

Hero glared at his employer. "I don't know anything more about it than that, since I haven't been able to work on it for days or even think about it, what with finishing constructing the whale and then all the commotion after the banquet. Not to mention that I've just started on this pressing new project." He waved his hammer at the collection of lengths of fine chain, cogs, scraps of leather, and an assortment of body parts made of hammered metal laid out on the dirt floor.

"A representation of a cart accident on the Mese?" Anatolius mused callously.

"They will be shaped into an exceedingly fine contribution to the festival, as you well know!" Zeno told his nephew in a severe tone. "Although how it and the other automatons could possibly be assembled without Hero's expertise and oversight I can't say!" He directed a meaningful stare in John's direction.

"I'm sorry, Zeno," John replied, "but unless Hero intends to be more cooperative, I'm going to have to order him kept confined for now."

"How can I tell you any more than I know?" Hero's voice rose to a shout but he made no effort to resist as the excubitors stepped forward to escort him away.

"Confine him to one of the spare rooms in the back of the villa," Felix instructed his men, "but see that it isn't anywhere near the one Briarus is locked up in."

"Do you think they were working together?" Anatolius wondered, looking after the trio as Hero was marched away.

John replied that he had no idea.

"The weapon was in Briarus' possession but it belonged to Hero, so therefore both are suspect," Felix told Anatolius. He barely looked at John, obviously still angry over their previous day's conversation concerning Bertrada. Zeno however was oblivious, continuing to complain bitterly like a child whose outing has been ruined by a sudden rain storm.

John, who had laid the strange prosthesis out on a work table, ignored Zeno's protests and examined the device closely.

"It's a complicated affair, isn't it?" Anatolius eyed the artificial hand. "Perhaps I shouldn't say so but by the look of the intricate workings, Hero must have spent considerably more time working on this hand than on that simple mechanical man spread out all over the floor."

Zeno looked offended. "This automaton is sufficiently complex to fire an arrow before it's tipped over the precipice into the sea, Anatolius. You should never judge by appearances."

John had picked up the mechanical hand and was tugging experimentally at one of its dangling leather straps. The action caused two of the fingers to curl realistically. Looking more closely he saw that the finger joints were hinged, held together by thin leather sinews.

"How could he possibly hope to operate the thing? Did he intend to hold the straps between his teeth?" Felix rubbed his great beard vigorously, as if the action might cause the answer to fall out of it. "Though it's recorded that when the general Marcus Sergius lost his right arm to the enemy, he ordered an iron hand be manufactured. According to Pliny, it was designed solely to hold the general's shield. So while it allowed him to resume battle it could do nothing more than that, and thus was quite unlike this strange monstrosity."

"How fascinating!" This interesting morsel of knowledge distracted Zeno from his annoyance. "You wield the scroll as well as the sword, then?"

"I've read a bit of history," Felix admitted. "One can always learn from the great generals." His emphatic statement was accompanied by a sideways scowl at John.

"But what reason could Hero possibly have had to kill Gadaric?" Anatolius put in. He sniffed. "It's the wretched smoke in here," he added apologetically.

"None whatsoever so far as I can see. The twins loved Hero," Zeno replied, "and he was very fond of them. He and Bertrada occasionally took them to the beach, for example, and sometimes he made toys for them. There was a jackal that ran about on little wheels. It was so funny to watch that I insisted he make one for my own collection. And he seemed to enjoy it when the children visited the workshop."

"But even if he did kill Gadaric, why would he hide the hand in Briarus' lodge?" Anatolius continued. "Then again, if Briarus was the culprit, how did he obtain the hand? Did he know Hero? And if it was Briarus, why would he hide the weapon in his own home? Also, if—"

John interrupted his friend. "All puzzling questions indeed, Anatolius, but I fear you've missed the most significant question. Where is Castor? After all, if Briarus is indeed guilty of murder then his master's unexplained absence suddenly becomes considerably more sinister, wouldn't you say?"

Zeno looked stricken. "Briarus's dictatorial style of estate management might have been modeled after Sulla's methods, but I am absolutely certain that he would never kill his master," he declared emphatically.

John did not care to argue with Zeno, who after all had spent most of his life on his estate, away from the court in Constantinople, and so had not been in a position to observe how remarkably often "never" seemed to come around.

"It's now even more urgent that we find Castor," he said instead. "I've thought of an excellent place to begin. Castor's account books will reveal the merchants with whom he habitually dealt. Anatolius, I fear you must be back in Constantinople, knocking on their doors and asking questions before night falls again."

Anatolius looked horrified. "But John, I've just arrived! I can't leave again so quickly. You're aware of the circumstances. My future romantic happiness hangs in the balance," he concluded pitifully.

"Duty must always come before affairs of the heart."

Anatolius' mission was soon arranged. A quick visit to Castor's estate to scan the account books, then on to Constantinople to interview those with whom the vanished man had done business. He sputtered protests and then fell into grief-stricken silence.

Only when he and Zeno had left the workshop did Felix speak. "Do you really suppose Castor might be absent on business, or did you just want Anatolius away on horseback before that young woman gets her claws properly hooked into him?"

John thought it a strange question coming from Felix, who seemed to be the quarry of another young woman. He refrained from mentioning it. There had been enough friction between him and his friend.

"I admit, it's a good opportunity to put him beyond Calyce's reach," he said, "but I still hope we'll discover Castor has gone off on business. I've been told he's often away for long periods. Quite possibly he may just have left without telling anyone."

"Not even his estate manager?" Felix shook his head. "In the old days, I would be betting on a more sinister explanation."

"It's true Briarus hasn't been very helpful. I shall have to insist he be more forthcoming." John turned his attention back to the heavy prosthesis he held in his thin, sun-browned hand. He frowned and pulled another strap, causing the artificial thumb to move.

"I think you've missed something," Felix commented. "If I could look at that?"

He took the device carefully but rather than testing the hand's leather straps like John, the big German gripped the extension that served as its forearm.

"While you were operating the fingers just now, did you happen to notice the hand's hinged at the wrist?" he asked as he squeezed the prosthesis as if operating pincers. It was a slight pressure but the fingers curled together with a loud snap.

The excubitor captain looked at the clenched metal fist with a military man's admiration. "Yes, anyone could commit mayhem with this. Indeed, if that long-ago general had been fitted with an iron hand such as this, he wouldn't have needed a sword."

❊ ❊ ❊

Poppaea woke late in the afternoon.

It was an abrupt and strange sort of awakening. The sick girl simply opened her eyes, sat up and began to babble gibberish like an oracle. At least that was how Bertrada, watching at the bedside, had frantically described it when she located John.

Familiar by now with Bertrada's tendency to paint events in overly vivid colors, John was surprised, when he arrived at Poppaea's room, to find the child's condition very much as depicted.

"Ah, here is someone very high at the court," Poppaea was saying as he entered the room. "How very good of you to visit."

John wondered that the girl recognized him. Then he realized that although her eyes were open they were not focussed on him or anyone in the room.

She rambled on, talking about a picnic, banquets, the garden. Her gaze darted back and forth as she turned her head back and forth as if addressing first this person and then another, but her blank stare never rested on John or Bertrada beside him, or on the only other person present, her mother, who stood trembling at the bedside.

Livia's round face was almost as colorless as her daughter's. "Where is she speaking from? Who is she speaking to? I fear Poppaea has left us, Lord Chamberlain. That's not my child speaking."

"Calyce has gone to get another potion from Minthe but we've said nothing about it," Bertrada whispered to John. "No doubt Godomar will be in here spouting prayers soon. He seems to think the girl is possessed."

"Your daughter is just delirious," John tried to reassure the distraught mother.

"Demons prey on those who are weak."

"Don't pay so much heed to what Godomar says," Bertrada told her impatiently. "Poppaea's been ill but now she's awake, she's going to get better. There's nothing more to it than that."

John addressed Poppaea by name. She made no acknowledgment of it but continued to talk to her invisible audience.

"...it was a fine picnic," she murmured. "Won't you try some of these? But they are so sweet... look...the queen is approaching..."

Sunilda had appeared in the doorway. "Poppaea," she exclaimed. "I'm happy to see that Porphyrio has cured you."

Poppaea looked away from an empty spot in the air and directly at her playmate. "Sunilda, welcome! Yes, the whale has indeed taken care of everything and now we are having a grand celebration, as you can see." She lifted her hand and gestured weakly around the room.

Sunilda smiled. "It is a very grand celebration indeed, Poppaea," she agreed.

❄ ❄ ❄

Godomar made the sign of his religion as he entered Poppaea's bedroom. It seemed to him that his moving hand was met with some slight, inexplicable resistance, as if the very air were ready to impede his mission, while the ecclesiastical stole draped ceremoniously over his shoulders and crossed over his chest felt as heavy as a wooden yoke.

"The Lord Chamberlain just departed with Bertrada," Livia informed him. "He tried to question Poppaea but the demon within her insisted on answering him with the most terrible blasphemies."

"Oh, Livia, she was just telling us about the party and Porphyrio," Sunilda said sharply. The girl was standing by the head of her friend's bed. "And now as you can see all that talking's tired her out."

She brushed a fine strand of hair away from Poppaea's closed eyelids. Delicate veins, like fine blue stitchery, were visible in the girl's linen-white skin.

Godomar stepped resolutely forward, convinced that he was in the presence of something evil. Yet was it any wonder, surrounded as they were by mechanical mockeries of the human form, not to mention constant talk of fortune-telling goats and pagan festivals?

"Please move aside, Sunilda," he said sternly. "I have come to abjure the fiend that has taken up residence in Poppaea."

Sunilda remained where she was and glowered at him.

"Please, Sunilda, Godomar must perform this ceremony." Livia timidly laid her hand on Sunilda's shoulder as she spoke.

The girl jerked away and glared. "I will not be touched in such a fashion by a mere servant! If I were queen such impudence would be worth your head!"

Livia burst into tears.

Godomar sidled up as close to Poppaea's bed as he could manage. Sunilda made him uneasy. Who would put such awful words on the lips of a little girl? Or perhaps he should more accurately ask what would do so?

He bent over and laid his hand on Poppaea's forehead. It felt as hot as if imbued with the fires of Hell. While Sunilda stood rigidly nearby, staring at him with what struck him as equally burning hatred, he murmured his adjuration, concluding more hastily than he had intended, "Leave this innocent one, in the name of He who suffered and died for all our sins."

"Poppaea is only sick," Sunilda remarked pointedly.

"I am doing what is necessary," Godomar replied softly.

"You are doing it for yourself," the girl replied.

Looking at her, Godomar had a sudden thought. "But as to you, Sunilda...."

Livia let out a ragged sob. "No! Not her as well!"

"It would be a wise precaution," Godomar argued. "She is after all descended from a line of heretics and such flesh, although blameless itself, may yet be prone to demonic infection. One cannot be too careful."

He took a swift step forward. As his fingertips reached the top her head, Sunilda gave a piercing shriek, grabbed his stole and yanked it with more strength than Godomar would have imagined it possible for an eight-year-old to possess.

He lurched forward and fell to the floor.

As she walked calmly from the room, Sunilda paused in the doorway to glance back at him.

"When I am queen, you will not be returning to Italy with me, Godomar. And while everyone seems to think I'm in danger, I can assure you, there are many here in much greater danger."

Chapter Nineteen

Since Poppaea's poisoning, Zeno's household had eaten almost as simply as peasants. Meals were plain, free of the possibility of camouflaging deliberately tainted food with spice or sauces, and all were prepared under the watchful eye of some person of undoubted trustworthiness, usually one of Theodora's ladies-in-waiting.

The breakfast of wheat cakes and wine well suited the Lord Chamberlain's taste, for his culinary preferences had never risen to match his high position at court. When they had finished their frugal meal, John and Felix retired to Zeno's study to discuss their two prisoners. Codices and scrolls were piled untidily on the desk. The room carried a hint of the dusty smell of desiccated papyrus.

"At least I've breakfasted as if I'm at home." John spoke first, breaking the uncomfortable silence they had maintained since their meal. "If only court ceremonial wasn't always accompanied by such rich repasts." He was thinking of the endless banquets he had not only to plan as part of his official duties, but also to attend. The recollection reminded him of those strange festivities in Poppaea's room that had apparently been visible only to her and to Sunilda.

His half-jocular comment, however, did not seem to thaw the frost in his friend's demeanor.

Felix sat heavily down on a low bronze stool behind Zeno's desk, almost vanishing behind a mountain of half unrolled scrolls. "A crust of bread and some watered vinegar can be a veritable feast when you're out on campaign," he complained, "but if I have to be nothing more than a child's bodyguard I'd just as soon eat better than that. Besides, you can poison a cup or a jug or a plate of food wherever it might be sitting. You don't need to skulk about in the kitchen to do it."

John agreed his statement was certainly true.

"We were wasting our time looking for Barnabas, just as I said," Felix continued. "He's long since run away. Did you suppose he might have contrived to be carted back into the villa concealed at the bottom of a basket of loaves? Or disguised as a large duckling? Not that anything that happens in this house would surprise me, I must say. But we've already got the two bastards responsible in custody, thank Mithra, so perhaps now my men and I can take them and return to the city."

"Not until they tell us what we need to know," John said quietly.

"Leave that to Justinian's torturers!"

John pushed the scene in Poppaea's room out of his mind. Turning his gaze to the study walls, where painted philosophers strolled along paths that appeared so realistic he might have walked down them directly into Zeno's untidy garden, he said, "I'm not certain it would be wise to take Briarus and Hero to Constantinople yet, Felix. We both know what fate awaits them in Justinian's dungeons."

Felix grumbled an unintelligible reply and yawned mightily.

"You need more rest, Felix," John said. "I'm beginning to wonder if your obvious exhaustion springs from something other than staying up all night patrolling over-zealously."

The captain muttered a ripe curse and hastily changed the subject. "You've already talked to the prisoners more than once, John. Of course they'll both claim to know nothing about murders or poisons, but surely you can't believe that Briarus knows nothing of his master's whereabouts? What's to be gained by keeping them locked up here? Once they're gone, Zeno will stop asking me about Hero and complaining about his wretched automatons not being ready for the festival every time I see him."

"I don't intend to question them further right now," John replied. "I want to give them another day in isolation to give them ample opportunity to contemplate what fate awaits them in Constantinople. By tomorrow morning, they'll doubtless be happy to reveal everything they know."

"You're too kind-hearted, John," Felix said without a trace of irony in his tone.

John allowed his gaze to wander the walls along the shaded paths as he contemplated the arrangements needed to transport the unlikely accomplices safely to the palace grounds.

A light step sounded in the corridor and he turned to see Bertrada peering around the ivy tendrils painted on the doorframe.

"Lord Chamberlain," the nursemaid whispered. "I'm happy I found you alone. I have a terrible confession to make. It's very embarrassing. Something I wouldn't want certain parties to hear."

Scrolls toppled off the desk and rattled to the tiles as Felix was suddenly on his feet and in full view. "It isn't necessary to be afraid, Bertrada."

The girl gave a tiny squeak of shock, and turned away to flee back down the corridor.

"Please," John told her, "come in, Bertrada. As the captain says, you have nothing to fear."

She bit her lip as she took a reluctant step into the room, glanced at Felix and then averted her eyes. "Lord Chamberlain, if I could speak with you alone..." she began hesitantly.

"If it is anything that concerns the safety of the household, then Felix will have to hear it," John said quietly.

Bertrada, who had been looking at the floor, pushed her hair back and looked up at John. "It's about Hero, Lord Chamberlain. He's innocent, I swear it."

"You have some proof of this?" John thought it was doubtful. "And if you do, why have you suddenly decided to come forward now?"

Bertrada looked toward Felix again, then quickly away. "Well, it was seeing him brought into the villa under guard, with half of the household gawking at him, just like Briarus. I thought surely someone would soon realize it was all a terrible mistake and he would be freed, but he's still locked up."

"I see," John said. "And why do you insist that Hero was not responsible for Gadaric's murder?"

The girl's eyes filled with tears. "It's shameful to admit, Lord Chamberlain, but I was with Hero at the time."

She stole a swift look at Felix. He said nothing but simply walked to the study door, moving as slowly as a condemned criminal going to his death.

As he passed by Bertrada she caught at his sleeve and looked at him silently.

John was struck by the incongruity. Felix, a big scarred veteran with a few streaks of white in his beard, Bertrada a young girl. It could almost have been a parting between father and daughter.

"Felix, don't be angry," Bertrada begged. "That's all over now, I swear it. Please..."

The excubitor captain shrugged her small hand off his arm and vanished down the corridor.

"I will order Hero released immediately, but he must not leave the estate," John finally said. "You were right to tell us, Bertrada, and I realize to do so has cost you greatly."

❄ ❄ ❄

Briarus yanked harder at the ornamental hanging. One of the nails attaching it to the wall popped loose and skittered across the tile floor but no sound came from the corridor. Evidently the excubitor had heard nothing or, more likely, his patrolling had taken him to the other end of the long hallway running the length of this wing of the villa.

Briarus smiled grimly. His temporary lodging was nothing more than a windowless room that had been decorated with a few wall hangings of little artistic merit in order to hastily convert it into a bedroom for one of Zeno's numerous summer guests. The dense, leafy vegetation depicted on the fabric was crudely sewn, neither natural in appearance nor pleasingly ornamental. Castor would never have allowed it to be hung in his house, Briarus thought, but much could be forgiven for the unpleasing decoration had provided him with a weapon.

He got down on his hands and knees to find the nail, which had bounced off the tiles onto the woven carpet stretched between bed and door. To his disappointment, the small length of metal was not only bent but also much shorter than he had hoped. At first glance it suggested no way it could be used to his advantage. It might inflict some damage thrust into an eye, perhaps, but he was unlikely to be able to get close enough to an excubitor to accomplish that. He stuck it into his belt anyway, just in case. Then he sat down on the edge of the bed and waited.

Briarus had not always labored as an estate manager. He had risen to that position largely by waiting. It had occurred to him early in life that although each day contained only so many hours, each one of those hours contained Fortuna's handiwork. Whole days of hours, even weeks or months of them, might stream by, all useless in accomplishing an individual purpose. But there were so very many hours and their flow so unceasing, that if one waited watchfully, eventually some opportunity would present itself. So, over the years, he had seized this chance and that, and then another.

Even as he worked in his comfortable post on Castor's estate, Briarus had waited for a better opportunity to present itself. So when disaster fell upon him and the excubitors had marched him off to this soft but secure room, he had simply gone on waiting, certain that one of the hours still between him and Justinian's dungeons would offer him the chance he needed to escape.

Nevertheless, being locked in the cramped room was burdensome. Aside from the bed and a small wooden table, there were only a clay lamp, a religious tract, and a chamber pot whose necessary use had rendered his surroundings somewhat malodorous. He intended to complain about that at the next opportunity, but unfortunately the Lord Chamberlain had not appeared to question him again.

Not that Briarus would have anything more to say about the matter, having immediately pointed out the noticeable lack of proof of any misdoing on his part. Unfortunately, he knew very well that this undisputed fact would not be something he could turn to his advantage once he was escorted to the palace.

Now the night was well advanced. Briarus fingered the tract but made no effort to read it. At this point he was more intent at avoiding eternity than in preparing for it.

During the day, listening occasionally at the door, he had overheard a man berating someone of the household for a dalliance and, later on, his guard sharing scurrilous jokes about the empress with someone with a booming laugh. Swift, light footsteps had run past once or twice, accompanied by childish laughter. He had eavesdropped on grumbling about the heat and learned that someone in the house liked to sing hymns, although unhappily in a dreadful, tuneless manner. Nothing that he had heard seemed useful in resolving his current dilemma.

Now as he sat quietly pondering the situation he heard a footsteps outside. They sounded almost too quiet. Stealthy, in fact. He padded over to the door and listened intently.

There was no sound of a key being turned but rather an odd scratching. Something was scrabbling at the wall outside.

Then Briarus smelled lamp oil, its light odor hitherto masked by the stench from the chamber pot.

Looking down, he saw that a stream of lamp oil had run in under the door and was rapidly soaking into the carpet.

He reacted quickly, reaching down to pull it away from the oil before it became saturated.

It was too late.

His hand closed on flames as a rivulet of fire raced into the room.

He grabbed the chamber pot and threw its contents over the carpet but it had no effect. The glowing fire spread rapidly across the floor as Briarus began to shout hoarsely, pounding at the door.

A wave of heat washed against his back. Turning, he saw the bed was catching fire.

Streamers of flame crackled up the wall hanging. Briarus opened his mouth to yell again and heated air poured down his throat like boiling water. Smoke filled his lungs.

Coughing and cursing, he kicked at the door frantically. Surely he would be heard and help would arrive. Where was his guard?

He screamed louder, choking on the swirling smoke.

Briarus was still waiting to be rescued when he lost consciousness and fell to the blazing floor.

Chapter Twenty

John raced across the atrium toward the sound of hoarse shouting and arrived at Briarus's temporary quarters to find Felix wielding an axe powerfully against its door. Splinters flew, then the onlookers were assaulted by a gust of scorching air carrying whirling sparks and a cloud of thick smoke out into the corridor.

Coughing convulsively, Felix pulled a body away from inside the room and the flames licking around the doorpost. He bent over the limp figure and gave a grim shake of his head.

"Suffocated," he growled to John.

Several servants rapidly formed a line and passed slopping buckets filled with water from the courtyard fountain hand to hand. The threat of fire had spurred Zeno's generally lackadaisical staff to efficient action. Unfortunately the buckets of water simply vanished into the room to produce clouds of hissing steam with no apparent effect upon the conflagration. A large scrap of flaming wall hanging whirled out of the smoke and landed in the corridor. Felix leapt forward and stamped the flames out, accompanying his heavy-booted dance with lurid curses.

Suddenly a noise like distant thunder rose over the crackling roar of the flames. Heat and smoke were forcing the men further away from the room as Zeno trotted briskly into view, closely followed by two husky servants pulling a cart carrying a deep wooden vat. The cart rumbled to a stop and at Zeno's order the two men sprang onto raised steps attached to each side of the cart and began vigorously working the narrow beam linking a pair of rods extending up from inside the vat.

It was a large water pump, John realized.

Zeno rushed to the front of the device and grasped the leather pipe protruding from its base. As the pumpers strained at the beam there was a clunking, wheezing noise as pistons started to do their work. Suddenly water gouted out of the pipe with enormous force.

Zeno directed the powerful stream first at the walls of the burning room, then into its corners, soon smothering the worst of the flames. Before long the bucket carriers were able to assume their work and eventually advance into the room to douse the smoldering remnants.

Zeno bustled over to John with a proud smile. "It's Hero's work, of course. A wonder, isn't it? A real life saver."

"It didn't save Briarus's life," Felix pointed out, "although it's certainly prevented the villa from going up in flames. Fortunately, the fire hadn't got into the walls."

Zeno looked stricken. "Castor will be devastated at this news," he said somberly. "He absolutely depended on the man, you know. Briarus was a good businessman and an excellent employee by all accounts. Yet a despicable villain too, as it turned out! Dare I say that it's only fitting that the gods gave someone who murdered a child such a terrible death?"

"We haven't definitely established that Briarus was the culprit," John reminded him.

"Well, John," Felix put in, "I have to say that if you'd taken my advice and sent both prisoners immediately to Constantinople, we would have had a chance to find out the truth of the matter. As it is, how are you going to explain this latest development to Theodora's satisfaction?"

Zeno blanched at the mention of the empress and observed in a timid voice that he trusted that there would be no repercussions over what was, in all truth, merely a terrible accident.

Felix grunted. "An accident? When one conspirator dies hours after the other is set free?"

John requested that a servant be sent to summon the Egyptian inventor for further questioning and that the rest be dismissed to their beds.

Likewise, the excubitors were ordered back to their duties with the exception of the man who had been on guard in the corridor.

"You were obviously not at your post when this fire broke out!" Felix barked at the latter. "Otherwise the alarm could have been given earlier. Where were you?"

"There was a suspicious noise in the back courtyard, captain. Since the prisoner was securely locked in, I went to investigate. I discovered that the statue of Eros was knocked over and its arm was smashed."

"That statue was a gift from a close relative," remarked Zeno. "The lady is deceased now, alas, so she won't mourn its loss."

"How long were you absent?" John asked the guard.

"There was someone moving about in the bushes so I searched them for a brief while, excellency, before returning to my post and immediately raising the alarm."

Felix scowled. It was obvious that a lot more would be said to his subordinate once the two men were in private. Meanwhile, he curtly dismissed the excubitor, who escaped thankfully down the corridor in the footsteps of the servants departing with their buckets.

John was inspecting the corridor wall beside the door of the damaged room when Hero appeared. He greeted the man coolly. "I am surprised you didn't arrive with that fire-fighting device of yours."

Hero lifted the stump of his arm. "I'm afraid I'm not much good at operating such machinery, Lord Chamberlain. Ironic, isn't it?"

Zeno broke into the conversation, effusively describing to Hero the ease of obliterating fires when equipped with such an ingenious water pump. He then hurried off "to calm everyone down," as he put it—a task for which the elderly and excitable man was particularly ill suited, in John's opinion.

"I am not quite so enthusiastic about your mechanical contrivances as your employer," John remarked as Zeno's orange-clad form disappeared from view. "Of late, they seem to be appearing rather too frequently in the general vicinity of those who have recently died."

Hero placed his palm in a protective gesture on the side of the vat. "What do you mean, Lord Chamberlain? If it weren't for this contrivance we'd all be standing in the garden watching the villa burn down like a city tenement."

"I wasn't referring to the pump but rather to this strange lighting contrivance." John indicated a recess in the wall by the door to what had been Briarus's room. The small niche and its contents were badly charred, with a black streak stretching from it to the water-puddled floor tiles.

"My self-lighting lamp? It's a clever device indeed, Lord Chamberlain. It's operated in a most cunning manner with the aid of a water clock, not unlike the automatically lit lamps inside the whale."

John observed quietly that he was less interested in discovering how the lamp worked than the manner in which it appeared to have malfunctioned. "From the stains on the wall," he continued, "it's fairly obvious that lamp oil was somehow spilt, caught fire and then ran under the door."

Hero inspected the blackened wreckage inside the recess. "Yes, that does seem to have been what happened," he admitted thoughtfully. "Its oil supply is in a container set into the wall but it couldn't have leaked accidentally. I have some expertise in designing such things and I can assure you that the arrangement was perfectly safe."

Felix and John regarded him silently. It was obvious they were thinking about the mechanical whale, which had also been judged to be perfectly safe.

Hero's jaws clenched in anger. "Surely it is clear that someone tampered with the lamp?"

"And who would know how to do that? Apart from a person with some expertise in these things—such as yourself?" Felix pointed out.

"Lord Chamberlain, this was a terrible event." Hero waved his hand at the wreckage visible through the doorway a few paces from them but did not glance down at Briarus, who lay even closer. "But whoever did it remains at liberty." He turned his gaze toward Felix although he continued to address John. "It is my opinion what whoever killed Gadaric murdered Briarus and as I believe you now know, the night that the boy was murdered, I was with Bertrada."

❄ ❄ ❄

At John's brisk knock, Bertrada angrily yanked her bedroom door open, her lips already forming a virulent protest. Recognizing the Lord Chamberlain, she hastily amended her manner.

"I thought it was Godomar, excellency," she explained in a nervous tone. "He's always creeping around to spy on what we're doing. He claims it's his duty to keep an eye on all of us. The Evil Eye is what I call it!"

John, thinking that Godomar no doubt had good reason to keep a close watch on the young nursemaid, stepped into the room. He gestured the girl to sit down on her rumpled bed. She was wearing only the flimsy tunica she slept in. It revealed a form that was still boylike and angular.

"You surely cannot have slept through the recent uproar?" John said.

"No, I didn't. It's certainly a terrible thing that has happened, excellency."

"And how do you know if you have not been out of your room?"

"I heard about it from a servant who went by a little while ago. Of course I heard all the commotion but I knew I should remain here with Sunilda," she continued, looking toward the door connecting her room with her charge's bedroom.

John suggested that apart from devotion to her duty, might she also have remained because she expected a visitor, perhaps one who could be described as a military man?

She blushed as she denied the charge.

A few brief questions elicited the information that no-one had visited her since her young charge had fallen asleep and she herself had retired to bed.

"But someone has tracked mud in on his boots," John nodded toward the obvious evidence on the floor.

"Sunilda's always playing in the mud." Bertrada shook her head and smiled. "I have often had to correct her about that. It's not at all lady-like."

"I ordered Hero released because I believed what you told me," John said, "which is to say that you were with him on the night Gadaric was murdered. Now, no sooner is Hero a free man than someone else is dead, and again through the agency of one of his mechanical devices."

Bertrada's face flushed as she insisted Hero was innocent of wrongdoing. "There is a room at the back of the workshop. We met there that night..." She hesitated, biting her lip for an instant, before continuing in a low voice. "Our entanglement was a mistake, I see that clearly now, excellency. Do you think Captain Felix was terribly hurt to learn about it? He is a fine man."

John ignored the question and instead instructed her to relate her movements on the night of the banquet in detail.

"Both children were put to bed early and were soon fast asleep," the girl replied, looking ashamed. "There were guards all over the place with the empress being here, not to mention many of the banquet guests had their own bodyguards. So I just assumed this villa was as safe as the palace."

"Indeed? As you now realize, it's exactly as safe as the palace, or in other words, not at all. So you crept out to visit Hero? Didn't anyone remark on your leaving the children unattended?"

"Why would they? I'm their nursemaid and it's not for servants to question me. Besides, Calyce and Livia sometimes take charge of the children. So has Godomar, on occasion."

John questioned her concerning the time when she had left the children asleep.

"I couldn't say exactly, but it was after the banquet had started. I could hear all the laughter and chatter going on and the clatter in the kitchen as I went out to the workshop. There were lots of servants scurrying about the corridors but they didn't take much notice of me."

The information was of little use, John realized, since the banquet had been in progress well before the whale appeared on stage. "Was Hero there when you arrived?"

She confirmed he was.

"He didn't keep you waiting?"

The girl shook her head. "Nor did he leave at any time, excellency, and neither of us emerged until we heard screams coming from the villa." Her face darkened. "Would you like me to describe further how we passed the hours?" she blurted out angrily.

"You would perhaps do better to describe that to Felix, Bertrada," John replied evenly. "It would prove most instructive for him, although not in the manner that you meant."

Bertrada looked stricken. "Hero is nothing to me, Lord Chamberlain. I was lonely, it was a whim, an accident. He is but a boy compared to Felix, I swear it."

John felt sudden fury boiling in his veins. Bertrada had been lax in carrying out her duty and a tragedy had ensued. Yet now, apparently, she was still more interested in pursuing affairs of the heart.

"The captain is of no concern to you nor can he ever be," he replied in an cold, controlled tone. "And as for boys, it is important right now that you assist in every way you can to find Gadaric's murderer. The boy was in your charge, remember. His family entrusted him to your care but you failed them. Now he is dead and they will never see him again."

Bertrada's eyes filled with tears. "I try not to dwell on thoughts of his death, for it is unbearable to contemplate."

Was that true? John wondered. Zeno had offered his own excuses for his seeming lack of concern over the boy's death. He was preoccupied with the upcoming village celebrations. If Calyce grieved, her hot pursuit of Anatolius gave no evidence of it. In general, the mood of the occupants of the villa seemed remarkably unaffected by Gadaric's terrible demise. Was it surprising? The boy's true family, those who might have cared, had sent him away to live among strangers and strangers could not feel the same as they would.

As he stepped out of Bertrada's room John glimpsed a movement at the end of the corridor. Someone passing by, or hastily retreating? A tall figure. Godomar?

He thought of pursuing but did not. Zeno's halls were always busy and especially tonight, with everyone roused by the fire.

He was struck by the uneasy conviction that with each passing hour events were running further out of his control. He could not be everywhere at once observing everyone at all times. Now two people had died. Barnabas was still missing and so was Castor.

A strange pairing, to be sure, but the key had to lie with the two missing men. Yet John could think of no other place to search for Barnabas, and as for Castor—whatever Briarus knew had just been extinguished with the estate manager's life. And while John found himself staring at a blank wall, it was entirely possible that someone, somewhere, was already embarking on a course of action that would result in yet more disappearances—or even deaths.

Chapter Twenty-one

The morning damp seemed to have settled painfully into Peter's bones as he accompanied Godomar down the coast road. He struggled to keep pace with the long-legged prelate who, it turned out, was long-winded as well.

"It is as the venerated Patriarch Chrysostom said to Eutropius, who was a patrician and a consul but withal a eunuch and corrupt." Godomar's booming voice carried easily back to Peter above the rush of waves. "Where are your banquets where the wine flowed endlessly, the tables groaning with overly exotic offerings concocted by your wasteful cooks? Where are the friends who were always so agreeable and now are nowhere to be seen? For was not all of it but dreams of the dark hours that disappeared with the sunrise, merely blooms of spring and lo, spring has gone?"

Apparently Godomar had requested Peter to accompany him to the village in order to serve as a congregation of one. But if that were the case, he had not chosen the topic of his remarks well. John's loyal servant was unlikely to be inspired by a homily disparaging both eunuchs and cooks.

Godomar was at least correct in declaring that spring was gone. Indeed, summer had suddenly fled as well—at least for the moment. A chilly breeze drove small clouds across the bright blue sky. Peter imagined them as a herd of ragged sheep. He would mention the image to the Lord Chamberlain's friend Anatolius, he thought. He might care to use it in one of his poetic compositions.

"Are you listening, Peter?" Godomar called from the other side of the road. This particularly loud peal of verbal thunder caught Peter's wandering attention.

"Listening? Oh, yes, yes," he replied. "As you say so eloquently, it is nothing more than a dream."

Godomar arched his eyebrows. "A dream? The path we go down to Paul's house is a dream?"

"Ah, I thought you were speaking in parables, sir." Peter hastily crossed the road as an ox cart came lumbering into view from the direction of the village. It lurched and dipped as it moved slowly along and had drawn almost level with the two men when it tilted sideways far enough to dislodge a small stool from atop a mound of household goods, sending the piece of furniture clattering to the ground.

The cart driver, a broad middle-aged man with the sunburnt skin of a farmer, stopped his cart. "Good sirs, would one of you be kind enough to hand that up? I fear to even set foot to ground now that I'm fleeing this cursed place."

Peter hobbled to the stool and hefted it back onto the laden cart.

The ox's massive head was veiled in a cloud of gently buzzing flies. Godomar waved an ineffectual hand back and forth in front of his face as he questioned the man about his remarkable statement. "What do you mean by cursed place?"

"Why, I mean the village, sir. It's doomed. I thought everyone knew that. You only have to look at the goats." The farmer pointed a work-worn hand toward the sharp peaks of the island. With his less than perfect eyesight Peter could just distinguish a vague peppering of what he supposed must be the famous goats, near the summit of one of the taller crags.

"But surely you realize it's all nonsense?" Godomar told the man firmly.

The man was unrepentant. "I might agree with that, sir, but even if it was just nonsense as killed the little lad and set fire to the villa, I don't want my family near it. So I sent them away yesterday to my brother's house. Heed the goats, sirs, that's what I would advise you both to do. The evil events are only just beginning. Why, I distinctly saw old Matthew's daughter walking about last night, not that it was that unusual when she was alive but after ten years in the earth..."

He fell silent and then urged the powerful ox and its retinue of flies forward as another fleeing villager came into sight, trudging up the road and struggling to carry a wicker cage stuffed with squawking chickens. The new arrival hurried past them without a glance or a backward look at the hearth and home he had just left behind, perhaps forever.

"I fear I've already learned much of what I intended to question Paul about," Godomar remarked grimly to Peter, "for I desired to discover the mood of the village as discreetly as I could."

The prelate fell uncharacteristically silent for a while, gazing after the man who was fleeing with the chickens. "What does your master think of all this superstition, Peter? I know his views are not... the same as mine."

"He has not confided his thoughts on the matter to me, sir."

"Indeed? I noticed that he hasn't had much use for your services these past few days. That's why I requested your company this morning. He keeps you informed of his whereabouts, doesn't he? So you can be on hand if necessary to bring a treat for Sunilda when he is spending time with the child, for instance, or perhaps to clean his room when he will be away for a few hours."

Peter, uncomfortably aware that the prelate was fishing for information about his master, shook his head. "No, I have had little to do since we arrived on the estate," he replied truthfully enough. "I think he intends me to rest, as if I could in such a place."

"Or he may realize that you are falling prey to the frailties of old age," Godomar pointed out. "I am told your master is a kind man. Surely it is time he allowed you to retire? He could easily engage a younger man to take over your domestic duties."

The suggestion horrified Peter. "I am a freed man, sir," he said in a dignified tone. "And even if I were not, my master would never discard me like that."

Godomar shrugged. "Perhaps not. But a man of your faith could always find a useful role in the church, you know."

By now the fleeing villagers had disappeared from sight. Godomar turned to lead the way down the path to Paul's house. "On consideration I wouldn't worry, Peter," he offered over his shoulder. "After all, the Lord Chamberlain is very preoccupied at the moment. Perhaps he doesn't realize he's left you with so few duties. I suppose he must have made a great deal of progress in his investigations by now?"

"He doesn't confide in me about such things, sir."

"Of course not. You are merely his servant. Even so, you are an astute man, Peter. If your master were making any progress toward finding this murderous mime, well, surely his demeanor would reveal it to one of your discernment?"

"Possibly," Peter said and then fell silent.

They reached the end of the path and walked around to the front of Paul's house. The old man, seated on a wooden bench by his door, was looking out over the sea. He stood to greet his visitors, spilling the fishing net he'd been mending from his lap to the ground.

Godomar wasted no time with pleasantries but got down to the business of superstitious nonsense and devilry immediately.

Paul scratched his chin. "I'd pay no attention to that story about old Matthew's daughter, sir," he finally advised. "People often go walking about on the headland, even at night. It has a strange attraction to some, especially since the poor woman threw herself over the edge, how many years ago was that now? I forget. And, of course, it's also where the straw man festival is held every year."

Godomar's lips tightened at this further proof that all was not spiritually what it should be in the village, but Paul seemed not to notice the prelate's disapproval.

"But then there's the matter of the little boy," Paul went on, "not to mention the fire. What with the goats grazing in worse and worse patterns every day, everyone's in an awful state. Some villagers are so afraid they're ready to be scared half to death by an egg with two yolks or any such oddity."

"We did see a man fleeing with his chickens just now," put in Peter. "Perhaps they were beginning to lay unnaturally?"

"Those goats are merely ordinary animals, simple and useful creatures, and all of them God's handiwork," Godomar declared.

Paul belatedly offered his visitors wine. "To warm you up for your walk back," he said kindly. "The air is cold this morning. The winds are changing, too, and that's a better omen of what's to come. Wind direction is a much more reliable oracle than any number of goats for telling what weather is coming. Still, despite the occasional foggy day, I'm hoping we'll have some hot afternoons for a little while longer." During their brief conversation the wind from the sea had begun to rise and the visitors were happy to go inside.

Godomar accepted wine but did not sit down. "I see you are a devout man, Paul," he said, with an approving glance at the wooden cross displayed on one wall. "Do you think that a special service might suffice to allay fears in the village?"

Paul shook his head. "From all I've heard, most of the villagers think their best chance of heavenly help will come from the straw man."

Godomar looked aghast at the very notion.

Paul, who had faced many angry seas in a small fishing boat, continued unperturbed. "It's but the simple truth. Some may be fleeing but most are staying in hopes the evil might be averted by the coming celebration. Begging your forgiveness, sir, but they see the animals as heavenly messengers, warning us all about—well, who knows what?"

"The Lord does send angels," Peter pointed out.

"Not cloven-footed ones!" Godomar snapped angrily.

"It may be that heaven speaks to ordinary folk in ways they can understand," argued Paul.

The prelate drew himself up to his full height. His head almost brushed the rafters. "I see that I am confronted by a pair of most learned and subtle theologians! Has the Patriarch of Constantinople convened a council in this dwelling? My advice to Zeno will be that this blasphemous festival be immediately cancelled. He shouldn't even be thinking of holding such a celebration hardly two weeks after an innocent child has died!"

"The straw man's a very ancient tradition," Paul replied. "It would cause a great deal of trouble if it was cancelled. It could be considered blasphemous, of course. However, I will say that I always enjoy watching the procession."

"Very well, Paul. Thank you for your hospitality. I'm certain you will do your best to remind your neighbors of where we must all look for true salvation. Now, if I may have a word before Peter and I leave..."

Godomar nodded toward the door leading to the other room and the two vanished inside. Peter could hear them speaking in low tones. To his distress, he thought he distinguished his master's name. Obviously Godomar wanted to warn Paul about the pagan Lord Chamberlain out of Peter's hearing, having already voiced similar concerns to most of Zeno's household.

Annoyed, the elderly servant glanced at the wooden cross hanging on the wall. There was a small shape burnt into its foot. Leaning closer, he saw a crudely rendered whale.

❄ ❄ ❄

Zeno was late arriving at the goat shrine, having spent longer than expected at the workshop trying to decide how to speed up construction of the automaton whose progress had been delayed by Hero's incarceration. Then too some of the household had begun to grumble about the celebrations. Livia had berated him over his apparent enthusiasm for the event, and that despite a poor child lying dead, as she put it. But what choice did he have? The empress had made it plain that she expected the festival to go ahead. It seemed heartless and indecent, but there it was.

Minthe was waiting for him, arms folded and shoulders hunched under a thin cloak. Although she had placed herself on the land side of the shrine, the wind found its way around its columns and whipped her long silver hair around her face, partially obscuring her sharp, wrinkled features.

"Did you see the goats at sunrise?" Zeno said eagerly. "Did they have an answer for my question? I'm looking forward to finding out—for entertainment only, of course," he added with quick caution.

"They had a most interesting reply." The woman pulled her cloak tighter around her shoulders. "Let us walk along the beach while I convey it to you, sir. I find as I get older even the gentlest breeze seems to cut to the bone."

Zeno agreed, adding dolefully that he experienced the same unfortunate effect from even the merest zephyr.

Soon the elderly pair was pacing along the high water mark. A passerby looking down from the coast road would have taken them for an old married couple walking the shore to collect driftwood for their brazier.

"I don't always understand the answers that I see," Minthe began, "but that's because I don't know the questions asked. The same applied to oracles in the older days, did it not? They merely conveyed what heaven told them. Very well, then. The pattern formed by the goats this morning was fragmented but in brief it conveyed that sorrow is to be expected."

Zeno furrowed his brow. "That's a very philosophical answer but I confess it's not exactly what I expected to hear. Not very entertaining, is it?"

His companion smiled gravely. "The goats also informed me that the tallest knows the answer you seek. Are you acquainted with any very tall people?"

"The tallest person I know is Godomar, although the Lord Chamberlain's not much shorter. However, neither of them knows any more about the matter I was inquiring about than I do, so the goats must have meant someone else. I must confess to some disappointment, Minthe. Perhaps the animals don't know as much as is rumored?"

"But there is one last thing, sir. According to the goats, the twin is to follow and will take high office."

Zeno looked astonished. "Sunilda? But surely that can't be the answer to the question I asked?" A tremor had crept into his voice.

The white-capped swells of the sea rolled hypnotically ashore to dash themselves on the beach with a dull roar, the muted thundering made by the hoofs of Poseidon's horses.

Minthe observed that during the decades she had interpreted the goats' oracles, they had often been worded extremely strangely and in many cases their answer sounded completely unconnected with the question asked. Yet, on looking back, they had never been proved wrong. "So, sir, what will doubtless happen is that in a few days or a few weeks you will see the true sense of their reply and be vastly entertained when you do."

Zeno thanked her and then said he understood that consulting the goats was a very old custom indeed.

"So it is," Minthe confirmed. "There are even those who claim the herd has been there since the days when humans were sacrificed to the sea for a fruitful harvest and for good fishing."

"An extremely regrettable practice, to say the least," Zeno observed, "although obviously that would be the origin of the straw man's role in the village festival. On the other hand, I'm puzzled as to how the area acquired this remarkable tradition concerning the goats."

"Nobody knows. Some say the goats were set there by the old gods themselves, others claim the herd was taken over centuries ago. Whatever the truth of it, their island is forbidden to all and the only time villagers set foot there is when they leave occasional supplies of food for the keeper of the goats. It's said that a villager left the beach on one such visit to explore a little, but that as soon as he set foot back over here he had a strange fit and fell to the ground. Ever thereafter, he could hardly lift his arms. It was and still is considered a fitting punishment for profaning the goats' island."

Zeno shook his head at the fate of the unfortunate villager. "But the patterns, Minthe, what method do you use to interpret them?"

"It's done according to the arrangement of the clusters of goats, taking into account the dominant color of the animals in each group. The height at which they're grazing is also very important."

Zeno observed that it sounded very complicated.

"Not really." A stronger gust of wind caught at their clothing and she shivered. "Different patterns symbolize different words and whoever requested guidance interprets the answer according to the content of the question they'd posed. Thus the message conveyed in any given answer means something different to everyone, since its sense would change according to the nature of what had been asked."

They had arrived at the rebuilt temple that was Minthe's home. Zeno hardly noticed where they were. His eyes gleamed with delight as he contemplated Minthe's words. "Absolutely fascinating! It's one thing to read about these ancient arts, but to see them still practiced on one's very doorstep is even more intriguing."

Minthe shivered again. "I'd be happy to discuss it further with you if you wouldn't mind stepping into my house, away from this wind."

"Of course, of course, I wasn't thinking of you freezing half to death while I stand here babbling away."

As they stepped into the dim interior, redolent of herbs, Minthe observed that many old customs lingered in villages though they were long forgotten in cities. "Take medicinal matters, for example," she went on. "City dwellers may speak highly of all manner of new and more effective treatments for old ailments but those of us who live in the country know that the ancient herbal remedies are often just as effective."

"There's no doubt that many are very efficacious," Zeno remarked. "Castor swears by them when his joints feel particularly rusty. The relief he gains is almost magickal, or so he claims."

"I am glad to hear that. However, my preparations are not magick despite what some may say," Minthe said. "Many such as I can make up an herbal mixture for someone with a cough or a fever or other ailment, but people should be cautious whenever they hear talk about magick. You'll find many who claim the ability to, say, provide you with a curse that will kill anyone you choose or a love charm guaranteed to bring the one you desire to you, willing or not. They'll charge a high price while they're at it too, yet very few can really accomplish what they promise."

"Magick may be nothing but trickery but it has its fascinations to a scholar such as myself."

"Magickal tricks are simple once you understand how they work, sir. People are gullible. They'll see what they want or expect to see. When the jeweler substitutes green glass for emeralds, people accept what appears to be genuine gems and never realize they're completely worthless."

Suddenly, Zeno wondered uncomfortably if the elderly woman considered him gullible—a foolish old man looking for answers from a herd of goats.

* * *

"Minthe made up this concoction for Anatolius." Zeno waved the small clay pot enthusiastically rather too near to John's nose. "I told her he suffered mightily from a malady brought on by proximity to certain plants. 'Elderberries,' she said. 'They're the best treatment for that particular misery.' I'll present it to him when he returns from the city."

John had met Zeno coming up the drive to the villa. The garden air was suffused with the faint smell of smoke, whether from the workshops or a lingering memory of the fatal fire it was impossible to say. The two men stood before the villa entrance while Zeno relayed, with some excitement, the goats' reply to his inquiry. Although he listened politely enough, John was relieved when his host abruptly changed the subject to Anatolius' affliction.

"From the odd smell of that mixture, you'll be fortunate to get Anatolius into the same room with it, let alone take it," John observed, "but I wanted to ask you again about Castor. Are you absolutely certain there is nothing more you can tell me about him?"

Zeno looked pained. "As I've already explained, John, I know nothing of the man's personal life."

"Even though he's been your neighbor for such a long time and visited you often?"

"Yes. Castor is a very private man. As I've told you, he collects antiquities and books, he's a scholar and a philosopher, a scientist—"

"He has many and varied interests, I know, but I'm interested in finding out more about the man himself."

Now Zeno looked puzzled. "But surely, John, what we think about is who we are. In the workings of our bodies we are all the same. It is only in our thoughts and beliefs that we differ."

John sighed. "There's some truth in that. But even Castor could not have sprung full grown from some desiccated scroll in his library."

"No, although it's a most interesting idea. Now, if I may leave you for a while, I'm in need of some nourishment and a bit of rest. I've had a rather strenuous walk."

John did not accompany Zeno into the villa but instead walked around the gardens. He had spent the morning making futile inquiries about Castor. It seemed that the man spent his time communing with written words rather than with people.

The Goths, not surprisingly, had barely glimpsed him in the short time they had been staying with Zeno. Castor had no neighbors other than Zeno. His estate was surrounded by fields, orchards, and vineyards. He employed the smallest of staffs, and all of his servants had apparently taken their orders directly from Briarus, who had been allowed to run the estate to even the smallest detail. They had had only the most minimal contact with their actual master. Setting a plate before him. Filling a goblet. Briarus had even decided the daily menu. Castor had more urgent concerns.

Not that it would be unusual for a wealthy man to confine his social contacts mostly to those he might see at court, but Zeno insisted that although

Castor might travel on business, he never set foot near the Great Palace. John had certainly never seen the man there. Castor appeared to be one of those who live by and for and through the written word, a kind of monk of the intellect.

The image of a monk had not come to John out of the air but from the sight of Godomar, who was watching gardeners at work clearing out the flower bed surrounding one of Zeno's ancient shrines.

"Lord Chamberlain," Godomar snapped in an outraged tone, "I really must protest. This structure is an abomination."

John mildly pointed out that since the estate belonged to Zeno, whatever was built on it was his alone to order.

Godomar looked even more upset. "I do not explain myself well. Erecting an edifice to house an idol and surrounding it with beds of the poppies its pagan worshipers love is wicked enough. But what's far worse is that I've found Bertrada inside this building more than once. I'm convinced that her interest is neither that of an antiquarian nor the student of ancient religions. This is a shrine to Hypnos, and..." He lowered his voice and leaned towards John "...the statue inside is...naked."

John suppressed a smile. "Well, after all, it is a pagan shrine, isn't it?"

"Oh, indeed!" Godomar nodded. "Now I have no objection to naked statues as such, even if they have wings on their shoulders such as grace the one in there. Its workmanship is certainly very excellent. But it is a male statue after all, and I fear that Bertrada's interest in it is...well..."

John sighed. Sensing that a discussion of naked pagan idols, with or without wings, would not prove useful he changed the subject and questioned Godomar about Castor.

"All I can tell you about the man is that he has an interest in blasphemous and impure works," was the curt reply.

"You have seen his library, Godomar?"

"No, but I've had the misfortune of discovering many of its volumes around Zeno's villa. Some of them were in the possession of my charges. I would prefer not to describe what Bertrada was reading—and she's still only a child."

"Is Bertrada acquainted with Castor? Has she perhaps visited his library?"

Godomar frowned. "You insult my vigilance, Lord Chamberlain. Do you think I would ever allow such a friendship? Fortunately we're only visitors and the sooner we are gone the better. The Lord willing, we'll survive to leave."

"It seems Castor's volumes are everywhere yet the man himself is nowhere to be found," John mused.

"The only time I've seen him was at the banquet, Lord Chamberlain." Godomar turned abruptly and walked toward the villa without a word of farewell.

John lingered for a while, watching the gardeners at work. A breeze picked its way through the shrubbery lining the path, rustling parchment-dry leaves. Perhaps, he thought tiredly, Castor really was just away on business after all.

John sighed again. His thoughts turned to Hypnos, who personified sleep—and whose twin brother was Thanatos, or death.

He could only hope that Anatolius' investigations were proceeding more fruitfully than his own.

Chapter Twenty-two

The red-faced shoemaker blustered on while Anatolius patiently made notes on a wax tablet.

"Castor is one of my finest customers, barring the emperor. Half the patricians in the empire wear my boots, you know. Quality recognizes quality, that's what I always say. However, Castor has not come by recently. Yet how can I be surprised? My boots will outlast the Hippodrome. Yes," Kalus lamented, "I am putting myself out of business with the quality of my wares."

Anatolius scratched through the name Kalus in the list on his tablet. Speaking of boots, he thought sourly, even though he had nearly worn out his own spending the entire day tramping around Constantinople visiting the merchants listed in Castor's account books, all he had ascertained was that the missing man had not recently conducted business with any of them.

Kalus led his visitor out of his office and back along the hallway to his wares. From unseen workshops behind them came the muted sounds of hammering. The heavy smell of leather, mingled with the acrid odor of the urine in which it was tanned, enveloped the establishment.

"He's very particular about what he orders, is Castor," Kalus went on importantly. "His sandal thongs must be the correct length and always dyed black. There again, he is a man of discerning taste. Like all of my customers." He glanced down at Anatolius' footwear and frowned. Although he said nothing, it was obvious he did not find it admirable.

The lowering sun spilled its deep red light into the shop and across its display of elegant boots and sandals. Kalus rearranged several pairs to show them to better advantage.

Anatolius politely thanked the boot-maker for sparing time to talk to him.

"Aren't you Senator Aurelius' son?" the other asked. "A fine man, if I may say so. It was my father who set my feet on the road to success. He was the wisest man I ever knew, sir. An army marches on its feet, that's what he told me when I was a young man. The wisest words ever spoken, don't you think? Armies will always need their feet well shod and I am proud to say that Justinian has placed his army's feet in my hands. Imagine that, in my hands, yet at the same time those very feet are in Italy! The streets of Ravenna will be happier under sturdy military footwear than beneath the crude sandals of barbarians, I'm certain. I ask you, where would Belisarius be without my boots?"

Anatolius indicated agreement with every word spoken by Kalus and managed finally to escape.

He strolled down the street, emerging into the Forum Bovis. As he crossed the open space's busy expanse he recalled that he had shared a cup of wine with more than one young lady while sitting near the great bronze head of a bull at its center. While a cup of wine would be very pleasant right now, there was one more call to make on John's behalf and he must not linger.

The last business belonged, so its plaque declared, to the scribe Scipio, whose emporium was discovered after traversing a narrow street that was not exactly a dim, dangerous alleyway but neither was it a broad, colonnaded avenue. The familiar odor of ink and parchment that met Anatolius as he stepped inside its shady interior felt welcoming after the long, hot day.

Scipio was a small man with a shaved head. His white tunic was a palimpsest of ancient and more recent ink splatters. As the scribe rose from his desk to greet his visitor, Anatolius noticed the right side of his nose was as black as a Nubian's. Disregarding the fact that a scribe always kept his hands clean, the thought came to him that the man must be left-handed, habitually rubbing his nose with his free hand while he copied. He wondered if his flash of insight was anything like those that John experienced while he was unraveling some knotty puzzle or other.

"Can I help you, sir? Is there a particular work you're looking for or have you something you wish to be copied?" Scipio's gaze moved toward the tablet Anatolius carried.

Anatolius replied that he wished to ask a few questions if Scipio would be kind enough to answer them.

"We are able to copy out ten pages for a semissis," the scribe answered quickly, anticipating the question usually put by his visitors. "A third of that is just for the parchment. Alas, the price for it just keeps increasing. Eventually it will ruin me, sir."

Anatolius made the same inquiry as he'd been fruitlessly making all day. The answer he received was little different from all the rest.

"Though I expect we'll hear from him shortly," the scribe added, "since we've almost finished the copy of the Enneads that he commissioned."

Anatolius looked around. The shop's few shelves held no more than seven or eight codices along with a few scrolls. He was inspired to ask another question. "Did Castor usually commission works or did he generally purchase items from your stock?"

"Both. In addition, he often calls upon us to produce copies of his own works."

Anatolius asked about the nature of these works.

"Philosophy, science, religion. Every imaginable subject. Castor is man of great erudition."

"Do you have any of these works on hand?"

"Not at present. However, I suspect he will be bringing more work soon since it has been some weeks since I last saw him."

"He is a very good customer, it seems."

"If only all my clients were like Castor! You'd be amazed at the number of students we chase away, not to mention common men of law and the like. They handle my excellent wares with no intent to buy. Nor even the means to buy them, if they were honest, not even if they had a whole year's salary concealed about their pitiful persons. They could scarcely afford the parchment we write on, let alone the writing itself. However, I see you know something of our profession and I suspect you're equally economical with your parchment."

Following Scipio's gaze, Anatolius realized there was a trace of ink on his forefinger, a remnant of recent labors. "You're very observant, Scipio," he said with a smile. "However, my master doesn't find it necessary to scrimp on the purchase of parchment."

Understanding dawned on Scipio's lined face. "Or to cut back on building churches and forums or conquering foreign lands?"

"Quite so." Any of the countless administrative clerks serving at the palace probably would have impressed Scipio by the fact they labored there but Anatolius did not inform the man how closely he worked with the emperor. Instead, he gave him the same instructions he had given the other merchants he had visited, which was to send an immediate message to the captain of excubitors at the palace should they receive any communication from Castor.

He had turned away to step out into the shadows lengthening along the street when inspiration struck him. "How long would it take you to copy out some poetry for me? I'd also like decorative borders with a motif suggesting the past glories of Italy, and leather covers."

"Ah, sir, I could see immediately that you are a man of refined taste," Scipio beamed. "But I'm afraid that it might be a little while as we're still overwhelmed with business generated by the emperor's codification of the laws. Every provincial town seems to think it ought to have a copy even though half of them don't even have a man of law who can read Latin. It's my opinion that they just sit whoever is hearing petitions on a bench in front of those volumes to lend some credence to his rulings. Not, however, that we're complaining about the amount of work."

Anatolius thanked Scipio, saying he would visit again to consult him about the copying and then slowly made his way through the deepening twilight back toward the Mese.

Around him men laughed and jostled, grimy workers returning home from their long labors in the sun, important persons conversing with their companions as they strode through the bustle, ignoring the beggars that sat at every corner and haunted every colonnade. The street sounds beat around his head, a ceaseless babble of noise that was beginning to give him a headache.

His thoughts turned toward his uncle's estate where it would be quiet and cool and there would be good food and wine as the night crept in over the sea to lay its kindly fingers across the garden. Yes, it would be wonderful to stroll there with Calyce. She would certainly enjoy his poems, he thought as he walked quickly along. Of course, it was true that he could copy them out himself, but he hardly had the time right now.

He realized his journey would cause him to pass not far from the house where Balbinus and Lucretia lived. Yes, he chided himself, he'd been foolish to imagine some ember might smolder beneath the ashes of time. His acknowledgement of the truth was bitter-sweet, but then again perhaps it hadn't really been an ember glowing in the darkness of memory waiting to be fanned into a blaze, but rather just a warm thought like a ray of sunlight, insubstantial and impossible to capture—or recapture. Strange were the whims of Fortuna, he mused, as he turned a corner and began to move briskly down a street leading directly into the Mese. If his affair with Lucretia had not been so ill-fated, he, not Balbinus, might well have married her and then he would never have found his true love, Calyce.

All the same, it would certainly be most helpful to John's investigation to visit the senator's house again and inquire of Balbinus if he had now heard anything from his missing nephew.

Indeed, he told himself, it was increasingly obvious that Castor was not just away on business but was missing. Just like Barnabas.

He turned to retrace his steps and saw a familiar figure moving quickly along on the opposite side of the street. The sight brought a sinking feeling to his stomach.

It was Balbinus returning home. To his wife. To Lucretia.

Anatolius wiped his suddenly watering eyes and looked again.

No, he had been mistaken. The pedestrian was someone he did not know. Strangely, the thought made him happier.

❊ ❊ ❊

Later—he could not have said how much time had passed but darkness had long since fallen—Anatolius found himself unexpectedly approaching the barracks across from John's house. He had been lost in thought. Thoughts of Calyce, of Lucretia, of events he wished he could change. He had no recollection of his walk down the crowded Mese nor of entering the palace grounds. His feet had followed the familiar route as automatically as one of his uncle's odd mechanical devices went through its movements. He was fortunate he hadn't been run over by a cart.

Lamplight shone brightly through the diamond-shaped panes of John's second story window, the window of the study in which the Lord Chamberlain was usually to be found when he was at home. It was puzzling, since at present John was supposed to be some stadia away.

Anatolius crossed the cobbled square, acknowledging the greeting of the excubitor guarding the barracks. On reaching John's door he raised his fist to rap sharply, the action reminding him of Hypatia's distress about her recent strange visitor.

Perhaps, he mused, that was why his feet had carried him here at this late hour. Perhaps they had more commonsense than his head.

He pounded on the door for a long while before it was opened. Hypatia greeted him warmly enough although she looked haggard. The flaring torches in the entrance hall and atrium, more torches than seemed necessary in a house currently occupied by a single servant, accentuated the shadowed hollows around her eyes. He had barely stepped inside before she had the door securely bolted.

She invited him to the kitchen and, as he began to follow up her upstairs, he glanced into the atrium. A dark shape, some small creature, was scuttling across the raised edge of the impluvium.

No, he realized. It was only the clay scorpion he had seen during his last visit, brought to a semblance of life by the flickering reflection of torchlight in the water. Or perhaps it was not the same scorpion, for there was another guarding the top of the stairway and yet another set on the floor beside the kitchen door.

"Have demons besieged you again, Hypatia? I see you have placed your guardians everywhere."

The young woman's offended expression told him that he would not be able to dispel her fears by making light of them.

He apologized. "I suppose this big house must seem rather frightening when it's empty," he went on. "It wouldn't echo so much if John would just get a few more furnishings."

He sat down at the kitchen table. Seeing the jug set on it, he hinted that while an unannounced visitor such as himself would hardly expect to be offered his host's favorite wine, on the other hand he would not be averse to sampling another vintage.

"You mean you don't wish to have a cup of the master's Egyptian wine, sir?" Hypatia said. "Then this will suit you very well. It was a gift from some ambassador or other and the master directed Peter and myself to feel free to drink it. I think that you'll find it less raw than the sort that the Lord Chamberlain prefers."

Anatolius took a sip of the wine she poured for him and nodded approval. "Perhaps John likes the type of wine he does because of someone with whom he once shared it. I'm only guessing, of course," he added hastily, realizing that he shouldn't be chattering about the Lord Chamberlain's personal life with a servant. Normally it would never have occurred to him to say such a thing, but somehow in John's household this sort of conversation seemed quite natural.

John's relations with his servants were, he reflected, extremely irregular but that was his own business, insofar as anything at Justinian's court could be said to remain one's personal business.

"Tell me what has happened, Hypatia. Have you had another night-time visitor?"

Hypatia nodded. "Last night. It was at the same hour as when it last appeared, only this time I didn't dare answer its summons." Her distress was obvious in the increasingly halting way she spoke.

"Immediately I get home I'll send one of my servants around to keep you company," Anatolius offered. "You really shouldn't be here alone, even if there is a barracks full of armed men just across the way. And if I may say so, if Peter comes back and finds any of your friends standing about," he said in an attempt to lighten her mood and with a nod toward the clay scorpion that still sat on the shelf, "he won't be at all pleased to see them."

At Anatolius' suggestion Hypatia had taken the opportunity to pour a cup of wine for herself. It had brought some color back to her face. "I notice you keep wiping your eyes, sir. Are you unwell? I would be more than happy to make up a potion for you."

Anatolius looked thoughtful. "Strangely enough, it seems that the longer I'm in the city the better I feel. Perhaps I should stay here myself tonight. I don't like to see you so upset."

He was recalling when he had initially met Hypatia. She had been a slave belonging to the Lady Anna, but the first time he had seen her he had not realized the fact. Not that a difference in social position was any bar to love. After all, Lady Anna had married a former tonsor. Yes, it was true, he thought, noting anew Hypatia's golden skin and large, dark eyes and finding himself wondering that if John were not as he was, might he...

Anatolius' impertinent speculations were abruptly interrupted by a loud banging on the door.

"It's probably just a message for the Lord Chamberlain, Hypatia. I shall attend to it." He got up and went down to the entrance hall.

It was not the authoritative, insistent pounding of someone whose duties commonly included rousting citizens out of their beds in the middle of the night. It was more frenzied than powerful.

Anatolius drew the knife he carried, the small blade that was an accessory worn by every prudent man who walked the streets of the city. Glancing over his shoulder, he saw that Hypatia had come to the top of the stairs. He waved her back.

The loud knocking continued. Blade at the ready, he slid back the bolt.

Silence fell.

He felt his heart racing. He did not believe in demons, but, on the other hand, it was rare indeed that good news came calling at such an hour and in such a manner. He cracked open the door and peered out.

The demon standing in front of the door looked back at him.

Or rather the woman, for he now saw by the lamplight seeping out into the darkness that the night caller was both human and demon. One half of her face was that of a woman while the other was a scarred mass akin to a melted candle.

"I am Pulcheria, your honor, and I wish to speak to the Lord Chamberlain." As the woman addressed him she pulled a veil over the ruined portion of her features.

❄ ❄ ❄

Before long Pulcheria was sitting in the kitchen providing Anatolius and Hypatia with details of what, according to her, had been a long and close working relationship with the Lord Chamberlain. Anatolius originally supposed she was exaggerating, but after close questioning it was obvious that she was sufficiently informed about John and his investigation of Barnabas to prove she was at least telling the essential truth about the commission she said had been given her.

"But how did you get into the palace grounds unseen?" Anatolius asked with great interest when Pulcheria had finished her explanation for her unexpected appearance at John's door.

"Do you not think that I was a guest here often enough before my unfortunate accident?" the woman replied with half a smile. "Besides, there are always ways into any place you wish to name, however secure they seem. Even the palace itself, as you see—or indeed as any rat could tell you."

Seated in the warm, bright kitchen, with her elaborate wrappings of colorful scraps of cloth and hair festooned with ribbons, she did not resemble any rodent Anatolius had ever seen. She was more like a peacock, or perhaps a pile of colored rags discarded by a dyer.

"So it was you who's been terrifying me?" Hypatia asked, apparently uncertain even now that the disfigured woman was only that and nothing more.

Pulcheria admitted she had come calling before. "I regret I could not visit at a more civilized hour," she concluded.

"I peeked out the window of the master's study and all I could see was...well...I thought..."

Pulcheria gave her frozen half-smile. There was no need for further explanation.

Anatolius held his tablet over the embers remaining in the brazier, obliterating all traces of his notes on Castor's business associates. Then the man whose occupation was transcribing the words of the emperor turned his skill instead to taking notes on the detailed ramblings of a beggar and street prostitute.

"So the great mime was born in the countryside not far from Zeno's estate?" Anatolius interrupted her, amazed at the woman's flow of information. "How could you have found all this out in such a short time?"

"I may no longer have my looks, sir, but I do have a way with people!"

Hypatia, Anatolius noticed, was sitting staring somewhat dreamily at the ceiling, another cup of wine in her hand. She looked pleasantly flushed, relieved of her fears now that her demon was inside and happily chatting with them.

"I haven't told you all that I have to tell," Pulcheria was saying. "I also heard it rumored that he has bedded more than one noble lady for whom he had performed. Or, to put it more correctly, they have bedded him. It seems he's very popular with the ladies."

"People working in the theater can be terribly attractive," put in Hypatia, her words slightly slurred.

Anatolius finished writing. He had almost filled his tablet despite the brevity of his notes and the tiny size of his script. "I'm sure the Lord Chamberlain will be most grateful for your efforts on his behalf, Pulcheria," he said, finally laying it aside.

The woman's garish rags rustled as she leaned forward confidentially. "There's one last piece of information for you to convey to him, sir. Barnabas is a great lover of literature and he has a large collection of scrolls and codices."

"An expensive interest indeed, even for a performer as well paid as he." Anatolius recalled his recent conversation with Scipio.

"Too expensive even for Barnabas, it seems," came Pulcheria's reply. "For I also hear that he has a habit of visiting the libraries of those aristocrats who hire him to entertain at their homes. Not just visiting them, you understand, but returning when their owners are not present to help himself to one or two choice items. I don't necessarily mean his patrons' wives, either," she added with a coarse laugh.

Anatolius observed that, aside from the matter of the wives, he did not think that Barnabas would continue to receive invitations to perform in aristocratic homes if he was suspected of stealing from their libraries.

"He's remarkably agile," Pulcheria observed. "It's child's play for him to climb through a second floor window in the middle of the night. So he's never observed and most of his wealthy patrons don't realize things are missing. If they do, they may well suppose they've been pilfered by one of their drunken guests. After all, why should a mere mime, even as one as brilliant as Barnabas, be suspected of aspiring to such culture? No doubt they would find the very idea laughable."

Anatolius saw Pulcheria away into the night after rewarding her more handsomely than he would normally have been inclined, but knowing how generous John could be for information.

As he went back upstairs he realized he would have to return to his uncle's estate with the dawn to convey to John what he had just discovered.

Could the visitor to Castor's library who had left the mud on its immaculate tiles that so outraged Briarus have been Barnabas? Even if it were, he could not see how it could be linked with the deaths on his uncle's estate. Still, if there were some connection, John would make it fairly quickly. Doubtless this other unexpected and useful information he had uncovered would be instrumental in aiding John to deduce why Barnabas at least had vanished. Perhaps they would now be able to run the fugitive mime to ground.

Chapter Twenty-three

Wheezing and cursing, Barnabas inched toward the island's craggy summit, hauling a large goat through the darkness. His toe was caught by a root, or perhaps the entrance hole to the burrow of a small animal. It hardly mattered what it happened to be this time. He fell heavily again and the cloven hoof of his caprid charge clipped his shoulder painfully.

He struggled from beneath the musty-smelling beast, uttering further imprecations as he gripped its damp body and felt one of the legs wobble. He tugged at it and a clump of goat hair came off in his hand. Finally he managed to shoulder the goat once more and continued to struggle toward the high meadow where a number of the herd glimmered in the pale moonlight.

The dwarf was strong and agile. For years—and to the delight of numerous audiences—he had performed amazing acrobatic feats, leapt and tumbled, brandished stuffed phalluses of exceptional size and weight, and dazzled onlookers with his agility, but he had never before been called upon to haul an entire herd of stuffed goats up and down dark crags.

Reaching the meadow, he thankfully set his burden down and surveyed the heavens. At least he had managed to get the albino goats assembled at one of the highest spots in good time. Having reasoned that he might be more easily spotted moving the lighter-colored beasts about as dawn came on, he had taken to relocating them first when they needed to be taken to higher elevations. There the grass grew less readily and offered less concealment than it did further down the slopes.

He turned away from the motionless animals and trudged back down the steep track.

❊ ❊ ❊

Dawn found Barnabas coaxing life from the remains of a wood fire, heartily huffing and puffing on them until glowing sparks formed a necklace of red that eventually burst into flames. The task made him look paler than usual since it coated him with gray flakes of ash, giving him the appearance of a demon. Fortunately the man lying on a pallet close to the hearth was not particularly concerned with outward appearances.

"Now we'll have some warmth to chase the fog out of our bones," Barnabas said, poking twigs into the burgeoning fire to feed its quickening life. "Then I shall get breakfast."

"And about time too," remarked Pythion from his bed. "And that reminds me, Barnabas. While it's true I've been known to curse my monotonous diet now and then, I must say I find the increasing presence of wrinkled turnips and shriveled radishes on my plate becoming rather tedious. Perhaps if you kept trying you might catch a fish or two and we could cook them?"

The man had somewhat the appearance of a wrinkled and shriveled vegetable himself, albeit exceedingly sun-browned, with the unruly hair and beard of a desert hermit and the rope-like muscles of a dock worker.

"It's not easy catching fish," Barnabas protested, omitting to mention he had not even attempted the task. "Especially when you have to be so quick to get them. I am constantly exhausted from moving those disgusting goats up and down the slopes."

"I know how difficult that can be," his companion agreed, "but you have to keep moving them around. It's my livelihood, you know! At least you don't have to worry about placing them in any particular pattern. Wherever the animals are standing, the person who interprets their message will always find something suitably vague, or vaguely suitable, to declare to anyone foolish enough to consult them."

Barnabas looked up from the fire. "It will be your skin as well, Pythion, if the villagers ever find out about the goats," he pointed out. "So it's just as well I got here when I did, what with your broken foot. Where would you be now without my help, eh, that's what I want to know?"

"And how did I break my foot? Scrambling down to the beach to see who my unexpected visitor might be!"

"You mean to say your goats didn't warn you I was about to arrive?"

The other only grumbled a bit more and then grudgingly expressed gratitude for the mime's assistance. "Now I know what's going on over there," he went on, "I realize this sudden stream of people consulting the goats is because Theodora's visiting Zeno's estate. Whoever would have thought that the empress would appear in these parts? Well, you can be certain that more than one of those high-ranking officials travelling with her is less interested in learning his fortune, under the guise of entertainment of course, than of taking advantage of a good excuse to get out of range of Theodora's presence for a while." Accepting a piece of bread he dunked it into his cup of wine and continued. "But you'll be able to stay long enough to see me back on my feet, Barnabas?"

"Yes, and even a little beyond that in case of unforeseen difficulties."

Barnabas had not mentioned the reason for his arrival on the island and had no intention of doing so. The keeper of the goats had enough to worry about, he told himself. Winter was coming on and there was a very poor crop to show for all the man's summer laboring in the small vegetable patch next to his hut, without his having to worry about possible repercussions if it were discovered he was harboring a fugitive, no matter how unwittingly.

Thinking about vegetables as he chewed on a stale bread crust, Barnabas considered a more pressing problem. With two of them to feed, the stunted cabbages, beets and leeks would quite possibly all be gone before spring came again. He wondered if it was his fate to starve to death on an island. Yet even that might be preferable to what could—no, most certainly would—happen to him if he were caught. The thought that he was at least still free, if not performing at the palace or sleeping in his own bed, brought a better flavor to his humble breakfast.

Hopefully, he thought, when their small stock of food was consumed the villagers would be generous in what they brought when they came to the island, provided of course that conditions continued to allow them to make the journey.

Then at the right time, and if Fortuna continued to smile on him, he would be gone. To Africa, perhaps, or off to Greece. He recalled wistfully his small room in Constantinople. Doubtless Brontes would enjoy using it but could he be trusted to take care of it?

Gnawing on his crust, he mulled over his plans concerning what he would do as soon as it was safe to slip away from the island. By the look of recent activity on shore, it appeared this might be further in the future than he had originally anticipated when, in a panic to find a hiding place, he had stolen a boat and rowed with all speed to his temporary sanctuary. However, he had not expected his continued personal safety to involve creeping up and down steep inclines and rocky paths carrying stuffed goats half the night and hiding in a small hut for most of the daylight hours. At least, he congratulated himself, he had had the wit to push the boat back out into the sea so that the current would carry it away. Even if it traveled only a little way down the coast before beaching, doubtless its owner would retrieve it thankfully enough, not to mention making certain that he pulled it further up the beach than before. No, he was safe from discovery as long as he kept out of sight.

He chuckled at the recollection of the revelation he had received upon assisting the injured goatkeeper into his hut.

"This is a terrible disaster," the man had cried, pulling off his boot and wincing as his painfully swollen foot was jarred by the action.

"Oh, I wouldn't say so," Barnabas had offered with callous cheerfulness. "I've broken more than one bone in my, er, everyday job and they heal quickly enough if you're fortunate and avoid physicians. You know what Martial said of Diaulus? He remarked that the man had been a doctor and then became an undertaker but even so he was doing the same job as he had when he was a medical man."

As he spoke he had hoped that the goatkeeper would not ask to be rowed to shore for medical attention and, it seemed, the gods had answered his prayer. For as it transpired returning to the mainland was the last thing that Pythion desired, as he immediately declared to Barnabas.

"Since you're here, I am supposing that you'll not mind staying for a few days?" he had said hopefully as he bathed the injured foot in not too clean water from a bucket in the corner.

Barnabas confirmed that he would be happy to do so.

"Then in that case," Pythion had continued in a stern voice, "I must remind you that this is a sacred island and therefore I shall expect appropriate behavior."

Barnabas, wondering if word of his stage act involving the enormous phalluses had somehow reached even this remote island, promised solemnly that he would ensure that he did not offend either his host's hospitality or the goats in any way whatsoever.

"You must swear absolute secrecy about anything you learn here," the goatkeeper had gone on urgently.

"Of course," Barnabas had replied, giving his oath while wondering if the man was afraid that he intended to learn the secrets of fortune-telling by goat and then set up a rival oracle in a more frequently traveled spot.

But, he reminded himself as he poured out more vinegary wine and filled their breakfast plates with radishes, it had turned out that Pythion had more to hide than Barnabas since the famous goat oracle was nothing more than a fraud perpetrated upon a gullible public.

Thus it was that Barnabas was now temporarily carrying out the injured man's role of moving stuffed goats here and there around the island, giving the animals the appearance of life by occasionally venturing out to push them along the stony ground while crawling through what for most people would be knee-high shrubbery.

"Thinking about them goats again, aren't you?" Pythion asked. "It may seem a bit underhanded, but you know what they say—you can't fool an honest Christian. It's all just entertainment, officially speaking, so obviously it's only pagans we're misleading. How they're dealt with in this transitory world is the least of their concerns."

Barnabas grinned. "If she found out about your efforts, Theodora would be just as likely to ask Justinian to appoint you to a court post than have you executed. She's always been one to admire a rogue, especially one who's successful, and you've been managed to fool everyone for years."

"Of necessity, may I remind you?" Pythion parried. "The herd died off during that drought a few years ago. According to tradition, the albino ones are more important than the black ones but they were the first to die."

"Interesting, that."

"Yes, but I had just arrived on the island and so I knew that the villagers were terribly impressed that the goats over here were flourishing while over there many of their animals, and even some people, were dying. The goatkeeper at the time was a man of great intellect—not to mention someone who didn't wish to see a very old custom die with the animals, or so he said to me."

Pythion stopped to give an admiring shake of the head at the previous goatkeeper's wily intelligence. "So," he went on, "as I told you, he very cleverly stuffed the animals' skins so that there would always be goats on the island and, more importantly, he would still have the job of keeper of the goats. After all, nobody said anything about them having to be live goats, did they?"

"You would make a good man of law, Pythion. He must have really feasted on all that goat meat, though. I wonder how he prepared it?" Barnabas mused, thinking wistfully of all the palace banquets where, after entertaining, he had partaken of many dainty and exotic dishes that seemed now the stuff of dreams.

"Not well enough," was the reply. "He died not long after I arrived. It was something he ate, apparently."

Barnabas looked up sharply. "You didn't mention that before. I thought you said he died of old age?"

"What I said was that he was very old when he died and that was true enough. I suppose I forgot to mention that it happened not long after over-indulging in goat stew. Who knows, perhaps the hot weather tainted it. I advised him to cure most of the meat and even made a smoking frame for him. But he was a hasty man, so I suppose you could say his manner hastened his own death. Still, the only stews I have eaten since then have been made out of rabbits."

Barnabas pondered his companion's words. It had not occurred to him before to ask what had originally brought Pythion to the rocky island, whether he too might have been fleeing from a pitiless pursuit. He knew Fortuna could be some-times be crueler than a cat with a field mouse. Had he then managed to escape Theodora only to find himself on a small island with a herd of stuffed goats, an inadequate food supply, and a murderer?

Chapter Twenty-four

Greetings, dear Aunt Matasuntha.

Has General Belisarius set Ravenna alight yet? I do hope not! Here we just had an awful fire. We would all have been burnt to ashes in our beds if it hadn't been for Hero's fire-fighting device. I'll draw you a picture of it some time. I did draw Hero's wine machine, as I promised. The top part was easy enough, being like a man, but it was hard to draw its goat legs. Godomar found the picture before I could hide it. He was very angry but I couldn't help laughing because I made its face look like his.

Anyway, I have decided Hero will come and live in my court when I am queen. He makes all sorts of toys and clever things and knows lots of interesting stories.

But about this strange fire. Bertrada says it was a horrible accident but I don't think it was. You see, the goats have been foretelling terrible things for some time now. I think the fire must have been what they meant, or at least some of what they meant. But nobody had taken any notice of what they said, so in a way it serves them right. Also there's an old statue that somehow got broken, but you could hardly call that a disaster. Zeno doesn't seem at all upset about it although he told me it was given to him by one of his relatives. He says he's not expecting this relative to visit him in the near future and laughed as if he had said something very funny. Godomar just looked disgusted, but then he looks disgusted a lot of the time. I wonder if he ever laughed when he was younger or if he has brothers or sisters?

But I'm getting away from what I wanted to tell you about the goats. Minthe says they have been making the worst patterns that have been seen for years and years. They're very clever, those animals, and know much more than most people. Yes, soon the villagers will realize they were not just foretelling the fire but also my departure.

People always seem to find a way to believe the goats are saying whatever it is they want them to say, but in this case they are telling only the truth because when I have gone a lot of people will be in great trouble. I wish I could be here to see it, but then if I were, there wouldn't be any trouble for them to get into, would there?

So, dear aunt, as you can see, it will be a little while before I can write another letter but I wanted to tell you not to worry. I am going with Porphyrio.

One night recently, I will not say when, I woke up and heard Porphyrio summoning me as he sometimes does. It's like someone blowing on a great horn, but so far off I can only feel the sound inside me, like when a cart rumbles past. I got out of bed and left the villa. I didn't have to creep past Bertrada because Porphyrio had cast an enchantment over her. All the way through the garden and the olive grove I could hear Porphyrio calling. Even though it was really dark, I had no trouble finding my way. My feet floated over roots and rocks as if I were a leaf drifting down a stream.

I came to the headland and went to the edge of the cliff. There was nothing to see except a great star-strewn sky, but looking down I saw the deeper darkness of the sea and the gleaming back of my friend Porphyrio. He looked so small I realized how far down below the water was, but I wasn't frightened a bit.

I was ready to cast myself over the edge to join him right then but he stopped me. "It is not yet time," he said in his deep, silent voice. "Hide where there is nothing between you and the sunrise, Sunilda, and then when the straw man comes to the sea, that will be a signal for you to fly to meet me."

And so we made our final plans, but I am not permitted to tell you more. I shall write to you again after I join Gadaric and can tell you all about my journey and what wonders I have found at its end.

Chapter Twenty-five

"But where is the straw man?" demanded Sunilda. "I want to meet him!"

John noted the exasperated look Zeno cast at the girl. They were standing in the workshop, looking on as Hero tinkered with the automatons Sunilda had asked to see and was supposed to be admiring.

"Why are you so interested in a silly bundle of straw when you can see these wonderful musicians and this shining archer?" Zeno made a sweeping gesture toward the trio of almost completed automatons set in the middle of the workshop. His flapping orange sleeve struck Hero, who was squatting nearby adjusting a length of bronze tubing. Hero glanced up, blinking rapidly and obviously annoyed.

"These mechanical figures are very nice indeed, Zeno," said Sunilda, "but the straw man is really the most important one, isn't he? It seems such a shame, really, that he's no sooner put together than he's dashed on the rocks. If I were Theodora I'd honor him before he was thrown off the cliff."

"I've never thought about it quite that way." Zeno looked as if the notion distressed him.

"If your entire life were spent leading a procession you might indeed have a short existence, but at least it would be a happy one," Hero remarked, tinkering with the innards of a lyre-player.

John took Sunilda's small hand and gave it a tug. "If you want Hero to finish what he's working on in good time, we'd best leave him to it."

Sunilda made an effort to pull her hand away but it was apparent John was not going to release his grip. "Oh, very well! We can go and see whoever's making the straw man, Lord Chamberlain."

"It's Minthe, John," Zeno put in. "I gave her one of my old robes to dress it in and a rather sad-looking leather ball for its head."

"We can't go any further than Minthe's house," John told the girl firmly as they left the workshop. "Bertrada expected you to have only a short visit with Hero and will be wondering where you are if we're away too long." He did not mention that he did not wish to take the girl into the village, since it was in an increasing uproar over the dire configurations of the goats.

The smell of smoke from the forge followed them outside along with the sound of hammering and a sudden muffled curse from Hero. Godomar might consider the automatons the devil's work, John thought, but it would take a miracle to see them finished in time to perform their allotted roles at the festival.

"Let's have a game of micatio!" Sunilda had managed to slip her hand loose from his and raised her small fist.

John sighed but made a fist himself. Playing micatio was not one of his official duties at court.

Sunilda smiled. "One...two...three..." she counted and shook her fist up and down. "Six!" she shrieked, unfolding four fingers at once. She gave a delighted laugh. The Lord Chamberlain had called "Five!" and extended two fingers.

"Your two fingers and my four make six," the girl explained importantly, if unnecessarily. "So I win this time! Do you want to try again?"

John smiled and made another fist. He had discovered during the last few days that he did not care much for children's games. Perhaps he would not have made a very good father had Fortuna permitted him the opportunity to help raise his child. Yet he had not minded pretending to race Sunilda around the garden and it had not occurred to him until afterwards that he must have appeared very foolish indeed loping along in his formal robe a few paces behind the little girl.

"Two!"

"Three!"

Sunilda clapped her hands with glee. "Again!"

They played the game for a while longer. John did not win one round. He wondered if she were cheating but could not see how.

She laughed again and looking down at her smiling face John chided himself. He was too familiar in dealing with adults, the powerful men and women at court who survived by such behavior, not little girls who took such pleasure in a simple game. "I'm afraid Fortuna smiles more often on you than me, Sunilda."

"Not at all," the girl replied solemnly. "I just know what's going to happen before it happens."

"I see." John amended his thoughts. His experience, or rather lack of it, of dealing with eight-year-olds obviously had little bearing on how he should deal with Sunilda.

They were still standing at the edge of the courtyard by the workshop. Loud and contentious voices began to drift out of the building. John urged Sunilda to hurry if she wanted to visit Minthe and see the straw man.

"I haven't played micatio for a long time," he remarked as they set off. "Who taught you how to play?"

"Felix showed me yesterday."

"Yesterday?"

"He and Bertrada are best friends again," the girl said seriously, "so I'm glad Poppaea is getting better. I'd like someone to play with. Bertrada will be talking all the time with Felix and reading to him now. Felix is funny sometimes but when I pulled his beard, he was angry with me." She looked contrite.

"I'm not surprised," John replied as they reached the coast road. "But as a proper young lady you should know that not only was it very impolite to do such a thing, but also unwise to annoy a ferocious excubitor captain."

❊ ❊ ❊

When John entered Felix's room its occupant looked up from the codex on which he was concentrating.

John did not mince words. "You are consorting with the girl Bertrada again?"

Felix replied shortly that his private life was his own affair.

"When it leads you to neglect your duties it is the entire household's affair, and especially mine."

Felix snapped the codex's leather covers shut and tossed it down on the bed in a manner much too careless for so costly an object. John assumed it belonged to Castor. Every other volume he had seen in Zeno's villa thus far seemed to have come from his neighbor's library

"If you weren't a good friend, I would draw blood for your suggestion that I neglect my duties, John," Felix said with a scowl. "Do you suppose I'm some dreamy poet like Anatolius? When I'm on duty, I'm on duty and not sewing a fine embroidery of romantic fantasies in my head."

"You wield an excellent metaphor for a military man!"

"What would you know of..." Felix caught himself. He shook his head. "I'm sorry, John. I do sound like Anatolius, don't I? Making a fool of myself over a girl. No woman should cause strife between two old comrades such as you and I."

"It's a common enough occurrence, my friend," John replied. "Of course, you need not fear me as a rival for her affections."

"I didn't mean—"

John gave a slight smile. "Then let's put our argument behind us."

He picked up the codex, noting that it was Cassiodorus' Gothic History, and leafed through a few of the pages. They retained a faint smell of ink.

"This is a heavy tome in more ways than one, if I may say so, Felix."

"And it's only the first of twelve," was the doleful reply.

"But you're not a Goth, are you? I hope you aren't supposed to memorize the history of all these tribes. There are scores listed here, what with the Aeragnaricii and the Ahelmil, not to mention the Vinovilith, the Suetidi—"

Felix gestured to John to cease reading. A faint smile flickered behind his unruly beard. "And none of them my kin either! However, like the Goths, my tribe has Germanic roots, so we're practically related, Bertrada and I." He looked at the floor and then suddenly asked, "John, do you ever grieve for an opportunity you failed to grasp?"

"In a word, no, or at least not so far as court goes. Or do you mean an opportunity to hear warm words from a young woman's pretty lips?"

Felix' jaw set firmly as his nascent smile vanished. "No, I didn't mean that, but since you mention it, younger eyes sometimes see more clearly than old and it's certainly true that I'm not advancing as quickly as I should."

"The emperor and the empress always see very clearly everything that might affect them, Felix, including discontent among the palace guards. Even the merest appearance of improper ambition is extremely dangerous. More than one such foolish dreamer's head has been set free to wander, as you should know." He paused, aware suddenly of the uncharacteristically cold tone in his voice. "I'm sorry, my friend. I'm getting short-tempered. I'm afraid I'm not advancing quickly enough with my current task." He waved the codex he was holding.

"And this has reminded me again of how utterly I have failed in my search to learn anything of the whereabouts of its owner."

"I'm sick of the cursed thing! Much as I love history, by the time I finish twelve volumes of it, I'll be history myself. If anyone remembers me, that is."

John leafed thoughtfully through the codex. "This set must have been an expensive acquisition. Why would Castor be so interested in the Goths?"

"He was interested in everything, John. Obviously he knew that Zeno had Goths as guests this summer and it piqued his interest."

"That's probably so." John snapped the codex shut. "But have you noticed, there's something exceedingly strange about all this? The murdered child was an heir to the Ostrogoth throne. And yet, look at those who have died or vanished since. A mime, a servant, an unworldly Roman patrician. None of them Goths or even politically involved. How often, would you say, is a royal heir murdered for reasons having nothing to do with succession?"

"I doubt you'd find anyone who would give you good odds on that. After all, innocent people often die when the powerful squabble."

John stood. "Well, I may not be able to question Castor personally, but since he apparently spent most of his time reading and had a tendency to annotate the works with thoughts on their subjects, through them he can tell us what he thinks. Let's go and make inquiries about his interest in Gothic history by consulting his library."

❊ ❊ ❊

While John scanned the library's shelves and alcoves Felix glanced through some of the notes piled on the table. "Look at this, John. It says, 'A Comment On Galen's Treatment of Digestive Disturbances.' It's just as you said. Castor had an opinion on just about everything."

"And apparently compelled to set them all down. Now, let me see..." John pulled a leather-bound volume down, twin to the one Felix had been reading. He leafed rapidly through the work, stopping now and then to consider notes scribbled into it by its owner. "There's one thing to be said for living in a world that consists of the written word, Felix. You can easily correct what's wrong with it." He paused. "Have you seen this?" he asked in a suddenly grim tone.

Felix leaned over for a closer look. "I don't think so. What is it?" John directed Felix' gaze to several scribbled lines in a small space left under the text at the bottom of the last page. The ink was darker and the crabbed writing not so meticulous as the hand of the scribe who had copied the book. "Is this Bertrada's writing?"

"What do you mean?" Felix looked confused. "What? These names here? This lineage?"

"Written as if someone were imagining a place for themselves in the Ostrogoth royal family."

"Mithra!" Felix expression darkened. "I don't know if it is Bertrada's writing. I've never seen it. It doesn't look much like a woman's hand to me. Surely you don't imagine we sit around and pretend we're king and queen like poor little Sunilda?"

"No. I don't. I just wanted to be certain."

There were several names arranged in rows, with lines linking some together. He recognized Theodemir, underneath which was written the name of his son, Theodoric, the Ostrogoth king of

Italy. Below Theodoric was inscribed Amalasuntha, Theodoric's daughter who had ruled as regent and whose murder had brought Belisarius to the gates of Ravenna. Beneath her name appeared those of her children, Matasuntha and Athalaric, while below Athalaric's were written the names of his twin offspring, only one of whom was still alive—and indeed, not that far away.

"But why shouldn't Castor write in his own codex if he wants to?"

"That isn't what troubles me. It's this."

John touched his lean finger to the parchment, pointing out a line from Theodoric descending to two other names—one of them familiar.

He slammed the volume down with an oath. "I am going to Constantinople at once, Felix. I wish to have another word with Senator Balbinus about his deceased brother and his missing nephew, Castor."

Chapter Twenty-six

John rode with all haste back to Constantinople.

Anyone who met him on the highway would have realized at one glance that he was absolutely furious.

Something akin to the black fog a young mercenary would allow to smother all civilized behavior on the eve of a battle had grown in him as he had read the incomplete family lineage scrawled in the back of Castor's history.

After a few quick words with Felix he had stamped off to leave immediately. Even Zeno, who had glimpsed him as he strode across the stable yard, could see by the set of his shoulders that the Lord Chamberlain was in no mood for polite conversation.

By the time he passed through the city gate, however, he had regained control of his emotions and presented his usual expression of quiet attention, honed through years in a court where one wrong look or gesture could cost a man everything.

Now after a journey marked by his steady stream of cursing under the regular clatter of hooves, the taste of a salty breeze in his mouth and sunlight flashing off water into his angry eyes, he was finally pounding on Balbinus' door to demand entrance.

John met the senator in the atrium. The gem-encrusted embroidery at the collar of Balbinus' unseasonably heavy dalmatic attested to the fact that he had been about to set out to attend to official business. John made it just as plain that the senator was going to have to change his plans.

"Lord Chamberlain, what a pleasant surprise," Balbinus began but noting the grim set of John's lips, his smile froze in an expression not unlike that of a malfunctioning automaton with faulty gears.

"Indeed?" John replied in a level tone. "I rarely find surprises to be pleasant but I'm glad you mentioned it as I wish to talk to you where we will not be surprised."

Wordlessly, Balbinus led him to a reception room whose walls were frescoed with mythological scenes.

"You have lied to me, senator," John stated without preamble.

Balbinus raised his eyebrows in an exaggerated expression of offended astonishment that would have been visible across the Senate's assembly hall before protesting that he could not even recall when they had last spoken.

"You lied to Anatolius, who informed you that he was seeking information on my behalf."

"Surely, by lie you cannot mean—"

"I do not care to be lied to," John broke in.

Balbinus' tone hardened. "Do you have proof of what you claim, Lord Chamberlain?"

"I don't need proof. I need only to speak one word to the emperor and that would be sufficient to condemn you. However, I wish to be fair. You will explain yourself."

Balbinus' shoulders drooped as he finally met John's gaze directly. "There are times when family responsibilities outweigh one's civic duties, do you not agree?" he began hesitantly.

"You may have to debate that statement with Justinian. I am not here to argue points of philosophy. What is the truth concerning your nephew Castor—or should I say the man you call your nephew?"

"So far as I'm concerned, Castor is my nephew," Balbinus replied with a defeated look in his eyes. "I've always considered him such and so have done my best to help him."

"Then you confirm Castor is not, in fact, your nephew?"

Balbinus nodded wordlessly.

"I see," John said. "He is, however, a great maker of notes, leading the reader to suspect that his is a lineage of Ostrogoth rulers."

Balbinus emitted a massive sigh. "Castor! That's just like him! How careless can a man become? At least he doesn't have his father's wild streak nor his eye for the ladies—and always other men's ladies at that."

He helped himself to wine from the green flask that sat on the table beneath the fresco depicting the judgment of Paris and drained his goblet, seeking courage from it.

"Concerning my older brother Bassus, Castor's father," he continued, his normally hearty, booming voice subdued. "As you know, the great Theodoric, who became king of the Ostrogoths, was a guest of the emperor just as his great-grandchildren are today. Or at least, as the surviving twin still is. A very sad business, that, Lord Chamberlain. At any rate, it has been over half a century now since Theodoric finally left Constantinople to return home."

He was silent, staring at the fresco, no doubt imagining a more recent past than that depicted there, and then filled his goblet again. "Theodoric was eighteen when he went back, Lord Chamberlain. A man. So it will hardly surprise you to know that he fathered a son during his time here."

"That would be Bassus?" John said immediately.

"Yes. Bassus was the product of a very unfortunate dalliance. It happened during the reign of Emperor Leo, ten years before I was born. Soon after Theodoric returned to his home land, it became apparent he'd left behind a woman pregnant with his child. That the child would be a bastard was of little consequence, since Theodoric himself was also one. However, it was expected that he would appoint his first born son to succeed him so it was decided that my family would unofficially adopt the royal bastard and raise him, knowing it was entirely possible that eventually he would be called upon to rule in the west."

John made no reply.

Emboldened by the wine, Balbinus continued. "I have been told that the story put about at the time was that my mother was experiencing a very difficult pregnancy, which took her to one of our country estates for an extended period for the sake of her health. Thus when she returned with a newborn child, it was not remarked. No doubt Theodoric's mistress developed some sort of similar affliction and left court for a while in order to keep the child's existence from public knowledge."

"In that she was certainly successful," John commented, thinking that Justinian must surely have known about the affair. Since it was obvious that an unknown heir to Theodoric's throne touched upon his orders regarding the safety of Sunilda, it seemed extremely odd that the emperor would have kept such a secret from him. Yet, he reminded himself, it was fruitless to question Justinian's withholding of important information. He was fortunate in that he could, and would, continue to interrogate Balbinus.

"Bassus did not live long enough to go to Italy," Balbinus confirmed in response to John's questioning. "He died young and in rather odd circumstances. It troubles me to say this of the man I still regard as my older brother but Bassus was a foolish and dissolute young man. He did not, I fear, bring honor to the family name for he too fathered a bastard, though it grieves me to term my nephew so."

"Therefore Castor is Theodoric's grandson and heir to the kingship," John remarked quietly.

"As you say, Lord Chamberlain." Balbinus took another hearty swallow of wine.

"Why didn't Castor come forward when Theodoric died? He could have claimed the kingdom rather than allowing it to be ruled by his aunt Amalasuntha."

Balbinus shook his head in puzzlement. "Possibly Castor did not desire to rule? After all, not all men lust for power. Perhaps Justinian did not wish it. Who can say? Castor has never been an ambitious sort of person. He's more of a dreamer, a scholar. Then there is the manner in which his father had died. Perhaps that made him very cautious about revealing their relationship."

"Under odd circumstances, you said?"

"Even for this city, Lord Chamberlain. Now it's true enough that soft young aristocrats who frequent places where they do not belong will often find themselves embroiled in deadly brawls. But drunken louts do not usually insert a blade quite so deftly between a man's ribs and then disappear down an alley in the wink of an eye while everyone in the immediate vicinity is immediately struck blind, even the young woman who enticed the dead man down that very same dark byway. It was fully investigated and a huge reward offered for information, of course, but despite that the culprit was never caught. Not but what it might have been only a fortunate blow, as you might say. Yet, given his lineage...."

"A fascinating history indeed, Balbinus. However, more importantly, where is Castor now?"

Balbinus looked down into the remaining wine in his goblet, studying it for an answer. "I will not reveal that, Lord Chamberlain," was his surprising answer. "Except to tell you that he has fled to a monastery. He intends to live out his days in obscurity so that they may be longer than otherwise."

He set the goblet gently down on the table. "He arrived here in a state of terror the morning after Zeno's banquet and asked for my help. He didn't explain the particulars of his predicament nor did I ask for any. Often it's often best to know nothing. I couldn't refuse him assistance, but there were certain arrangements to be made before he could be on his way to safety. That was why I didn't reveal anything to Anatolius. As I suggested to you earlier, Lord Chamberlain, there are times when family responsibilities outweigh one's civic duties, although I do not expect you to agree with me about that." He paused. "I intended to inform you about this in a day or so."

John did not reply. He was certain that Balbinus had not intended to do any such thing, but he also had no doubt that the senator had not questioned his nephew further about the reasons for his flight. In fact, there would have been no need. There were only two people in the empire who might frighten a very rich man like Castor so much that he would panic and go immediately into self-exile. Given the obvious origin of the threat, the circumstances were immaterial.

Balbinus filled the silence with another nervous burst of conversation. "Surely you don't suppose he is your murderer? It's been thirteen years since Theodoric died. The grandson he appointed to succeed him died a few years ago and although the boy's mother had been ruling as regent, she's now dead as well. As you just pointed out, Castor could have advanced his own claim long ago if he'd wished to do so."

He gave a grim laugh. "I seem to be speaking of my nephew in the past tense, Lord Chamberlain," he continued, "as if he were dead rather than merely gone to a monastery. Are you certain you won't have some of this wine? After the third go around it starts to taste as if it's Falernian." He tipped the decanter over his goblet again.

"And the identity of Castor's mother?"

"I don't know," Balbinus replied shortly. "However, thanks to Bassus' royal blood, Emperor Leo aided my family in setting up suitable financial arrangements for him. Fortuitously enough, at just the critical time, some poor fellows apparently failed to validate their wills correctly in just the sort of oversight one sees happening more and more these days. So although their original heirs found themselves without some very attractive holdings, Bassus suddenly gained a house here in the city and an estate on the other side of the Marmara as well as the one next door to Zeno. Of course, Castor inherited them in due course but apart from the estate where he lives, the original properties have long since been sold at very handsome profits."

John remarked that Castor had been fortunate indeed to be able to arrange matters so that he could live in the obscurity he seemed to crave. "Although his father would doubtless not have been happy to see so much property sold away within one generation, even though he was heir to an entire kingdom," he concluded.

"I wasn't close to my brother, Lord Chamberlain, so I cannot say. Remember, I was barely fifteen when he died and I had interests other than estates and inheritances. Then, too, my family owned a number of properties that I rarely visited. Now they're all mine, since my parent's wills were all correctly witnessed. Or should I say that at the time the emperor was not interested in finding some pretext to prove otherwise." Balbinus reached unsteadily for the wine decanter and looked surprised to find it empty.

The voice that came from the doorway was not loud but it was it was nevertheless firm. "Balbinus, guard your tongue and put away the wine before it makes you hand your head to the Lord Chamberlain."

Lucretia was standing there. Balbinus looked abashed but set down his goblet.

"I was passing down the corridor and overheard some of your conversation," Lucretia went on, addressing John rather than her husband. John wondered how long she had been listening to their conversation, just out of sight along the hall.

"My family and Balbinus' have always been close friends," she was saying. "We often visited each other's estates and our marriage entwined the two families even closer together. As it happens, my old nursemaid Nonna is still alive and might possibly recall something from those long ago days that would be of assistance. She lives in a street just off the Forum Constantine."

❄ ❄ ❄

Nonna fluttered around her tiny apartment in a state of voluble agitation, apologizing for the humbleness of the surroundings, the coarseness of the bread, the age of the cheese, and the dent in the silver plate holding the food. She fanned at rays of sunlight slanting in through the window and decried the dust motes they revealed descending inexorably toward the chair where her important visitor would have to sit.

John smiled and tried to put her at ease by complimenting her furnishings which, although few, would not have looked out of place in a fashionable villa. The old woman, looking pleased, explained they had been gifts from her former owners upon her manumission and retirement.

John convinced her, finally, to sit down. She looked at him apprehensively. Her skin was wrinkled as a dried apple, but through a wispy halo of gray hair her scalp looked as pink as a baby's.

"And how is my dear Lucretia?" she asked. "I haven't seen her for what seems like years. Young people think nothing of time, sir. They do not realize how little of it they have to fritter away."

"Lucretia is very well." John detected a tinge of sorrow in Nonna's tone and felt certain she would much rather be entertaining her former charge, regardless of how honored she might be by the possibility of assisting a Lord Chamberlain. He quickly explained the reason for his visit.

"Oh, I see," Nonna replied. "Yes, we often went for long visits to Master Bassus' estate. It was across the Marmara, a lovely place indeed."

"Do you remember anything unusual?" John suggested "A scandal? A regular visitor from court who suddenly stayed away for a few months?"

"It's hard to think back after all these years," Nonna replied, looking ready to cry.

"Were there rumors?" John persisted gently. "Servants always talk about their masters. Perhaps you heard something?"

"That's true, sir, but as a Christian woman I would not think of repeating such tattle, and especially to a high official such as yourself."

"I do understand your feelings, Nonna, but let me assure you that I have seen and heard much worse than anything you might possibly tell me."

The old servant's wrinkled face reddened. After hesitating for a short time, she spoke.

"None of it was anything but youthful prattle and foolishness, Lord Chamberlain. Just young people making up silly stories, dreaming of being better than they are. After all, romance with the high born is not for servants, so when the stable-hand talked about how he planned to entice the young mistress into the straw or some wretched cook's assistant prattled about putting a love potion in the master's wine, I never paid any attention. Besides, I was a nursemaid. I spent more time with the family than with the other servants."

John took a sliver of cheese. He had not eaten all day. Perhaps that was why he was developing a raging headache. "I imagine that you recall Balbinus and his brother well from those days?"

Nonna's expression immediately brightened. "Both very fine young men, sir. Lucretia is fortunate indeed to have married Balbinus."

"But young men will be young men," John ventured with a slight smile.

Nonna scowled to hear his implication. "Balbinus was not that sort of wild young man, Lord Chamberlain. It was the young ladies who would set their eyes on him. Of course, he is a most handsome man with a profile to tempt a classical sculptor, but the girls were always disappointed." She gave a fond smile.

"But perhaps his brother Bassus did not disappoint them?"

"It was so long ago, you know, and all the summers I spent on that estate seem to have melted into a single golden season. However, I do recall there was one foolish young maidservant who declared most firmly she was going to throw herself into the sea because one of the young masters had looked crossly at her or some such nonsense. But was it Balbinus or Bassus who made her so distraught? I have forgotten. In any event, she didn't do any such thing of course. That I do remember. And then there was a young vixen from the kitchen who was always letting her hair come undone at opportune moments. Very long it was, and the color of ripe wheat. A vain girl she was, always trying to catch someone's eye, usually the eye of someone who was wealthy. As a result of her efforts in that direction, the family were always pulling hairs out of their food."

John suppressed a smile. He had seen similar behavior at court on more than one occasion and knew that sometimes it achieved its purpose. He asked Nonna what had happened to the two temptresses.

"They were only there for the one summer and then were sold away to another estate owner. I wish I could be more helpful, sir, but as I get older, my memory is not what it was and I can't recall where they went." The woman was genuinely distressed at her inability to assist her visitor.

John had finished the small chunk of bread. "You have helped me by offering me a good meal," he quickly assured her. "I'd have fallen off my horse from lack of nourishment within the hour otherwise." He set a coin on the table, enough to pay for a great quantity of bread and cheese, and then rose to leave.

"And you say that Lucretia is well?" Nonna asked wistfully.

"She is very well."

Nonna beamed. "A good marriage is a blessing from heaven," she said and began to ramble about how happy Lucretia and Balbinus must be together.

John thought of the frescoes with their theme of frustrated love on the walls of Balbinus' reception room and wondered if the choice of subject matter revealed something about the household. He hoped not.

As he emerged into the hot street in front of the solid masonry apartment building where Nonna lived, he resolved that the next time he saw Lucretia he would recommend that she go to see her old nursemaid. At least his visit today would then have served some useful purpose.

He was suddenly aware of how hastily he had departed from Zeno's estate. He was aware also that his increasing fatigue seemed to have placed weights in his boots. Given the manner of his leaving, however, rest was out of the question. He would have to return as quickly as he could.

He therefore set off immediately, offering a quick petition to Mithra that he would not find another disaster had occurred in his absence.

Chapter Twenty-seven

John had hoped to reach some useful conclusion before he arrived back at Zeno's estate, but as he rode along by the gradually purpling sea, he found the meaning of the facts he had accumulated, even the strange matter of Castor's royal lineage, to be as indecipherable as an oracle. The only thing that was certain was that with General Belisarius poised to create a vacancy on the throne in the west, the number of Ostrogoth candidates in the east had been reduced to two. Perhaps he was simply too fatigued to reason properly.

He contemplated Anatolius' search for news of Castor, a search that John now knew would be futile, although perhaps not entirely wasted as the task had at least removed the young man from the vicinity of Calyce.

When he finally reached Zeno's estate, he was waved in by an armed guard he had not seen before but who obviously recognized the Lord Chamberlain despite the fading twilight. Approaching the stables, John saw the explanation. Several imperial carriages were drawn up in the yard alongside heavily laden wagons while groups of soldiers mingled with the slaves unloading luggage or tending to horses and donkeys.

Theodora had returned to the estate while he had been gone.

The empress always traveled with enough of a military escort to take a small city by force if her safety, or, for that matter, her comfort, required it. By contrast, to the emperor's oft-voiced chagrin, the Lord Chamberlain had long since dispensed with the sort of guards considered necessary by others holding lofty court positions. Having spent time in chains, John had no desire to be fettered to an entourage.

As he dismounted stiffly, a spectral figure emerged quickly from the shrubbery at the edge of the yard. It was Zeno. His garishly colored robe made a smudge of light in the increasing darkness.

"I see you're under occupation by the legions of the empress, Zeno. I hope the pillaging is being kept to a minimum."

"John," the elderly man panted, "thank the gods you're back. The most dreadful thing has—"

The crunch of boots on gravel announced the appearance of a detachment of guards. Armed guards, and all strangers to John.

In an instant John was surrounded. The smell of leather and of breath soured by a soldier's vinegary wine ration assailed his nose. He took a step toward Zeno but an impertinent hand fastened upon his shoulder.

He turned and glared at the man who had dared to do such a thing. It was the guard commander.

"This way!" the man ordered, unabashed, "and quickly!"

John was marched off into the garden, leaving a helpless Zeno staring after him.

"I am Justinian's Lord Chamberlain and under his orders," John stated curtly. "Why have I been arrested?"

No reply was given as he was escorted deeper into the garden. Balbinus must have reported his visit to Justinian, John thought. Had the emperor decided to rid himself of his Lord Chamberlain for having disobeyed his explicit instructions to remain on the estate?

The company was moving deeper into the inky shadows. But, John thought, what if Justinian were not involved? What would he do when he discovered that his beloved wife had ordered John executed? Doubtless nothing at all. Or perhaps he would never find out and John would become another mysterious victim, dead or vanished, just like Briarus, Castor, and Barnabas.

John considered drawing the weapon in his belt but dismissed the thought. Against this group of trained men his small blade would bring nothing but instant death. He would wait and seize his chance to escape if one presented itself.

One of his captors yanked his arm, directing him down an overgrown side path. John felt the muscles in his back tighten as he braced himself for the sword thrust that would surely soon end his life. It seemed inevitable.

Take me to you, Lord Mithra, he prayed, and guard my family when I am gone.

Then he was abruptly shoved through a thick wall of rampant, thorn-filled bushes.

He stumbled forward, blood trickling down his scratched face, and realized with a combination of relief and fury that the whole thing had been just one of Theodora's horrible jests.

Or was it a warning?

He had been marched in a circular path and was now facing the torchlit colonnade of the villa where Theodora stood waiting, surrounded by a knot of guards. Zeno was beside her, looking as pale as a demon.

"Lord Chamberlain," Theodora said with a gloating half-smile, "I do hope that you enjoyed your little evening stroll even though I understand an old goat sought to bring you a prophesy of doom." Her eyes glinted in the torchlight as she glanced toward Zeno.

John effected an all but imperceptible bow of the head. "My apologies, highness, for having kept you waiting. If I had known you would require my presence, I would have been at your disposal much sooner."

"The emperor will doubtless be pleased to hear that you are so much more solicitous of my concerns than you are of his," Theodora replied as she stepped forward. A torch guttered at her passage, sending a cloud of moths into the night. "You were explicitly ordered to guard Sunilda at all times. I could have you executed on the spot for your disobedience, Lord Chamberlain."

The features of her guards betrayed no emotions. They were automatons, prepared equally to kill or not, at Theodora's order. It was obvious to John that he was not yet completely out of danger.

"The emperor must be the proper judge of my actions, highness," he replied softly.

His comment elicited no response from Theodora but Zeno emitted a muffled peep of horror.

The empress slid toward John with a faint rustling of silk. He could smell her exotic perfume. It did not quite mask the acrid sweat from her long, hot, carriage ride. He was reminded of an animal moving closer for the kill.

"It was insult enough that you should allow a murder to occur practically in my presence," she said, "and now I return only to find you have lost another." Her breath was sour with wine.

"Briarus's death was—"

"Briarus?" she snapped.

"Castor's estate manager, highness," John explained. "The man who burned to death."

Theodora laughed. "I must say, Zeno, that the excitement never ceases for those living, not to say dying, on your estate. The village festival will seem dull by comparison. However, I was referring to the girl, Lord Chamberlain."

John felt a stone form in his chest. He glanced at Zeno. In the flickering torchlight the elderly man resembled a bloodless wraith.

"Poppaea?" John asked. He did not want to hear the news he feared from Theodora's lips.

Zeno shook his head mutely.

"Oh, the useless little peasant is doing perfectly well," Theodora said, "or so my lady-in-waiting Livia insists on constantly telling me. No, I was referring to Sunilda. Zeno informs me that a particularly thick sea fog rolled in late this afternoon and by the time it dissipated she had vanished."

***

The stone in John's chest had grown to the size of a boulder. As he and Felix quickly made their way to the Ostrogoths' apartments, John kept hoping the girl would jump out from a shadowy doorway, laughing, to explain that her disappearance had all been a prank.

"We've looked everywhere," Felix told him, "and after the search we made for Barnabas, we know everywhere there is to look."

"If I had been here to help guard the girl—"

"Yes, but all the same it's me and my men who carry the burden of securing the estate. It's ironic, John. As a soldier, I would far rather die by losing my head on the battlefield than for failing as a nursemaid!"

A red-eyed and trembling Bertrada met them in Sunilda's room. She looked desperately toward Felix for an instant but the excubitor captain avoided her glance.

Perhaps he did not dare offer her the comforting words she sought—at least not in front of John.

John asked her bluntly how she could have allowed Sunilda out of her sight. "We have had this conversation before, Bertrada," he added. "I hope the answer you give is not going to be the same as the one you gave last time."

He glanced at Felix, who had reddened above his bristling beard.

"You offend me mightily, John," his friend snapped. "Do you think I can't separate pleasure from duty?"

"Usually I trust your judgment implicitly, Felix, but there seems to be some sort of malign enchantment over this entire estate. I'm not certain I can be sure of anything right now."

"You can be absolutely certain that neither Bertrada nor I have neglected our duties. Tell the Lord Chamberlain what you told me, Bertrada."

Bertrada nervously ran her hand through her disheveled blonde hair.

"Go on," Felix prompted her irritably.

"But it all sounds so unbelievable. You see, Lord Chamberlain, what happened was that an intruder broke in and carried her off."

"And what did this intruder look like?" John asked patiently.

Bertrada shook her head. "I don't know."

"Surely you saw whoever took the girl? Are you saying you didn't get even a glimpse?"

Bertrada blinked back tears. "Sunilda insisted we stay indoors because of the awful fog, Lord Chamberlain. She said she did not feel too well and indeed she looked rather pale. She stayed in her room and I lay down to rest for a while. I fell asleep and when I woke up, she was gone. There was evidence of a struggle." She put her face in her hands and began to sob.

Felix stepped toward the girl and put an arm around her shaking shoulders. "That's all she's able to tell you, John. I've already questioned her at great length."

"Zeno's estate seems to have become more dangerous than Constantinople's worst alleyways." John glared. "We'll have to discuss this further, Felix."

He had a sudden vision of Sunilda, chatting away happily as they walked along the beach, and the boulder in his chest shifted painfully, almost cutting off his breath.

"We'll find her," Felix said grimly.

"Just as we've managed to find Barnabas?"

❄ ❄ ❄

Like giant fireflies, bobbing torches spread out from the villa into the night. An owl flying overhead would have observed bright patterns form and reform as groups of excubitors combed the garden, crashing through shrubbery and spinneys, trampling on the flower beds and through the olive grove, meeting now and then in clusters of torchlight to consult each other on where next to proceed in their futile search.

Zeno flapped back and forth among them, an anxious orange-plumed bird bearing constant reports back to Theodora who, with her ladies-in-waiting, occupied the villa's main reception room.

After another fruitless foray and a quick word with Felix, who was standing on the colonnade directing operations, Zeno returned to the large room to find Theodora sitting by a window looking out into the night. The pearls along the hem of her robe mirrored the color of the pale moon rising above the dark, twisted mass of the olive grove.

She turned to look at her host. With a sinking heart, Zeno noted that although the empress' perfectly made-up face was in repose and her hands were folded quietly on her lap, one small purple-shod foot was tapping impatiently.

"Highness," Zeno began, suddenly realizing there were three ladies-in-waiting in the room and valiantly trying to suppress hysterical laughter at the notion, "Captain Felix has directed his men to spread out along the coast road and search the shore and the village while my servants continue to criss-cross the estate. I'm certain that we'll soon find the girl." His voice trailed off.

Calyce directed a wan, encouraging smile at the elderly man but Livia, seated beside her on the red upholstered couch, merely glared venomously. Whether she was angry with him in particular or at the prospect of being kept up in attendance on the empress all night, Zeno could not surmise. Nor did he particularly care at that instant about the opinion of anyone in the room other than that of the empress.

"It would be best if the girl were found sooner rather than later," Theodora said in a voice as cold and smooth as the snow that occasionally fell in the hills. "For everyone's sake, but for yours and the Lord Chamberlain's in particular." She looked out into the darkness again. "I am not pleased with his dereliction of duty."

Zeno's heart sank into his boots. "Highness, the entire blame cannot be laid on the Lord Chamberlain's shoulders—" He stopped at a quick gesture of warning from Calyce. "That is to say," he continued hastily, "it may be that Sunilda is merely hiding somewhere, playing some silly childish game, rather than some harm has come to her."

"Yes, that's true, Zeno," Theodora said. "But little girls do not inconvenience empresses and when she is finally found, we will make certain that she remembers that in future. However, beyond that I intend to personally request the emperor to ensure that the Lord Chamberlain will not have the opportunity to fail in his duties again."

The other two women blanched. Zeno began to feel nauseated.

"And in order that the emperor will not be forced to suffer further embarrassment," Theodora went on, "naturally I shall recommend that his solution be a permanent one, which is to say that the Lord Chamberlain and his head should part company as soon as possible."

To Zeno the air in the room was suddenly, unbearably hot. He felt a wave of giddiness and looked at the floor. He knew the empress and Lord Chamberlain had been at cross purposes many times but he had always thought that John would remain immune from her enmity because he was so much in the emperor's favor. But it had hardly been two decades since another eunuch Lord Chamberlain, Amantius, had been put to death by Justin, Justinian's predecessor, for his alleged designs on the throne. And many of his associates had suffered as well. Zeno remembered those events well. He forced himself to look up and saw a smile curving Theodora's thin scarlet mouth into a sickle that matched the rising moon, a sickle hanging uncomfortably close over his head as well as John's.

❊ ❊ ❊

John made his way quickly along the twisting garden path. He reasoned that Sunilda might well have taken a familiar route if she had decided to play a joke on everyone and so he was retracing the route he and his young charge often followed during their walks. It looked different at night, with thick vegetation reduced to solid walls of darkness receding from the flaring light of his torch. Of all the flowers that brightened and sweetened the daylight hours, only a few light-colored blooms could be picked out, glowing with a uniform whiteness from the scanty moonlight.

More than anything else John noticed the quiet. Instead of Sunilda's constant chatter flowing like a river in his ears, there was only the sound of his footsteps, his breathing, the slight susurration of his robe as it brushed past twigs encroaching on the path.

"Sunilda!" He called again but there was no answer. Would he, or anyone else, ever hear her voice again?

He continued at a brisk pace, half-hoping to see her sitting on the marble bench where they often paused for a while or beside the fountain where she invariably insisted on throwing a pebble into the water. The visions of her in all these places leapt so vividly from his memory that when he turned this corner and that to find only shadows, her absence seemed all the more foreboding.

He returned to where Felix was stationed. The captain had a grim reply to John's inquiry about the progress of the search. While his excubitors could be relied upon to conduct it diligently, he pointed out, it was now almost certainly too late.

"If someone wishes to harm the girl, they're not going to lurk around in the vicinity waiting to be apprehended, are they? I'd guess she's nowhere near here. It's more likely she's half way to Constantinople by now."

"If she's even still alive," John responded somberly.

"It's as if the intruder entered the villa by magick." Felix sounded uneasy. "Even so, with Theodora breathing down our necks we'd better be seen to be searching." He lowered his voice as a pair of Zeno's servants passed by, torches in hand, calling Sunilda's name. "So just in case I've dispatched several of my men back towards the city, John. With everyone milling around, even

Theodora won't notice a few guards are gone, assuming she even knows how many were here to begin with."

"Theodora never misses anything but I agree you're right to look beyond the estate. I'm off now to talk to Minthe. She was friendly with the girl and could well know something useful."

Felix gestured toward a nearby group of excubitors waiting for orders but John shook his head. "No. I'll go alone."

In a short while John was on the shore road, looking down towards the village. He could see bobbing lights marking progress from hut to hut as the search for the girl continued. The murmur of breaking waves formed a peaceful lullaby as he loped swiftly down the hill toward Minthe's house. An observer might have mistaken him for a young man running to meet his lover at this late hour, anticipation quickening his stride.

No lamplight shone through the window of the woman's strange dwelling. John cut across the herb beds, whose crisp, clean smell of thyme mingled with the musky smell of decaying seaweed lying on the beach.

He stepped carefully around the fallen column Minthe used as a bench. It was not hard to imagine the resident of such a strange house practicing magick. Perhaps there lingered in the remaining pieces of the original building's walls some trace of the power of whatever god had once been worshipped here.

His flickering torchlight glanced off the glossy, blackberries hanging heavily on a bush under the dark window. The house door stood open to the surrounding night and the mournful sound of the sea.

John drew his blade, tossed his torch through the door and then leapt inside after it.

His caution was unnecessary, however, for the small room was empty, its atmosphere even more pungent than that hanging above the herb beds outside.

John scooped the torch from the stone-flagged floor, sending shadows slithering around the walls and across the bundled herbs hanging from the ceiling beams. The flickering light passed over a low bench and an array of clay pots on a table.

An arm extended from the shadows under the table.

His torch revealed a rotund figure clothed in a worn but finely made orange dalmatic, sprawling limply, its limbs twisted at unnatural angles. Its head was a shapeless mass.

For a heartbeat John feared it was Zeno. Then realization flooded in and with it the grim prospect of returning to the villa to inform the empress that all he had been able to locate was the straw man.

Chapter Twenty-eight

"So, Lord Chamberlain, you have failed in your search." Theodora was seated on a red couch by the window in Zeno's main reception room.

John bowed his head wordlessly, wondering if the two dismissed ladies-in-waiting were listening outside the door. The only people now in the room were himself, the empress, and her unfortunate host, Zeno.

Theodora gave a particularly unpleasant smile. "Yes, Justinian will not be pleased to hear that our dear young guest has disappeared while in your personal charge." She paused. "Not to mention while she was also under the guard of Captain Felix."

John's face remained impassive. He well knew that, despite the truth of any given situation, punishment was commonly meted out according to imperial whim. Thus quite often the innocent suffered along with those who, if not guilty by design, had failed in their duty—or had been judged to have failed.

"Highness," he replied curtly, "no punishment would be sufficient for my neglect of my duty."

He was pleased to see that his answer surprised Theodora, although few except him would have noticed the transitory narrowing of her eyelids or the almost imperceptible tightening of her reddened lips.

"I am quite certain an appropriate punishment can be devised, Lord Chamberlain," she replied coldly. "However, I will admit that I am curious. Why do you admit to this negligence?"

John squared thin shoulders and looked her directly in the eye, a liberty that few attempted. Of those who had, most had soon regretted it. "I neglected my duty because I allowed anger to control my actions, highness. That is never acceptable."

Theodora's hard expression changed to thoughtfulness. "That's true enough, and that you should admit it makes me almost respect you. Yes, almost."

In the ensuing heavy silence, John spared a quick thought for Felix, hoping he did not need to be reminded of the danger in which he also stood.

Then his mind turned to Sunilda, so young and far from her home and family. She might well already be dead. The thought sickened him.

The truth of the matter was, he admitted to himself, that he had become fond of the girl. Now she was gone, perhaps forever, he felt as if he had first gained, and then lost, another daughter. The thought caused him more pain than he would ever have anticipated.

Theodora suddenly smiled. For an instant John imagined she had somehow read his morbid thoughts and was reacting to them with pleasure.

"At least you managed to find the straw man the herbalist was commissioned to make for the festival," she commented ironically.

"We will have no need of it, highness," Zeno spoke up at last. "Obviously all these frivolities will have be put aside while we search for the child. In all fairness, I should like to say that not all of the blame should be laid on the Lord Chamberlain and Captain Felix, for I have realized as the hours have gone by and Sunilda has not come home that I've been too caught up with my automatons and not attentive enough to my responsibilities to her."

Theodora rose from her seat. "I admire your loyalty to your friends, Zeno. However, we will not compound your errors by disappointing the villagers. I ordered that the festival go on. I do not repeat orders. Indeed, why should the sorrows of the rulers of the empire ruin their subjects' quaint little joys? They've worked long and hard and the festival I have come here to witness will be held for that, if for no other, reason. Who knows, perhaps we shall be able to find a companion to accompany their straw man on his watery journey."

Her gaze lingered on John's face as she spoke.

❄ ❄ ❄

"John!"

John turned to see Anatolius hurrying toward him.

His friend's expression was troubled. "I heard about the girl when I arrived. When did you sleep last? You look half dead. And why is your face all scratched?"

"Never mind about that, Anatolius. We have bigger worries to cope with right now."

As John spoke, he briskly strode down the corridor, leaving Anatolius to follow close behind. Navigating the vestibule without incident, they crossed the threshold and set off across the garden. Around them, figures could be dimly seen moving through the shrubbery in the graying darkness that heralds dawn.

"There is someone I must speak to," John said. "I don't know why it didn't occur to me earlier, but something Theodora said made me think of it."

"I'm coming along with you, John. You look as if you're hardly fit to cross a cart track by yourself right now."

They cut through the olive grove. It lay under the chill, empty silence that gathers at the very end of the night and in the shadowed interiors of mausoleums. Gnarled roots along the way caught at John's feet. He had never noticed such obstacles before. His legs felt as heavy as his eyelids. He thought of relating to Anatolius what Balbinus had revealed about Castor but decided it was not the time. There were more pressing concerns. Besides which, he knew his friend would immediately blame himself for not seeing through the senator's lies.

Anatolius quickly described the results of his most recent visit to Constantinople. "I fear I learned more about the price of parchment than I did about Castor." As Anatolius related his futile interviews with various city merchants first one bird sleepily called, then another. From the direction of the village there came the confident crow of a rooster.

When the young man's report began to approach epic proportions, John halted him with a word of thanks. "Clearly you were very thorough in your inquiries."

"I did learn something from Pulcheria, but even then it was about Barnabas and not Castor."

"Pulcheria?"

"She came to your house and nearly scared Hypatia to death."

"Pulcheria's scars are visible. In that regard, Fortuna treated her less kindly than some. But what were you doing at my house?"

"Checking on Hypatia's safety, nothing more than that, John. You know I have cast myself at Calyce's feet."

"Only too well. Now, what is this about Barnabas?"

Anatolius related the entire conversation, something for which John noted the young man had a particular facility. It was doubtless born from several years' experience in accurately recording Justinian's words, a task requiring an excellent listener and a better memory than most.

They had reached the headland where Paul's stone hut overlooked the sea. Their feet stirred silvery wisps of mist hovering here and there just above the rough grass.

"So that's how Barnabas assembled his collection of scrolls and codices, by stealing them? That's very interesting."

"At the prices mentioned to me he could hardly have afforded to buy very many, I assure you. But what's so interesting about that?"

John was distracted from their conversation. Was that a movement? The faint moonlight limned bushes along the coast road but failed to penetrate into their dark mass of leafy branches. Even so, he could distinguish a shape, a figure, the pale oval of a small face.

"Sunilda!"

He ran forward.

Suddenly the ground disappeared from under his feet. He had just enough time to realize he had stepped into the ditch but not enough to extend his arms to fully break the impact of his fall before he slammed down on one knee, then onto his hands, their palms scraping painfully on stony ground.

For an instant he was dazed. Then he pushed himself up to his knees, the burning wetness of blood soaking through his garment and grit stinging in his abraded skin.

What had attracted his attention was not a small, pale face but rather a clump of white seabird feathers clinging to a branch waving slightly in the sea breeze.

❊ ❊ ❊

Paul shuffled out of his stone dwelling carefully carrying three cups of wine. The steady breeze from the sea carried the tang of salt. The three men might have been standing at the prow of a great ship instead of on a weedy outcropping.

"If I knew where Minthe's gone, I'd suggest you consult her about a poultice for that, excellency." Paul handed a cup to John, who took it gingerly in his injured hand.

John looked in the direction of Minthe's house. Already the air was noticeably warmer. Soon the night would be gone. Rays from the still invisible sun rising beyond the island caught its jagged peaks, tinting them with reddish gold.

He asked the former fisherman to tell him more about Minthe, now that Sunilda was not present to eavesdrop.

"Well, Minthe certainly knows every use for all the herbs and healing plants the Lord has given us," Paul replied slowly, "although she also thinks she can interpret the future, which is another matter entirely. Only the Lord knows our futures."

John said that he was interested in the woman's personal history.

Paul shrugged. "I'm not one to put my nose uninvited into the affairs of others, sir."

"You've lived here a long time?"

"That's so." Paul drained his cup and then wiped his mouth on his sleeve. "Even so, no one seems to know very much about her."

"People always gossip," put in Anatolius.

"They do indeed. One thing that's caused a lot of talk is that she never goes near the church. Some claim she wouldn't dare, that she's a demon. Mind you, more than one person who's whispered that abroad has asked her to put a question to those goats she pretends to speak for." He held up his hand, extending a crooked forefinger. "But you see that? I ran a fishing hook through it. Minthe pulled it out and dressed the wound with some strange-looking mess. Three days later the skin was healing, yes, even though I've seen more than one man lose a finger after an injury like that."

"Has she been accurate when interpreting the messages of the goats?" Anatolius wondered, looking toward the sea. "Is that why people consider her a demon?"

"I think she's encouraged that rumor herself," Paul admitted. "Fear keeps people away from that blasphemous hovel of hers and she has always liked her privacy."

"But she doesn't seem to mind Sunilda's visits," John pointed out.

"I can't explain that, excellency. She's a woman, of course. Women like children, don't they? Or perhaps she's getting lonely, living on her own for so long. Me, now, I've spent most of my life out there on the water, so solitude and I are old friends. What some may fear, others love. Many men are afraid of the tempest, but sometimes I wake up during the night in a panic because my pallet is lying still. I'm afraid I've run aground, you see. I suppose in a way I have."

Strange to imagine, John reflected, that someone might actually fear not sailing on the vast bosom of the sea. "So Minthe has no family?"

"No. She's not from the village," Paul said, "and now I think about it, it must be twenty years since she showed up here. That house she lives in was once a temple. It had been in ruins for as long as anyone can remember. You can probably find bits of it in walls all over the village. A stone here, a stone there, very handy indeed it was. In fact, it's said the marble for the path to the church came from there as well."

"Just think of that, John," commented Anatolius. "All those devout worshippers treading on stones that once echoed to blasphemous abominations."

John silenced his tactless young friend with a glance.

"The Lord triumphs over all," Paul replied simply, ignoring the young man's attempt at humor.

"So Minthe simply appeared and moved into the ruin?" John prompted him.

"That's right, sir. Let's see, it was at the end of the winter, a very wet winter it was, with rain pouring down day after day and keeping people indoors more than usual. I'd mended all my fishing nets twice over."

Paul squinted toward the sea, whose swells were beginning to flash in the strengthening sunlight. "One day the rain stopped," he continued, "and there was smoke blowing along the beach. The woman had moved in. During the rains she'd transformed the place. Piled up stones, boarded up gaps, repaired the roof. It was like magick, which is probably what she wanted us all to think because she immediately started healing with potions and herbal remedies. She's lived there ever since."

"And did she wear her hair exceedingly long then as she does now?"

Paul gave John a puzzled look. "I suppose she did. She's still a striking looking woman, even though she's aged. I can't deny that."

John was already turning to go back to the coast road. He had to speak to Poppaea again.

Chapter Twenty-nine

"Potions? Do you mean Poppaea has been subjected to the ministrations of an ignorant village herbalist without her mother's knowledge?" Godomar had risen from the chair in which he had been seated reading scripture aloud when John and Anatolius entered Poppaea's room.

"I thought everyone knew, Godomar," stammered Anatolius. "In fact, Calyce predicted Minthe's potions would make the girl stronger and you can't deny they have." He gestured toward Poppaea, who was sitting up in bed, looking pale but alert.

"You may attribute her recovery to magick," Godomar told them. "But I drove the unclean spirit from her frail body." He glared at Anatolius.

"I must speak to Poppaea concerning Sunilda," John said sharply, too fatigued to practice the civility he prized.

"I doubt you'll ever find her," Godomar returned.

"You know something useful concerning her disappearance?"

The prelate's bloodless lips tightened into a smile suitable for a death mask. "I fear the demon was too willful and I could not drive it out of her, Lord Chamberlain. Isn't it obvious? It would have been better for her poor soul had she died with Gadaric. Now the foul spirit has taken her away somewhere beyond our reach."

"I see. I regret I must now ask you to take yourself away, Godomar," John replied curtly. Seeing that the prelate was about to protest, he added, "and as Justinian's Lord Chamberlain, you may consider my order to be his own."

Godomar strode out of the small room without a word.

Anatolius idly fingered the codex Godomar had left open on the table by the bed. "It's the tale of the Gadarene swine," he noted. "I must say that's a poor choice of something to read to a child."

"Godomar's read it to me more than once," Poppaea said gravely. "He says I had a demon living inside me, just like those poor pigs did."

John sat down on the chair. "A few morsels of tainted food is all you had inside you, Poppaea."

"Would I know if I had something bad living inside me?"

"Of course you would, but you didn't, so don't let the notion give you nightmares," Anatolius replied.

"Do you remember much about your picnic?" John asked the girl gently.

"Yes. It was very nice. Bertrada got honey cakes and apples and sweetmeats for us. She said the cook was very cross to be asked to find such things so early in the morning."

"And then after the picnic?" John prompted.

The girl made a show of thinking hard, pursing her lips and frowning fiercely. "I went to a grand party but I don't remember much about it. I got sleepy and my stomach hurt. Sunilda was at the party too. Why don't you ask her about it?"

"But there weren't any demons there as well, were there?" Anatolius put in.

Poppaea shook her head vigorously.

"So, you see," Anatolius said with a smile, "there couldn't be any lurking about to jump inside you, could there, or else you would have seen them." He paused. "Was Minthe at this party?"

The girl shook her head again. "She wasn't invited."

"Did you see her on the day of the picnic?"

Poppaea shook her head a third time.

"Has she come to your room to give you any potions?"

"No. She's Sunilda's friend, not mine," the girl replied firmly. "But Calyce keeps making me take some horrible tasting mixture."

"It was for your own good, as people are so fond of saying," Anatolius said with a smile.

"And you can't recall anything about the party?" John asked.

"No, I can't." Poppaea looked unhappy. "It all seems like a dream."

John said he understood and, changing the subject, asked her if she had any idea where Sunilda might be hiding.

He did not really expect her to know, but she did.

"Oh, yes. I think she's hiding in our secret place."

"A secret place?" Anatolius echoed with interest.

"We found a place to hide that only we know about," the girl explained with an impish smile. "We play there a lot. And Sunilda keeps her letters there so Godomar can't read them. He's always poking about peoples' rooms, you know."

"Letters?" John hid his surprise.

The girl hesitated.

"That sounds like a fine jest," Anatolius observed. "I'm certain Godomar would have loved to read them! But who were these letters for, Poppaea? Don't worry, we won't tell!" he added in a conspiratorial whisper.

Poppaea giggled. "Sunilda often writes to her Aunt Matasuntha in Italy, but Zeno told her it wasn't any good sending them because Belisarius was 'beseeching' Ravenna and they wouldn't get there. So Sunilda decided to keep them safe till he was done 'beseeching.'" The rush of words stopped for a short time. "Only we knew about our hiding place," she went on, "and Gadaric did too. Oh, and Barnabas as well. Gadaric insisted on that. He thought Barnabas was very funny and just had to show him where we hide."

"Will you tell us where this secret place is, Poppaea? I think it could help us find Sunilda and bring her safely home," John said softly.

Poppaea started to speak, then stopped, looking distressed. "But if I tell you it wouldn't be secret anymore, would it, and besides I promised Sunilda I wouldn't tell anyone."

"But you see, Poppaea," John replied, "I must ask you to tell because it's also the emperor's business."

"Couldn't you tell the emperor about my promise?" the girl replied slowly. "If you did, I'm sure he'd understand. Everyone says we have to keep promises, even Godomar."

"John," Anatolius interrupted. "Let me have a few words with Poppaea, would you?"

John got up and moved out of earshot by the door as his young friend whispered for a few moments with Poppaea, then beckoned him into the corridor.

"I believe I know where she means." Anatolius kept his voice low. "She didn't tell me directly, of course. She just answered a question I posed to her."

❊ ❊ ❊

The two men made their way to a far corner of Zeno's gardens where tangled thickets of laurel and rose bushes rioted in a manner that would have made even the stoutest-hearted gardener pale if faced with the prospect of pruning them.

Plunging into the thick and thorny jungle, Anatolius got down on his hands and knees to squeeze along a natural tunnel under the mass of entwined vegetation and limbs. John followed, uncomfortably reminded of the short tour of the garden Theodora had so recently arranged for him.

When he was finally able to stand he found himself some distance from the path, in a cramped clearing invisible to any passersby. The small space was almost filled by a moss-encrusted marble structure whose open entrance revealed a narrow stairway leading down into the depths of the earth. Three large birds, obviously ravens, were carved over the doorway.

It was a mithraeum dedicated to Mithra, John's god—not to mention that worshipped by Anatolius as well as Felix and most of the excubitors.

"Uncle Zeno built this years back when he had an enthusiasm for exotic, not to say proscribed, religions," Anatolius explained. "Although as usual he did not entirely follow tradition. I mean, look at those coraxes over the door. One of his little personal touches, I suppose."

"An appropriate motif for a doorway, though, since each Mithran enters the order as a corax," commented John, who had reached the high rank of Runner of the Sun. "At least it's well hidden from official eyes."

"Its concealment is probably more from neglect than design, John. Uncle isn't one of those subtle thinkers. It's just as well he doesn't live at court."

"Even though it's said that a raven brought sad news to Apollo," John replied, "I can't help feeling that that trio of birds is a good omen. They remind me of that strange rhyme I heard so long ago in Bretania. You know the one, I've mentioned it before. 'One for sorrow, two for joy, three for a letter...' Of course, there were those who declared vehemently that three was for a girl but I've found that there's always disagreement over even the smallest things. Yet if Lord Mithra has been kind, we'll find Sunilda hiding down there, safe in His care. Tell me, though, what made you think of it?"

"I found myself wondering if this could be what Poppaea was talking about, so I asked her if their secret place was underground." Anatolius pulled bits of twigs from his hair as he spoke. "She nodded but would say no more. Of course, she didn't realize what she'd revealed. This is just the sort of hiding place that children love, John. In fact, when I was a lot younger I played here myself, in a manner of speaking."

"And that means...?"

"I would hide here with one of the girls from the kitchen," Anatolius replied, with a grin. "Let me go first. The stairs were in sad repair even then."

As Anatolius paused beneath the doorway the sound of stealthy movement floated up from the depths of the small building.

The missing girl?

A small shape raced up out of the mithraeum and skittered away. It was a small, striped cat. Obviously frightened, it vanished into the thick undergrowth pressing in around the clearing.

Anatolius called Sunilda's name as he led the way down the crumbling stairway.

Sunilda was not there.

It was obvious from a cursory glance that the area at its foot had originally been an antechamber. Now only a few fragments of the woven wickerwork screen that had separated it from the rest of the mithraeum remained. From where they stood, the whole of the narrow room with its rough plastered walls, far smaller in size than the mithraeum concealed in a cellar on the grounds of the Great Palace, was visible in the greenish light filtering down the steps. An odor of decay hung heavily in the small chamber's thick air.

Anatolius started forward but John placed a hand on his shoulder, directing him look down.

There were small, muddy tracks on the cracked flagstones.

"The children's footprints!" commented Anatolius.

"All that's obvious is that they are small footprints," John replied thoughtfully.

Anatolius was struck by inspiration. "Barnabas! Of course! He was hiding here!"

John made no reply.

They stepped over a dead rat that lay at the foot of the stairway, accounting for the rank smell that had greeted them.

"Evidently we disturbed that little cat at its supper," Anatolius commented idly as they walked slowly up the narrow space between low benches set along the two longer walls. A quick glance revealed that the benches were formed of thickly plastered solid slabs with no hiding places beneath.

The stone altar in front of the far wall was carved with bas reliefs of Mithra. Reaching it, the two men paused and bowed their heads briefly in honor of their god, who had acquired a holy place in an unexpected manner.

Stepping away, they glanced around again.

Anatolius picked up a clay pot. It rattled as he up-ended it and the skull of a small animal, perhaps another rat, spilled out.

"Sacrifice or some spirited play?" Anatolius wondered aloud. "But it shouldn't be left here to pollute Lord Mithra's house. I'll get rid of it and the rat when we leave. And what's this?"

A board game was hidden behind the altar, along with a pair of small ceramic plates and two cups.

John examined the ceramic ware. They all bore the mark of Zeno's household.

"The children obviously borrowed these from the kitchen to play with, Anatolius. You'll recall Poppaea talked about a party. I thought she was referring to their picnic but now I'm beginning to think she wasn't. Perhaps she meant that they had played here later that day?"

The wall behind the altar was decorated with the traditional sacred scene depicting Mithra killing the primeval bull. The wall painting would have originally displayed brilliant reds and greens, but now it was faded. Patches of plaster had fallen off, leaving much of the scene missing, and the blade in Mithra's hand had been reduced to little more than a few flakes of pigment clinging to the rough surface of the wall.

Anatolius slipped into the cramped space between wall and altar.

"I made this little hiding place before I realized it was blasphemous and an insult to Mithra," he confessed shamefacedly. "I'm sure He understands that I was but a child at the time and that it was not meant as an affront to Him."

A slight scraping ensued as he quickly pulled an irregularly shaped piece of stone from the back of the altar, exposing a small niche in which nestled a sheaf of parchments.

The letters Sunilda had written to her besieged aunt in Italy.

John rapidly scanned them when they had emerged back into the green-tinted light of the small clearing.

The girl's handwriting and grammar were certainly very accomplished for one of her age, he thought. As for her imagination, as he read Sunilda's visions of her future as a queen, her descriptions of conversations with Porphyrio the whale and accounts of marvelous events and astounding adventures that simply could never have happened, he found it difficult to credit that a child could possess such powers of invention. Surely she must simply be describing the world as she truly saw it, however mistaken such a view might be.

He remarked on this to Anatolius, adding, "I suppose we all live in different worlds. The one I live in now is not the one I inhabited as a young man."

Then he abruptly stopped scanning the neat lines of writing and reread the passage that had startled him.

"What is it?" Anatolius asked.

"It seems Mithra has indeed smiled upon us," John replied. "For indeed his sacred ravens were right, whichever version of that old rhyme you accept, Anatolius!"

"But how can that be?"

"Because from this letter I know where to find the girl," John said rapidly. "She's gone to meet the whale. Apparently it's promised to take her to Gadaric. She describes her plans to her aunt, right down to the last detail."

Anatolius sadly shook his head over the girl's mistaken notion of being reunited with her brother, characterizing it as a childish fantasy. "But at least we now know where she is. Where is that, John?"

The parchment crackled as John's fingers tightened around it.

"We'll find her hiding near the headland when the straw man festival is under way."

"That's at dawn tomorrow! This is wonderful news! But how does she expect to meet a whale on a cliff top? Does she suppose it will fly up to carry her off?"

"Hardly, Anatolius," John replied. "Unless we can stop her, it seems she intends to throw herself into the sea at the same time as the straw man—just like the Gadarene swine."

Chapter Thirty

The sea was the bright and unnatural green of a hand-blown glass vessel, its frozen waves, far below, flaws just underneath the bright surface. Sunlight glanced off the swells with the painful brilliance of the dog days of summer yet the rocks beneath John's feet felt cold. He could not remember how he had come to the precipice or why, yet he had the distinct feeling that if he stepped over its edge he would soar out across the water like a raven. Some urgent matter pulled at the edge of his memory. He had to be in attendance at a particular place at a specific time. But where? And at what hour? He couldn't recall. Looking down at the solid sea made him giddy.

Suddenly a sluggish line of light rippled across the green, glassy seawater.

He leapt from his bed, blade in hand before he was fully awake.

"Master!" Peter's flickering oil lamp made his shadow huge as he advanced a few steps. The room thus illuminated was now better furnished than it had been when John had moved into it. Although the Lord Chamberlain did not care much about comfortable beds and good furniture, his servant knew what was fitting and proper for one of such standing and had requested them for his master.

John sat on the edge of his bed. The dream lingered, sea and precipice submerging the room for a few heartbeats until the vision flowed away into the darkness like a wave from a beach, leaving behind only the racing of his heart.

"You have overslept, master," Peter said.

John thanked him, glancing toward the ceramic water clock set in the corner. Its water level showed it was still the middle of the night.

"Anatolius is waiting for you in the atrium," Peter went on, bustling about the room, laying out clothing.

John dressed rapidly. An alarming twinge of pain in his knee reminded him of his recent fall on the road.

Peter followed him into the corridor, which, despite the hour, was thronged with Zeno's servants mingled with the small army of attendants and guards accompanying Theodora. Darkness pressed silently against the windows.

"Even you need to sleep occasionally," Anatolius remarked when John greeted him with apologies for his tardiness. "You aren't Justinian, you know, who apparently manages to rule the empire without the need for any rest at all."

"I shall not require anything to eat, Peter," John said wearily in answer to his servant's inquiry.

"I will find you a bit of bread at least," Peter insisted, moving off toward the kitchen before John could order otherwise.

Anatolius informed John that Felix had the headland guarded as requested.

"And along the road from the village?"

Anatolius nodded silently.

They picked their way through the crowd into the garden. John did not speak again until the two men had emerged into a clearing where they could not be overheard if they kept their voices low. Even then, he bent to put his mouth to Anatolius' ear as he quietly sketched Balbinus' confession concerning Castor's parentage.

Anatolius looked stricken. "The senator lied to me!" he managed a choked whisper. "Why didn't you tell me yesterday? There I was telling you what I'd learned from my investigations, which was practically nothing, and—"

"How could you have possibly known? He was only forced to admit it when I presented him with proof that had not fallen into your hands."

"Castor having royal blood!" the other marveled. "And to think I always considered him a younger version of Uncle Zeno, as alike as two peas in a pod—and eccentric peas at that." A fresh thought struck him. "But who could have been Castor's mother?"

"Minthe," John replied and smiled at Anatolius' astonished expression. He could guess the question he was about to be asked, yet he knew that if challenged he could not adequately explain the origin of his insight to himself, let alone to someone else. Still, his friend was obviously interested in how he had reached such a startling conclusion.

"My thoughts began to march in order when I learned about Bassus," John began. "It's not always the case that one fact points to another and that to the next and so on. Solving this particular puzzle involved the accumulation of several pieces of information until I had gathered enough to reveal a pattern, or a mosaic if you will."

"But how...?"

"It's a complicated business indeed, Anatolius. The Goth heir Gadaric is murdered. What's the first thing you inevitably think of when something like that occurs?"

"Who else is in the line of succession to the throne, of course."

"Exactly. Now, when confronted, Balbinus confirmed that the man he called his brother, that is to say Bassus, was actually the illegitimate son of King Theodoric and so had a closer claim on the Italian throne than the twins' father Athalaric, who after all was only Theodoric's grandson."

Anatolius said he agreed with John's reasoning thus far. "But Bassus is dead," he pointed out.

"As you say. However, Balbinus also revealed that Bassus had fathered a son and that this son was Castor. So if Gadaric's murder was connected to the matter of succession and there seems no doubt that it was, then obviously it involves Castor, a hitherto unknown heir."

"Who ran off immediately after Gadaric's murder!" Anatolius choked back his excitement. "It sounds so obvious when it's explained, John, yet I still don't understand how you could possibly have seen a familial connection between Castor and Minthe."

John waited while several heavily armed imperial guards passed nearby, their boots clattering with the staccato sounds of one of Hero's automatons.

"Normally I would regard my chain of reasoning to be as flimsy as cobwebs," John went on, "but consider what I was just saying about patterns. We have established Castor as an heir to the throne. We know the identity of his late father. But what about his mother? Castor was obviously not ambitious or he would have declared his lineage long ago, but as history has repeatedly shown, mothers are often murderously ambitious for their children."

"That's certainly true."

"So I cast about for a possible candidate to fit into the mosaic I was constructing, to see what sort of picture it made. I was looking for someone near Bassus, someone who would not be noticed carrying Bassus' child. Remember, he had been killed in very odd circumstances. Given his lineage...."

Anatolius looked thoughtful. "Yes, I can see it would be highly dangerous for both mother and child."

John quickly related what he had learned during his visit to Nonna. "She described a very vain slave with exceptionally long hair, who had, let us say, social ambitions but who was sold away to another master."

"Slaves are always invisible, aren't they? And so are their children....But what made you think of Minthe? Castor's mother could have been anyone."

"I considered the people living on this estate and in the village. Minthe had long hair, and she was not from the village. You'll recall Paul mentioned that she moved into that odd little house near him some twenty years ago. Then I remembered you had said that Castor and Zeno had been friends as well as neighbors for a couple of decades. I suspect that Minthe had been keeping her eye on Castor from afar and moved to be near him when he came to live out here."

"Well..." Anatolius said dubiously.

"Consider, too, how close she had managed to become to the twins. An ordinary village woman and two royal children form rather an unusual friendship, wouldn't you say? But useful if harm is intended. It's often those nearest the victims who strike the fatal blow. After all, they have easier access to them than everyone else."

"Looking at it like that, I suppose it's not surprising that Minthe appears to be the missing piece." Despite his agreement, Anatolius still sounded dubious. "However, I can see a very large flaw in your mosaic, John. How could a slave such as Minthe move around so freely?"

"Slaves can be freed, Anatolius. Am I not myself one such? However, I will admit that what finally convinced me of Minthe's involvement was when she disappeared at the same time as Sunilda."

Anatolius leapt to the conclusion John had already reached. "Mithra! She's kidnapped Sunilda! She intends to kill her as well!"

John nodded. "She's already attempted to poison the girl."

"The plates and cups in the mithraeum! Of course!" Anatolius frowned. "But how could Minthe possibly have known about the children's secret hiding place?"

"She didn't have to, Anatolius. You'll recall that after the abandoned picnic Zeno found Sunilda safe with Minthe. Given everything else that's transpired, it is not beyond the bounds of reason to assume that before he arrived, Minthe gave Sunilda a poisoned treat to bring back here. Now, the swine fed the remains of the picnic are all still alive, but there was a dead rat in the mithraeum. Dead rats are not unusual, of course, but what if in this instance the animal ate the remains of the treats for the grand party Poppaea talked about—a party we had dismissed as mere delirious ramblings—including whatever remained of what was meant for Sunilda?"

"But surely Sunilda would have eaten it too," Anatolius argued, looking even more perplexed. "And she didn't even get ill. It was Poppaea who almost died."

"But what if it contained nuts, like the honeyed dates Peter sometimes prepares for me? Sunilda mentioned in one of her letters to her aunt that the twins were not permitted to eat nuts. Apparently it's because they provoke some undesired effect in them, just as proximity to certain plants does to you."

"You amaze me, John! I could never have thought of such a convoluted theory!"

"Nor would I," John admitted, "if Minthe hadn't directed the gravest suspicion at herself by vanishing at the same time as Sunilda. It was too much of a coincidence not to be connected with what has taken place here. In effect, she had accused herself and as soon as I realized that, all the fragmentary information fell into place and I saw the whole."

"But we must be too late to save Sunilda now, she's been gone so long!" Anatolius frantically burst out, all thought of discretion forgotten.

John shook his head. "You've forgotten that Sunilda wrote about her plan to join Gadaric. It will begin when the straw man is tossed off the headland and that won't be for a while yet since it's not yet dawn. Unfortunately, if Sunilda balks I'm absolutely certain Minthe will be only too happy to assist her to carry out her fantasy."

Anatolius pointed out that Minthe must have known she could not fail to be hunted down and executed.

John shrugged. "I may be able to hazard a guess at what someone has done or may be planning to do, but as to how such a one would propose to escape from such a certain fate I confess myself puzzled. Perhaps this is one of those situations where once the desired object is accomplished, nothing else matters and so the perpetrator's plans extend no further beyond that."

"Eliminating the twins would certainly remove even the remotest possibility of any impediment to Castor assuming the throne." Anatolius lowered his voice again, even though they were standing well away from the general flow of pedestrians. "Of course, given the enormous crushing power that Hero's accursed artificial hand is capable of exerting, it would be easy for Minthe to employ it to kill Gadaric. To think of her using it on the boy's throat...."

John remained silent.

"Why didn't Poppaea die, John? Minthe is, after all, a very knowledgeable herbalist."

"Since she was responsible for the poisoning attempt, she knew the antidote to administer when the wrong person ate it," John replied, turning at the sound of Peter's shuffling approach.

"You must be hungry, master. I've been hunting for you for some time." The elderly servant ceremoniously offered John a hunk of bread and a piece of cheese from a small silver plate that reminded John of Nonna's recent hospitality.

"I regret that this was all I could obtain for you," Peter went on in an outraged tone. "Theodora's entourage appear to have scoured the kitchen as cleanly as a plague of locusts."

John quickly ate the frugal meal. When he had been requested to attend Zeno's grand banquet in honor of the twins he had not expected the invitation to lead to the consumption of so much bread and cheese—for once, almost too much. As he finished and handed the plate back to Peter, Godomar loomed out of the darkness and, to John's well-concealed annoyance, paused to converse with them.

"Lord Chamberlain," he began with a slight bow. "I sincerely hope you do not intend to take part in this blasphemous festival. It would be unconscionable enough at any time, but when an innocent child is dead and another has vanished, to even contemplate holding it is unspeakable."

"As a matter of fact, we are about to resume our search for Sunilda," John replied.

"Then you won't be in attendance at the service I have arranged for the villagers? Needless to say, I consider it my duty to offer an alternative to this hideous pagan rite, for it's obviously no more than that."

John noticed Peter directing a furtive, sorrowful glance him. "You are free to go if you wish, Peter," he told his servant, knowing that it was his, John's, pagan beliefs that worried Peter much more than his master's absence at the service just announced.

"What of Calyce? Is she going?" Anatolius asked with over-elaborate casualness. "And Livia?" he added hastily.

"The empress has decreed that all of her attendants, including the ladies-in-waiting, will accompany her to the event. No doubt they'll be much educated in the ways of wickedness after witnessing it!"

"That's a lesson Theodora would be well qualified to teach, if it weren't that her ladies have already been long enough at court to be well practiced," muttered Anatolius as Godomar departed for the village with Peter trailing behind.

Watching his servant leave, it struck John, not for the first time, that the aging Christian—who was after all a freed man—might well decide to end his days contemplating the world from a monastery rather than cooking meals for a pagan master with the culinary tastes of an ascetic. Should that come about, what would his house be like when it no longer sounded with Peter's tuneless singing of lugubrious hymns as he scrubbed the kitchen floor or his scolding when his master did not eat what he considered adequate nourishment?

He quickly drew his thoughts back to the immediate problem of Sunilda. There, at least, was a loss that it might be in his power to prevent. He had to find her before she had the chance to harm herself.

Unfortunately, children loved to play hide and seek. And they were experts at it. John had remained ignorant of her intentions for too long and now, if he were to save the girl, he had only until sunrise to discover her hiding place.

Chapter Thirty-one

John left Anatolius to stand watch with the guards at the villa and set off down the shore road toward the village.

The road was as crowded as the Mese at midday, with villagers either making their way to the headland where the celebration would culminate or claiming good places from which to observe the procession as it passed by. John saw no one he recognized except Paul, who was standing at the end of the path to his house. A quick exchange between them confirmed that the man had seen no sign of Minthe or the missing girl.

"I expected you to be attending Godomar's service," John observed.

Paul took a long time to respond. When he finally spoke, his words were hesitant. "If it were being held at any other time I'd certainly be there, faithful follower that I am. Godomar himself invited me as he went by a little while ago. Quite a flock he'd gathered already. But the straw man goes to the sea and the sea is ancient and all powerful. And though you may say I'm just a foolish old man, still...." His voice trailed away.

John did not press him further. It had struck him on more than one occasion that the Christians' rigid insistence on their god's exclusive sway, so at odds with human nature, would finally prove to be their undoing.

He continued on his way. The dark sky was strewn with a dusting of stars against which loomed the black masses of trees and bushes. An owl called from the towering shadows of a stand of pines as he passed.

Just before the road passed through the center of the village, John arrived at an open space illuminated by a huge bonfire. In its shifting light he saw Zeno supervising the drawing up of the procession. Flapping back and forth, long hair flying, the elderly man was directing groups of his servants, villagers, and Felix's excubitors into their places with equal and enthusiastic impartiality.

Two of Zeno's younger servants stood at the head of the line. They wore golden-colored tunics and were harnessed to a cart decorated with fragrant greenery and bundles of straw on which the well-stuffed sacrificial figure was laid out, surrounded by piles of vegetables and fruit. The cart was brightly illuminated by torches held by two men, dressed entirely in red, who flanked it. The sight of the duo immediately reminded John of Mithra's torchbearers. The notion was strangely comforting.

Behind the straw man's cart three or four young village women, dressed in long white garments with chaplets of olive leaves on their hair, were chattering. Their role, Zeno explained to John when he dashed up for a quick word, was to dance in celebration of the straw man's fate.

"It's customary for the rest of the villagers to carry torches and follow behind the young ladies and sing as they walk to the headland for the final ground event. This year, of course, it will be even grander. But I see I am needed. A small problem, perhaps. If you would excuse me..."

Zeno hurried away. John strolled along the line. Two husky men were standing at its mid point, each grasping one end of a stout pole passing through the center of a wooden wheel to which bundles of brushwood were tied. The bundles would, John guessed, shortly be set afire so that when the wheel was trundled along it would present the appearance of a whirling mass of flames.

"It's a sun-wheel," Zeno confirmed, having reappeared at his side. "I wonder what Lord Mithra's foolish followers would make of such a thing? I can certainly imagine what Godomar would say about it."

"Fortunately for all concerned he won't see it, Zeno."

"And Sunilda hasn't been found yet?" the other said in a worried tone. "You know, John, if everyone gathered here were to forsake the procession and join in the search...but there are Theodora's orders to be considered. If the empress wants the festivities to go forward, what choice do any of us have?"

Their walk had brought them to an ox cart on which sat a trio of Hero's automatons, two holding lyres and the third grasping a flute. Hero was crouched in the middle of the cart, making small adjustments to the flute player. A gust of wind coaxed a faint, discordant noise from the lyres. It sounded like a far-off groaning.

Felix, standing nearby, grimaced and tugged at his beard. "I hope these musicians produce a more pleasing sound once you start them up," he complained to Hero. The inventor, intent on his task, did not answer. Felix lowered his voice for John and Zeno's benefit. "I must say that that strange sound matches the look of them. They're extremely odd creatures."

The automatons had metamorphosed from the skeletal beings John had last seen in the workshop. Now they were dressed in deep blue dalmatics, their metal skulls sporting wigs of horsehair. Only the metallic surface of their faces and sightless glass eyes betrayed their lack of breath. Hero, of course, would bring them to life at the appropriate point.

The breeze elicited more moans from the mechanical musicians' instruments as four burly villagers arrived on the scene, carrying a small litter. Its tasseled curtains were tied back to display another automaton sitting in solitary splendor. Dressed in green and sporting long, fair hair, the creature's metallic hand grasped a bright emerald-colored bow in which was notched a long gold-painted arrow.

"Is this all not absolutely magnificent? Everything was completed in time!" Zeno exclaimed. "It is such a good omen that I can hardly believe Sunilda will not reappear soon, safe and sound. I think that all our preparations are completed now. Hero, if you would be so kind as to give the signal?"

For the space of a few heartbeats nothing happened. Then there was a creaking noise and the head of the flute-player turned slowly as its stiff hands raised the instrument to frozen lips. Silvery notes filled the night air.

"Mithra!" breathed Felix.

As the procession slowly began to move forward, John glanced at him. The excubitor was closely scanning the area. "I'll follow along for a while and keep an eye on things, John, in case the girl attempts to slip into the procession," Felix said. "She might try, so she could get up on the headland among the crowd."

John left him at his post and swiftly strode along the length of the slow-moving line as it snaked towards the road.

Now the fire wheel was set alight, flinging sparks into the starry sky. As the sound of lyres joined the cascading music of the flute, Theodora arrived. Far larger and more ornate than that of the mechanical archer, the empress' litter announced its presence by the chiming of small bells hanging along its sides. Naturally, her place was at the head of the procession.

Among the attendants, servants, and soldiers accompanying Theodora John noticed Bertrada and Calyce. Livia was some steps behind them, firmly holding Poppaea's hand.

John stepped forward and asked the child how she was faring.

"She insisted on observing this abominable ceremony," snapped Livia, keeping her voice low. "Theodora thought it was a splendid idea as well, but then our dear empress has never had to worry about a sick child going out in cold night air, has she?"

"Oh, mother!" Poppaea said in an exasperated tone. "I am quite well now."

"Look, Poppaea." Livia yanked her daughter's hand impatiently. "You see that wheel of fire? There are those who worship fire, you know, but such people will see enough of it in the hereafter, as Godomar will tell you. I wish you to be attentive. Tomorrow you will relate to him the lessons you have learned from this disgusting pagan exhibition."

Poppaea stared obstinately in the opposite direction.

John stepped back into the shadows and watched the procession depart. Theodora, he noted, was leaning out of her litter, staring intently back toward the blazing fire wheel. He smiled thinly at the sight. The noisy ceremony was akin to many that the ancient shore must have seen since the world was young, and yet here was the wife of the ruler of an avowedly Christian empire completely enthralled by it, to judge from the curve of her scarlet lips.

Now that the procession was finally under way it formed a striking sight indeed, with its doomed straw man in his ox cart, women dancing lightly back and forth behind it, their flowing robes whipping in the rising breeze that presaged dawn. And following them were all the rest...dozens of villagers ambling along holding torches and laughing and talking, another cart carrying the stiffly moving automatons playing their shrill melody, the blazing wheel shooting sparks everywhere.

But neither Sunilda nor Minthe was anywhere to be seen.

Now the villagers began to sing, enthusiastically waving their torches. They sounded much more fervent than might be expected of rustic laborers attending an ancient festival officially regarded merely as entertainment as their voices rose with the smoke into the star-sprinkled sky.

The straw man liveth once again
He journeys to the sea
And thus we offer him with praise,
O, Harvest Lord, to Thee

By his sacrifice we beg
From Thy heavenly hand
A goodly harvest from the sea
And Thy blessing on the land

Summer ends and die he must
Die he must, as all who live
Accept him now, O Harvest Lord,
And all Thy bounty give

Staying well back, John loped rapidly along the roadside, scanning the procession and various groups of villagers waiting to see it pass. Armed soldiers were everywhere. There did not seem any way in which Minthe and the girl could reach the headland undetected, nor any place they could hide.

Then he was racing back past the empress' litter, not caring whether she saw him or not, barely feeling the burning pain shooting across his knee.

Several of Felix's men had swords already in hand as he reached the cart carrying the reclining straw man and leapt aboard. Zeno, striding along beside it carrying a torch and singing enthusiastically, waved them away. He shouted a question which John ignored. Hero stared speechlessly from his seat by the driver.

The procession kept moving. Perhaps the villagers mistook John's precipitous arrival for a new part of the spectacle.

As he clambered onto the cart, John saw the straw man's painted features leering up at him from the battered leather ball of its head. He grabbed the front of the effigy's bright orange dalmatic, ripped the fabric open and thrust his hand into its plump chest.

He found only straw.

He quickly punched here and there at the well-stuffed effigy. There was nothing but straw. Sunilda had not hidden herself inside it. For once his sudden surmise had been wrong. He had leapt in the wrong direction.

A wave of shouting came down the road. Torches were being waved about even more enthusiastically. Hero, seemingly oblivious to John's strange actions, pointed toward the dark mirror of the sea.

Out there a gray phantom moved and a translucent pillar rose into the night.

It was the whale Porphyrio, blowing water into the air. Beyond this ghostly vision an inky blotch was outlined against the sky: the goats' island, crowned with jagged peaks etched in faint moonlight.

John's thoughts took another leap forward. He dropped from the swaying cart and began running back down the road, setting his teeth against the pain it caused him. The death of the boy Gadaric had been preceded by the spouting of a mechanical whale. The superstitious might predict that the real whale had just heralded another death.

But though the superstitious might make such a claim, John had realized that if Sunilda indeed came to harm he would have only himself to blame.

Hadn't her letter been perfectly clear? Hadn't she said she would throw herself into the sea from a point where nothing lay between herself and the rising sun? Why had he so foolishly gone with the procession accompanying the sacrificial straw man?

There was something else that lay between the headland and the sun. The island inhabited by the goats. And now that it was almost certainly too late, he had to find some way to reach it before sunrise.

Chapter Thirty-two

The two men dragged the tiny boat down to the beach. Although he had been prepared to take it out alone if necessary, John had found Paul lingering beside the shore road, idly watching the tail end of the procession as it passed brightly and loudly by.

Paul was eager to assist with the launch but his aging body was reluctant. When they reached the water's edge, he came to a halt, grimacing, his gnarled hands painfully grasping the small vessel's gunwale. Lowering his head he muttered a brief prayer to his god. Or perhaps, John thought, it was addressed to the sea.

He glanced up at the procession, now marked by a fiery line bobbing slowly along the headland. Here and there he could make out an indistinct figure enveloped in a nimbus of smoke. Looking seaward, he saw thickening pre-dawn fog was rolling in, forming a low, faintly luminous wall rising against the sky.

The susurration of the sea against the beach whispered its eternal threat as he waded into the shallows.

"No need to hesitate, excellency," Paul said. "My little boat doesn't look much but it's a lot sounder than I am. I built it myself. It will carry us faithfully where you want to go."

John made no reply. It wasn't the boat. There was no boat, or ship, however large and seaworthy, that could allay John's fear of water, the terrible element that had taken the life of a comrade so many years before. John forced himself to take another step forward, concentrating on the task at hand in an attempt to shut out all thought of the hungry, deep stretch of water waiting.

As they waded further into the shallows, he tried to imagine he was simply stepping into the pool at the baths, although he in fact avoided cold water even there. A pause to steady the craft and then they had clambered into it.

Paul began rowing, working the oars as smoothly and mechanically as one of Hero's automatons.

Waves sloshed and gurgled against the sides of the little boat as they moved across the water surrounding them with an undulating floor of polished ebony marble. Tendrils of fog came slithering across its glassy surface to meet them. Before long the men were engulfed in a chilly blanket that seemed to draw a cold luminescence from the stars.

"The island?"

"It's straight ahead," Paul replied. "There's a strong current towards it and we're already in it. Can't you tell?" His voice sounded strained.

John shook his head, wishing he had insisted that he row rather than the older man. It was too late now to change places, so he was forced to sit rigidly, hand clenched on the gunwales, staring into the blank face of the drifting fog. His fear of deep water was drawing time out as the dead of winter draws out the hours of the night. But there was nothing he could do but endure the endless journey.

A breeze was beginning to blow landward now, just strong enough to stir the fog into swirling, ghostly shapes without dispersing it. As it shifted, snatches of the faint, discordant music made by Zeno's metallic players and the lusty singing of the villagers were carried to them from the headland.

John muttered a prayer of thanks to Mithra that the festival was still in progress, had not yet been ended by the rising of the sun that might also end Sunilda's life.

The oars continued their regular dipping into the water. The boat groaned and creaked as if ready to burst apart. John was suddenly aware of his weight pressing down perilously on the thin wooden floor, all that lay between him and the waiting water. Visions of shadowy horrors moving through the blackness below filled his thoughts.

The boat abruptly rolled sideways.

"Only a swell," Paul assured him quickly.

Another sickening lurch. This time Paul offered no reassurance. John peered into the mist, straining his eyes to see something, anything.

The small vessel shuddered and spun around, throwing John sideways. For a sickening instant his upper body hung over the edge of the boat before he could pull himself back to safety, scrabbling at the wet planks, one hand slipping into the water, so horribly close, that waited patiently for him.

Something huge was moving out there in the fog, but rather than dissipating into swirling coils of mist it solidified into a half-seen massive shape that slid by them some way off.

It was Porphyrio.

Perhaps, John thought, the beast really had come to meet Sunilda.

Swift on the heels of his thought the fog roiled around the gigantic shadow that could now be seen rising toward the unseen sky.

There was an explosive slap in the rolling bank of whiteness and John glimpsed the beast's powerful tail sliding back into the water as Paul said swiftly in a strangely calm voice, "The whale's closer to land than I've ever seen it. When we capsize, try to cling to the hull, excellency."

John had seen elephants brought to Constantinople to entertain at the Hippodrome on several occasions. They would have been dwarfed by any part of the whale. The tail alone could have knocked one of those enormous animals off its feet.

Yet again came the sound of rushing water. A huge wave slammed into the boat, accelerating it forward. Spray stung their faces. All around their small craft the dark water boiled. Paul grimly clung to the oars, his eyes tight shut and his face drained of color.

Then their craft gave one last shudder and burst through the wall of fog. They were facing the dark bulk of the island. The gray light that precedes dawn revealed jagged rocks jutting from the surf on all sides. The boat's momentum carried it toward the shore until it finally hit an underwater rock and capsized.

The men fell into the cold water.

John had no time to think before all the sounds of the world were replaced by a muffled roar. His mouth opened in an involuntary gasp and the sea choked him as he fell, rigid with horror, into its obscene embrace.

Downward he floated, hair and clothing spreading out under the touch of the sea's watery fingers. Trying desperately not to gasp for air, John kicked his legs, praying fervently that he would not die this terrible death. His arms flailed. He did not know whether he was moving upward toward life or deeper toward his death. The roaring in his ears sounded louder, a droning dirge. His lungs were burning. He felt as if they would surely burst.

Over and over he slowly tumbled through the freezing, dark water in a seemingly endless fall towards oblivion.

He knew that he could not hold his breath much longer.

Perhaps he should let go and accept his fate as serenely as he could...

A hand suddenly yanked painfully at his hair, pulling him back up into blessed air and the roar of the waves.

It was Paul, who had somehow found the strength to bring John to safety.

Half-blinded and gasping, the two men reached the island. Their sodden clothing dragging like lead weights, they crawled, shuddering with cold, beyond the eager reach of the waves and collapsed on the beach.

Shingle crunched beside John's head and he found himself staring at a boot.

A child's boot.

Looking up, he realized that he had finally discovered the whereabouts of Barnabas, who had indeed crossed the waters, just as the goats had informed Zeno. But the mime had only fled as far as the island where the oracular animals resided.

❄ ❄ ❄

The rutted path to the island's summit seemed full of holes waiting to trap the careless foot or loose stones eager to cause the unwary scrambler to slip and fall. John continued grimly on at the best pace he could manage between shock, cold and a throbbing knee but moved hardly fast enough to keep ahead of Paul. As John slogged upwards, for the first time since his flash of insight he wondered if, in fact, Sunilda and Minthe were not on the island.

"I haven't seen them," commented Barnabas, who was leading the way, "but then small as this island is there are plenty of places to hide, and I have to stay inside most of the day anyhow."

John grunted, concentrating on finding his footing.

"You'll appreciate that I had no choice but to flee, Lord Chamberlain," Barnabas went on, stepping smartly along. "I'd spied on Theodora and Castor. I don't think she saw me but what if she had? After all, what's the theft of a few scrolls compared to running off with one of the empress' secrets?"

Barnabas had quickly described the scene in Castor's library as they huffed along, confirming what John had begun to suspect. Although Justinian habitually turned a blind eye, Theodora's proclivities for amorous adventures were well known, not to say notorious, in Constantinople.

Wandering Zeno's garden unattended, as Zeno had mentioned she had lately been in the habit of doing, allowed her not only a breath or two of fresh air but also the opportunity to slip unobserved through the private door to Castor's estate. Why else had the empress chosen an eccentric, elderly scholar to be host to the twins for the summer when any estate would have served as well and there were several closer to the city? Clearly it was because Zeno was Castor's neighbor.

And given Castor's claim on the Italian throne, John had a suspicion that Theodora's interest had not been entirely carnal.

Hardly out of breath as he forged ahead, Barnabas continued with his rapid explanation. "I grew up in this area and knew that the villagers don't dare set foot on the island. They're a superstitious lot. I intended to hide here for a while and then take ship for foreign parts as soon as it was safe."

He then admitted to hiding in the mithraeum on the night of the banquet.

"Unfortunately," he continued, "even though it's very well hidden, the search seemed to be getting too close for comfort. So I scaled the wall and hid on Castor's estate for a while and then stole a boat and came over here. Been here ever since, hauling these wretched goats around."

They had come to a tiny, rugged field, hardly more than an indentation in the side of the peak. Its rough expanse was strewn with several of the stuffed animals. On the opposite side of the uncropped grass the rocky and crumbling cliff resumed, rising jaggedly above them. A bird called from somewhere in the straggly brush growing at its base.

John's throat clenched as he looked upward.

"Don't worry," Barnabas assured him, "there's a path up to the top. You'll see it when you get closer. It's extremely steep, though. Watch out for loose stones and...."

"It's too late," Paul gasped breathlessly, pointing a shaking finger to the top of the cliff as he spied what John had already glimpsed.

Two figures were nearing the top of the precipitous path, picking their way slowly as the smaller helped the other.

Now, too, a blood-red line of incandescence was touching the summit.

John's leap of deduction from the darkness of doubt to the light of certainty had been correct, but had it come too late?

He limped at as rapid a pace as he could manage across the open space populated by departed goats. He was bound to attempt the climb, although he saw with a sinking heart that the path was a series of switchbacks, an impossible distance to traverse quickly even on two good legs.

Mithra aid me, he muttered, plunging up the stony track as quickly as he could. He glanced over his shoulder, expecting to see Barnabas about to overtake him, but the mime wasn't even on the path. Instead he was running off towards the base of the cliff.

The dwarf's short legs gave him an awkward gait. Under other circumstances it might have been a comical sight. Now, with a child's life at stake, his inexplicable action was horrifying.

Then John understood as Barnabas carefully chose his spot and began working his way up the side of the rocky precipice. John would have said it was a nigh impossible feat, but Barnabas was somehow finding unseen hand-holds, his powerful arms and legs pulling and pushing him quickly upward as surely as they had propelled him through hundreds of the comical acrobatic stunts for which he was justly famous.

John continued painfully on a journey that seemed to take an eternity. Each time the crumbling track began to point directly to the cliff top it soon looped back on itself, forced away from its course by a sheer rock face or an impassable outcropping. He could have climbed Mithra's seven-runged ladder faster, John thought grimly, as he fought his way up the hellish incline.

As he finally emerged between two boulders marking the end of the path, a wash of sunlight stabbed out over the windswept rocks forming the flat peak of the island.

And there, at the edge of a precipice overlooking the sea, stood Minthe, her torn garment testimony to a struggle. Her long silver hair streamed down her back.

A small distance from her Barnabas crouched, holding Sunilda firmly in his arms.

The girl looked over his shoulder at John with eyes that might have seen a hundred lives.

"Lord Chamberlain," she greeted him calmly. "I am very happy that you and Barnabas have arrived, for I am afraid that Minthe has betrayed me. Porphyrio has not appeared despite his promise. In fact, there's nothing below this high place but jagged rocks. I conclude from this that Minthe intended to kill me and that she is not, after all, my friend."

Minthe made no reply.

From the mainland came a rousing cheer. So unexpected and loud was the sustained sound that John's gaze was drawn back toward it for an instant.

Sunilda screamed shrilly.

John whirled. The child was lying almost at the edge of the precipice with Barnabas' hands clamped around one of her thin ankles.

Minthe was gone.

"She jumped," shrieked Sunilda hysterically. "I didn't want her to die. I tried to grab her." Now she was sobbing. "Minthe, Minthe, come back! I didn't mean what I said!"

"She squirmed out of my arms," Barnabas explained. "I only glanced away for a heartbeat..."

John hurriedly pulled the bitterly sobbing Sunilda away from the drop, away from anything that might be visible below.

As he turned back towards the path, he saw Paul standing silently between the boulders, staring at the girl with a strange expression on his face.

Sunilda grew quiet and deathly still. It was the sort of shocked reaction John had seen soldiers experience after a battle.

Barnabas helped the girl back down the path. John and Paul followed slowly. As they left the summit, Paul turned to stare toward the precipice where Minthe had been standing not very long before.

"What is it?" John asked in an undertone.

"Nothing, excellency, nothing. I'm just sorry I arrived too late to help save that poor creature from flinging herself into the sea. Although to tell the truth, I imagined that I saw the girl...but no, my eyes are old and dim and surely I was mistaken. Now, thank the Lord, we can forget this terrible nightmare. It is surely ended now."

Chapter Thirty-three

Choppy waves rocked the boat as it carried Paul, John, and Sunilda back to the mainland. The girl seemed to have recovered with remarkable rapidity from her ordeal and showed them where the boat that had brought Minthe and herself to the island had been hidden.

John did not voice his thought that for Minthe to navigate the dangerous strait between land and island during a thick fog indicated how pressing she considered the mission to be accomplished. The effort must have cost her enough to allow Barnabas to scale the cliff before she and Sunilda could make the climb to its brink. And he, too, and Paul, had risked all in the same mad crossing.

Now the girl was talking of her friendship with Minthe. The men remained silent as she poured out her love for a woman who had treated her as her own child and was now gone forever.

"She has gone to join Gadaric," she insisted. "You shouldn't have stopped me following her, Barnabas. And as for you, Lord Chamberlain, I am not at all pleased with your interference."

John was silent, intent on rowing.

"You see," the girl went on, "Minthe was the only one who really cared about me. She was very clever, too."

It was not what Sunilda had said about the woman a short while ago. The girl was, John thought, already constructing a much more pleasing reality for herself. He also sensed that once they reached land, Sunilda would never again speak of the lost woman, so he took his opportunity to inquire how the seemingly magick abduction had been accomplished.

"It was easily done," the girl replied with a slight smile. "Minthe gave me a sleeping potion to put in Bertrada's wine. Then I knocked over a stool, threw the bedclothes around, and crept away into the fog without any of the other servants even noticing me leaving." She finished and sat staring silently at her feet, her face as blank as a block of stone waiting for the chisel.

The journey seemed to John to take much less time than their voyage to the island. The tide must be on the turn, he thought, assisting their passage. Paul, who already looked uneasy at being carried along by the labor of one so highly placed as John, looked more and more disturbed the faster the small boat cut through the water.

"It's not natural," he muttered at last. "The current's all wrong."

John, concentrating on getting back to solid ground as quickly as possible, did not mention his gratitude for the sea's assistance in his task, replacing the whale.

As they approached the shore, he could see knots of villagers still clustered on the headland despite the fact that the ceremony had ended. Doubtless they were waiting for Theodora to withdraw to the villa, signaling permission for them to return to the village. Godomar's service would have concluded by now. John wondered if Peter had found it at all enlightening.

Although from his viewpoint most of the coast road was blanketed with trees and bushes, John's eye was caught by movement half concealed by the vegetation. He had the impression of a group of people moving purposely toward the headland.

Then his attention was diverted by a thump against the side of their boat. Sunilda let out a brief shriek.

Looking down into the water John saw what it was—the half deflated leather ball that formed the head of the straw man. Seawater had made its painted features run into a leer. The rest of its body was nowhere to be seen.

"Look!" Sunilda pointed up at the looming headland as the keel finally grated on shore nearby. "Bertrada's waiting for me."

The faint sound of bells came to their ears. It was very strange, John thought, because they sounded exactly like the ones suspended from Theodora's litter which, he could clearly see, still sat on the headland. Furthermore, there was no breeze.

In fact, the air had become preternaturally still.

Paul made his religion's holy sign as he stared out toward the island.

"The goats..." Paul muttered, his superstitious fears seemingly undiminished by his discovery of the creatures' true nature.

John now realized what he could not have noticed while surrounded by the murmur of the sea and the creaking of the oars. No birds were singing to welcome the dawn.

Sunilda leapt out of the boat and started up the path to the headland, calling out to Bertrada.

John stepped quickly out to follow her, relieved to be standing on solid ground once more.

Except that the ground was trembling slightly and the bells on the empress' litter were jangling even louder.

John started after Sunilda as, on the headland above, a raw-boned young man with straggling hair leapt onto the seat of the cart carrying Hero's mechanical musicians.

"The prelate is right. It's these accursed figures!" the man shouted. "They must be destroyed before a disaster happens!"

There seemed to be a great many people gathered on the headland, more than John had noticed while rowing back. He could distinguish one familiar form, taller than the rest.

John recalled the group he had glimpsed moving up the coast road. Had Godomar decided to lead his congregation forth to do battle with the evils he had railed against?

A grinding roar suddenly filled the air, whether from the mob or from the stronger shaking of the ground or both John could not say.

A familiar voice rose above the clamor. It was Felix, barking orders to his men. A phalanx of excubitors immediately picked up Theodora's litter and moved swiftly away from the precipice.

The ground shook sluggishly again. The excubitors swayed like drunkards. John saw Livia running beside Theodora's litter, dragging an hysterical Poppaea. Bertrada, weeping, trotted behind them, accompanied by a perfectly composed Sunilda.

Even so, the child was still John's responsibility, especially now that Felix was otherwise occupied. John looked around, quickly gauging the situation, and then back toward Bertrada and her charge.

But they had vanished in the general confusion. For now he would have to trust the nursemaid's good sense. He had no other choice.

"These ceremonies are blasphemous. The Lord is displeased!" the young Jeremiah was telling everyone in a voice rivaling that of Godomar.

By the time John arrived on the headland Zeno was struggling feebly with the young man on the cart while Felix and his remaining excubitors expertly herded the screaming crowd away from the headland.

"We must destroy these machines of Satan!" the malcontent shrieked. He shoved Zeno down, seized one of the lyre-players and began dragging it towards the precipice.

A few steps more and then he had tipped the automaton over. A moaning noise drifted up as the strings of the falling lyre vibrated with the swift passage of air through them on the way down to the sea. The automaton's companions soon followed.

John glanced around rapidly. The panicked crowd forced back by Felix and his men was streaming back toward the village, although several had left the main mass and were running through the olive grove. More than a few had fallen in their haste.

"Have you seen Sunilda?" John shouted at Zeno as he helped him up.

"They ran away towards the villa, John," Zeno gasped, looking dazed and as pale as a lily. John made his way there as quickly as he could. As he approached, he could see cracks had opened in its façade. Part of the colonnade had collapsed. Amid shouting and lurid curses, villagers were rushing in and out.

Two red-faced men appeared, dragging the serpent-slayer automaton by its feet. Its head was missing but it blindly and repeatedly shot an arrow that had long since flown elsewhere.

John ducked inside the building, to be greeted by more yelling and the noise of breaking pottery. Between his expression and the blade in his hand those he met in the corridors fell back. Once Felix's men arrived the place would soon be secured, but his immediate task was to find Sunilda and her nursemaid.

He rapidly made his way to the Ostrogoths' apartments. Here and there he passed by one or another of Hero's constructions lying on the floor, making futile repetitive movements like dying men on a battlefield. Several of the mechanical figures had smashed heads. There was no doubt they would never work again.

Rounding a corner he found Hero seated on the floor beside the tilted torso of his wine-dispensing satyr. In his lap was a cloven hoof, in his one hand a goblet. A painfully loud grating emanated from the figure as wine gushed at regular intervals from its wineskin. Hero's goblet moved mechanically back and forth from the geyser of wine to his mouth. His eyes appeared more glazed than the glass eyes in his creation's metal face.

John's quick glance through the Ostrogoths' rooms showed no sign of the nursemaid or her charge.

The workshop!

He climbed quickly out the broken window and limped rapidly around to the back of the villa where the noise was even more intense.

Crossing the courtyard, he met several villagers, led by the man who had instigated the riot and who would doubtless be parted from his head before too many days had passed. They were pulling the mechanical whale on its wheeled platform.

Zeno, also arrived from the headland, was protesting but to no avail. Standing outside the workshop, he wept at the destruction going on around him.

Another swift search revealed no trace of the missing girls.

Cursing luridly, John made his way quickly through the villa and back to the coast road. He wondered briefly if Theodora was enjoying this unexpected turn of events. By the time he had got back to the headland the rioters had managed to pull the mechanical whale to the edge of the cliff.

He stood well back. Several villagers were clustered near the whale and he was alone.

"Harvest Lord, we have brought another offering," shouted their leader, who had apparently taken it upon himself to preside over an impromptu ceremony.

As if in reply, the ground vibrated slightly. Its movement evidently upset Hero's finely balanced machinery, for the mechanical beast's mouth slowly opened and a watery plume shot up from its broad back.

Then, unexpectedly, a deafening roar filled the air. The whale toppled sideways and a huge crack snaked across the ground as the edge of the headland majestically crumbled away, carrying the beast and its tormentors down to the sea in a black cloud of dust that continued to rise slowly, in a towering pillar, into the clear blue morning sky.

John turned and started back toward the villa.

"Master?"

It was Peter. He emerged from the olive grove, holding Sunilda's hand. "I found her all alone," he continued in a quavering voice. "I told her she had to come back to the villa with me but then that mob came running towards us with the whale and we hid so they wouldn't see us. They were in a very ugly mood."

The girl regarded John impassively.

"Where is Bertrada?" John asked her.

"Don't be cross with her, Lord Chamberlain," the girl replied. "I ran away from her so I could see all the excitement. I was just taking a walk when Peter found me."

John looked at Peter.

"She was indeed taking a walk, master, just as she says. Right towards the edge of the headland."

The girl scowled at the elderly servant but said nothing.

"I left Godomar's service before it concluded," Peter went on. "He seemed intent on stirring up the congregation and I didn't want to find myself caught in the middle of a mob. Besides which, well, I wanted to see a bit of the straw man festival. But by the time I arrived, it was over. However, thank the Lord I was just in time for something else, for as I said, I found Sunilda wandering about on her own and who knows what further tragedy might have ensued?"

❊ ❊ ❊

"I must commend you, Zeno. Even the Hippodrome has never seen such thrilling events! The goats were correct after all!" Theodora surveyed the ruined dining room strewn with fragments of painted marine life fallen from its walls. A light coating of plaster dust covered everything, while in the bushes outside the base of a toppled statue could be observed from a window that was no longer quite straight.

"Thank you, highness," Zeno muttered with a slight bow.

"I expect you to provide a suitable sequel next summer, Zeno. I shall look forward to it." Although some time had passed since the earthquake Theodora was still flushed with excitement.

She turned her attention to John. "I must also commend you, Lord Chamberlain, for discovering the identity of the murderer. Who would have imagined a crazed old woman could inflict such damage on her superiors? Yet she managed to accomplish two deaths as well as a near-fatal poisoning. One must admire her resourcefulness and ingenuity, I suppose."

To this strange remark John made no reply.

"My carriage is ready," Theodora declared. "I shall request the emperor to order the Patriarch to hold a special service at the Great Church on behalf of the village. Justinian will also arrange assistance of a practical nature, of course." Turning to go, she pointedly remarked to John, "And, yes, I am quite confident that the Great Church will still be standing when I arrive back in Constantinople. The emperor employed only the best architects and the finest building materials."

After the imperial carriage and its accompanying guards and carts, including one carrying the litter that had unwittingly acted as an oracle, had rumbled away down the coast road, John paced thoughtfully off into the garden. It was an hour or so before Anatolius located him.

"I've finally found you, John! Why do you keep running away when people want to talk to you? I have wonderful news to impart!"

"I didn't see you during the empress' farewell speech."

"I wanted to talk to Calyce before she left and managed to persuade her to leave her duties for a while."

John replied with an inquiring look.

"You'll be pleased, John. I've come to realize the whole notion of any romantic involvement was foolish. Fortunately, Calyce wasn't too upset." Anatolius sounded hurt at her implied rejection of his affections. "She tells me that she feels she needs to devote her entire attention to the service of the empress. However, I think the real reason is that she hopes to return to Italy some day whereas I have absolutely no desire to go there. What is Rome these days? Nothing but ruins, so I hear."

John expressed agreement with the young man's decision.

Anatolius looked disappointed. "You don't sound very enthusiastic about my sacrifice, John."

"My apologies. It's just that my thoughts are of an exceedingly dark nature."

Anatolius inquired as to their content.

"It's a terrible fate for a child to lose a parent, Anatolius," came the surprising reply. "I've been thinking about my daughter. It wasn't my wish that I never knew her, yet it still saddens me greatly that I didn't. I can't help wondering if her life has been poorer for my absence. I hope it hasn't. And now think of the twins, taken from their family and living far from their homeland. Always moving from place to place, pulled this way and that by servants and ladies-in-waiting, by men of religion, by the emperor and empress. Children without parents need guardians whose first concern is their charges' welfare, not how to use them to further their own selfish interests and ambitions."

"I suppose these are the sorts of thoughts you always have after an earthquake?" Anatolius replied in a puzzled attempt to lighten their conversation.

"I'm sorry," John said wearily. "I've been forced to take an extremely hard decision and in considering it, my thoughts began running here and there and ended up galloping in some odd directions indeed. So you won't be surprised to hear that I went and sat in Zeno's mithraeum for a while."

"You asked Lord Mithra to guide you?" Anatolius guessed shrewdly.

John nodded. "Still, it was a struggle to take the right course, and even now...I don't wish to deprive Poppaea of her mother, so I haven't had Livia arrested for Briarus' murder."

Anatolius could only gape at his friend.

John stopped and looked at the sky, gathering his thoughts from the clouds. "It's true there's no proof that could be used against her," he admitted, "yet my order would suffice to have her detained and there would soon have been a full confession, as we both know. However, if she is correct in her religious beliefs she will answer to her god soon enough and in the meantime her daughter will still have a mother."

"But why, John? Why would Livia do such a terrible thing?" Anatolius finally managed to blurt out.

"Livia left the basket containing Hero's hand in the pile of boxes and baskets deposited beside the gate to Castor's estate. She was afraid that Briarus might have watched her leaving it. Even if he didn't know who she was, once he was arrested and brought to Zeno's villa it was quite possible he'd see her at some point and identify her as the person who left the hand there. He had to be silenced as soon as possible. She admitted she killed him when I questioned her just before Theodora and her entourage departed."

"Ah," the other replied. "And there I was, convinced that Briarus' murderer gained entrance to the villa through the malfunctioning automatic doors while an accomplice outside distracted Briarus' guard. Of course, it wasn't nearly as complicated as that. It rarely is, is it? Livia was already inside the villa. All she had to do was draw away the guard by creating a disturbance in the garden and then she could strike."

They had reached the road and stood in silence for a while, staring at the jagged length of new coastline. Birds wheeled and mewled in the cloudy sky above them. The sea was calm, keeping its secrets.

"Something troubles me a great deal, John," Anatolius finally said. "I can see Livia would have been in a panic to get rid of the murder weapon before she was discovered in possession of it and how this led to Briarus' death. But what reason could she possibly have had to kill Gadaric?"

John shook his head. "It is best if you know nothing further about this tragic affair, my friend," he said firmly.

Epilogue

When John finally met him, Castor turned out to be a short, unremarkable-looking man. His undyed garments were not ill-fitting enough to hide a slight paunch nor did his cropped hair lend any air of asceticism to the face half concealed by a straggly beard.

Castor's living quarters were plain but not the barely furnished hermit's cell John had expected. The room's narrow window overlooked a steep drop to the beach, reminding him uneasily of the headland near Zeno's villa.

"I know what you're probably thinking," Castor told John abruptly. "How could the empress have been attracted to such an ordinary, middle-aged fellow? The truth, I fear, is that she saw me only as a useful tool, a playing piece in an imperial game. Or perhaps even a weapon against Justinian, for I don't believe he knew she was urging me to come forward and claim the Italian throne. He supported the boy Gadaric as heir, of course."

John said he had thought as much.

Castor sighed. "Yes," he went on reflectively, "Theodora ordered me to meet her secretly on a number of occasions. She beguiled me with all sorts of inducements and encouragements to declare my ancestry. Wealth and power to begin with, but at the end all she offered was a chance for me to keep my head on my shoulders! Nothing more carnal than that, thank heaven. After all, would you wish to couple with a scorpion, Lord Chamberlain?"

Castor's servant padded in, placed a jug of wine on the table and then left the room after shuttering its window.

"You do not find this new life too burdensome?" John inquired.

"As you see, even here wealth eases one's way through life although my servant didn't like having to grow his beard to be allowed to sit at table."

John had sailed across the Sea of Marmara on an early summer day as dark clouds gathered over the sunlit water. He had been careful to ensure that his taking ship from Constantinople went unobserved.

From the sea, the monastery Balbinus had reluctantly identified as Castor's hiding place—and then only at Lucretia's insistence—loomed above the rocky shore like a fortress or a continuance of the rugged cliffs upon which it stood. Its lower stories displayed featureless masonry walls punctuated higher up by slits of windows, while along its roof bristled a profusion of turrets, domes and crosses. Yes, a man who passed into anonymity behind its forbidding doors would be lost forever.

Castor had greeted him warily at first. Then, realizing he had nothing to fear from this particular visitor from court, he had asked eagerly for news of the world he had left behind. John described in detail the rest of the tragic events at Zeno's estate and their aftermath.

Castor looked extremely upset. "How could I possibly find my quiet life burdensome after such a terrible tale, Lord Chamberlain? Many a king and emperor has ended his days in peaceful contemplation. The fortunate ones, at least. And I shall spend my remaining time in the same way without having had the onerous task of actually ruling anything beforehand."

"You have salvaged part of your library, I see." John indicated the low shelf holding a pile of codices.

"Some of my favorites, yes," the other replied. "So although my body may be confined to this monastery, my world is without limits. Balbinus kindly retrieved them from my library. He's running my estate for me. Mind you, there's one volume he couldn't find that I do rather miss. It's a history of beauty written by a very obscure philosopher by the name of Philo. He was one of those pagans teaching at Plato's Academy years ago."

John gave his thin smile and remarked that he had heard of the man. "Do you suppose Barnabas shares your taste for philosophy and made away with it?" he went on. "I understand he recently came back into Constantinople and took ship, but where he is now I couldn't say. I've no doubt he found the island too confining, especially since he told me he had begun to wonder by what means the current keeper of the goats had supplanted his predecessor. I wouldn't have thought that the guardians of oracular animals would indulge in murderous intrigues against one another. On the other hand, doubtless Barnabas' views have been shaped by all the gossip he's heard when performing at the palace."

He did not mention that he knew of the mime's flight because first the stentorian-voiced actor Brontes and then an anonymous Egyptian ship captain, both of whom had spotted Barnabas as he crept away to safety, had arrived separately at Felix's palace office to demand the reward John had promised them for this very information months before.

"So Fortuna has smiled on Barnabas, if I may be forgiven for saying so in this holy building," Castor mused. "Few who find themselves in Theodora's bad graces survive to tell their story."

John poured them both more wine. "Theodora has ordered the Ostrogoth entourage moved to another estate some distance further down the coast," he said, "and perhaps it's just as well."

He recalled that upon hearing of their relocation Felix had valiantly tried to appear relieved, remarking that he considered the departure of Zeno's guests exceedingly fortunate since military men could not afford to get romantically involved with anyone. Perhaps, John thought, Felix would eventually persuade himself that this was the truth. Meanwhile, John's recollection of that conversation reminded him of matters of war.

"Belisarius has finally won his way in Ravenna," he told Castor, "but as yet there's been no indication that Justinian plans to put Sunilda forward as Theodoric's heir."

"Perhaps his plans are more subtle than that?"

They sat in silence for a while, sipping their wine. A gust of the rising wind rattled the shutters.

"When Balbinus brought your codices, did he tell you about Minthe?" John finally asked.

"Yes, Lord Chamberlain. It grieves me greatly that I never knew her. She would have had a far easier life if I had. But nobody ever told who my mother was or what had become of her. It was a matter that was never to be discussed or even mentioned. Of course, I occasionally saw Minthe from a distance. I feel as if I should grieve for her since she was, after all, my mother, but somehow I can't quite convince myself...it all seems unreal...I am not describing this very well, I fear."

John wondered if his own far-off daughter would feel the same way about him should some stealthy blade finally find his back.

"But you surely realize that by attempting to remove Sunilda she was seeking the same high position for you as Theodora?"

Castor's eyes filled with tears. "No, Lord Chamberlain, I had no notion, no idea at all...."

"Apart from everything else, consider what she claimed the goats were telling Zeno. According to a recent conversation I had with him, they said that, first, sorrow was to be expected."

"Every life has sorrow in it and some have a lot more than others," Castor observed. "I would not make much of that, Lord Chamberlain."

"As you say. Then they supposedly claimed that the tallest knew what Zeno sought. Such a vague statement sounds mysterious and important but of course means nothing."

Castor agreed. "Surely all this nonsense about goat oracles is your usual case of interpreting vaguely worded statements to fit a given situation?"

John shrugged. "But now consider the third answer provided to Zeno, which was that the twin would follow and take high office. Naturally, Sunilda sprang to mind. However, Castor, you are named after a mythological twin. Obviously this third statement was another ploy by which Minthe contrived to prepare the way for you."

Castor nodded. He wiped his eyes with the back of his hand. "But to accomplish it by such means...." He hastily gulped down the rest of his wine and then tried to push back his grief by taking refuge in scholarship. "From your description, I'd guess a distillation from poppies was involved. Zeno grows them around one of those pagan shrines of his, you know. You can make an excellent sleeping potion from poppies but it's deadly in larger doses. Fortunately, however, there's an antidote. It's belladonna."

John gave him an inquiring look.

"Some years ago I made an extensive study of poisonous plants," Castor explained. "I've always been curious about the world and all its wonders, as you've probably heard."

John nodded silently. It had obviously not occurred to Castor that by preparing a deadly potion from a plant found on Zeno's estate but not in her own garden, Minthe had cleverly arranged to deflect immediate suspicion from herself. As for its antidote, well, while it was true it was a well-known poison, its popularity with Theodora's ladies-in-waiting as an eye cosmetic provided a legitimate excuse for Minthe to keep a supply on hand, in order to replenish theirs as needed.

The two men were not alone in the room. John could feel another presence, the unspoken thing that both knew must finally be said aloud.

"You know, don't you?" John asked quietly.

Castor took a quick sip of wine, spilling a few drops on his chest. "Yes. Theodora told me after the banquet. She said it had been an accident but then she went on to say that since Gadaric was now dead, it fortuitously meant only one other heir was left. I am not a violent man, Lord Chamberlain, and certainly not a murderer of little girls."

The wind banged the shutters even harder and the lamp on the table guttered as a draught found its way into the room.

"I'd already left for Constantinople before her lady-in-waiting delivered Hero's artificial hand to my estate," Castor went on. "No doubt Theodora intended it as a warning of what would happen if I refused to carry out her order."

"Indeed."

Castor belatedly asked John how he had deduced Theodora's role in Gadaric's death, not realizing that his admission had indirectly provided John with confirmation of what up to then had been merely speculation.

"I originally debated who would want the boy dead," John replied. "But later I realized it was fruitless to pursue that since the boy was not the intended victim."

He explained this astonishing statement by relating how the solution had begun to coalesce around Castor's library, the library of an estate neighboring the property where Theodora had insisted the twins spend the summer, the library of a man who, as it turned out, was another heir to the Italian throne—and a library that would doubtless be irresistible to a bibliophiliac mime.

"When I was able to question him," John went on, "Barnabas confirmed what I suspected, which is to say that he had observed you and the empress in your library late at night."

Castor sighed. "Yes, Lord Chamberlain. She would take Zeno's key and slip through the private door between my estate and his."

"As it happened, on this particular occasion she left the mud and leaves on your library floor that so distressed your estate manager. Briarus had to brush similar vegetation off his clothes after he showed us your caper beds and the door itself, but of course I didn't attribute any significance to it at the time."

John stopped to collect his thoughts before continuing. "So the question to be answered turned from who might have wanted Gadaric dead to who might have desired Barnabas dead? Barnabas didn't think the empress saw him peeking into your library window, but he still thought it best to flee rather than take that particular gamble. Subsequent events proved it was a wise decision. Even though he's a favorite of hers, she wanted him eliminated to protect her own interests, if not yours."

Castor turned pale at the thought and took another hasty gulp of wine. "Does he suspect Theodora of killing the boy?" he finally asked in a faint voice.

"I think he must. Naturally, he didn't say so to me."

"But how...?"

"It's reasonable to suppose that Theodora stepped into the workshop to get a closer look at the mechanical whale before the banquet or perhaps to talk to Hero. He wasn't there, being otherwise occupied with Bertrada, but she heard someone moving around inside the whale. Now, nobody was allowed to touch the contrivance except Hero and Barnabas. Who else then could it be but the mime who was, after all, due to portray Jonah very soon and would be expected to be making one final check to see that everything was in order for his performance?"

Castor nodded wordlessly.

"It was probably a sudden decision," John continued. "Hero liked to talk about his ingenious constructions and during one of her previous visits would certainly have shown her the artificial hand. She'd been quick to realize its murderous possibilities. It wouldn't have taken long to find it, open the trapdoor in the whale's head and then, seeing the small shape sitting down there in the dark mouth of the beast—for the lamps lit automatically and it was not yet time for them to flare into life—to extend the artificial hand downward..."

Castor hastily stopped him.

"When I spoke to him, Barnabas revealed that when he climbed into the whale during the performance and discovered what was inside, he got out immediately. Naturally the other actors were puzzled, but he's nothing if not ingenious. He explained that another scene had been written at the last moment especially for him, one that required him to reappear not from the whale but under the banquet table. You can imagine the coarse humor that such a notion provoked. Then he set the beast in motion and seized his opportunity to flee while he still had time," John concluded.

"It's long been preying on my mind that if I'd refused to entertain any notion of claiming the throne when Theodora first brought up the subject, Gadaric would still be alive," Castor said sorrowfully.

"The empress committed the murder, Castor, not you. In fact, by ordering Livia to take the basket to your estate, she's also indirectly responsible for your estate manager's death."

"But what led you to suspect Livia of killing Briarus?"

"I'd been told that Theodora customarily employed her for fetching and carrying. So Livia hurrying about with a basket would not be remarked upon, even if anyone noticed in the first place. Nor do I think the empress would have entrusted such an important task to anyone else."

John quickly explained Livia's subsequent actions as he had to Anatolius, carefully omitting to mention that the latter had immediately—and naturally—assumed that Livia was also responsible for Gadaric's death. It was misapprehension John had not corrected since, as he had said at the time, it was safer for Anatolius to know as little as possible.

"And of course Livia is under Theodora's protection! To think that neither of those murderous women will ever be called to judgment," Castor burst out furiously.

"No," John said softly. "But you should remember also that Livia knows one of Theodora's secrets and that's extremely dangerous." He fell silent for a space before continuing. "It is ironic that only Minthe, who didn't even succeed in her murderous plans, and in fact spared Poppaea's life, has been punished."

Castor sighed heavily. "And yet, Lord Chamberlain, is it possible that you're not entirely certain of your deductions? You have fitted together many pieces of information into a most convincing picture, but could they not also be assembled into another? It's little wonder Theodora looked so horrified and shocked when she realized it was the boy and not Barnabas who had died. Her reaction was genuine enough and the same as that of everyone else present, it just wasn't for the same reason. But where is proof that would persuade a court of law of her guilt or, more importantly, persuade Justinian? Would even you dare to suggest that the empress was a murderess?

"As to the rest of it, what if Livia lied to you? Or Barnabas? Or someone else? What if I've lied to you, for that matter?"

"Have you lied?"

Castor ignored the question. "I believe you've constructed an explanation with which you can feel comfortable, Lord Chamberlain, rather as Sunilda appears to have created an imaginary world for herself, one where she rules, one that remains untouched by tragedy."

John stood to make his departure. "I don't think that I'm wrong, Castor," he replied brusquely. "And indeed I sincerely hope I'm not."

For the first time, Castor noticed the haunted look in his visitor's weary eyes.

The wind howled even louder around the high building. Heavy drops of rain rattled against the shutters and from the sea came the thunderous rumble of an advancing tempest.

Glossary

Glossary

AESCHYLUS (c 525-c 456 BC)

Greek playwright regarded as the father of Greek tragedies. He wrote dozens of plays of which only a handful are extant, including *Agamemnon* (458 BC), considered by many to be the greatest surviving Greek drama.

AGAMEMNON

See AESCHYLUS.

AMALASUNTHA (498-535)

Daughter of THEODORIC and mother of MATASUNTHA and ATHALARIC. She served as regent for ATHALARIC when he became king of the OSTROGOTHS while still a child. Like her father, she supported Roman culture and maintained friendly ties with the Eastern Roman Empire. Following ATHALARIC's death in 534 she was unable to maintain her position in the face of opposition to her policies and was murdered in 535.

APOLLO'S RAVEN

According to Greek legend, Coronis was unfaithful to the god Apollo while she was carrying his child. A raven informed Apollo, who killed Coronis although he saved their unborn son. Until then ravens had had white plumage but in his rage Apollo scorched the bird who had told him of Coronis' infidelity and thereafter ravens had black feathers.

ARIANISM

Christian heresy originating in the fourth century, holding that Christ was not divine but rather a created being. Although proscribed, the belief persisted until the seventh century among certain Germanic peoples, including the OSTROGOTHS.

ATHALARIC (c 516-534)

Grandson of THEODORIC, son of AMALASUNTHA and brother of MATASUNTHA. Shortly before his death in 526, THEODORIC named Athalaric heir to the OSTROGOTH throne with AMALASUNTHA to serve as regent while he was still a child. He died in 534, the year before his mother was murdered.

ATHENAEUS (known c 200)

Greek grammarian born in Egypt whose *Deipnosophistae* (*Banquet of the Learned*) is his only extant work. Written in fifteen volumes, ten of which have survived intact and the remaining five in summarized form, it quotes extracts from several hundred writers, including many whose works are otherwise lost.

AUGEAN STABLES

According to Greek mythology, the stables belonging to King Augeas were so filthy that Hercules could only accomplish the task of cleansing them in one day by diverting the raging waters of two rivers through them.

BATHS OF ZEUXIPPOS

Public baths in Constantinople. They were named after a Thracian deity whose name combines Zeus and Hippos. Erected by order of Septimius Severus (146-211; r 193-211), they were rebuilt after the Nika Riots (532) by order of JUSTINIAN I. Situated to the northeast of the HIPPODROME, they were generally considered the most luxurious of the city's public baths and were famous for their classical statues, numbering between sixty and eighty.

BELISARIUS (c 505-565)

JUSTINIAN I's most trusted general. His exploits included retaking northern Africa and Italy.

CASSIODORUS (490-c 585)

Roman statesman, historian, and, in later life, monk who helped preserve the culture of Rome while serving under the OSTROGOTH kings in Italy. His writings include a twelve-volume *Gothic History*, of which there survives only a mid sixth century abridgement written by the Gothic historian Jordanes.

CICERO (106-43 BC)

Roman statesman, lawyer, and writer who was famous for his powerful orations.

CONCRETE

Roman concrete, consisting of wet lime, volcanic ash and pieces of rock, was used in a large range of structures from humble cisterns to the Pantheon in Rome, which has survived for nearly 2,000 years without the steel reinforcing rods commonly used in modern concrete buildings. One of the oldest Roman concrete buildings still standing is the Temple of Vesta at Tivoli, Italy, built during the first century BC.

CYBELE

Phrygian Mother Goddess represented by a sacred black rock, possibly a meteorite. Her son and lover Attis died but was resurrected. Roman rites associated with Cybele included the felling of a pine tree symbolizing Attis. Cybele was sometimes shown riding a lion or in a chariot pulled by a team of these animals. Her priests were castrated.

DALMATIC

Loose overgarment worn by the Byzantine upper classes.

DAPHNE PALACE

Main building of the GREAT PALACE. Nothing is known about its appearance.

ENNEADS

Written by Plotinus (c 204-270), an Egyptian philosopher who in 244 moved to Rome. His works were edited by his student Porphyry (234-305) into six sets of nine books under the general title of *The Enneads* (from ennea, nine).

EUNUCH

Eunuchs played an important part in the military, ecclesiastical and civil administrations of the Byzantine Empire. Many high offices in the GREAT PALACE were typically held by eunuchs.

EXCUBITORS

The GREAT PALACE guard.

FALERNIAN WINE

Considered one of the finest Roman wines.

GADARENE SWINE

Large herd of swine into which Christ drove numerous unclean spirits that had possessed a man.

GREAT CHURCH

Popular name for Constantinople's Church of the Holy Wisdom (HAGIA SOPHIA). One of the world's great architectural achievements, the Hagia Sophia was rebuilt by order of JUSTINIAN I to replace the church burnt down during the Nika Riots (532). Completed in 537, the structure is most notable for its immense central dome, which is about a hundred feet in diameter.

GREAT PALACE

Lay in the southeastern part of Constantinople. It was not one building but many, set amidst trees and gardens. Its grounds included the DAPHNE PALACE, barracks for the EXCUBITORS, ceremonial rooms, meeting halls, the imperial family's living quarters, churches and housing provided for court officials, ambassadors and various other dignitaries.

HAGIA SOPHIA

See GREAT CHURCH.

HERO OF ALEXANDRIA (lst century AD)

Egyptian mathematician and inventor, whose writings included works on surveying, water clocks, geometry and engineering. His PNEUMATICS describes how to construct useful, unusual, or amusing devices such as musical instruments played by air or water, a solar-operated fountain, a self-trimming lamp and automatic wine dispensers. He is also known as Heron of Alexandria.

HIPPODROME

U-shaped race track in Constantinople. The Hippodrome had tiered seating accommodating up to a hundred thousand spectators. It was also used for public celebrations and other civic events.

IMPLUVIUM

Shallow pool in the center of the atrium of a Roman house. Situated under the compluvium (a square or oblong opening in the atrium roof) the impluvium caught rainwater for household use or decorative purposes.

JUSTINIAN I (483-565; r 527-565)

Justinian I's greatest ambition was to restore the Roman Empire to its former glory. He succeeded in temporarily regaining North Africa, Italy and southeastern Spain. He ordered the codification of Roman law and after the Nika Riots (532) rebuilt the Church of the Holy Wisdom (see GREAT CHURCH) as well as many other buildings in Constantinople. He was married to THEODORA.

LEO I (c 401-474; r 457-474)

Leo I followed a military career, reaching the rank of tribune before being acclaimed emperor after the death of Emperor Marcian (396-457; r 450-457).

LORD CHAMBERLAIN

Typically a EUNUCH, the Lord (or Grand) Chamberlain was the chief attendant to the emperor and supervised most of those serving at Constantinople's GREAT PALACE. He also took a leading role in court ceremonial but his real power arose from his close working relationship with the emperor, which allowed him to wield great influence.

MARTIAL (?38-c 103)

Epigrammatist who was born in Spain and moved to Rome. He wrote twelve books of epigrams, many satirical in nature and often containing cutting observations on contemporary society.

MASTER OF THE OFFICES

Official who oversaw the civil side of imperial administration within the GREAT PALACE.

MATASUNTHA (known c 530s)

Grand-daughter of THEODORIC, daughter of AMALASUNTHA and sister of ATHALARIC. She was married to WITIGIS, with whom she was taken to Constantinople after the fall of Ravenna. She later married Germanus, JUSTINIAN I's cousin.

MESE

Main thoroughfare of Constantinople. Enriched with columns, arches, statuary (depicting secular, military, imperial, and religious subjects), fountains, religious establishments, workshops, monuments, public baths and private dwellings, it was a perfect mirror of the heavily populated and densely built city it traversed.

MIMES

After the second century AD mime supplanted classical Roman pantomime in popularity. Unlike performers of pantomime, mimes spoke and did not wear masks. Their performances featured extreme violence and graphic licentiousness and were strongly condemned by the Christian church.

MITHRA

Persian sun god. He was born in a cave or from a rock and slew the Great (or Cosmic) Bull, from whose blood all animal and vegetable life of the world sprang. He is usually depicted wearing a tunic and Phrygian cap with his cloak flying out behind him and in the act of slaying the Great Bull. He was also known as Mithras. See also MITHRAEUM, MITHRAISM and MITHRA'S TORCH BEARERS.

MITHRAEUM

Underground place of worship dedicated to MITHRA. They have been found on sites as far apart as northern England and what was later the Holy Land.

MITHRAISM

Of Persian origin, Mithraism spread throughout the Roman empire via its followers in various branches of the military. It became one of the most popular Roman religions during the second and third centuries AD but declined after Emperor Constantine's conversion to Christianity. Mithrans were required to practice chastity, obedience and loyalty. Parallels have been drawn between Mithraism and Christianity because of shared practices such as baptism and a belief in resurrection as well as the fact that his followers believed that MITHRA, in common with many sun gods, was born on December 25th. However, women were excluded from Mithraism.

Mithrans advanced within their religion through seven degrees. In ascending order, these were Corax (Raven), Nymphus (Male Bride), Miles (Soldier), Leo (Lion), Peres (Persian), Heliodromus (RUNNER OF THE SUN), and Pater (Father).

MITHRA'S TORCH BEARERS

Representations of MITHRA show him accompanied by the twin torchbearers Cautes and Cautopates, statues of whom were also part of the sacred furnishings of a MITHRAEUM. Cautes always held his torch upright while Cautopates pointed his down. The twins are said to represent the rising and setting of the sun. Another interpretation is that they symbolize the twin emotions of despair and hope.

MONOPHYSITES

Adherents to a doctrine holding that Christ had only one nature (a composite of the divine and the human) rather than two that were separate within him. Although condemned by the fourth ecumenical council in Chalcedon (451) it nevertheless remained particularly strong in Syria and Egypt during the reign of JUSTINIAN I. THEODORA championed the Monophysite cause.

NOMISMATA

Plural form of nomisma, the standard gold coin at the time of JUSTINIAN I. See also SEMISSIS.

OSTROGOTHS

Germanic people that, along with the related Visigoths, was at war with the Roman Empire for centuries. Under THEODORIC the Ostrogoths established a kingdom in Italy towards the end of the fifth century. During the latter part of their existence the Ostrogoths converted to ARIANISM. By the mid-sixth century, as a result of JUSTINIAN I's campaign to reconquer Italy, they had ceased to have a national identity.

OVID (43 BC-17 AD)

Best known for his erotic verse, Ovid was the author of the *Art of Love* and also of *The Metamorphoses*, a mythological-historical collection in fifteen books.

PATRIARCH

Head of a diocese or patriarchate. At the time of JUSTINIAN I these were (ranked by precedence) Rome, Constantinople, Alexandria, Antioch and Jerusalem.

PNEUMATICS

See HERO OF ALEXANDRIA.

POLUS (4th century BC)

Greek actor famed for his performance in Sophocles' *Electra*, during which he carried an urn containing the ashes of his recently deceased son on stage in order to enhance his enactment of grief.

PORPHYRIO

Whale that, according to the sixth century Byzantine historian Procopius, inhabited the seas around Constantinople for more than half a century.

QUAESTOR

Public official who administered financial and legal matters in addition to drafting laws.

RUNNER OF THE SUN

One of the highest degrees in MITHRAISM.

SEMISSIS

Coin worth half a nomisma (see NOMISMATA).

SETESH

Egyptian god epitomizing evil. He was also known as Set or Setekh.

SILENTIARY

Court official whose duties were similar to those of an usher and included guarding the room in which an imperial audience or meeting was being held.

STADIA (singular: STADE or STADIUM)

Ancient Greek measure of distance. As adopted by the Romans a stade equaled 606 feet 9 inches, the length of a foot race at the Olympic Games.

SULLA (138-78 BC)

Roman politician, appointed dictator in 82 BC following a civil war.

THEODORA (c 497-548)

Influential wife of JUSTINIAN I. It has been alleged that she had formerly been an actress and a prostitute. When the Nika Riots broke out in Constantinople in 532, she is said to have urged her husband to remain in the city, thus saving his throne.

THEODORIC (454-526; r OSTROGOTHS 471-526; r Italy 493-526)

Known as Theodoric the Great, he was educated in Constantinople, having been taken there as a diplomatic hostage at the age of eight. Ascending to the OSTROGOTH throne on the death of his father Theodemir in 471, he eventually regained control of Italy from the barbarians who had won it from Rome almost twenty years before. During his reign he favored Roman methods of government and law. As an OSTROGOTH he practiced ARIANISM.

VITRUVIUS (1st century BC)

Roman architect, engineer and author of the ten-volume treatise *De Architectura* (*On Architecture*), the only surviving Roman work on the topic.

WITIGIS (known c 530s)

General elected OSTROGOTH king in 536, who unsuccessfully attempted to resist JUSTINIAN I's reconquest of Italy. He was married to MATASUNTHA, with whom he was taken to Constantinople after the fall of Ravenna. His subsequent fate is unknown.

To receive a free catalog of other Poisoned Pen Press titles, please contact us in one of the following ways:

Phone: 1-800-421-3976
Facsimile: 1-480-949-1707
Email: info@poisonedpenpress.com
Website: www.poisonedpenpress.com

Poisoned Pen Press
6962 E. First Ave. Ste 103
Scottsdale, AZ 85251